THE LAST QUEEN OF SHEBA

Other titles by Jill Francis Hudson

Fiction

Rabshakeh (Lion Hudson)

Zoheleth (Lion Hudson)

Hadassah (Lion Hudson)

A Fortress Among My People (Lighthouse)

Devotional

Esther: For Such a Time as This (Kingsway)

THE LAST

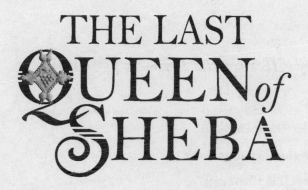

QUEEN of SHEBA

Jill Francis Hudson

LION FICTION

Published by Lion Fiction
an imprint of
Lion Hudson plc
Wilkinson House, Jordan Hill Road,
Oxford OX2 8DR, England
www.lionhudson.com/fiction

ISBN 978 1 78264 097 4
e-ISBN 978 1 78264 098 1

First edition 2014

A catalogue record for this book is available from the British Library

Printed and bound in the UK, February 2014, LH26

With the deepest gratitude as always to Keith, without whose continual support, computing skills and research assistance I could not have completed this project. And with special thanks to Karoline Kuhn at Gerth Medien, for suggesting it to me in the first place.

PART ONE

Chapter One

Dawn was scarcely a hint upon the desert horizon when the procession began to form outside the gates of the silent city. The priests of Almaqah gathered first, their fluid white robes and turbans all that could be seen of them in the deep shadow of the city walls. Then, as the rising sun turned the black dunes purple, and the jagged mountains and soaring mud-brick mansions and tenements of Marib emerged from obscurity, the ensigns they carried became visible too. Each was surmounted by the symbol of the Sheban god: a full moon resting on the horns of a bull.

Once the priests had taken their places, it was the turn of the musicians to assemble with their pipes, lyres, sistra and drums. They made no music as yet, for once they struck up with their dirge there would be no respite for hearer or performer until the embalmed body of the queen had been laid to rest in its rock-cut tomb, and a boulder the size of an elephant had been hauled across the doorway. But this would not be accomplished until the sun had set once again and the full moon of Almaqah had risen high above the mountains.

After the musicians came the mourners, male and female, who would take from them the cue to begin their ululations, and after the mourners, companies of boys and girls who had not yet come of age, chosen for their beauty and clad in the meagrest of ceremonial vestments. Above the waist they wore nothing but great golden collars, from which the late queen's monogram hung heavy on their chests, with a counter-weight dangling behind. Their long smooth legs were bare but for bulky golden anklets; bangles likewise adorned their wrists and upper arms. When the musicians played and the mourners wailed, these youths and maidens would prepare to dance the dance for the dead. Its every movement had been prescribed by the ancients, who had learned from the god what must be done if the soul of the deceased was to pass unscathed into the afterlife.

Now from the opened gates spilled the mass of the common people, compelled by custom and by their feudal overlords to lament their late queen's passing whether they cared to or not; few of them would ever have set eyes on her before today, let alone come to love or revere her. For the queen of the Shebans was forbidden to be seen alive outside her own palace. She would leave it only by curtained litter and then for no other reason than to travel to Sirwah, the seat of her summer palace in the mountains. Tradition dictated that the queen's person must be shrouded in mystery; she must remain aloof in her crenellated tower like the gods who dwelt above the firmament, and only in death would her face be uncovered. In truth, her subjects were likelier to hate her than to love her, for her father and his kinsmen – who were really their rulers – taxed, coerced and oppressed them without mercy until they feared for their very lives.

To keep the recalcitrant masses in order, an elite regiment of infantry had already marched out through the gates in close formation and deployed itself to either side of the swelling multitude. It remained only for the members of the current royal house and of the other noble families to be escorted to their places of honour by their attendants, and then the queen's handsome corpse on its open bier would be brought to the head of the column. The grave goods with which she would be buried would be carried in her wake like the bridal train she had never had, and her whole formidable cortège would head off to the valley of the tombs where she would rest for ever with the queens who had gone before her.

"Master, it is time we were leaving." Hami, my manservant, bustled up behind me and stood on tiptoe to drape my cloak about my shoulders. Though later in the day the heat would be stifling, mornings were chill and, as Hami was fond of reminding me, there was little spare flesh on my long thin bones. As cousin to Rafash, chief of the Banu Habesh, and as one of the richest and most respected men in Sheba in my own right, I was entitled – and indeed expected – to grace the ranks of the nobility with my presence on the march. Rafash himself would be conspicuous only by his absence. Our tribe having crossed the Red Sea many lifetimes ago to found colonies in Africa, he lived far away in his fastness in the highlands of Ethiopia, and like as not had yet to receive the news that the queen was dead. I was only in Arabia myself because I had been on my way home from a trading mission to the kingdom of Israel when the news had broken.

For I am Tamrin the Merchant, and in the days when this story begins I had five hundred and twenty camels and seventy-three ships to my illustrious name. Many of these camels, temporarily relieved of their precious cargoes, were with me in my camp on the plain of Marib. There were also many of my agents and servants, and their servants, and the mercenaries I hired to protect us all from the hazards of the road; all of them were no doubt as sorry to be held up here as I was myself.

"Come, then, Hami," I bade him, and together we left my pavilion, escorted by a sizeable company of attendants, which as the representative of a noble house it was only fitting for me to have with me on an occasion such as this. I was no fonder of the ceremonial than I was of unavoidable delay; having embarked upon a lifetime of travel to escape the burden of my own bereavement, I seldom came so close to contentment as I did roaming the desert roads or sleeping rolled in a rug beneath the glorious canopy of heaven. The Bedouin say that if you don't like living in the desert you aren't fit to live at all, and I am inclined to agree with them.

Stewards of the royal house directed me to my place; Hami and the rest of my entourage would join the retinues of my peers, close behind. Now that the sun had fully risen and the eastern horizon shimmered with the lure of the Empty Quarter beyond it, the faces of my fellows were clearly visible, in so far as they allowed them to be seen between the swathes of their headgear. In the main they were not pleasing to look upon. Hardbitten by greed, by ambition, by corruption and distrust, these were the faces of men who had no more affection for each other than they had had for the woman in whose honour they had reluctantly come together.

Only one person present showed any sign of genuine grief. Lady Ghalilat, the dead queen's niece, groomed by her virgin aunt to assume Sheba's throne in her turn, stood among the foremost of the nobles weeping kohl-stained tears that disfigured her face like angry scars. She was swathed in black from head to ankle, but her feet were bare, and would be blistered and bloody by the time she had walked the stony route to the necropolis and back. Perhaps she grieved for the love, marriage and children she would never have as much as for the aunt who had destined her for greatness. Yet rumour would have it that she coveted the throne she had been promised as much as any normal woman might want the things which this one had had to forgo.

Suddenly the morbid silence was shattered as the priests started up with their wailing drone, the drums began beating, and the mourners trilled their tongues against the roofs of their mouths until the very walls of Marib seemed to vibrate with their unearthly hooting. It was as though the entire plain had become haunted by the ghosts of thousands of screech owls trapped there by demons who added their own preternatural voices to the cacophony. Surreptitiously I reached into the folds of my garments and took out two tiny balls of screwed-up linen which I had brought for the purpose, and slipped them into my ears. They did not shut out the hubbub completely, but went some way towards preserving my sanity along with my hearing, which was in any case no longer as sharp as it had been.

And so, like an awakening behemoth, the great column lurched into motion, and as it ground its inexorable way along the road to its destination, the suburb of tents fell away behind us, the sun rose higher, and ahead of us loomed the rugged peaks and cliffs into which the royal tombs had been cut. The dead queen's tomb had been hacked out years before, and the stele inscribed with her monogram had been erected in readiness almost as soon as she had come to the throne. We Shebans are not as obsessed with death as our Egyptian neighbours; we neither spend as many months embalming our rulers' corpses nor speed them on their final journey accompanied by as much gold. But we understand the importance of recording their names for posterity, since no man knows for certain the fate of the soul once the body is dissolved, and the name each of us leaves behind may turn out to be all that survives once our bones have crumbled away.

Though perhaps, I mused as I walked with my eyes downcast to protect them from the sun, there is *one* man who knows the answer to the question of whether and how we can live beyond the grave and perhaps be reunited with those who have passed on before us. Solomon of Israel, from whose court I had so recently returned, had already answered many other such questions which had plagued me for longer than I cared to recall. He had summoned me in the first place to negotiate with me about the furnishing of the temple he had been building to his mysterious invisible god, but we had wound up discussing very much more than the price of the commodities he was seeking. He had recognized very quickly that I was seeking something too, but that what I hankered after was not a thing which could be bought or sold. Both of us, being richer than most folk can even imagine, had long since concluded that there has to be more to a man's life than material prosperity and fathering sons to whom he may bequeath his name and his fortune.

But unlike me, Solomon seemed to have some idea as to what this "more" might consist of. And what a paradise he had created for his fortunate subjects, or so it seemed to me, as a result of the philosophies he had adopted! What order and harmony I had beheld there, what freedom from the bitterness and bickering that blighted the politics of Sheba! How I had longed to spend more time in dialogue with the scholarly king, and in marvelling at his subjects' enlightened customs. But Solomon himself had bid me return to my homeland to fetch for him sapphires, ivory, obsidian, rare red gold, and logs of the hard African ebony which no worm or insect can devour. These things he desired for the embellishment of the house of his god, and when it was finished, he promised me, I should be invited to its consecration.

All this felt very far away just now, with the sun beating down on my head and the sand as hot as embers beneath my sandalled feet. The further we advanced into the wilderness, the gladder I became that our column was flanked by soldiers. As a seasoned desert traveller, I was only too aware that bandits as well as Bedouin herdsmen roamed the dunes, and that behind any one of the numerous rocky outcrops beside the road, disaster might be lurking. Pretty pickings the dead queen's treasures would have made, to say nothing of the dancers' gaudy trappings. The kind of desperadoes who ransack tombs would think nothing of attacking a funeral train or of hacking off the hands and feet of innocent adolescents to abscond with their adornments.

Sometimes, when our path sloped downwards, I could see the queen's body quite clearly; her shroud had yet to be wrapped around her, and presently hung loose from the bier. Her arms were folded across her chest, her thick black hair under its diadem was twisted behind her head, and her face, though the brow was lined, retained something of its former beauty. But the set of the mouth was hard, and the lips too thin, at least to my half-African eyes. I had noted the same hardness in the kohl-stained face of her niece.

Despite my unease, and thanks no doubt to the presence of the soldiers, we made it to the place of the tombs without interference. Then what had been a marching column reorganized itself like a flock of migrating birds into a semicircle many ranks deep, to form the arena where the burial rituals would be conducted. The drums changed their beat and the flutes their mode; the mourners howled, and the dancers twisted and swayed in a ring around the bier, which the priests who bore it had placed on a great stone platform in front of the cliff. To the music and the wailing the priests now added their chanting, and on each of four altars surrounding the platform fires were lit and offerings made. The windless desert air grew thick with the stench of burning flesh and the perfume of incense, for Sheba is home to the trees whence incense and myrrh are collected. To these, along with my reputation for integrity, I owe the greater part of my legendary wealth.

So loud was the mourning and so effective the plugs I had rammed into my ears, I did not notice at first that some of the chieftains standing around me were using the cover of the noisy spectacle to mutter among themselves rather than reverently witness the rituals. Once I had marked what they were doing I took out my earplugs at once, for a man in my position must see and hear everything, and I pay a veritable swarm of spies to gather in high places what intelligence I cannot glean for myself.

"So we are all agreed that Mafaddat's brat must not be confirmed as queen? That the Crown Council must reject her nomination as inappropriate?"

"There can be no question about it. To have two successive queens from the same tribe, from the same *clan*, no less... far too much power would be concentrated into too few hands. It is imperative that another suitable woman be identified with all speed."

"Woman? The new queen should not even *be* a woman yet. She should be a girl-child, innocent and untutored, one whose virginity is not open to question, and who cannot possibly have been indoctrinated with rebellious nonsense by her predecessor. This Ghalilat is almost twenty-five years old, by Almaqah! Her succession would make a mockery of our traditions; it would jeopardize everything they have evolved to protect. It is in the sharing of power among the Seven Foremost Families that Sheba's strength has always lain."

Her strength, or the seeds of her downfall? I wondered cynically, but was not permitted to dwell upon this thought any further, for one of the nobles remarked with a sneer, "*Eight* Foremost Families now, my friend, or had you forgotten? Rafash of Yeha now controls sufficient territory and rules enough subjects to qualify for inclusion among the nobility, and for membership of the council. He must be present when the council sits, or any decision it makes may have to be declared null and void."

"Rafash will not come here. He is too happy hunting his elephants and hippopotami to want to waste time on affairs of state which he does not believe concern him."

"On the contrary, Rafash will be on his way here even now. He is neither as stupid nor as lazy as he looks, mark my words. He has his spies to keep him informed of political developments, just as we do. He will not miss out on a chance to prove himself as important as the rest of us."

After that they took to swapping scandalous stories about Rafash, clicking their tongues and wagging their heads in grim disapproval. I ceased to pay any attention to what they were saying, as the unwelcome repercussions of what they had said already were giving me quite enough to think about. If Rafash were coming here, I would have no choice but to await his arrival, since I could not procure the goods I needed for Solomon without Rafash's permission. (I would have sought this as a matter of course had he been resident in Yeha when I got there.) A further tiresome delay was surely now inevitable, as was my having to be civil to the cousin I despised.

To distract myself from depression, I tried to take refuge in the ritual ecstasy erupting all around me. As the flames on the altars flared up and the incense burned, and the dancers writhed and leapt and fell down foaming at the mouth under the influence of their familiar spirits, I closed my eyes and breathed in the heady fumes, and sought to lose myself in holy oblivion. But it did not come. In the end I looked around for Hami, and had him lead me aside to a place in the shade where we could wait until the whole irksome proceedings had drawn to a close and we could return to our pavilion without causing offence.

"Master, you have overtaxed yourself!" cried Hami in dismay, simultaneously helping me sit down upon a rock and fanning my face with his sleeve. "You are not used to walking in the heat of the day. It has done you no good at all."

"Nonsense, Hami," I rebuked him good-naturedly. "I can walk as happily as ride when I choose to. No, I am not ill. I simply need time to gather my thoughts, since it seems that we must presume upon the hospitality of our hosts at Marib a little longer than we were intending."

"Really, master? And why is that?" Hami ceased fussing over me and took to fanning himself instead. His round, still boyish face was as red as a pomegranate, for in truth he was no more used to standing around all day in the full glare of the desert sun than I was myself.

My cousin Rafash would have boxed the ears of any servant who dared to ask such a direct question in such a forthright way. But I was not Rafash, nor was Hami just any servant. He had been with me all his short life, and his father had served me too until his death not so many years ago. Neither had given me cause to reprimand him harshly, and I would have trusted either with my life without a moment's hesitation.

"Because, Hami," I told him candidly now, "Rafash my kinsman is almost certainly on his way here to claim his place on the Crown Council, and it would be very ill-mannered of us to attempt to avoid him. Besides, we need to see him on business of our own, or rather on business of the king of Israel. But it appears that the session of the council for which he has sacrificed the pleasures of the chase is likely to last a good deal longer than either of us could have anticipated, since his fellow chieftains have made up their minds to reject the queen whom the last one saw fit to bestow upon them."

"Reject the royal nominee? Surely they are not entitled to do such a thing?" Hami was fanning himself more furiously than before, but his face had turned even redder.

"Oh, but they are, my young friend, they are. It has happened more times than enough in Sheba's history, particularly when the young lady in question has been likely to prove difficult to manage. What they may find more difficult still is to come up with a suitable alternative."

"Then perhaps we should thank the gods that Rafash has to make such a long journey to get here. Otherwise he might have been tempted to go home again and fetch Makeda."

"Makeda, to be queen of Sheba?" I laughed out loud, for one of Hami's most endearing gifts was his unfailing ability to bring a smile to his master's face without intending to do so. Makeda was Rafash's only daughter, as beautiful in my eyes as her father was ugly, and as innocent as he was depraved. But she was also as black as her dead Cushite mother, and lame in one leg as a result of the terrible accident which could so easily have killed her. Makeda was about as eligible to become queen of Sheba as I was myself, and for that I did indeed thank the gods, as it was not an honour I would have wished upon any girl for whom I cared.

And I did care for Makeda, very much. Having begotten no children of my own, I had always cherished a soft spot for the little girl growing up without a mother, and especially after the accident, when for such a long time she had been in great pain and unable to walk at all. I had made it my business to cheer her up by bringing her little presents from my travels: usually miniature idols for her private shrine.

I had wanted to bring her a likeness of Solomon's god too, but when I had learned that no image of him was permitted to be made, Solomon himself had had one of the royal goldsmiths craft for her a tiny model of a thing he called the Ark of the Covenant, which he said was the symbol of the presence of his god among his people. The model was a box no longer or wider than the palm of my hand, but it was made from solid gold and had two winged angels facing one another on its lid. I thought Makeda would like it for keeping her earrings and nose-rings in; exotic objects delighted her, for she said they were the next best thing to being able to travel herself. Whenever I left on one of my expeditions she would beg me to take her with me, and I might even have done so, on the shorter trips at least, had her father allowed it. But Rafash, who cared nothing about her at all, claimed that she might be kidnapped by outlaws and he didn't want to be embarrassed into paying out the dowry he had set aside for her marriage just to prevent them slitting her throat.

He would be needing this dowry sooner rather than later, for to his immense relief he had recently succeeded in getting her betrothed. Soon she would be another man's responsibility; then I too would have to cease thinking of her as a lonely little girl who needed to be loved. She was sixteen years old, after all, and even though I was her kinsman, once she left her father's house it would no longer be appropriate for us to be friends.

Dreaming wistfully of Makeda I must have fallen asleep among the rocks, for the next thing I knew, it was dark and Hami was shaking me and hissing in my ear, "Master, wake up! It is time to return to the city."

I was taken aback, and reluctantly accepted that the sun must have gone to my head after all, for I had slept through the interment and the sealing of the tomb. No offence would have been given, as it happened, for it was perfectly acceptable at a Sheban funeral for any number of the guests to collapse and lie insensible with grief or excess of religious fervour. As the column reformed in the moonlight I was not the only man leaning heavily on his servant's shoulder. And Ghalilat, daughter of Mafaddat, having torn her clothes, her hair and her face in a drug-enhanced frenzy, was having to be carried back home on a litter.

"Hami, you must wake me early again tomorrow morning," I told him as he set me on my feet. "We must offer a goat to Shamash at daybreak, as penance for failing to acknowledge his sovereign power, else we shall both pay dearly for our presumption with raging headaches."

I had long since come to revere Shamash, god of the sun, above all others. Though the moon god was patron of my people, it had not escaped my notice that mankind as a whole owes considerably more to the sun, source of all light and life. He controls the seasons, ripens our crops, and exposes injustice wherever it lurks; indeed it was Shamash who inspired Hammurabi, the legendary king of Babylon, to draw up the law code by which I had resolved to live my life. Moreover, the sun has the power to burn us all to cinders if we do not placate him aright. Yet Solomon had merely inclined his head graciously when I had expounded my theology to him, and informed me that his nameless, invisible god had *created* the sun and the moon, along with everything else in our teeming universe and the laws that govern it, simply by speaking them into existence.

Our procession, as it made its way back to Marib, lacked something of the formality of its outward journey. Nevertheless a modicum of order had to be maintained, since we still needed the soldiers to guard our flanks until we reached the safety of the city. Now it was the moon shining down from overhead rather than the sun; Almaqah's wan, white face cast an eerie light upon the dunes, and the rock outcrops silhouetted against the sky looked like nocturnal creatures poised to pounce. I was convinced we were being spied upon by malignant eyes, but perhaps it was only the rocks that kept watch as we passed by.

Contrary to my custom, I allowed Hami to help me undress, then I lay for a while wide awake, having slept too much in the daytime. Hami, rolled in his blanket across the entrance to my pavilion, was already snoring contentedly while I was still rearranging my pillows.

When I did sleep, Makeda once more filled my dreams. This time she was a child again, perhaps seven or eight years old, and she was strumming on the half-sized, six-stringed lyre which had once belonged to her mother. Her mother had been teaching the little girl to play, before Rafash had sent her back to her own father's house to die of shame and a broken heart. Now Makeda bent low over the instrument to tune it; she had coiled her long braided hair in a twist at her neck to keep it back, and her brow was furrowed in concentration. Suddenly she looked straight at me with her doe-brown eyes and said, "Uncle Tamrin, won't *you* show me how to play?" So I smiled, and took her on my knee, and placed my fingers over hers on the strings. And we played together, and presently she sang; only her voice was no longer the high-pitched piping of a child, but the low, sweet voice of the marriageable girl she had since become. She sang of the things she loved: flowers and mountains, and the stars she and I would stand and gaze at together, and her forthcoming wedding, and she reminded me so strikingly just then of my own lost bride that I woke with a start and found that my pillow was damp under my face.

I slept only fitfully after that until just before dawn, when I was sleeping like the dead and Hami hadn't the heart to rouse me. This dubious honour was reserved for Bijo, chief of my spies, who strode in over Hami's protestations and growled at me in his coarse Cushite accent, "Master Tamrin, wake up! I have urgent news which cannot wait. Please, we must talk at once."

Chapter Two

"Not before I have breakfasted, my friend," I rebuked him mildly. So he stood there chafing at the bit while I splashed cold water in my face and had Hami bring in bread and dates and melon, and cups of warm honey wine, without which no day should begin. I invited my guest to breakfast with me, but he waved my hospitality aside as though life were too short to waste on food and drink. Bijo was small and swarthy, with narrow little eyes which never stopped moving, and ears that missed nothing worth listening to. But since he was also as surly as a camel driver, he himself was seldom deemed worthy of anyone's attention. I could not have wished for a better spy.

"Well," I said at last, dabbing at my chin with a facecloth, "you had better hurry up and tell me this news which has been eating away at your patience. Though I do hope it is not something I have learned for myself already, such as what a bad queen the Lady Ghalilat would make in some folks' opinion, or how my worthy cousin Rafash is about to turn up here any day now and start throwing his considerable weight about, to who knows what effect."

Bijo's little slits of eyes went briefly round; it was only when he was taken by surprise that you could really see them at all. He said, "Master, you know for certain that Rafash is on his way here? This isn't just a rumour you are repeating?"

"It may be no more than a rumour, for all I know," I confessed with a smile. It was wrong of me to make fun of Bijo for my own amusement, but he did so much hate not being first with the news.

"In that case, I *do* have something to tell you, master. Rafash *is* coming here, and his brothers with him; I have spoken with men he sent ahead of him to arrange their accommodation. He intends to sit with the Crown Council as is his right, and to speak in support of those who reject Ghalilat's nomination for the throne. I have also spoken with servants of the chieftains of all seven of the other tribes. *None* will support Ghalilat, except her own father."

"But has any viable alternative been suggested? If every eligible girl from every branch of every one of the Foremost Families has to be considered, I dread to think how long the council will have to remain in session. With all these chieftains and their escorts in residence, before long there will not be a single loaf of bread or pitcher of water to be found in all Marib. At least *we* shall be able to leave, once I have seen Rafash and gained his approval for our deal with Solomon."

"Alas no, master." Bijo cast a furtive glance to either side, as though he feared that some stranger might have slipped into the tent unobserved. Then he took a step closer to my couch and said, "Rafash wants you to attend the council too. As his first cousin you are entitled to be there even though you have no vote, and he will insist that you are."

"*I* attend the council? Whatever for? I am a merchant, not a politician. What possible use could my presence serve?"

"I don't know, master; nor did Rafash's servants have any light to shed upon the matter. But he himself will be here by noon tomorrow, so if you wish you may ask him to explain his reasoning to you directly."

"Hmm." Frankly, I could not imagine a situation in which reasoning and Rafash would have anything remotely to do with one another. But aloud I said only, "Thank you, Bijo. You may go now, unless you have any further contribution to make to the ruining of my day."

"No, master." Seeing my mood, Bijo bowed himself out as quickly as he could, though in fact I have never been given to taking out my frustration upon others. It has never been my way.

But Hami too gave me space before venturing to be of any assistance. I sat morose upon my couch, briefly feeling that I must be the unluckiest man in the world, even though I had eaten my breakfast from silver dishes, my couch was upholstered with Oriental silk, and the antique tapestries and carpets with which my pavilion was adorned could have bought me several of the tenement blocks which towered over Marib's city walls. Then I shook myself free of my self-pity and said to Hami, "Come, for we have a sacrifice to make, or had you forgotten?" And we set out into my encampment to collect a goat to present to Shamash.

Poised between the desert and the mountains, Marib owed its existence to the small hinterland of green where from time to time rivers would deposit the mountain rains before the sands of the Empty Quarter swallowed them up. Ramshackle dams had been erected here and there by enterprising farmers in an effort to capture and regulate this sporadic bounty, but most of the time a large and desperate population fought over very little water, and when the rains did come they were as likely to sweep away dams, buildings, livestock and even people in a terrifying deluge as they were to bring fertility or prosperity.

As we passed inside the city gates with our goat, the appalling bustle and smell of concentrated humanity assailed us, and Hami hid a smile when I covered my nose with the loose end of my turban. The narrow streets were thronged with tradesmen, porters, messengers, darkly veiled women, and sheep and goats being herded to market. Beggars swarmed about us, and we gave them what bread and victuals we had been able to carry with us for the purpose. Above our heads on all sides the bizarre mud-brick towers rose up, shading us from Shamash's penetrating glare; it had long been the custom in Marib to build high rather than out, partly against the heat, partly for fear of the encroaching wilderness. From the outside at least, the homes of the rich differed from those of the poor only with respect to the number of people who lived there; a multi-storeyed tower might house a single affluent family, or else there might be dozens crammed many to a floor. The palace of the queen was a tower like all the rest, albeit higher still, and located in the very centre of the settlement. There she would live with her handmaids on the uppermost floor, while the menfolk of her family plotted and planned and entertained below.

The temple of Shamash stood close to the palace, as did that of Almaqah. Though the latter was constructed on a much grander scale, they closely resembled one another in design. Each was predominantly open to the sky, as was fitting for a structure built to honour one of the heavenly bodies. Outside the entrance there were free-standing square-cut pillars, beyond which a flight of steps led to the sacred enclosure. It was with profound relief that we ascended these steps, emerging from the teeming crowds to exchange their stench for the sweet-smelling spaciousness of the holy precinct, furnace-hot though it was.

At the far end of it we could see the sanctuary which housed the baetyl of the god – and I say baetyl rather than statue, for neither Shamash nor Almaqah was depicted in the form of a man. Shamash's baetyl was a great black stone which was said to have fallen from the sky long ago, in the days before records began. I myself have never seen it, for the sanctuary may only be entered by priests.

Of course, there are still Shebans who venerate the images of mortal beings: of men and women, of animals, and of creatures with animals' heads and human bodies, or the other way about. Rafash himself was one such deluded soul: he worshipped Sando, the hideous serpent god of his Ethiopian ancestors. I regret that I shall have to say more about Sando in due course. But since the mere thought of this god, and the things he requires his devotees to do, makes my stomach churn like the sea in a storm, I shall return for now to the more congenial subject of my sacrifice to Shamash.

The altar on which we would offer him our goat stood not far from the sanctum, in the open air. Other altars stood round about it, for the pouring of libations or the burning of incense and myrrh. Two priests came forward to meet us; they inspected our goat for imperfections and, finding none, presented me with a consecrated knife to slit its throat. Two young acolytes held it firm while I did what I had to do. It scarcely struggled, and its death was swift – an excellent omen, which went some way towards lifting my spirits. The blood which spurted from its wound was caught in a goblet and handed me to drink. I took a tactful sip, the minimum required, for as I have indicated already I don't have the strongest of stomachs. (I am not the only ship owner who much prefers travelling over land.) Then I made my apology to

Shamash for taking his benevolence for granted, and returned with Hami to our camp to await my cousin's arrival.

Some of the time I had to kill I spent reading in my tent as is my wont, for wherever I go I search out scrolls in which are recorded the words of the wise and holy. From Solomon too I had sought to buy books, but he had told me that in his opinion the only ones worth reading were the writings of the great prophet Moses, and copies of these were far too scarce and sacred to be sold to an inquisitive traveller, regardless of the price he was prepared to offer. No; if I wished to learn more about the God of Israel I must return there, and Solomon himself would undertake to teach me. In the meantime, he said, he was compiling a wisdom treatise of his own, and for what it was worth, when it was finished he would present me with a copy for nothing.

As a change from my reading, every few hours or so I would go out into the camp and walk abroad among the tents and tackle, to talk with whichever of my employees or their servants I came across with a moment or two to spare from their chores. I had always considered it important to enquire after the well-being of those who worked for me, and to listen to any grievances they might have. Sauntering to and fro, I contemplated how wonderful it would be if our new queen and the menfolk who ruled on her behalf were to think the same way about their subjects. Then I shook my head; one can always dream, but I recognized that some things are simply too much to hope for.

It was only appropriate, perhaps, that Rafash should arrive the following day in a sandstorm. They sweep over the plain all too often, and especially just after noon; the sun is dimmed, the wind blasts sand into everything, and desiccated shrubs are uprooted and hurled about as though by children in a tantrum. I had only just made it back to my tent to escape the worst of it when Rafash strode in unannounced, as was his custom, caked from head to foot in dust, with his turban wrapped tighter round his face than the bandages of a pharaoh's mummy. A bevy of his brothers muscled in behind him, none of them as tall as I, but each twice as broad across the shoulders.

Hami, having risen to request them to wait outside, swiftly thought better of the idea, and hung back behind my couch awaiting orders.

"Cousin Tamrin, well met!" declared Rafash, tearing off his turban and springing forward to crush me in his ape-like embrace. "How glad I was to learn that you had not departed already, for then I should have had no choice but to fetch you back to share with me the honour of sitting among Sheba's nobility for the first time in the history of our people. To think that I, Rafash of the Banu Habesh, have so greatly increased our tribe's size and influence that you and I now belong to the aristocracy." Though most of our tribe's rise to eminence had taken place under the auspices of Rafash's late father, the son's boast was not entirely without substance. He had begotten enough bastards on his maidservants, willing or not, to increase its size significantly. If only his wife had been similarly fecund.

"You have certainly acquired a formidable reputation, Cousin Rafash," I assented, indicating that he and his brothers should make themselves comfortable on the couches and cushions ranged about the tent's interior. I sent Hami to fetch food and drink and some pretty slave girls to serve it; unlike Bijo, there was no way that Rafash's party would turn down a free feast when it was offered. "But I have to confess," I went on, attempting to disguise my distaste as the loutish fellows sprawled inelegantly over my furniture, covering it in sand, "I fail to understand why you should want *me* to share in your hard-earned glory, when I have done nothing to deserve it."

"Because," announced Rafash, slapping his thighs, then suddenly leaning forward and dropping his voice conspiratorially, "you are a scholar, that is why. These gentlemen of the council, with their flowery words... a plain-speaking man such as myself can all too easily have the wool pulled over his eyes, Tamrin. You will be there to make sure they don't try any tricks."

Well, I thought, at least he recognizes his intellectual limitations these days, which I suppose is something to be thankful for. But I said, "I scarcely think that playing tricks on you is going to be a major priority of the council on this occasion. It does have rather more pressing concerns to address."

"Yes, well, that may be so." Rafash waved one horny hand dismissively, as though swatting a bothersome fly away from his face. "But things have a way of going in unexpected directions, do they not? When men get together to make decisions, no matter how clear-headed each man is when he's by himself, sometimes with a council it seems that the decisions are somehow making themselves, and the outcome is something no one seemed to be arguing for at all. Now, you would see that coming, Tamrin. You're used to dealing with clever men who are out to deceive you. Bribery, corruption… you would smell them from a mile away. You could even make things go in *your* direction, if you wanted to."

"These things may also be true," I acknowledged, for undoubtedly they were, and bribes had certainly exchanged hands over the choosing of queens in the past. "However, I fail to see their particular relevance here. With your seat of power being far off in the jungles of Africa, it will hardly matter to you *who* reigns as queen in Arabia. To all intents and purposes you are your own king, and will remain so, whether the throne goes to Ghalilat or to another. I cannot see the chieftains of *any* of the Arabian tribes wanting to mount an expedition across the Red Sea and cause trouble for you in Ethiopia, when they have troubles aplenty of their own."

Rafash did not respond at once, because the food and drink had arrived, and the slave girls. Any of these things would have distracted him, but taken together they severed his train of thought entirely. Platefuls of lamb roasted with garlic and herbs, spicy mutton slices and freshly baked bread with hunks of goat's cheese which my cooks had been preparing all morning in readiness, vied for his attention with wine and mead and the breasts of the girl who bent down to serve them. The inane grin which took possession of his coarse features did nothing to improve my disposition towards him, though it spread very quickly to the faces of his brothers. Soon they were helping themselves with raucous abandon, licking their fingers and wiping them on the upholstery, and fondling the girls' buttocks through their gauzy skirts as they passed by.

Eventually Rafash remembered that I was there, cleared his throat, and said, "Well, cousin, it's true that the Red Sea forms a very useful barrier between the Banu Habesh and the Arabian motherland we came from, but what goes on over here isn't quite as uninteresting to me as it used to be. This business of choosing a new queen, for example. It intrigues me, I have to admit. Yet I know so little about how it's really supposed to be done."

Now, I myself am particularly fond of history, and I am inclined to take a little too much pride in exhibiting my knowledge when given the excuse to do so. I said sagely, "Well, in the olden days the throne went automatically to the first female born to a woman of one of the Seven Foremost Families after the accession of the previous queen. But this method was abandoned when on one occasion the child in question was born deformed and simple. After that the queenship rotated among the families, who took turns to choose a successor to the reigning queen from the ranks of their own unmarried daughters. Then there came a time when the family whose turn it was couldn't supply anyone suitable at all, and at that point things became… rather less orderly."

"Is that so?" This was the first time I had known Rafash to show the remotest interest in Sheba's heritage, yet suddenly it seemed to hold more fascination for him than any of the slave girls' quivering bosoms. Knitting his brows and stroking his grizzled chin, he was evidently thinking ferociously. The spectacle was frankly comical, but I ought to have been more anxious than amused.

Since the conversation seemed in danger of flagging at this point, I took the opportunity of enquiring after the health of his own daughter, Makeda. At this he gave me a very strange look indeed, but when I merely stared back at him nonplussed, he shrugged his great shoulders and said, "I should imagine she's as well as she ever is. I'm sure her women would have told me if there was any cause for concern." So I knew that he had seen no more of her recently than he ever did, and I began to be sorry all over again that I wasn't going to be able to visit her as soon as I had hoped and cheer her up with the little golden ark and my tales of travel and adventure.

Not that Rafash took any notice of my disappointment. The fact that I had sunk into silence freed him and his brothers to return to the serious business of getting drunk on my wine and mead, and enjoying the favours of the slave girls, most of whom were only too happy to oblige in return for a signet ring from a stubby finger or the promise of a pretty scarf to be sent along on the morrow.

When at last my guests had departed, or rather been escorted away on my orders, I was left with a distinctly unpleasant taste in my mouth and a vague but nagging sense of disquiet in my stomach. Hami fussed around me ineffectually; in the end I told him to summon Bijo, even though by then it was getting dark and the camp was beginning to settle down for the night. Bijo came hotfoot, his sharp little eyes going round again at the sight of the mess in my tent, which Hami hadn't yet finished clearing up.

"Bijo," I said, "I want you and your assistants to find out everything you can about Ghalilat, the daughter of Mafaddat, and about Mafaddat himself. Then I want the names of every girl or woman the council could conceivably consider a serious candidate for the throne. And you must work swiftly; now that Rafash has arrived, the council may be convened at the shortest notice."

"Yes, master. At once, master." Bijo's eyes glinted as they narrowed once again, for this was the kind of challenge he relished the most.

After that I went back to reading and reflecting, since I didn't want to make myself conspicuous by poking my own nose into the chieftains' affairs. In the morning I was notified that the council would convene at sunrise the next day, so Bijo would indeed have little time to conduct his research. But I wasn't worried about that. He had never previously failed me, and I was confident that he would succeed in this latest mission also.

He presented himself to me in the early hours of the morning on which the council was due to meet. Unable to sleep, I had been reading by lamplight, so I was alert and ready to receive his report. It did not make for easy listening.

"Master, the Lady Ghalilat is every bit as ambitious as we had been led to believe. She considers the throne to be hers by right, and from what I have learned, there is nothing she would not do to secure it. Her father is as ruthless as she is; he murdered five of his own brothers in order to become chief of his tribe, the Banu Marthadam. The other chieftains claim they would rather see *anyone* become queen than accept Ghalilat, yet the mention of any name whatever has led to such jealousy and squabbling already as you would not believe."

"And Rafash? What part has he played in all this wrangling?"

"None at all, as far as I am aware. He and his brothers have kept themselves to themselves. That is to say…" Bijo attempted to cough delicately, but sounded more like a man who has something stuck in his throat. "It's to say, Master Tamrin, that they have kept themselves to the girls you so generously provided for their entertainment."

I could think of no suitable comment to make upon this less-than-startling revelation, so I made none. Instead I said, "These other names to which you referred, Bijo; I should like to hear them, if you don't mind."

"Certainly, master. The one I have heard most frequently is that of Kanan, daughter of Kahalum of the Banu Waren. She is a girl-child ten years old or thereabouts, but every one of the other chieftains has a reason why she will not do. Then there is one Lilah, daughter of Salamat of the Banu Wahab, but she is only a baby, and her own father is unwilling for her to be considered. There is Bahalat of the Banu Hawbash, and her sister Mentewwab, and Rihannan of the Ygdad, and *her* sisters…" and so the list went on, but no name stood out as being worthy of special attention. It was beginning to look horribly likely that Ghalilat would be chosen after all, in the absence of any credible alternative, and because only she and her father possessed the will and wherewithal to have their own way.

Eventually, when Bijo's stream of information had dried up, leaving me none the wiser, I said, "Thank you, my friend. You have done well, but I fear that we shall have to wait until the council meets to see what the future has in store for us."

Chapter Three

At the crack of dawn a contingent of royal guards arrived to conduct me to the palace. The proceedings of the council would take place on one of its upper storeys; the lower floors, which would have been occupied by animals and foodstores in a lesser house, largely consisted of empty space, one of the most sought-after commodities in Marib and hence a symbol of the highest status.

Of course, every wall was hung with tapestries, alongside which even my own collection might have failed to impress, and anything which could be overlaid with gold or ivory had been. Scuttling along in my wake, Hami was gawping from side to side like a child at a festival. It wasn't that he hadn't seen such splendour before, but rather that it usually belonged to me. I recalled that he had reacted in much the same way when we had been received at the court of Solomon.

Having been ready long before my escorts arrived, I was one of the first to take my seat in the council chamber. I hadn't been back to bed after talking with Bijo. Since my bereavement I had rarely slept a whole night through, and as the years have gone by I have sometimes found that I can manage for several days with very little sleep at all.

Only three council members were present when I got there: a chieftain who was very much younger than I was, and two men seated beside him whom I assumed to be his brothers. Our servants and anyone else not authorized to be present had to wait in an airless antechamber until the proceedings were over. The council chamber itself was kept cool by tongueless slave boys wafting huge feathered fans over the heads of those assembled, and between them stood armed guards, whose function, I surmised, might not be exclusively ceremonial.

31

Once I had made myself comfortable among the cushions, I was well placed to watch the other council members arriving. The name and credentials of each was announced as he stepped across the threshold and stacked his weapons by the door; I made it my business to remember every name and tribal affiliation as it was given out.

Kahalum of the Banu Waren was the first to take his seat after myself. Decked out in full ceremonial regalia he presented a fearsome aspect, intensified by the grim expression on his face. His regalia consisted of an enormous pectoral monogram, and a sceptre so formidable that I rather thought it belonged by the door with the weapon-stack. Like the young chief already seated, he had brought two brothers with him; like me, they would have no right to vote when the time came, but they were permitted to address the council at their chieftain's request, as was I.

After Kahalum had taken his place, the other members of the council arrived in quick succession. There was no buzz of conversation, however, but rather an increasingly oppressive quiet as the chieftains and their kinsmen glowered at one another from beneath their beetling brows. Though all but Mafaddat remained united in the conviction that Ghalilat must not be crowned queen, in the days since I had heard them talking at the funeral they had been doing very little but disagreeing with one another about pretty well everything else.

Rafash and his brothers were the last to arrive before the gentlemen of the current royal family were announced. For a man who had allegedly passed most of his time at Marib in reckless dissipation, Rafash looked remarkably fresh and alert; indeed, disconcertingly so. His brothers too looked wary, or perhaps shifty, depending on your point of view.

A blare of trumpets announced the father and uncles of the deceased queen. This was the last occasion on which they would preside as royalty. By the time the council was dissolved – whenever that was – we should not only have a new queen but a new royal family as well.

The dead queen's father, whose name was Yuhafri, was probably the oldest man present. He had to be helped to his feet to deliver the inaugural address, and although he affected to encompass all those gathered with his penetrating gaze, he was in reality almost blind. His voice quavered as he welcomed his fellow noblemen and recited the required formulae which stated the council's business. Once the opening remarks were concluded, it was his prerogative to give his own opinion regarding the succession, and this he did.

"Esteemed princes of Sheba, it is without reservation that I commend to you Ghalilat, daughter of the illustrious Mafaddat of the Banu Marthadam here present, as the worthiest of those among whom we must seek our new queen. She is of peerless birth and unimpeachable reputation, and her candidacy for the throne was expressly endorsed by her predecessor, so recently taken from us. There is no reason why this council should not ratify Ghalilat's election at once, and invite her to appear among us to indicate her acceptance of the crown which we would confer upon her."

Of course, he spoke as though he himself had no vested interest in the matter whatsoever, despite the fact that everyone present knew perfectly well that he had been chief of the Banu Marthadam in his own right before abdicating in Mafaddat's favour. Yuhafri had passed on his duties as tribal chief when his daughter had assumed the throne; it was not mandatory for the queen's father to do this, but it had happened often enough in our history, especially when the territory of the tribe which the chieftain headed was located far away from Marib.

Yuhafri sat down again, with assistance, once he had finished, and for an interval no one spoke. Then Kahalum of the Banu Waren rose to his feet, his imposing bulk seeming to fill out even further as he did so. "With all respect," he thundered, with no respect at all, "there is *every* reason to reject the nomination of Mafaddat's child. To begin with, she is not a child at all, but a full-grown woman. Whoever heard of a woman old enough to have a marriageable daughter of her own becoming queen over our people? Secondly, she is of the same tribe as the queen we have so recently buried, may Almaqah receive her soul! Whenever was *that* kind of travesty permitted by our ancestors? And thirdly, she is not like a real woman at all. She is a man in a woman's guise, with ruthless ambition and intentions of her own. Who *knows* what disasters she would bring down upon our heads? To crown Ghalilat queen would be like inviting a jackal bitch to nurse the pups of your prized pedigree hound. I say we rule this dangerous woman out of the reckoning forthwith, and I call upon every true son of Sheba to stand with me."

For a moment the entire assembly was too cowed to do or say anything at all. Then as Kahalum continued to glare about like a warrior challenging the enemy to send a champion against him in single combat, the young chief who had arrived before me arose and stood at his side.

"I second Kahalum's proposal," he said in a quiet but resolute voice, and a moment later every chieftain was on his feet, and their supporters with them, excepting Rafash who maintained his chary vigilance, and Mafaddat himself, who appeared to be puffing himself up like an almighty bulge-eyed frog. Suddenly he stood up too, and strode across the floor to confront Kahalum face to face.

"And since when has it been acceptable for the last queen's words to be disregarded like a common washerwoman's, for her wishes to be waved to one side like a moth that has the audacity to flutter in the flame of your candle? There is *no* reason why my daughter should not be queen, except that *you* want *yours* to be chosen, so that you can lord it over the rest of us and claim all the taxes that should be shared among us for yourself! I know how greedy you are, Kahalum, but do these other men here know you as well as I do? Shall I tell them the size of the dowry you demanded when your son was wedded to the daughter of my friend? Shall I tell them about the taxes you levy on your own tribesmen, how you demand such an exorbitant share of the harvest that you leave your people starving or drive them to sell their children into slavery? How every day you seize a hundred poor men's oxen and have them slaughtered for your own table, merely because you have conceived a craving for their tongues?"

"Oh yes? As if *you* didn't have five hundred of your own *tribesmen* slaughtered because they dared to question your right to rule over them when Yuhafri became Queen's Father? As if you didn't execute your own wife because one of your henchmen ventured to look her in the eye when he came to do obeisance to you? Or perhaps you had good reason to dispatch her, Mafaddat. Perhaps you couldn't control her any more than you will be able to keep your wildcat of a daughter in check. Perhaps Ghalilat isn't even *your* daughter at all."

Mafaddat had had enough. With his eyes all but bursting from their sockets, he grabbed Kahalum by the throat and spat in his face. In return, Kahalum wrenched off his rival's turban and seized him by the hair, at which Mafaddat butted him full on the nose with his great hard head. There was blood all down both their chests; Mafaddat took to shaking Kahalum by the shoulders without mercy, until there were flecks of blood all over everyone else as well. All this had happened too fast for the guards to prevent it, but now at a sign from Yuhafri, who had sensed if not seen the violence erupting, they dragged the opponents apart and threw them down unceremoniously in their places. Mafaddat surged up again at once and threatened to leave, but this could not be condoned. No voting member of the council could be allowed to depart until its business was concluded, else the new queen's election would be invalid.

When things had settled down and Kahalum had been provided with a wad of cloth to take care of his bleeding nose, the young chief who had previously risen to second his proposal stood up again. He spread his arms wide in a gesture of appeal and said, "My fellow princes, have we not witnessed evidence enough just now to convince us that Mafaddat is not the kind of man we could respect as father of the queen? Kahalum's arguments against Ghalilat's appointment were sound, yet he was viciously attacked as though he had no right to speak his mind. Kahalum is a man of principle, who is unafraid to stand up for the truth. I say that his daughter Kanan is the one we should crown as our queen. She is a maid without blemish, not yet eleven years old. What finer choice could we make?"

This suggestion took everyone aback; for one chieftain to recommend the daughter of another was all but unheard of. Then I remembered Bijo speaking of one council member whose daughter was a baby, upon whom he did not want the burden of royalty to fall; his name was Salamat, and this was he. No doubt he was thinking of himself as well as of his child, and I had to admire him, for it seemed that he was one of those rare men who recognize that they already have all the power they can effectively wield. To govern an unruly tribe is demanding enough, without volunteering for the weighty and often conflicting duties the queen's father is obliged to discharge. To see the daughter of Kahalum ascend the throne might well seem to Salamat the lesser of many evils.

I was even beginning to reach this same conclusion myself, except that what Maffadat had said about Kahalum's greed was disturbing, and in spite of Mafaddat's obvious jealousy his words had somehow rung true. So Salamat's suggestion failed to find the support he had been hoping for, and we were back to square one.

Thus it came about that the first day's deliberations got us nowhere, and by nightfall nothing had been decided except that Ghalilat the daughter of Mafaddat was not to be elevated automatically to the exalted position she had been led to expect. Not even this decision could be announced officially. There was to be no divulging of the council's proceedings until the new queen had been elected.

But Ghalilat must know, I realized, as I was escorted to the upper room in which I was obliged to spend the night. I would be under constant surveillance just like every other council member, for it was decreed that none of us must speak to any outsider before we reconvened, or indeed to each other. This was a precaution against corruption, against private deals being done under cover of darkness. Not even Hami was permitted to wait upon me. Instead, a mute palace slave was sent to attend to my needs, and two armed guards were posted outside my door.

No, I reflected; if Ghalilat had been going to be crowned as queen after all, the decision would already have been taken and given out, and she would have been summoned so as to be the first to hear it.

So by now she must know that the future she had looked forward to could never be, and that all the sacrifices she had made had been for nothing. She would die a frustrated spinster without power or progeny, for she was far too old to marry now. With nothing left to lose, I dreaded to think what her next move might be.

That night I dreamed that the Crown Council had to remain in session for ever, because no new queen could be found. We all sat and stared at one another without blinking, while our hair and beards grew long and white, and our toenails and fingernails resembled those of certain holy men in India who think that the more unkempt they look, the more saintly they must be.

When the council members gathered again in the morning, Mafaddat was the last to take his place. His face was set, its expression unreadable, but it seemed that a cloud hung over him so dark and thick it could almost be seen with the naked eye.

All day we sat while names were bandied to and fro, suggested and rejected, weighed and found wanting. One girl was ugly, another weak-eyed, others too short, or too fat, or too thin, or hadn't got the sense they'd been born with. So many insults were hurled and curses exchanged that I began to marvel that Sheba survived as a nation at all. At one point it seemed that Salamat's baby daughter might be chosen even against her own father's wishes, and that he himself might be forced to take on the role he shunned whether he liked it or not. Fortunately, common sense prevailed, for the reason why Sheba *did* continue to exist was that its various princes knew that they were stronger together than they were apart. Only together could they keep rival powers such as the vassal state Hadramaut in its place, and maintain their control of the spice trade that had made them rich.

Then, as the heat of the sun was abating and all of us were weary enough to have elected a crocodile as our queen, one of the brothers of Rafash rose to his feet.

"Princes of Sheba," he began, and his accent was so unlike that of any man who had spoken so far that everyone paid him rapt attention, weariness notwithstanding. "It seems to me that the claim of every girl of noble birth in the whole of Arabia has been considered and discounted. But Arabia and Sheba are not one and the same, for across the Red Sea live the Banu Habesh, who in years gone by you have regarded, and rightly so, as insignificant and unworthy even to be called a tribe. Yet now we are as numerous as the stars in the sky, and our chieftain, my brother Rafash who is sitting here beside me, possesses as much gold and land and wealth of every conceivable kind as any Sheban lord. It is only on account of his comparatively recent acceptance as head of a noble family that he has not so far ventured to speak. But now on my distinguished brother's behalf I ask you to consider the possibility that Rafash's daughter, Makeda, his only child, could be the one for whom you are searching."

A look of astonishment came over every face except those of Rafash and the rest of his brothers. So with sinking heart I recognized that it was no sudden inspiration that had prompted our kinsman to speak. This was exactly what Rafash had been planning all along, and only my own contempt for his coarseness had kept me from seeing it. And there he sat, looking as deferential and unprepossessing as he could manage, leading everyone to believe that it was modesty that had moved him to allow his brother to speak on his behalf, rather than the fear that he would open his mouth and put his dirty great foot right in it.

Silence descended, and the longer it lasted the more horribly convinced I became that the calamity I hadn't even bothered to dread could indeed come to pass. Eventually Rafash's designated spokesman ended the silence himself, launching into an exhaustive list of well-rehearsed reasons why the aforementioned Makeda would make the perfect choice. She was chaste yet beautiful, clever yet refreshingly naïve, and exemplary in her obedience to her esteemed father. Never before had a member of her family sat upon the throne of Sheba, so whichever timeworn tradition you invoked, it could not be argued that the turn of the Banu Habesh to supply Sheba with its queen had not yet come around.

What was I to do? Rafash had allegedly invited me along to prevent the momentum of the council running away with itself and somehow taking us all along a road down which none of us really wanted to go. Yet here we all were plunging headlong in *his* direction, and it was apparently I alone who found myself wanting desperately to run the other way.

Not that it was for myself that I was afraid. It would make little difference to me, I thought, whether Makeda became queen of Sheba or another man's wife. My concern was entirely for her: that she would have her betrothal annulled (her father had always begrudged her her dowry, after all) and be forbidden so much as to speak to a man who was not her kinsman ever again. Then she would be taken away from everyone and everything she had ever known and loved, to live like a prisoner in a garret, albeit a garret embellished with gold and ivory. No more would she be surrounded by forests and flowers, waterfalls and lakes; from her tiny windows all she would see would be mud-brick walls and the desert beyond, until she herself became as dry and shrivelled as everything around her. Could I simply sit back and let this happen? Yet if I attempted to stand in Rafash's way I should likely be torn to pieces by the entire assembly, and Makeda would be no better off than if I had held my tongue.

No; there was one way only in which Makeda could be saved from this fate worse than death. She must be brought from Ethiopia for all the council to behold, so that they might see for themselves how much more African she looked than Arabian, and how badly she limped when she walked. She would have to endure the humiliation of their laughter, but this ordeal would swiftly be over; if she were chosen queen in her absence – in itself an abomination entirely without precedent – the whole of the rest of her life would be ruined.

So when Rafash's brother had finally run out of superlatives with which to describe her, I got up from my place and obtained permission from Rafash to add my own endorsement to this lavish testimonial.

"My lords," I said, "I perceive from your silence that you doubt such perfection can exist. And how wise you are to be sceptical, when all that my cousin has said about the daughter of Rafash must seem too good to be true. Yet happily for you, our laws dictate that no queen can be elected until she has appeared before the council in person and been examined for any fault or disfigurement that might render her unworthy of your choice. Since I myself am beholden to King Solomon of Israel to fetch him merchandise from Ethiopia at my earliest convenience, with the council's permission I could deliver her to you before the new moon after next."

Briefly the chieftains considered my offer without reacting; then I saw them begin to purse their lips, stroke their beards and nod their heads as they saw the sense of it. Of course, it would necessitate their remaining at the palace for several weeks, but they would be sumptuously entertained, enjoying the finest food and drink, and the favours of the fairest slave girls – or boys, according to their taste. Though I myself was a council member I was one without a vote, and therefore could conceivably be granted leave of absence to undertake the council's business, provided that I exercised complete discretion in conducting it. Only Rafash stared at me with narrowed eyes; I supposed he couldn't work out whether I was volunteering to do him a favour or not.

Presently Yuhafri, our president, was helped to his feet once again. Swivelling his sightless eyes around the room he announced, "The proposition of Tamrin the Merchant is accepted. You will leave for Ethiopia at first light tomorrow, and return with the Lady Makeda forthwith. But you will tell no one the purpose of your mission, not even the lady herself. She and those responsible for her in her father's absence must be told only that her father has sent for her. Is that understood?"

"Perfectly, my lord. The council's wish is my command."

Chapter Four

By sunrise the next morning my caravan was on the move.

I had stayed up most of the night organizing my affairs. I secured permission from Rafash to have the commodities I needed to satisfy King Solomon's requirements gathered together back in Ethiopia. Then I despatched the chief of my commercial negotiators, whose name was Mahiko, with a team of fast riders to go ahead of me. They would ensure that everything was assembled for me to inspect upon my arrival in Rafash's capital, thus achieving the swiftest possible turnaround.

But I sent no message to Makeda. I did not want her worrying for days that her father had perhaps been taken ill, or that she was being summoned because she had displeased him in some way. I wanted to tell her myself about the journey she would soon be undertaking, and to give myself time to decide what exactly I was going to say about its purpose.

Although as a rule travel is a pleasure for me, and I enjoy the journey as much as I relish reaching my destination, on this occasion I longed only for the tedium to be over. I scarcely noticed the wide desert skies, and utterly failed to appreciate the grandeur of the mountains through which we had to pass to reach the Arabian coast. I forgot to feel sick when we crossed the Red Sea on the ships my agents had made ready for us, and my heart forgot to leap when I set foot once again on Ethiopian soil and began the ascent from the scorching coastal plain into the gorge-riven highlands where I had grown up. All I wanted was to see the smile that would illuminate Makeda's face when I stepped across her threshold, and for the gods to permit me to bring this whole sorry business to a conclusion that would not see that smile dimmed for ever.

Like Marib, Rafash's fastness of Yeha was set in a landscape of cliffs and mountains, but here the similarity ended. The little valley where the city had been built was itself higher up than the summits of what pass for mountains in other parts of the world, so the climate was mild and the fields green and fertile. Lofty fig trees with great spreading crowns gave shade to the flocks of sheep and goats that grazed placidly on the verdant pasture. Directly above the city reared a mountain that the inhabitants fancied had the form of a lion; long before the worship of Almaqah had arrived with the colonists from Arabia, the native people had imagined this lion to be their protector. And it was true that it did seem to gaze down benignly upon the little square houses that huddled at its base and some way up its lower slopes. Unlike the houses of Marib, these were built of red stone, not mud-brick, and were two storeys high at the most, with flat roofs you could walk on and from which you could admire the views of farmland and forest and the misty distances beyond. As the outline of the lion-shaped mountain emerged from the haze, and the low red blur at its feet became a city, with walls and gateways and houses both inside and out, my heart lurched. A few days hence, Makeda would have to leave all this behind. I could but pray that it would not be forever.

Just as at Marib, my caravan established its camp outside the city walls, but this time on land I owned myself. All became a flurry of activity, with camels and mules being unloaded, watered and fed, and the merchandise we had brought with us from Arabia and Israel being sorted and stowed until the time came for it to be offered for sale.

So well-schooled were my employees and their servants that there was little I needed to do myself about the pitching and ordering of our camp. On the morrow I would send for Mahiko to see how he was getting on with fulfilling Solomon's order, and to find out whether it was ready yet for my inspection. Today all I really needed to do was visit Makeda, which under any other circumstances I would have made haste to do, with a spring in my step.

But as it was, I found myself postponing my visit for any number of trivial reasons. My favourite camel had been behaving a little skittishly when I'd been riding her on the last leg of our journey, so I thought I had better check that she was well. Then I remembered that Hami had complained of having blisters between his toes; I ought to ensure that he had had them attended to so they wouldn't fester. There were some figures I should verify with my chief accountant, and some vases I wanted to be sure hadn't been damaged in transit... and so on and so forth, until I realized that if I did not go up to the palace soon the day would be gone, and Makeda would be going to bed with her heart downcast, because by then she would have been told that her uncle Tamrin was camped outside the city, but he had not been to see her.

Accompanied only by Hami – whose blisters had miraculously ceased to trouble him as soon as he'd demolished a hearty meal – I entered the city late in the afternoon, as the tradesmen in the marketplace were packing up their wares, women were bringing back water from the river in pots on their veiled heads, and shepherds were driving their flocks home through the streets. But even now I couldn't bring myself to go straight to the chieftain's residence.

"Hami," I said, "we must call first at the temple of Shamash to give thanks for our safe arrival. I will go there directly; take this gold piece and buy us a lamb or a kid to present as an offering. I'll meet you there."

Some astonished herdsman would think that his own name had come up before the gods when he received a piece of gold in return for a single animal. But I have often heard it said that Tamrin the Merchant has more gold than he knows what to do with, and I do so enjoy sending a poor man home to his wife and children rejoicing because for once he can afford to put meat on their table instead of tendering everything worth having to his landlord.

The temple of Shamash in Yeha was a more modest affair even than its counterpart in Marib, especially when compared with Almaqah's. Yeha had a shrine to every god you could think of: lion gods and serpent gods, gods with the heads of birds or the tails of fish, or in any other shape which could be imagined. For the gods of Yeha were like its people, a wild mixture of Sheban and African, where the Sheban tended to come out on top but were in constant danger of being toppled from beneath. So the temple of Almaqah was the largest, most frequented and best endowed, but its priests had so far failed to wean Yeha's inhabitants from bowing to his rivals as well as to Lord Almaqah himself.

Once Hami had gone off on his errand, I quickened my pace – for I had other business I wanted to do at Shamash's temple besides giving him my thanks, and I wanted to do it without my servant around.

The courtyard was surprisingly busy with other worshippers, but the temple staff knew me well and I was escorted swiftly to the priest I needed to see. His name was Fasiladash and he was an ancient grizzle-headed sage even blinder and more decrepit than Yuhafri, but his reputation for seeing into the future was second to none. He was said to read it from the entrails of sacrificial victims, from communing with the dead, or simply by drawing lots from a quiver of marked arrows. And he had frequently challenged my own natural scepticism with the remarkable accuracy of predictions he had made for me. With his second sight he saw me now, knowing it was I who approached him when I was still some distance away. He rose and held out his arms and I embraced him, for we had often talked together of the gods and of the mysteries of life and death and what may await us in the world beyond. He started to ask politely after my health and the success of my mission to Israel, but I said, "Fasiladash, my friend, I need you to look into the future for me – or rather, not for me, but for the Lady Makeda."

His sightless eyes were still capable of registering surprise, and did so now, no doubt at the urgency as well as at the nature of my request. He said, "But you have never known whether to believe the predictions I have made for you before, Tamrin. Why should you suddenly trust them now?"

I said, "Let me make up my mind once I have heard what you have to say."

"But these things cannot be hurried. Surely you know by now that you must undergo purification, and that if you sleep tonight in

44

the sacred precinct the god may reveal your future to you in a dream, without my having to say anything at all."

"When it is not my own future I wish to learn? Come, come, old friend, I know *you* well enough by now not to be put off by your priestly prevarications. Just burn your herbs and chant yourself into one of your trances, and tell me what I want to know."

"But you haven't told *me* what you want to know. What is it about the Lady Makeda's future that has aroused your interest? Do you wish to learn whom she will marry, or how many sons she will bear?"

"Just read her future, Fasiladash. It is for the god to put thoughts into your mind, not me."

"Very well. Come with me." And he led me inside – not into the sanctuary of the god, but into a private windowless chamber of his own, where a boy sat feeding a fire against the darkness, and the stale air was heavy with the reek of incense and whatever it was he burned with it to conjure the spirits with which his master would commune.

Fasiladash bade the boy throw more of this potent mixture into the bowl that was suspended over the flames. Then he sat and composed himself upon a stool so close to the fire that its feet were smothered in ashes, and the smoke that rose up from the bowl hid his face from my view. He and the boy began chanting together in unison, in a language utterly unlike any of the several I could speak. Then as the boy kept up the incantation, the voice of the ancient seer became changed. It was neither a growl nor a wail, but some unearthly mixture of the two, which made me want to bolt for the door. Yet I knew I must not, or the spell might be broken, and I was afraid that something dire might befall Fasiladash himself if his communion with the spirits were disrupted.

Then quite unexpectedly the old man started to laugh. It was a strange kind of laugh, guttural and distorted, so that I could not work out if he were still entranced or not. Suddenly, while I cowered rigid with fear, he lunged towards me as though he himself were something supernatural that had materialized in the flames. He seized hold of my shoulders with claw-like hands and said, "Tamrin? I should never have thought you had it in you."

"Had it in me? Had what in me?" Did he think I was possessed?

"To influence the spirits like that, so that you could have the last word after all."

"Influence the spirits? I can't think what you are talking about. Fasiladash? Are you all right? Whatever did you see?"

For all at once he was tottering on his feet, and the hands that grasped my shoulders were shaking, not as any old man's hands might shake, but violently, so that I was shaking too. Then abruptly he released me and backed away against the wall, where he stood leaning against it and staring at me with incredulity, respect and amusement all at the same time, as though he were no more blind than I was.

I said, "Fasiladash, you had better tell me what you saw, before I am tempted to beat it out of you."

"No, Tamrin. *You* tell *me* what I saw, since you know as well as I do."

"*I* know? How could I possibly know?"

"I have no idea, my friend; all I know is that I don't need to tell you, and so I shall not, for Shamash has not constrained me to do so. We must each of us wait and see what the future has in store for Makeda, and for you. Then depending on how things turn out, perhaps I shall ask you again one day to tell me what I saw, and then we shall know which of us can truly command the spirits."

He left me to grope my way out in a daze. Hami found me wandering haphazardly about the temple court like a man walking in his sleep. With the sacrificial lamb wriggling and kicking under one arm, he somehow steered me to a bench with the other, and began fussing ineffectually as was his wont, asking me repeatedly what had happened, but getting no coherent response.

I was in no doubt as to what Fasiladash had foreseen for Makeda. Yet he found it so implausible that he imagined that someone – even I – was playing tricks with his mind. Stricken, I sat with my head in my hands, while Hami said, "Master, we should make our offering before this lamb gets away from me and starts rampaging all over the temple."

So I let him lead me to one of the open-air altars, where the priests helped me to go through the motions of thanking Shamash for blessing our journey. But it was all empty ritual, for I no longer wanted to thank him for anything.

I did consider postponing my visit to Makeda even further by going to the temple of Almaqah to elicit a second opinion. But what would be the point? If the priests of Almaqah saw something different, I should scarcely be reassured, for this would only serve to convince me that everything about the gods was bewildering and obscure. Besides, by now the sun was beginning to set. So reluctantly I directed my steps towards the palace.

Unworthy of comparison with the fabulous royal palace of Marib, Rafash's residence was nevertheless imposing and in its own way, beautiful. Built of rose-red stone which took on a golden glow in the evening light, its second storey stood proud of all the cottages clustered around it, for it was set on a high stepped platform and its ceilings too were high, supported on forests of square-cut pillars.

As soon as I was spotted and recognized, the soldiers on guard let me pass, and then excited servants vied with one another to usher me into the presence of their master's daughter, because they all knew how much she loved me. Hami was led away to be entertained in the palace kitchens, and I was taken to Makeda's chambers.

She did not notice me at first, because she was standing by a window watching the sunset. Her back was towards me, and her thick black hair plunged down it past her waist, all bound up in tiny beaded plaits. She wore a plain linen tunic, sheer and white after the fashion of the Egyptians, and I had to avert my eyes momentarily on realizing how much more like a woman she appeared than the last time I had seen her. Her handmaid, Sabla, stood beside her and noticed me first; she tapped her mistress on the shoulder and at once Makeda was a girl once again. She gave a gasp of pure childlike joy and flew into my arms.

"Uncle Tamrin! Uncle Tamrin, you're here at last! You have been gone so long, I thought you were never coming back. You wouldn't believe how much I've missed you, how *lonely* I've been without even

Father here to torment me. Oh, Uncle Tamrin, did you see him on your way home?"

"Yes, I saw him," I assured her when I could get a word in, never ceasing to wonder why she should care, when he showed no sign whatever of caring about her.

"And have you brought me a present? Another little god or goddess for my collection, perhaps?" For the first time she loosened her embrace enough for us to survey each other's faces; hers was so bright with expectancy that my heart lurched again, as I feared for a moment that in my wretchedness I had forgotten to bring the little ark with me. Then I remembered that I had been carrying it in the pouch at my waist all along. I undid the drawstring and took it out, holding it on the palm of my hand for her to see. "That," I said, "is the nearest thing the people of Israel have to a statue of their god. It's a copy of the symbol they keep in their temple in Jerusalem; King Solomon had it made for you himself."

"King Solomon? For *me*?" Momentarily she just stared at the little box in wonder, before reaching out and taking it tentatively between delicate fingers. She opened the lid and looked inside, but it was empty.

"Well," she declared, "I don't suppose it is much different from a baetyl, though it's certainly the strangest one I've ever seen. But it's gold, isn't it, right through?"

"Yes it is, though the real one is made from acacia wood with a veneer of gold on top, else it would be much too heavy to carry."

"They carry it about, then, at their festivals?"

"Not any more, but their ancestors carried it through the desert on their way home from slavery in Egypt."

"And the real one is empty, just like this?"

"No. They say it contains the Ten Commandments of their god, and perhaps a staff that belonged to one of the leaders of their people, and a pot of miraculous food. But no one knows for sure, because anyone who tries to look inside is struck down dead on the spot."

Her lovely eyes opened wide, and I saw for the first time that they were painted with kohl. She was indeed growing up. Hurriedly she replaced the box's lid and said, "Uncle Tamrin, you might have warned me! Well, at least we know now that my little model hasn't been imbued with the same magic. I shall keep my special jewels in it; just the ones Minash has given me."

Minash – the name of her betrothed. My heart sank further and my despondency must have shown in my face, but Makeda was too excited at my mere presence to see me properly at all. She thrust the ark at her handmaid to put away, and pirouetted spontaneously on the spot, clapping her hands as she did so. "You know, Uncle, it's less than two months now until my wedding? I've been practising walking without a limp so that Father won't be too ashamed of me when he presents me to my new husband. Sabla has been teaching me. Watch!"

Holding her head erect like the women I'd seen bearing pots upon theirs, she walked gracefully to the window, turned and walked back, and it was true, you could hardly see her limp at all. Now my heart fell so far down in my boots that in spite of her own abounding joy, Makeda could not fail to notice that something was wrong.

"Oh, Uncle Tamrin, I'm so sorry. How heartless of me to keep talking about my wedding, when you..." Tears sprang into her eyes and she hugged me so hard once again that I feared I might cry too. For I knew that she had drawn the wrong conclusion; she thought it was grief for my own late wife that was making me look so downcast.

I held her tight but said, "Makeda, do not distress yourself on my account. The pain of loss recedes with time. After all, you no longer grieve for Angabo."

"Angabo?" Briefly she seemed confused, then her smile returned and she said fondly, "Yes, I suppose I did love Angabo. But I was only a child. How can a child not love the hero who has saved her life?" A silence fell between us, as each of our minds travelled back to the appalling accident which neither of us wanted to remember. Then she said, "You are right, of course, Uncle Tamrin. Time can comfort, even if it cannot heal. But if it is not my aunt for whom you grieve, what is it that is making you so sad?"

"It is nothing, Makeda. Or rather – " (for I could see from her knitted brows that she was not about to let the matter drop) "rather, it is something your father said when I saw him, but he expressly forbade me to tell it to you."

Of all the explanations I could have given her, this was possibly the most foolish, but under the intensity of her gaze I found that I could no longer think straight at all. Her beauty and her innocence conspired to undo me, and unable to withstand them any longer I looked away in desperation at Sabla, her handmaid, who stood saying nothing but taking everything in. She had served Makeda since they had both been small children; she was the daughter of another cousin of Rafash who had owed him a large sum of money and given him his daughter as a slave in lieu of paying the debt. So this girl, who should have been betrothed to a wealthy man herself, was in thrall to Makeda, and she was as fiercely jealous of her mistress as she was haughtily obedient. Now she regarded me with smouldering, malevolent eyes, and I realized that she had grown up too, but not into someone I could trust or respect, or who was likely to help me out now.

"Is Father in trouble?" Makeda was demanding, and I realized that she was tugging at my sleeve, piqued that my attention should be anywhere but fixed on her. "Have the other Sheban chiefs banded together against him? I did tell him it might be dangerous to go to Arabia when he has never sat with the council before."

"So he told you where he was going?"

"Of course he did. I can always extract the truth from him if I really try. Just as I shall with you." For a second the gleam in her eye was anything but innocent, but then concern for her father took its place once more and she said, "But how I wish you wouldn't try to hide things from me, either of you. I do believe you're as bad as each other, thinking I'm still a little girl when I'm not. If Father is in danger, or sick, or in need of any kind, you have to tell me, Uncle Tamrin, if you love me at all."

She stood on tiptoe before me and put her arms up onto my shoulders; her kohl-painted eyes were troubled and her lips, reddened with berry juice, were parted and moist in her anxiety. I closed my own eyes and placed my hands over her trembling fingers in reassurance and said, "I love you dearly, Makeda, but your father is not in trouble. You must believe me."

"I do believe you." I opened my eyes to see her nodding earnestly; then with the same solemn intensity she said, "Actually, I know why Father was so keen to go to Arabia when he heard that the old queen was dying. I know he wants the council to make me the queen of Sheba. But the idea is totally ridiculous, and if this is what is upsetting you, Uncle Tamrin, you can stop worrying now. You know how stupid my father can be, as well as I do. How could an ugly lame black girl from the jungles of Ethiopia become queen of the Arabians?"

I was genuinely lost for words. How could I have anticipated that she might have discerned what her father had in mind from the outset, when I myself had had no such inkling? And what would be the good of my telling her that my initial reaction on learning the truth had been exactly the same as hers? Except, of course, that I knew she wasn't ugly and couldn't imagine that she truly thought so either. While I stood there stricken with bewilderment and misery in equal amounts, she kissed me merrily on both cheeks and said, "There! You have no reason to be sad any more, Uncle Tamrin. You must be happy. In fact, since you seem to think I am to be your queen, I *command* you to be happy. Because our dreams have come true: when you go back to Arabia I'll be travelling with you at last! I'll see the lakes and forests, elephants, leopards and antelopes. I'll see the *sea*, Uncle Tamrin, and then deserts where it's so hot you can't even put your feet on the ground. I'll meet hunters, and sailors, and nomads..."

I opened my mouth to bid her calm down, but she said, "Of course I'm coming with you; the chieftains will have to see me before they can make up their minds to reject me. As long as we get going soon, I'll be back in plenty of time for my wedding. I must pack for the journey straight away. What do you think I should take?"

How could I tell her she had better take everything she had ever valued or would ever want again? How could I explain that once she was queen she would never travel anywhere again, except in a litter with curtains so thick she wouldn't be able to see the light of day, let alone the wonders of creation? How could I convince her that she would never walk in a garden and smell its flowers, or feel raindrops on her face, but have to live as a prisoner in a lonely tower until she died of old age or despair?

But then, as she began to bounce about her chambers pulling dresses out of chests and piling up a heap of sandals and slippers in the middle of the floor, forgetting entirely not to drag her crippled leg behind her, I found myself daring to hope that everything might turn out all right after all.

Chapter Five

On my way home from Arabia I had scarcely taken note of my surroundings, or of anything that had happened en route. Travelling back there with Makeda I noticed everything, because I saw it all as though through her eyes, for the very first time.

The forests lush and the rivers swollen with recent rain, plunging down their gorges in swirling torrents; the brilliant plumage of parrots, jays and finches; the grace of bounding antelopes; the valiance of ibex jousting on tiny ledges, then leaping away from us, startled, up the jagged cliffs… so much beauty, so many wonders more spectacular even than my traveller's tales had led her to imagine.

And yet there was such poverty and misery too: the half-starved peasants labouring in fields they did not own for men who did not care; small boys seeking pasture for skinny goats, driven away by sticks and stones to the barren margins of the farmland where overgrazing had left them nothing but dust and thorns for fodder; rival bands of mangy youths shedding each other's blood over some senseless family feud or the right to butcher an animal they had hunted but to which some other clan laid claim. I saw it all more clearly than ever before, and Makeda saw it too, in alternate fascination and dismay.

For although these were her father's domains and people, she hadn't had the remotest idea of what anything looked like or how anything was done beyond the bounds of the quiet valley in which she had been brought up. To her, nature had consisted of the palace gardens which she herself helped to tend, and the manicured fields just outside the city walls, most of which belonged to me and were therefore farmed by tenants who were not exploited or oppressed. But the further we left Yeha behind, the harsher the landscape became, as did conditions for most of those who lived there. Rafash himself neither knew nor cared how his tribesfolk lived, as long as they paid him his taxes and caused him no trouble, and there were enough greedy officials and soldiers and owners and managers of land doing very nicely, thank you, out of the status quo to ensure that it was preserved.

I suppose I could have tried to protect Makeda from the stark realities of life for the rural poor a little longer; I could have tried to insist that she travel in a curtained litter, to practise being queen. But I knew she would not have obeyed me. From the beginning she pestered me for a mule of her own, and one for Sabla to ride behind her; when they had learned to ride these proficiently, she informed me, she would ask for camels instead.

If it had been up to me, I should have had her haughty slave girl walk, as Hami was accustomed to do. Yet for some reason Makeda was as indulgent towards the sullen little wench as she was devoted to her neglectful father.

For the first few days, our road took us through mountains and forests. It was not too hot in the daytime and the nights were distinctly chilly, so the tents had to be erected each evening and fires lit to banish the cold as well as to keep wild animals at bay. Makeda shared a tent with her handmaid, as I did with Hami, and I had guards posted outside her tent door, not only for fear of kidnappers but also because I had marked the way that some of the mule drivers looked at her and at her maid. Makeda didn't seem to notice but Sabla certainly did, and she wasn't making any complaints.

Each morning while Hami prepared breakfast for the four of us, I would get out the little portable altar I always took with me on my travels and set it up in the direction of the rising sun. Then I would pour a libation to Shamash to beg his continued blessing on our journey, and most days Makeda would join me.

For there were many dangers we might conceivably encounter along the way, from stampeding elephants to marauding baboons, hyenas, wolves, and venomous snakes, to say nothing of hostile tribesmen. Fortunately my caravan was large enough and sufficiently well protected to deter most warbands from attacking us, but baboons are not as circumspect as men, and will try their luck in almost any situation if they see there is food to be had or some interesting object to be carried away. I have heard stories of baboons stealing babies from their cradles, and even pushing grown men over cliffs. But then again, they are probably blamed for a good many crimes that were committed by human beings all along.

Another ritual that had to be performed every morning was the bathing and dressing of Makeda's leg. Sabla did this – just as she had had to do daily for almost half her life – and always in the privacy of their tent, for Makeda strove constantly to keep her disability and her suffering secret. Sabla didn't complain aloud about the distasteful chore any more than her mistress did; in fact, I was sure she drew perverse comfort from the fact that while she was a slave and her cousin free, at least she was whole and unblemished. If she *had* still been free, I regretted ruefully, *she* might have been going to Arabia to be made queen instead of poor Makeda. But when I contemplated the coldness in her eyes and the hardness about her mouth, I was forced to concede that she would have been no better than Ghalilat.

After almost a week in the highlands, at length our road began its descent towards the coast. But before we reached the sea at the port of Aduli we would have to cross the deadly searing dustbowl that Egyptian travellers have nicknamed Seth's Basin, after their god of destruction, for they say it is the hottest place in all the world. Here our camels would prove their worth, since any water that flows down into this basin from the highlands dries up at once, and what seem from a distance to be lakes are great expanses of desiccated salt.

For Rafash this meant wealth, for salt is almost as precious a commodity as incense. But for the wretched salt cutters – mostly slaves and convicts – whose lot it is to extract and pack it up to be transported, salt means only death, due to endless backbreaking toil in the burning sun with so little water to drink that when they expired their corpses looked like monstrous shrivelled locusts. This is why I have never dealt in salt myself.

If all went according to plan, we should be able to cross the deadly depression in a matter of days.

"So now Sabla and I *must* exchange our mules for camels," Makeda announced with satisfaction; and certainly most of the mules we had brought with us thus far would shortly be turning back. The food they had borne had already been eaten; anything else they had been carrying would henceforth be added to the burdens of the camels.

I separated out two of the more accommodating camels from the rest and redistributed their loads. Then I chose two of the least uncouth drivers to lead them. These bade their gangly charges kneel down on the ground for the girls to mount. Makeda, whose driver was a wizened old man of few words, mounted without any difficulty, in spite of her handicap; Sabla, whose driver was young and – I saw now – rather handsome, struggled and giggled and required an inordinate amount of help. Swiftly I sent him back to his companions and picked out another man to take his place.

In this furnace of a landscape it behoved us to strike camp early each morning and keep riding late into the evening, so that we could stop and wait out the hottest part of the day resting in the shade of semi-erected tents, for there were no trees or bushes for miles around. But in spite of my precautions, I began to worry about Makeda's physical well-being for the first time since leaving Yeha. She had stopped pointing and commenting on interesting things that she saw, and frequently rode with her head bowed and her eyes closed against the glare. She winced frequently, too, for the gait of a camel is very different from that of a mule, and it wasn't doing her damaged leg any good at all. But when I suggested we rig up a litter she recoiled in horror, and for the next hour sat rigid, staring fixedly ahead like an Egyptian statue.

But her fortitude crumbled shortly before we were due to stop for our siesta, when we came upon a crew of salt cutters hard at work beneath the midday sun. There were women among them, and children as young as five or six, but the overseers who were with them carried whips, which they used without mercy on anyone who showed signs of flagging. When one little boy keeled over not a spearlength away from her, Makeda could stand it no more.

"Stop!" she ordered her driver, and when the taciturn old fellow affected not to hear, she cried, "Stop, I beg you!" with such anguish in her voice that he reined in the camel at once, fearing that Makeda herself was on the point of collapse. He brought the beast to its knees and Makeda slid off the saddle, making straight for the boy who lay motionless by the roadside.

There was nothing I could do but call a halt; our behemoth of a caravan stopped in its tracks, and briefly the startled overseers ceased their slave-driving and gawped at Makeda, a finely dressed rich man's daughter kneeling in the dust with the head of a salt-caked urchin cradled in her lap.

"Water! Sabla, fetch some water!" Makeda shouted, but for once Sabla made no move to obey her. Silently I motioned to Hami, and he took one of the waterskins and handed it over with the stopper pulled out.

Gently Makeda wet the boy's parched lips. I saw his eyes open and then widen in fear and confusion at the sight of the anxious, delicately painted face looking down into his. Then his stare became fixed and his mouth slack, and his head lolled to one side.

She did not grasp at first that he was dead, never having seen a person die in front of her before. She kept begging Hami to help her get water down the wretched child's throat, but of course Hami was well aware that there wasn't any point, and we didn't have water to waste. When he prised the waterskin from her she almost fought to get it back, with the poor dead boy still draped across her lap.

In the end I got down myself and made them both give up the waterskin to me. Then I laid the body of the boy on the ground, closed his eyes, and crossed his arms decently over his chest. I commended his spirit to the gods and, without another word to anyone, scooped up Makeda in my arms and sat her on the front of my saddle, to ride with me.

She didn't say a word either. I knew she was weeping, but she wept in silence, with no shaking of the shoulders or unseemly heaving of the bosom. Meanwhile Sabla looked at her sidelong, her nostrils wrinkled as though she could smell on her mistress's breath the stench of contamination from the corpse we had left by the road.

Only when we stopped for our siesta did Makeda pass any comment about what had happened and what she had done. She left Sabla asleep beneath an awning and came to find me; I led her away from our companions, out of range of flapping ears, and we sat side by side in the sliver of shade provided by the jutting load of a camel that had hunkered down to rest. Makeda leaned her head on my shoulder and said, "If only we had come past sooner, Uncle Tamrin. Then we might have saved that boy's life."

"Yes, we might," I agreed. "But only for a day or two, or even less."

"No! We could have taken him with us. When he got better he could have helped Hami with his chores."

"But he didn't belong to us, Makeda. He was someone else's slave."

"Then at least we should have buried him properly. We should not have left him by the wayside for the rats."

"And how were we to dig a grave in solid salt? Besides, the next team of workers to come through would certainly have dug him up."

"But no child should have to die like that, or to work like that! Not even a grown man should have to endure it."

"Not even a bandit, or a murderer? A man who has tortured others? Most of the salt diggers are convicted criminals, or slaves who have run away from their masters."

"No! I mean yes, perhaps, but… oh, Uncle Tamrin, when there is so much evil and suffering everywhere, and so many poor people, don't you feel that you should *do* something? Don't you feel guilty to be rich?"

"I do what I can when I can, Makeda. I make sure that my own workers and servants are not ill-treated. And I plead poor men's causes before your father if I know they are in the right."

She sighed, and leaned her head in closer to my neck. "I suppose you do, Uncle Tamrin. And you had Hami bring me water when Sabla was afraid to. Thank you at least for that."

I was certain it wasn't fear which had held Sabla back, but I did not say so. Instead I said quietly, "You were very brave today,

Makeda. And not only in the matter of the boy." For I had seen that she was rubbing her leg; she stopped at once when I noticed.

"This is nothing compared with what other people suffer. I know that now. I'm ashamed when I think how much I've let it bother me."

"I have never heard you moan about it once."

"Maybe not, but I moan when I'm alone, to the gods. I shouldn't be so ungrateful." Suddenly she pulled her skirts up over her knee to reveal the bandaging round her calf, and the scarring that extended above and below it – a thing she had never done in my presence before. "Do you think these scars will ever fade away, Uncle Tamrin? Do you think the skin will ever stop breaking open in the place where the bone came through?"

What could I say? I was already feeling decidedly queasy; I wished she would talk about something else, yet I could not help but be touched that she should want to share with me her hidden pain. When I didn't respond, she said, "Sometimes I think the scars are getting fainter, but today after all that riding... you know, Uncle Tamrin, when this happened to me it was the second time I could have died in one year? Angabo was so brave, rescuing me from Sando's temple when Father wanted to give me to the god. I know he shouldn't have helped me, but after what happened this morning, I think I know why he did."

This was the one thing I wanted to discuss even less than the accident that had left her crippled all those years ago. But I could not prevent myself from exclaiming, "Shouldn't have helped you? Whatever do you mean?"

She left off examining her scars, covered them again with her robes, and turned to stare at me. "Why, Uncle Tamrin, what Angabo did was terribly wrong. To interfere with a sacrifice, to disrupt a holy ritual in the temple of a god! It was the will of Sando that I be given to him; Father had been told that very clearly."

"It was the will of a god that you be left in a pit of poisonous snakes to die a horrific, agonizing death? It was the will of a god that a beautiful, innocent little girl should die, just because her abominable father wanted sons instead of a daughter? It was the will of a god that – "

"Uncle Tamrin, don't get angry! Please, don't talk about Father like that…"

I could see she was going to cry all over again, but I *was* angry and could do nothing to hold it in, for I had repressed it as long as she had been repressing her pain. I could see the whole nightmare unfolding before my eyes even now, like a mirage in the midday heat; I could hear the screams of Makeda's mother when Rafash had beaten her black and blue for bearing a stillborn child after Makeda, and then no children at all; I could smell the rankness of his breath when he had drunk himself stupid after the priests of his malignant serpent god Sando had told him that the only way to get himself sons was to give up his only daughter to death in exchange. I saw him dragging her off to the temple when he was so far gone in his cups that he could barely stand; I heard his rabid laughter ringing round the sanctuary when they had cast her into the snake pit, and he had yelled, "Sons, Sando! Give me sons! Take this useless bitch-whelp and give me sons!" But Angabo, who had played with Makeda since they had both been babies, and whom she worshipped already as a hero, had run to the temple and somehow got her out with a rope while the priests were entranced and oblivious, and Rafash had passed out cold on the very lip of the pit. Once her disappearance was discovered, the priests had declared it an omen and refused to perform the ritual a second time.

"I don't know why you should care, Makeda!" I heard myself shouting, incapable of restraining my railing tongue. "Your own father gave you up to die."

"It was the will of heaven; he had no choice – "

"And then he drove your poor mother out of his house so that she died too, and married a woman as poisonous as Sando's snakes, who gave him no more sons than your mother had done, and who made no attempt whatsoever to behave like a mother to *you*. He would have slain Angabo as well, if the boy hadn't run off into the jungle, never to be seen again! By any god there is in heaven, Makeda, your father was not performing some pious duty when he dragged you to Sando's temple. He was sacrificing you on the altar of his own ambition – and now he is doing it again!"

For a long time after that she sat stunned into silence, never having seen me lose my temper before. I knelt with my head in my hands, in spite of my wealth and repute feeling like a worthless worm. I had failed to protect Makeda from her father's caprice in the past; now here I was actually doing his dirty work for him, though he would have seen me as a failure too, because he would think that I had not kept the reason for our journey a secret from his daughter as I had been told to. Like as not he would have me executed too when he found out about my ineptitude, but it would be no more than I deserved. The world I inhabited was riddled with wickedness, and not only was I doing precious little to counter it, but I was adding to it myself.

At last she said very gently, "Don't be distressed, Uncle Tamrin. I know you think they will make me queen and I'll never be happy again. But they won't; there's no way they will be able to, once they have seen me. What matters is only that I abide by the will of my father, to make up for all the grief I have caused him over the years. If I tell him I'm prepared to do whatever he asks of me, he may be able to love me after all. And perhaps the gods will even grant him sons."

And perhaps elephants will fly, I thought bitterly, and golden rain will fall from heaven. But I'd long since stopped believing in miracles. I'd also stopped believing in capricious gods who savour the smell of human blood. At least the sun and the moon floated way above the sordid mess of worldly affairs; they at least would accept an animal's blood as an offering in place of a man's. But whether they ever really heard the prayers of their devotees I did not rightly know. How I wished I might talk again with Solomon, even now. Perhaps his counsel would have been able to soothe my tortured soul.

Not that Makeda didn't continue to try. Though it was I who should have been comforting her, she did her best to lift my spirits, as she had so often been able to do. But she chose to attempt it by returning to the subject of her wedding, reiterating how confident she was that it would go ahead as planned, until I wanted to grab her and shake her and insist that it was time for both of us to face reality.

Yet the more she talked, the more the truth began to steal upon me that she wasn't really in love with Minash, her betrothed, deep down, for all that she prattled about him incessantly. Rather, she was in love with love, with the fact that in spite of her lameness a man had been found who was willing to give her status and children and a household to manage, so that other women should not despise her. In fact, what she really wanted from marriage was a reason not to despise herself, and this she might acquire even more surely by becoming queen. But I didn't find the thought reassuring.

Eventually she tired of trying to distract me, and accepted that for once the cloud of my depression was too thick to be dispersed by the usual means. Planting a kiss on my forehead she got up and returned to the spot where she had left her maidservant asleep.

A moment later she was back, breathless and distraught.

"Uncle Tamrin, Uncle Tamrin, come quickly. It's Sabla. She's gone."

And indeed she was; when Makeda dragged me back with her to their awning there was no sign whatsoever of her handmaid. But neither was there sign of a struggle, and no one had heard a thing. So she hadn't been kidnapped or abducted by ravening beasts.

It didn't take me long to work out why she was missing, but it took a good deal longer to track her down. Our caravan was of considerable size; there were pack animals and men in their hundreds, and tents and awnings everywhere. In the end they were caught in the act: Sabla and the handsome young camel driver I'd had the good sense to redeploy, but not soon enough. They were so intent upon their pleasure that they didn't even notice when Hami and I tore their awning down about their ears, and they had to be dragged apart like fighting dogs.

I had the youth flogged and put on a diet of bread and water until we reached Aduli; he would not offend again. But what to do with the intractable Sabla? She was unrepentant, that much was clear, and from the smug defiance in her eyes I surmised that this was not the first time she had had knowledge of a man. But she was Makeda's servant, not mine, and it was for Makeda to decide her punishment.

And Makeda as usual chose to let her off the hook.

"Poor Sabla will *never* get married," she explained to me sadly, when I ventured to question her judgment. "It would be cruel of me to deprive her of what little love she can find."

I thought: love had no more to do with Sabla's latest exploit than it was fear that prevented her from bringing you water for the dying boy. But all I said was, "You mean that she has transgressed in this way before?"

Makeda answered with a sigh, "I could not say for certain, but she has gone missing before, back in Yeha, and more than once. Now it all makes sense."

I went back to my brooding, because it seemed that a little more of Makeda's innocence had been lost along with her handmaid's virginity.

Three days after that we reached the port of Aduli. Nowadays it is a sizeable settlement; back then it was scarcely more than a fishing village with a reasonable harbour, where a flotilla of my own ships lay at anchor ready to carry us across to Arabia. But the sea was rough from recent winds; we should have to wait until things were calmer if we didn't want to risk losing half our cargo at the bottom of the sea, not to mention my stomach.

So we were obliged to pitch camp once again, though I wished it could have been otherwise. For sailors are no less predatory than the drivers of camels, and Makeda would insist on engaging them in conversation at every opportunity, asking about their lives and the places they had visited, and how their families managed without them when they were at sea. Meanwhile Sabla ogled and flirted, and they flirted back, but they seemed to sense somehow that this was not the way to treat Makeda. Having been busy with Mahiko, inspecting the loading of Solomon's consignment onto the ships, I came back to find Makeda singing and playing her lyre to a bunch of brawny seafarers who were sitting enraptured, for once paying Sabla no attention at all.

But the sailors' stories tugged at Makeda's heartstrings as insistently as the plight of the salt cutters. Many had been sold to ships' captains as beardless boys, to pay off a debt, or during a famine. Some had left wives and children to go on a distant voyage and had come home to find their families murdered by bandits or their wives seduced away by other men. Nor were sailors and fishermen Aduli's only inhabitants: abandoned children roamed the harbourside begging for their bread and looking for a chance to stow away on a boat that might take them to a new and better life. I gave Makeda food and clothing to share among them, as a result of which they took to following her everywhere like a pack of hounds. She didn't seem to mind, and though Sabla chased them away repeatedly, they always came straight back.

Makeda had the good sense not to tell them who she was, however. After she overheard a couple of drunken ruffians roundly cursing her father for taxing them into penury she kept her identity a close secret.

When at last the time came for us to set sail, a huge crowd had gathered on the harbourside to wave us off – or rather to wave goodbye to Makeda. How much more there was to my young kinswoman already than the sweetness and simplicity for which I had long admired her myself.

I soon discovered she was a better sailor than I was, too. While I spent most of the crossing closeted away with my head over a bucket, she was helping the crew coil ropes and hoist sails, and swinging from the rigging like a monkey. Since none of the men were particularly young or good-looking, Sabla sat in the stern with a scowl on her face, until Hami made her a doll out of knotted rope. I should have thought her much too haughty to appreciate so childish a gift, but she favoured him with such a dazzling smile that I had to warn him to give her a wide berth.

Though the winds had died down, the blue-green sea was still choppy and flecked with foam. Sea birds circled and called overhead, leaping dolphins competed to escort us, and the air smelt of salt and the plentiful fish the crew caught for us to eat. Makeda found the whole experience enchanting, though she was by no means oblivious to the dangers with which our captain and his helmsman had to contend. The Red Sea is bedevilled by unpredictable currents and hidden reefs upon which many an unwary voyager has come to grief.

Makeda's keen eyes were the first to spot land as the Arabian coast emerged from the haze on the eastern horizon. "Look! Uncle Tamrin, Sabla, come quickly. We shall soon be there," she sang out, her excited cries echoed by those of the gulls above her head. Sabla ran to lean over the bow beside her, and it struck me all of a sudden how alike they looked from behind, with their plaited black hair, slender build and similar height. They might have looked alike from the front as well if Sabla had pouted less, and worn less paint on her face. It was she who had taught Makeda to use cosmetics, though Makeda by instinct favoured subtlety over ostentation. Not that this prevented Sabla from reinforcing her mistress's belief that she was ugly. "I know you can't help it," I had been astonished to overhear her say one day. "But you might at least try to make more of your better features." Though I had willed Makeda to slap the little vixen's rouge-daubed face, she had only looked sad and turned away.

But there was no time now for such tawdry concerns, for the Arabian coast was drawing ever closer; we could see the balsam and cassia trees that adorned the seafront and the teeming mud-brick houses that comprised the port of Muza. For this was no fishing village with a harbour. Muza was a city, grown fantastically rich through trade, as I had myself. Any moment now, Makeda, wide-eyed maid of Africa, would step onto the shore of the fabled land whence her forefathers had come.

Chapter Six

When at length we arrived in Marib, however, my wide-eyed maid was looking distinctly the worse for wear. There had been more mountains to cross, more extremes of temperature to be endured, more harrowing sights to sap one's morale. Worse than the harshness of the climate was the evidence of men doing evil to one another. We saw despairing farmers mourning their shrivelled crops, the water that should have nurtured them having been stolen by others further uphill who had built rickety dams to capture all the flow for themselves. We saw starving children with great distended bellies squatting by the roadside plagued by clouds of insects, too listless to beg or even to cry. And in Marib itself we came upon these children's elder sisters huddled in doorways in the forlorn hope of doing business with their own emaciated bodies. The arrival of our caravan in town had them scrambling to their feet and fighting like stray cats over the attentions of so many men of relative substance who hadn't touched female flesh in weeks.

I had always regarded such creatures as spiders in human form, in whose webs my camel drivers and muleteers were caught like so many hapless flies. Yet to Makeda they were fallen angels in desperate need of rescue, but whom she was powerless to help. Every pauper and prostitute she was obliged to pass by added his or her burden to the load of guilt and grief Makeda was carrying, so that when the time came for me to take her to the palace she looked as weary and downtrodden as any of the wretches for whom she had been weeping. All of which was to the good, I thought, for now a girl bearing less resemblance to an Arabian queen would have been hard to imagine.

But if I thought I could present this haggard, careworn Makeda directly to the Crown Council to have them dismiss her out of hand,

I was wrong. No, she was to be whisked away by the palace women and made to look her best whether I liked it or not. I tried to take courage from this, for surely the women who prepared her must discover that she was not a spotless lamb after all. Yet if the council had as good as made up its mind already… Her appearance before it was scheduled for the following day, and only then would I see her again when I sat with the princes of Sheba who had waited so long to find out whether Rafash's claims about his daughter's comeliness and purity were true.

I did not spend the interval in idleness. First I talked with Bijo, whom I had left in Marib to keep track of developments.

"Well?" I said to him. "Has Rafash succeeded in turning them all against him in my absence? Has he let them push him out on a limb, without understanding how he has done it, as he feared might happen at the outset?"

"Regrettably no, master," Bijo replied, knowing full well what outcome I desired. "Nor has any other contender for the throne emerged while you were away. At the moment, Makeda is Sheba's only hope."

I said, "But while the women are preparing her they will see… Bijo, Makeda is not… unblemished. There was an accident, when she was small."

"That may be," Bijo replied. "But if Makeda is judged unsuitable we may be left with Ghalilat after all."

"Ghalilat? Surely she gave up her royal pretensions long ago."

"Indeed she did. Yet with so much time having passed and no serious rival having emerged, her hopes have been rekindled. They say she was starting to doubt that you would ever return; indeed her father, Mafaddat, has been petitioning the council to re-examine her case on the grounds that Sheba has never been so long without a queen, and that the princes of our vassal state Hadramaut may take advantage of the situation to rebel."

"So she won't exactly be pleased now that I am here with Rafash's daughter after all. Still, if she happened to catch a glimpse of Makeda on our arrival, the sight may have set her mind at rest."

"Possibly, master," Bijo conceded, but I had never seen anyone look less convinced.

After that I walked abroad in my camp as was my custom, talking with any man who had time to spare. But already I missed Makeda tagging along in my wake, even if it did mean that I wasn't perpetually being made to feel as though all the world's problems were my personal responsibility.

That night I did not even bother to get ready for bed, since I knew I would not sleep. Instead I studied my books of wisdom and wished that more of it had rubbed off on me.

At dawn I was escorted once more to the palace, and once more I took my seat among the assembled chieftains and their supporters. But this time there was no wary silence. Rather, the sultry air thrummed with anticipation, and until his daughter made her entrance, all eyes were fixed on Rafash.

As soon as she did appear I was undone, for in her shimmering golden gown she might have outshone the Mother Goddess herself. Her oiled skin gleamed like ebony, her hair, released from its many plaits, tumbled past her waist like a cape of scrunched black silk. Her face, at once proud and lovely, drew every eye in the room to itself, and as she looked back, her gaze was quite without fear or guile. For a time she simply stood in the doorway taking everything in, waiting for the invitation to step forward. Then as old Yuhafri, the late queen's father, bade her approach him, she walked forward into our midst, and even I who knew of its existence could detect no trace of her limp. All was lost, I was sure of it, but when Makeda turned momentarily to catch my eye, though she must have perceived my distress, she only smiled.

"You know why you are here, my dear, do you not?" Yuhafri quavered, reaching out to take each of her hands in his. I noticed that although his hands shook as he extended them, in her firm but gentle grasp they grew almost steady.

"Of course, my lord," she answered, but when his sunken eyes began to narrow she added, "Tamrin the Merchant did not tell me. He didn't have to." So it seemed that I wouldn't lose my head after all, but I wasn't sure I really cared.

Did she know already that Sheba's princes had made their decision? Or did her confidence stem from the conviction that there was still no way she could be chosen? Perhaps she expected to be subjected to interrogation, during which she could expose the reason for her ineligibility even though the women who had made her so beautiful had evidently chosen not to reveal it. Certainly *I* was expecting a lengthy discussion, and that we should all be sitting here for most of the day at least while opinions were bandied back and forth.

Yet the chieftains had had little else to do in my absence than to ask Rafash all the questions they could think of. All that had remained for them to do was to see his daughter in the flesh; this they had now done, to their eminent satisfaction. Yes, she was dark, but her complexion and facial features were flawless. Yes, she was of a family only recently ennobled, but this might have distinct advantages, and besides, she carried herself like a queen already. Rafash might lack political experience, but this meant that he wouldn't get away with bullying his fellow chieftains in the way Mafaddat would undoubtedly have done. In fact, Mafaddat was now the only man who might stand in Rafash's way.

So I sat there willing him to try; nor did he disappoint me. When, like me, he saw which way things were going, and that this was his final chance, he rose to his feet and began to speak, without asking Yuhafri's permission, as he presumably suspected it might not be given.

"Noble princes of Sheba," he began in his deep, booming bullfrog-like voice. "I beg you, pull back now before you plunge headlong into disaster like game driven over a precipice. Do not entrust our ancient and distinguished nation to upstarts who know nothing of history or diplomacy or even of Arabia itself. Will you make this black minx of a girl your queen when you know nothing of her *own* character, or even whether she is chaste? I demand that at the very least she be examined by physicians to ensure that her maidenhead is intact. Did not our ancestors decree first and foremost that our queen be a virgin? Yet we have only this African upstart Rafash's word for it that his daughter has not slept with every man in Ethiopia."

I feared we might have another fight on our hands at any moment, but evidently Rafash had decided to prove himself worthy of his peers' respect. With remarkable self-restraint he said, "Go ahead, Mafaddat. Have her examined by whomever you please. But I would stake my own life on her virginity; indeed I *do*. If her virginity is found to have been compromised, you may have my head nailed to your city wall and *my* private parts served up on your dinner plate." Except that he didn't say "private parts"; decency prevents me from repeating his words exactly. But they achieved the desired effect. His peers roared with laughter; one particularly jovial fellow thumped him hard on the back and bellowed, "Well said, my friend, well said! *I* say we subject this exquisite young lady and her father to no further scrutiny, but that we proceed directly to the voting, since I for one know already how I shall be casting mine. What say all of you?"

A murmur of assent passed around the room; Yuhafri held up a hand for silence and said, "Well? Are there any objections to the voting being held at once?"

I toyed with the idea of intervening. If Makeda had so much as thrown me an appealing glance I would have done so, whatever the consequences. Yet she merely smiled at me once again, so that I was left still wondering whether she had suspected all along that this was how things would turn out.

"Very well," Yuhafri announced. "Since no one has objected, we shall proceed. But first I must ask the Lady Makeda and her father to leave us, along with all members of the council who are not entitled to vote."

This took me by surprise; I had not realized that non-voting members would be required to leave the room. Briefly I dared to hope that I might snatch a private word with Makeda while the election was in progress, but she and her father were led away to wait elsewhere.

The woman I did see on my way out was Ghalilat. She had been lurking with an attendant at the back of the antechamber where the servants of the council members sat dicing and dozing as they awaited their masters, and plainly she had not expected anyone to emerge from the council chamber quite so suddenly. Since I was first through the door, I was possibly the only one to mark her swift departure. The sight of her sent a shiver down my spine.

I found Hami among the servants and beckoned him to follow me out, for the room was stuffy and I did not care to stay there. Guards appeared from nowhere to escort us from the palace, but once we reached the ground floor with its cool spacious hall I bade Hami sit down beside me on the bench that ran along the wall, and ordered one of the guards to see that I was informed once the momentous decision had been taken. I might have no vote, but I was Tamrin the Merchant, one of the most celebrated men in Sheba, and only the most obtuse of officials would not rush to do my bidding.

Hami did not dare ask me how things had gone, but my face must have told its own story. When the guard duly brought word that Makeda had been elected all but unanimously I barely reacted. Her coronation would take place on the morrow; tonight she would be made ritually pure and then sleep in a special chamber by herself, with two royal guards posted by her doorway. Not even Sabla would be permitted to share her room.

But I had a very strong feeling that Hami and I should not quit the palace to return to our encampment. I requested a guest room, to which I was eminently entitled, and then had Hami go in search of Sabla and bring her to me.

She came grudgingly, having been consorting with the handmaids of the previous queen, who would now be Makeda's maids too. Sabla would have pride of place among them, an arrangement with which she would be more than happy.

"Sabla," I said, as kindly as I could bring myself to address her, "you must find out for me exactly where Makeda is to sleep tonight. I fear that her life may be in danger."

"I beg your pardon? Who would dare to threaten the queen-elect?"

"Don't argue with me, Sabla. Once she is crowned, no one *will* dare to threaten her, since she will be under Almaqah's special protection. Until then… let us say we cannot be too careful."

"Very well, Master Tamrin. I shall find out." And she bobbed out of my presence with a flurry of crisp new skirts.

When she returned presently with the information I wanted, I said to Hami, "We shall wait until well after nightfall when everyone is asleep. Then we shall find a place to conceal ourselves near to Makeda's room. If we do not do this, and something happens to her, I shall never forgive myself."

"But master, we cannot follow her around for ever. She will have her own guards to protect her, and besides, must we not return directly to Israel?"

"It is as I said to Sabla, Hami. Once she is queen, her life will be sacrosanct, and only an imbecile with no fear of gods or men would dare lift a finger against her. Before that, it is a different matter."

So when night had fallen and the palace was sleeping, Hami and I slipped out of our chamber and followed the directions Sabla had given us, carefully evading the few guards who patrolled the corridors; though the palace was heavily guarded against intruders, within its walls few security measures were thought necessary. The main thoroughfares and stairways were reasonably well lit by torches burning in brackets at regular intervals, so we could find our way without carrying lights of our own, but once or twice we had to dive into pitch-black side passages to avoid casting telltale shadows on the walls.

At last we came within sight of the room where Makeda had been closeted away. As Sabla had indicated, we could tell we were in the right place from the presence of two armed guardsmen who stood with spears erect to either side of the doorway. Hami and I hunkered down in an unlit alcove and prepared to spend an uncomfortable night cramped on the floor.

After a while I began to feel rather foolish. Did I imagine that Ghalilat was going to materialize from thin air, simultaneously stab two fully armed soldiers to death, and then murder Makeda in her sleep? Not even with her brawny father to help her would she stand the remotest chance of success. Nevertheless I did my best to stay awake, but having had not a wink of sleep the night before, my eyelids inevitably started to droop.

I was roused by piercing screams. Instantly alert, Hami and I made straight for Makeda's bedroom, on whose threshold we almost fell over the prone body of one of the two guards. He had evidently had his throat slit by the other, who now had Makeda cornered.

Things clearly hadn't gone as he had planned, though, for he hadn't been quick enough to butcher her in bed. She must have heard him come in and leapt up before he could grab her; now there was a large table between them, over which he could not reach her.

"Drop your weapon!" I yelled at him from behind, hoping only to distract him long enough for Makeda to flee the room. Fearing he had been apprehended by a party of soldiers and not by an unarmed merchant who scarcely knew one end of a sword from the other, he wheeled round to face me, and that would have been the last I knew had not Makeda's screams brought the men of the nearest patrol charging in like a herd of elephants. They wrestled the traitor to the ground, disarmed him and prepared to finish him off, but I shouted, "Take him alive! We need to know who he was working for." For it was hardly likely that he had been acting on his own initiative.

They dragged him to his feet and took him away for interrogation. Makeda ran into my arms and buried her face in my shoulder.

"Oh, Uncle Tamrin, where would I be without you? You must stay with me always and be my chief adviser, or my high priest, or anything, to keep you here with me."

"Makeda, you know very well that I am under oath to return to King Solomon. Do not ask me to break my word."

"But if you hadn't been here; if you had not heard…"

"Ghalilat will not dare to harm you once you are queen. Or rather, *she* might, but no man would agree to do her bidding."

"Ghalilat? You think *she* was behind this?"

"I am sure of it, though we may never find out for certain."

And indeed we did not, because the guard who had been arrested had a phial of poison hidden in his clothing, which he drank before he could be questioned. He knew he was marked out for death regardless, and poison was better than torture.

But when the day of Makeda's coronation dawned, both Ghalilat and her father had vanished without trace.

The coronation went ahead nonetheless, though some of the purification rituals had to be repeated. It has always been the Sheban custom to hold the coronation as soon as possible after a queen's election, and since the chieftains of all the tribes but one were in residence already there was no reason to delay. The ceremony was to be held in Almaqah's temple; hence there would be a procession there from the palace.

Teeming crowds thronged the streets, for this was the one chance they would get to catch a glimpse of their new monarch before she was whisked away to her tower in the sky. Of course there was no need for Tamrin the Merchant to mix with the seething throng; I had a ringside seat in the temple court, behind which stood Hami, whose view was equally good. Makeda was borne through the streets in a litter, open to public view, because until she was crowned there was no embargo on the people seeing her face. And as she stepped down, it betrayed no sign of last night's ordeal, though I could not begin to imagine what was going through her mind.

She wore a heavy white robe with narrow pleats; her hair hung loose down her back but for a portion which had been twisted up in a coil on the top of her head, and against which the royal diadem would rest. Her eyes and mouth had been impeccably painted, more heavily than she would have thought of doing it herself, yet the effect was majestic rather than crude. She was escorted by Yuhafri (who had to be assisted in his turn) and by Luqman, her predecessor's grand vizier, who would now be hers. I could not but feel a twinge of jealousy, for it was a role I might indeed have coveted had it been possible for me to perform it. But he was a solemn, sagacious-looking man, not noticeably shifty. I had to trust that I would be leaving Makeda in responsible hands.

In her train walked her ladies-in-waiting, Sabla to the fore. Sabla was turning this way and that, enjoying the crowd's attention as though it were directed at her. Perhaps she thought it was; she was a pretty girl, after all, and perhaps she really did think her mistress was ugly, though I doubted it very much.

Before the great altar in the courtyard, open to the sky, the prescribed words were spoken and offerings made, and Makeda's brow was anointed with incense and myrrh. Then she received the royal regalia: not only the diadem, but a massive necklace of office with the royal cipher suspended over her breast, and its counterweight behind. Then there were quadruple bracelets for each of her arms and ankles, and immense gold earrings which would surely have sheared through the lobes had they not had brackets which hooked around the tops of her ears as well as the standard fixings. Once the insignia were all in place and the declaration was made that Makeda, daughter of Rafash, was now the rightful queen of Sheba, the priests began throwing some substance on the altar which created a huge pall of smoke, hiding the anointed from the sight of all. When it cleared, Makeda had gone; all that could be seen was her litter, and its curtains were tightly closed. It was very likely that even I should be prohibited from ever seeing her again.

In the event, I saw her that very evening, because she sent for me. Clearly she had begun in the way she meant to go on.

The queen's private apartments were many storeys up in the palace tower, but there was an audience chamber on a lower level to which a few privileged men and women might be admitted, of whom I was to be one. When I was led inside, Makeda was seated on Sheba's throne on an elevated dais at the far end; no doubt it was made of gold and encrusted with jewels, but just then I did not notice, since I had eyes only for her. I could hardly fail to notice Luqman and Rafash standing to either side, but they weren't there for long.

"Leave us," she bade them, and when Luqman's eyebrows lifted she said, "I have not read of any law which denies the queen of Sheba her privacy when she desires it, or keeps her from associating with the members of her own family. Leave us, please, gentlemen. You may return when Tamrin the Merchant has been dismissed."

Each of them bowed and retreated; protocol required even her father to bow before her, though he and Luqman were the ones who would wield the power, or so they assumed. As soon as they were gone, she jumped down from the throne and raised me from my knees, to which I had fallen before her, as was fitting. She hugged me and led me to the dais, where we sat side by side on the steps as we had sat so very recently in the shade of a camel's load. Already that felt like another world.

"Your Majesty – " I started to say, but she interrupted with, "Makeda, Uncle Tamrin. Don't be silly."

"Makeda, I'm so sorry. I ought never to have brought you here. This has all been my fault."

"No, Uncle Tamrin. None of this has been your fault. It is my father's will that I am doing, not yours. But in any case it is my destiny, and you knew that even before we left Ethiopia."

"But how…?"

"I can read you like an open scroll, and I knew you would have been to the oracle before you came to me."

"But your wedding, Makeda, and poor Minash…"

"He doesn't love me; not like that. It is because of who my father is that he wanted to marry me, not for myself."

"But you will *never* have a husband, never have children…"

"All the people of Sheba will be my children, Uncle. Surely I won't need any more."

I didn't know whether to be awed at her resignation or afraid that she was embarking upon a flight of fantasy from which she was destined to come crashing down like Icarus, the Greek boy in the legend, the moment I left for Israel. Impulsively she took hold of my hands and squeezed them as hard as she could.

"Only promise me that you'll return from Solomon's court as soon as you can," she begged me. "As long as I know that each day that passes brings me a day closer to seeing you again, I shall be content."

"I shall come back with all speed, I promise. But the journey to Israel is long and arduous, much longer than the journey we made to get here. It will be eighteen months at least before I return."

"By which time you fear that I shall have been thoroughly spoiled." And when I hesitated to comment, she added, "I hope that doesn't mean you won't bring me a present this time."

I still didn't know what to say, which made her laugh and squeeze my hands more tightly than ever. "Oh, Uncle Tamrin, what a misery you are, always fearing the worst of everything. I do believe that if a genie offered you three wishes you would refuse to use them in case everything went horribly wrong."

Would I? This certainly wasn't the way I was accustomed to seeing myself. I should never have made my fortune if I hadn't trusted that at least some of my ventures would be successful. Perhaps it was the fact that riches hadn't restored my lost happiness that was causing me to stop believing in happiness altogether. Makeda was still young and foolish enough to think that things were bound to turn out all right whatever happened, and it would be cruel of me to disillusion her.

So I just smiled and nodded my head when she said, "Just think of all those poor people we met on our travels. Now I'm queen I shall be able to help them." I agreed that she was right when she claimed that there would surely be enough water for all the Marib farmers if some of them weren't so greedy and careless. I let her prattle on to her heart's content about how she would make sure that everything was shared out fairly so that there would soon be no beggars or prostitutes on Marib's streets any more. In fact, I bit my tongue so convincingly that she finished up by declaring, "There; even you can see that my election was no accident."

And she was still buoyant when at last I took my leave of her, determined to get a full night's sleep before commencing my preparations for the long journey ahead. I let Hami help me into my nightclothes and before I lay down he undertook to massage my neck and shoulders so that sleep would come more easily – a skill in which he had had plenty of practice.

"Hami, you are truly a gift from the gods," I told him as I felt the tension ebbing away under his expert hands.

"Master, you know that to serve you has always been a pleasure," he replied, then added after a moment, "Do not worry about the Lady Makeda, master. As well as Sabla she now has all the servants anyone could ever want. She has her father to keep her humble, and Luqman to assist her with affairs of state. And she won't be expected to *do* very much, I don't suppose."

"She won't be expected to, no," I agreed. "But she will want to. She will not be satisfied with presiding over religious rituals and judgments of disputes in which her own opinion will not even be solicited. She will want to change things, Hami, and she won't be able to."

"Well, she wasn't able to change things when she lived in her father's house in Yeha. So she shouldn't be any more frustrated than she ever was."

"But she hadn't *seen* so much before. She hadn't seen injustice, or poverty, or any of the evils that come about when rulers rule only to please themselves, to indulge their own hunger for power and luxury. Nor were the atrocities she did witness being perpetrated in her own name. Each time a new queen ascends the throne, the poor and downtrodden dare to hope that things will change, but they never do and never can, because the men who are Sheba's real rulers are all as bad as each other, and the officials who do the work of government on their behalf remain in post from one queen's reign to the next."

"At least Rafash is strong in body and will. He will be able to keep the princes of Hadramaut from threatening to revolt all the time and rob Sheba of the income from their incense and myrrh. And he'll be able to keep the other Sheban chiefs from quarrelling and fighting among themselves and pursuing blood feuds whose cause no one can even remember. That in itself could make things better."

"It may make things more orderly, but not necessarily better. And it won't make anything better for Makeda. Oh, Hami, can you imagine her being happy, held like a prisoner in that tower, from whose windows she can see only buildings and sand? She will have no gardens to walk in, no mountain views to lift her gaze beyond the tedium of her mundane existence. She will pine for Ethiopia and her highland home, and it may be two years before we can do anything to help her."

"With respect, master, Makeda is her father's responsibility, not yours. Might it not be that you are fretting on your own account rather than on hers?"

"Perhaps I am, Hami, perhaps I am. It is true that I have come to see her as the child I never had. If only my Zauditu had lived longer, how different my own life might have been."

"You would have made a good father, master, if the gods had granted you children."

I smiled, and patted Hami's hands as they kneaded my grateful shoulders. "That we shall never know," I said. "But I do know that it will feel good to be on the open road again, and to be headed for Israel. Who knows what opportunities for trade and commerce we may encounter en route? Then we shall get back to what I really *can* do well."

Chapter Seven

The journey back to Israel took nine months almost to the day. Much of it I enjoyed as I'd hoped that I would, yet the prospect of arriving at my destination made me happier still, and the nearer we drew to the borders of Solomon's kingdom the lighter my heart became.

It wasn't that the scenery was any greener or more fertile – from the south one approaches Jerusalem through the Negev desert, and a more barren and less hospitable landscape one could scarcely imagine. Nor was it simply a yearning for the comforts of civilization after nine months' privations, or even the anticipation of fulfilling the obligation under which I had been placed. Rather, my heart was glad because in Solomon it had encountered another that seemed to beat in time with itself, and soon we should be meeting once again.

Every morning without fail I offered up my prayers and libations to Shamash for protection from the dangers of the road, but I couldn't help but contrast the detachment of this businesslike transaction with the intimacy Solomon had claimed to enjoy with the God of Israel. In the flurry of Makeda's coronation I had temporarily forgotten how eagerly I had longed to talk with Solomon again about such things. Never since the death of my beloved Zauditu had I encountered such a kindred spirit.

And what was still more astonishing was that Solomon in all his glory seemed as keen to renew our acquaintance as I was, and not solely because of the treasures I had brought him from Africa. Long before my caravan crossed over into his territories it had been spotted by the king's scouts and a guard of honour had been dispatched on swift white horses to escort his honoured guests up to the capital. There my closest associates and I would be feasted in sumptuous style and later taken on a tour of the magnificent Jerusalem temple to appreciate how far the work on it had progressed. As a personal friend of the king, I myself would be accommodated at the palace and eat at the king's table for the duration of my stay – which could last for as long as I liked.

Nor was the banquet that was held to welcome us the stiff, formal kind of affair where there is little real conversation but only the exchange of pompous pleasantries. The king's couch was drawn up so that he would be able to recline at the same table as everyone else – and not the king only, but his consort too, until later in the evening when the wine would flow more freely, and she and her ladies would retire to their apartments.

"Tamrin, my friend, I do not believe that you had the opportunity on your previous visit of meeting my lovely Egyptian wife," Solomon enthused in fluent Sheban as he bounded into the hall where the banquet was about to be served, embracing me and kissing me on both cheeks in a single fluid gesture. I wondered at how youthful he looked for his thirty-odd years, and how carefree, for a king. "Makshara, my dear," – and here he switched effortlessly to Egyptian – "allow me to present to you Tamrin the Merchant, by far the richest and wisest man in Africa. Tamrin, meet the Lady Makshara, daughter of Pharaoh Siamun of Egypt."

"Queen Makshara," I murmured, embarrassed by Solomon's fulsome and exaggerated description of me, and somewhat overawed, because the bejewelled young lady to whom I was being presented was quite the most stunning creature I had seen in all my life.

But Solomon laughed, "Lady, not queen, Tamrin. In Sheba you have only queens; among us Hebrews the title is not used even for the king's consort. Women know how to have their own way with us men quite well enough, without needing titles to help them."

Makshara's welcoming smile did not waver, but I marvelled that the pharaoh should have married his daughter into a dynasty where she would not be addressed as royalty. It showed what a formidable reputation Solomon had carved out for himself, or else how far Egypt had fallen from her ancient glory – or conceivably both. In her prime, Egypt's kings had ruled a mighty empire and prided themselves on never marrying their daughters to foreigners at all; nowadays Pharaoh Siamun would have been happy if he could have claimed to be in control even of the Nile Valley, half of which was ruled in effect by the priests of Amun at Thebes.

When the king and his glittering partner had taken their places at the low central table, the meal was served. There was a bewildering array of the strangely delicious bloodless meats for which Israelite cooks are famous. There was every kind of fish, the bounty of the many and varied seas and lakes to which Israelite fishermen enjoy access. There were vegetables and fruit in abundance, for although the Negev desert is arid and hostile, the hills surrounding Jerusalem and the countryside to the north of it are well watered, and anything will grow there.

Much of the food was heavily spiced, apparently in my honour, for Solomon had heard that this is how Shebans like it. He told me that the Tyrians like spices too, especially ginger, which they say stops sailors getting seasick. But there was no pork, no shellfish, and no cheese served with the meat, because the Israelite god is very particular about what his people – and therefore their guests – are allowed to eat.

He doesn't mind them drinking wine, though, and there was plenty of that, mostly served after the food had been cleared away and the ladies of the court had departed. At other royal courts there would have been spectacular entertainment laid on to go with the drinking: dancing girls clad in meagre costumes, acrobats with rippling muscles, fire-eaters and the like, to give everyone a night to remember. But Solomon had arranged only for a homely looking boy in modest attire to strum a lyre and sing quietly in a corner so that conversation might continue unimpeded. Bijo, Mahiko and their colleagues might have preferred something a little less highbrow, but I was well content.

"And was your journey as enlightening as it was successful?" Solomon enquired of me, once I had assured him that I had brought with me all the treasures he had requested.

"I'm not sure that 'enlightening' would be the right word," I responded. "It was certainly interesting, but not quite in the sort of way I might have liked."

"This all sounds most intriguing." Solomon reached for a bunch of grapes, and began munching his way happily through them. So I found myself telling him the whole story of Makeda and her coronation, and how guilty I felt at having abandoned her to her dismal fate.

"Your niece must be an exceptional woman if she cares more about injustice than she does about clothes and jewels," Solomon observed with a mischievous glint in his eye.

"Yes, but would that it were otherwise, for she will have all the clothes and jewels any woman could desire, yet no freedom to pursue the desires of her own heart." I did not explain that strictly speaking Makeda was my cousin and not my niece or that she was still more girl than woman.

"So perhaps it is time she asserted her right to be queen in truth and not in name only," Solomon suggested, but I merely grimaced in reply, because this was exactly what I feared she would try to do.

"Well, I myself have been studying and thinking a great deal since last I saw you," Solomon said, as I seemed to be letting our conversation flag. "And I have been working hard on my own book of wisdom; don't you remember I promised you a copy when it is finished? For research I have been reading the Law Code of Hammurabi of Babylon; I believe you know it?"

"It is one of my favourite books," I agreed readily. "If a nation could truly be governed according to its precepts, its people would be fortunate indeed."

"Yes, but it is astonishing how similar many of these precepts are to the statutes of Moses by which I seek to govern here. Sometimes I wonder if it's possible that Hammurabi received his wisdom directly from God just as Moses did."

"He couldn't have got it from the same god, surely? Hammurabi venerated the sun god Shamash, which is why I have long sought to do so as well."

"You know, Tamrin, the older I get and the more I learn, the more I begin to think that the God of Israel is the God who reveals himself to every man who truly seeks him, wherever he comes from and by whatever name he believes God should be called."

"But how can that be? There are as many gods as there are peoples – indeed more, for in some places they worship many gods at the same time."

"But are not the gods of the various nations very like to one another, only with different names? Egyptians, Babylonians, Shebans... do they not all have gods of war, and storms, and earthquakes, and the like? Do they not have goddesses of love and childbirth, and are not their attributes similar? Could not all these attributes be regarded as different aspects of one, almighty God who is more than male or female, and encompasses all the rest? After all, the annals of my ancestors tell me that the God of Israel once stopped the sun on his way across the sky so that his people would have time to achieve victory over their enemies in battle. How could this have happened if the sun himself were not subject to Adonai's power?"

"Adonai's?"

"The word means 'the Lord'; it's one of the ways in which we Hebrews have come to refer to the God whose true name is too holy to be uttered aloud."

"And who plays a part in your history as well as in your rituals." I recalled on my previous visit to Israel having been amazed at the way the Israelites believed that their god had actually delivered them from slavery in Egypt and enabled them to win back their ancestral lands which had been occupied by Canaanite invaders during the time of their enslavement. Then I thought again and said, "But the gods make conflicting demands upon us; they all have different desires and expectations, just as we humans do. How can your one almighty God be divided against himself?"

"Perhaps it is we who have not understood him correctly. After all, he does not always speak to us as straightforwardly as we are speaking to each other now. In all my time as king he has only addressed me once in audible words."

"Solomon, you are uniquely favoured if he has personally addressed you in any way whatever! But what do you mean? You had a vision of some sort? God appeared to you in a dream?"

"It may have been a dream, for it happened at night, but it was much more vivid than any other dream I have had, either before or since."

"But what did he *say*, for heaven's sake? Have you told anyone else of your experience?"

Solomon smiled, and topped up my half-empty wine cup himself, without asking a slave to come forward. "All my subjects know of my experience, for they needed to hear of it in order to understand the source of the wisdom by which I strive to rule them. You see, Adonai appeared to me after I had been offering sacrifices on my people's behalf; he bade me ask whatever I wanted from him, and he promised to grant my request."

"Really? It sounds too good to be true! Whatever did you ask for?"

"Isn't it obvious from what we have been saying already? I asked him for wisdom, Tamrin; wisdom for ruling his people with equity, because I was young and near the beginning of my reign, and did not feel adequate for the task ahead of me. And he told me that since I had not asked for riches, or the destruction of my enemies, he would give me both wisdom and everything else a king could need besides."

For a while I sat amazed, simply shaking my head. Perhaps he thought I didn't believe him, for he added, "And so far he has been true to his word, Tamrin, in all respects except one."

I raised an eyebrow to invite him to continue, still not trusting myself to speak without implying disbelief.

"I have asked him for many sons, from whom I may choose a worthy successor, but though my wife and I have been married for eight years – almost as long as I have been king – so far we do not have a single one."

"Well, I have met other men in my travels who have waited longer than eight years for the arrival of their first child," I assured him, grateful that at last I had something helpful to say. "Besides, in the case of a king, too many sons can be as much of a curse as too few, for rivalry among princes – or indeed among princesses, if you are a Sheban – is a sure harbinger of bloodshed."

"True enough," Solomon conceded. "And I should know, for there was bitter rivalry between me and my brother Adonijah when my father David was dying, and even after David was dead and I was established on the throne, my brother did not give up. In the end he left me no choice but to silence him for ever." He paused briefly, his cup halfway to his mouth, even now visibly grieved by what he had felt obliged to do. "Yet no child at all in eight years… I cannot help but be concerned, Tamrin. Many men in my position would have divorced their wives and remarried, or taken another wife alongside the first. But the Law of Moses does not advocate this kind of behaviour – and besides, when one is married to the daughter of the pharaoh of Egypt, rejecting one's wife in favour of another is scarcely to be regarded as expedient."

Deciding that any comment I could make to this would almost certainly be inappropriate, I steered our conversation back towards God and the gods, and we spent the remainder of the evening amicably discussing whether we thought the future was already determined or whether as mortals we can influence the hand of fate – or the hand of God, depending on how you think of him.

The following morning Bijo, Mahiko and I, each accompanied by a servant, were given a guided tour of the temple precincts by Solomon himself. Bijo and Mahiko had had little to say for themselves at the banquet, having been considerably out of their depth. This morning they had rallied somewhat, finding themselves on firmer ground; indeed all of us felt more familiar with the idea of a god who lived in a temple than with one who masterminded history.

Actually there was much that was familiar about Solomon's gleaming limestone edifice, not least because its architect had been a Tyrian, and Tyrian temples are much like those of other pagan peoples. So there was a great open courtyard with an altar and an enormous cauldron borne on the backs of twelve bronze oxen, which would be filled with water for purification. There was a sanctuary building with freestanding pillars by its entrance, within which was hidden the holiest place of all, where instead of an image or baetyl, the mysterious Ark of the Covenant would be housed.

For now we were allowed to see inside all these places, for nothing had yet been consecrated, and everywhere there were craftsmen – both Tyrian and Israelite – and labourers – mostly Israelite – going about their business. Some were laying long planks of cypress on the floor of the sanctuary while others worked on the cedarwood panelling for the walls, and still others walked back and forth fetching tools and materials. As we made our way around, Solomon explained how the treasures we ourselves had brought from Ethiopia would be incorporated into the design and furnishings; most notably the gold was to be used to line the walls of the Holy of Holies and to plate the olivewood cherubim that would stand guard over the Ark of the Covenant; their eyes would be made from our sapphires.

Solomon also paused frequently to chat with the workmen, as I was wont to do with my own employees, and I was impressed by how many names he knew and by the interest he showed in these rough men's lives. (He spoke the Tyrian language with the same fluency as Hebrew, Sheban and Egyptian, and with a good accent.) I was also impressed by how quiet and orderly everything seemed to be for a building site; there was no hammering and banging, and no audible swearing. Noisy work was to be done elsewhere, and every care had been taken to create and maintain a reverent atmosphere, even though the god was yet to take up residence in his earthly home.

"So where has the ark been kept until now, Your Majesty?" Bijo wanted to know. All morning his little eyes had been darting this way and that as they sought to take in as much information as they could.

"When my ancestors were returning from slavery in Egypt, the ark had its own special tent, known as the tabernacle," Solomon answered. "After that it was kept for a while at the house of a pious man called Abinadab, who was pretty much the only fellow anyone knew who could have resisted touching it in all the time it was in his keeping."

"It is forbidden even to touch it?" I exclaimed. "I thought it was only removing the cover that incurred divine punishment."

"That's what Abinadab's son Uzzah thought too. He reached out one hand to steady the ark when it was being carried from his father's house to its present temporary accommodation in Jerusalem on *my* father's orders – and he was struck down dead on the spot."

"Surely that was quite uncalled for," objected Mahiko, who as my chief negotiator had a finely tuned sense of fair play. But Solomon only shrugged his shoulders as if to say: God is God. Who are we to judge him?

But Solomon himself was passionately interested in justice too, as became clear to me within days of my arrival in his capital. A large amount of his time was spent in hearing cases and finding equitable solutions to disputes among even his lowliest subjects, all of whom had the right of appeal to the king. He was gifted in proposing resolutions that no one else could ever have come up with, and he frequently found in favour of a peasant, a woman, or even a slave against a wealthy landowner, even if the latter had offered him a bribe. One rich farmer accused a landless neighbour of stealing his crops; Solomon merely reprimanded the farmer for not leaving the poor man anything to glean, as the Law of Moses said he should. A master complained that his slave had run away; Solomon asked how long the man had served him, and whether or not he was Israelite-born.

"Yes, he's a Hebrew," the master replied. "He has served me more than ten years, and nothing like this has happened before."

"In that case you have been lucky," Solomon informed him. "For doesn't our law state that a Hebrew slave must be freed after seven years? He has given you three extra years already, so now let him go."

The more I watched him in action, the more I knew that the most important present I could take back to Makeda this time was a portion of Solomon's wisdom. I began to write down every example of it that I could.

Not that I spent every hour of every day following Solomon around, though he would not have minded if I had. As my Hebrew improved (for a merchant should always be a linguist) I made other friends too, among the men who served him; in spite of my promise to Makeda to return as quickly as I could, my own men and beasts needed time to recover from their arduous journey, and Mahiko needed time to negotiate with his Israelite counterparts on my behalf. I spent time with Zadok, Solomon's high priest, a spare and austere man of middle years, who said little but knew much. Then there was Zabud the king's adviser, and Ahishar the palace steward, each of whom was prepared to share with me his perspective on what made Solomon an exceptional ruler. One particular friend I made very early on was a certain Jehoshaphat, who was Solomon's chief recorder and who administered the archives relating to Solomon's reign and to his father's. From him I learned as much about Solomon as I did from the king himself, for Jehoshaphat adored him and talked of him incessantly.

"Solomon is blessed indeed if all his subjects revere him as fervently as you do," I said with a smile, when Jehoshaphat had been extolling his royal master's virtues once again. We were sitting in the leafy courtyard of Jehoshaphat's house, in the shade of a vine which his gardener had trained across a trellis above our heads. Jehoshaphat's two youngest sons played contentedly around our feet; my servant Hami was pulling grotesque faces at them and making them laugh.

"Well, I can't pretend that *everyone* reveres him," my new friend conceded. He was a genial, portly little man who loved his food and wine as much as he loved his king. "Those who consider it their right to make money in whatever way they please, by oppressing their workers, cheating their customers and walking all over their rivals, don't think much of Solomon at all."

"No, I don't suppose they would. He must have some pretty formidable enemies as a result, for the sort of men whom most kings would take care to cultivate, he abhors, and I can't imagine that they take it well."

"He does have enemies, but in any country the rich are few and the poor are many, so his friends vastly outnumber those who hate him."

"But powerful enemies can make connections abroad, with kings and princes who think more as they do. Does Solomon not fear trouble arising from some such quarter?"

"Certainly there are men to watch. There is a character by the name of Hadad the Edomite, who thinks he has a right to Edom's throne. Edom is one of our vassal states; if Hadad gained control there he would undoubtedly foment rebellion against Solomon's suzerainty."

"And is he likely to gain control?"

"He might, since when he was driven out of Edom in the first place he was given sanctuary by Pharaoh Siamun and lives at his court. Siamun even gave him his sister-in law as a wife, and the couple have a son."

"But Siamun's daughter is Solomon's wife!"

"So Siamun is shrewd enough not to put all his eggs in one basket – and who can blame him, when you think what an enfeebled kingdom *he* inherited."

"I see. And is Hadad the only such threat?"

"No, not by any means. There is Rezon of Aram, a warlord who has set himself up in some fortress near Damascus with a band of rebellious rogues who are just as violent and unscrupulous as he is. He would do anything to oust Solomon, given half a chance. But at present Solomon is a good deal stronger than he is. Solomon has chariots and horses by the thousand stationed in his garrison cities. Unlike his father, David, he is not by inclination a man of war, and would never attempt to attack or annex territory from a neighbouring state. But he would certainly be prepared to defend his own borders if he had to, and he has the means to do so."

"Well, I suppose if he believes that this land was given to his people by God, it is a sacred as well as a political duty for him to preserve it intact."

"He owes it to God and to his people to keep his inheritance not only intact, but peaceful and secure. Solomon sees himself as the shepherd of his people, Tamrin, and a shepherd is not only responsible for the sheep in his care but answerable to the owner of the flock. The people do not belong to Solomon but to God, as indeed does the land. Solomon is *accountable* to God. He is not his own master, or above the Law of Moses, any more than his subjects are."

I was thinking that as soon as I returned to my room that evening, I would add all these insights to my written account. But Jehoshaphat was still pontificating, for Solomon's unique understanding of kingship was his favourite topic.

"He *consults* his subjects too, Tamrin, which many wise men have cited as the hallmark of a truly great king. Solomon is not afraid to ask the opinions of others, and to weigh them carefully before reaching a decision. Because of that, we his counsellors feel free to speak our minds candidly rather than to tell him merely what we think he wants to hear. For example, there was serious disagreement among us as to the wisdom of building a port at Ezion-geber on the Red Sea. I for one thought we might be in danger of overreaching ourselves. In the end the project has gone ahead, but there was never any ill feeling between the king and those who had sought to dissuade him from pursuing his plans."

"Ezion-geber?" I leaned forward with renewed interest, for I had not heard of this development, which might have serious repercussions for Sheba and hence for the relations between Solomon's nation and my own.

"Why yes; Solomon is creating a fortified harbour and building a city there, right at the Red Sea's head, so that he and his ally Hiram of Tyre can send trading ships down the coasts of Africa and Arabia. Up until now their ships have had access only to the markets of the Western Sea. But you know that Solomon has copper mines at Timna, less than a day's march to the north of Ezion-geber? If he could export copper and other commodities to the south as well as to the north – "

"Of course." There was no need for Jehoshaphat to tell me why Solomon might want to do such a thing, for it was perfectly obvious. But I didn't like the sound of it, and Rafash and his tax-gatherers would like it even less. Ezion-geber lay at the southernmost tip of Solomon's territory, almost in Arabia. If Solomon and Hiram had ships plying up and down the Red Sea, they would no longer need to rely on camel caravans trekking the full length of the Arabian peninsula risking countless attacks by bandits – and being fleeced by taxmen at every oasis through which they were obliged to pass. They might even be able to source their incense and myrrh directly from Hadramaut, and other commodities from India or southern Africa, and leave out Sheba altogether. This was a matter of grave concern, and one I thought Solomon ought by now to have mentioned to me.

So as soon as I could politely do so, I made my excuses to Jehoshaphat and took my leave, with Hami scuttling after me. But I didn't return to my rooms to write down the insights the recorder had shared with me; instead I went directly to the palace and requested an appointment with the king.

"But you are the king's friend, Lord Tamrin," I was told. "You don't need an appointment. His Majesty will receive you as soon as he has dealt with the case in progress. Please, take a seat, make yourself comfortable." And servants began bustling around me, offering to wash my feet or bring me refreshments, so that I felt rather guilty for making my petition a matter of such apparent urgency.

Before I had had time to enjoy any of the sweetmeats that were thrust upon me, I was ushered into the king's presence. Solomon sprang from his throne, clasped me in his arms, then sat down with me on the cushioned bench that ran the length of one of the walls of his throne room. (As throne rooms go, this was not an exceptionally grand one; Solomon had not yet built his own palace, but was using his father David's.)

"Tamrin, my friend; I had not expected to see you until this evening," he greeted me. "Is everything all right? Is there something of which you are in need? You have only to speak and it will be done for you."

Feeling guiltier than ever, I said, "I beg Your Majesty's pardon; I had not thought to make you drop all your business on my account. But since you have done so, I shall tell you directly what is on my heart. I have heard that you are building a port city at Ezion-geber on the Red Sea, and was distressed that you had not seen fit to inform me. Is it true?"

Solomon regarded me quizzically, as if taken aback. Then he said, "Yes, it is true, and no secret. But you have only been my guest for a matter of days, Tamrin. There will be plenty of time for politics later on; first I wanted you to enjoy my hospitality and to have the opportunity to explore my beautiful city to your heart's content. Have you not been well looked after? Have you not been shown everything you have asked to see?"

"Solomon, my lord, I did not mean to complain! I have been welcomed by all your ministers and officials, and have been entertained as though I were a king myself."

"Then I am reassured; all is as it should be. But do you still wish to discuss Ezion-geber here and now?"

"Not at the expense of other men, my lord, no. I do not wish others' appointments to be postponed because of me."

"Tamrin, as a foreigner in their country you are their guest as much as mine, and therefore your needs must come before theirs. So stop calling me your lord, and tell me the cause of your anxiety."

So I explained to him why I was concerned, and warned him of the strife I could foresee. I finished up by stressing how sad it would be if this venture were to drive a wedge between our two nations, which had so recently become friends, just as Solomon and I were friends ourselves.

"But Tamrin, surely this represents an *opportunity* for Sheba, not a threat; a chance for our two nations to cooperate as never before? Every ship which sails down the Red Sea headed for India or southern Africa will have to pass through the straits which divide the Red Sea from the ocean to the south; this is where taxes and tolls can be levied, so that the full sum will pass into Sheba's royal treasury, instead of being siphoned off by bandits. And in return for Sheba's guarantee of safety for my ships, *I* can guarantee safety for any caravans you or your queen or countrymen might wish to send through *my* domains, so that for the first time you will have access to the markets of Tyre and Sidon, Damascus, or even Greece, Troy and beyond. A safe harbour and a city at the head of the Red Sea will mean that goods can easily be transferred from ship to camel and vice versa; Ezion-geber will be a staging post for everyone – Israelite, Tyrian and Sheban alike."

His excitement was infectious; momentarily I glimpsed the splendour of his vision in all its potential, and understood a little more again of what made Solomon great. But then my own gift for seeing pitfalls before I fall into them asserted itself instead, and I said, "It all sounds very fine, I grant you, but the rulers of Sheba will not think so."

"I thought your mistress Makeda was the ruler of Sheba? Surely you could help her understand?"

"Makeda is not the ruler of Sheba, Solomon! I thought I had already helped *you* understand that her father, Rafash, and his brothers and cousins are the ones who wield the power. And may the gods forgive me for saying so, but it's well nigh impossible to get *them* to understand anything at all."

For a moment Solomon weighed my words, stroking his neatly groomed beard as he did so. Then he said pointedly, "But you are a cousin of Rafash, are you not? It seems to me that the time has come for a shift in the balance of power in your historic kingdom, for its own sake as well as that of its queen. Times are changing, Tamrin; in a modern nation, government by feuding tribal chiefs is no longer viable. If Sheba wishes to retain the respect of its neighbours and its prominence in international affairs, it must adapt and move forward. Conflict between Sheba and Israel would be good for neither; in cooperation our two nations could become the wealthiest and most powerful force on earth. Egypt and Babylon are shadows of their former selves; this is *our* chance to conquer the world – and not with military might, not by oppression and cruelty, but by creating prosperity and opportunity for all. Just imagine: Sheba and Israel hand in hand, dispensing justice and the knowledge of God to the world… I could even marry your Makeda to seal the union, and then everything would be perfect!"

My jaw must have dropped visibly as I tried to work out whether or not he was joking. By now he knew as well as I did that the queen of Sheba must be a virgin, and I knew as well as he that the Law of Moses requires one man to be married to one woman. And had not Jehoshaphat, his royal recorder, been at pains to convince me that in Israel not even the king is above the law? Yet Solomon's father, David, had had many wives, and I knew that Solomon was troubled by his failure so far to beget an heir with Pharaoh's daughter.

While I was still sitting there, perplexed, Solomon laughed out loud, so I concluded that he had spoken in jest after all. He said, "Tamrin, you worry far too much. Anxiety is corrosive to flesh and spirit, and makes us old before our time. You must put your mind to enjoying the remainder of your visit, which I wish could be indefinitely prolonged. But you must also be present for the consecration of my temple next year, and if you are to have time to return to Sheba in between, you must soon be on your way."

"You would seriously invite me, a pagan, to the dedication of Adonai's house?"

"But of course! How could I not want you to be there when you are my dearest friend, and you have provided me with the means to make the place as beautiful as it is possible for an earthly building to be? Besides, you are no pagan, Tamrin. God looks upon the heart, and is not in the least disconcerted by your having failed to be born a Hebrew. It is the mission of Israel to spread the light of God's truth and love among the nations; what better way to begin than by having seekers after truth such as yourself present to see Adonai take up residence on his holy hill?"

"I am honoured indeed," I murmured, and meant it, for I was deeply moved. "I shall do my best to be there. And when I return I shall bring with me representatives of my government who are empowered to negotiate on behalf of my queen and her council about trade agreements and military collaboration, and to espouse any other enterprise in which our two nations might seek to cooperate with one another. Who knows? Perhaps a formal alliance could be drawn up, requiring Israel and Sheba to assist one another on every level."

"Only one thing would please me more, Tamrin, and that would be to learn that you yourself were one of the men so empowered. You are honest and shrewd, you have the wherewithal to see beyond the end of your own nose, and you are related to your queen, just as her father and his brothers are. The time has come for you to claim your birthright, my friend – for Makeda and your people. And I myself need you to do so."

Chapter Eight

Travelling back to Marib, I spent even more time than usual in study, thought and prayer, for Solomon had given me a great deal to think about. It was not only his own legendary wisdom that had challenged me, or the many new things I had learned about his God, and the Law of Moses, and the principles by which he sought to rule over his people. No, Solomon had challenged me personally to think that I could and should be more than a merchant; that I could and should do more to support Makeda in her determination to see Sheba changed for the better. Instead of despairing of her youthful idealism and counselling her to abandon childish dreams, I ought instead to be looking for ways in which to help her make them come true.

But just as my heart had grown lighter the nearer I had come to Jerusalem, so it grew heavier and gloomier by the day as my caravan wended its way through Arabia, back to the seat of Sheba's government. Not even the prospect of seeing Makeda again could cheer me, because I was so very afraid of what might have become of her in my absence. I sacrificed daily to Shamash on her behalf, as well as petitioning him to keep my caravan safe on the road. When my prayers seemed to dissipate with the incense into the thin desert air, I even tried calling on the God of Solomon, addressing him as Adonai, and trying to believe that the whole of the world was under the control of this one almighty and benevolent being. But it didn't seem to do any good.

And was it my imagination, I wondered, or had life for Sheba's poor actually become harsher still in the time I had been away? There seemed to be more abandoned children begging by the wayside, more wild-eyed men driven to banditry, and women to prostitution. We passed whole villages left desolate, where once crops had grown

99

and animals had found pasture, but which had now fallen prey to the encroaching sand. The families who had lived there we met trudging along the road with their meagre possessions strapped to their backs, in the forlorn hope of finding work, or water, or anything else that might sustain their fragile lives. We came upon the clean white bones of those who had set out before them and already given up the ghost. I feared that by the time we arrived in Marib, any spark of joy or hope within me that Solomon had fanned in Jerusalem would have been snuffed out, and I would have nothing left to share with Makeda at all.

Yet even in my lowest moments I had not anticipated anything like the situation that confronted me on my return to Makeda's palace. For I was told that she was not there at all; she had been sent back to Ethiopia for the sake of her health, and ensconced upon Sheba's throne was her father, Rafash, himself.

"Her health?" I repeated faintly to the servant who had given me the news. "But what is the matter with her? Is she terribly sick? Are there no doctors in Marib who can treat her?"

"Oh yes, there are doctors. But they say the desert heat is not good for her; she needs the fresh mountain air of Yeha to set her on the road to recovery. No one knows when she will be able to return or resume her royal duties."

I was distraught. Makeda was desperately ill, and I had not been there to comfort her; I had lingered in Israel indulging my passion for philosophy when my own beloved cousin was at death's door with no one to hold her hand.

"Master, you must not torture yourself like this," Hami counselled me as he gave me my nightly wash and massage – in my pavilion; I could not bring myself to stay at the palace as a guest of Rafash. "It is not your fault if Makeda is ill. You are not a doctor; you couldn't have done anything to help her, even had you been here. If the best doctors in Marib were at a loss as to what to do for her, there's nothing you could have done even if you had been at her side all along."

"We don't know that, Hami. Body and mind are closely

connected, as I shouldn't have to tell you, for you see for yourself every day how the anxiety in my mind is reflected in the tension of my muscles. If I had been here to protect Makeda from loneliness and disappointment…"

Hami only sighed and started kneading my neck and shoulders more strenuously than before. Meanwhile I resolved that on the morrow I would call Bijo and his agents to account for not having found out about all this in advance. I would also confront Rafash and demand to know by what right he had been appointed his daughter's regent, for such a decision should have been taken by the Crown Council and apparently it had not been reconvened.

I did gain permission to see Rafash, but for me the interview was as pointless as it was humiliating. Resplendent in gold and purple, Rafash lolled upon his daughter's throne with one leg thrown up over its arm and his great beer-swiller's belly bulging in all directions over his jewel-studded belt. He ate and drank constantly throughout our conversation without offering me any refreshment at all, and gave me to understand that I was now utterly superfluous to his requirements – as indeed was Makeda.

"But there are mountains here in Arabia," I protested doggedly, determined that he should not dismiss me before I had made my point. "Her party must have had to cross them in order to get home to Ethiopia. Could she not have stayed *there* to recuperate? Then you could have visited her regularly instead of banishing her from your presence, and she could have begun to take part again in affairs of state once she felt able to do so."

"Come, come, Tamrin. Was the queen of Sheba to be billeted with goatherds? Besides, you know as well as I do how little she and I have ever had to say to one another. She doesn't need me to visit her all the time any more than she needs to worry her pretty head about politics. She is much better off where she is, in the place where she grew up, far removed from the stresses and strains of court life. I can take care of everything for her here."

"But that is precisely my point, Rafash. Makeda is queen. You ought not to be appropriating her responsibilities for yourself."

"Really? And since when has the father of Sheba's queen *not* considered it his duty and his right to relieve his daughter of the burden of keeping her subjects in order? Do you seriously mean to suggest that Makeda would be happier closeted away in this suffocating pile of a palace than enjoying her precious garden in Yeha?"

Of course, I wasn't suggesting anything of the sort, but with Rafash leering down at me triumphantly and the combined weight of his objectionable brothers squaring up behind him, there was little to be gained, and potentially a great deal to be lost, by seeking to prolong our fruitless discussion. Accordingly I had to agree that her father knew best, and turn my attentions to Bijo instead.

When he bowed his way into my presence later that morning the wiry, wary little spy cringed and cowered even more nervously than usual, for he was all too aware that he had failed me. Yes, he had been with me in Israel so could not be expected to have learned of Makeda's infirmity at first-hand. But he had men in Marib and in Yeha who should have got a message to him somehow so that we might not have been caught so conspicuously wrong-footed on our return.

"Master Tamrin, I crave your pardon," he pleaded with me when I challenged him. "But it seems that Queen Makeda's departure to Yeha has purposely been kept secret. No one here knows of it except for Rafash and his kinsmen at the palace, Luqman the grand vizier, and a very few of the senior ministers of government. None of my agents or their contacts were aware that she wasn't still living with her handmaids in her apartment."

"And in Yeha? Surely your contacts there must have known that she was back."

"Not at all, master. She was taken there by stealth, and must have been held under house arrest ever since."

So this explained how Rafash had assumed total control without consulting the Crown Council. None of the other chieftains had any idea that it wasn't business as usual.

I let Bijo go unpunished, because although arguably his men might have been more observant, he could not fairly be blamed for their credulity.

So, what to do next? While I was pacing to and fro in my tent trying to decide whether to go on to Ethiopia straight away, and with what kind of an escort, I received a distinguished visitor.

He had come alone and incognito, with a great scarf wrapped around his head like a desert warrior. Though he had sought to disguise his height and dignity by stooping, I was in no doubt as to who he was the moment Hami led him into my presence.

"Lord Luqman." I bowed low before him, for as grand vizier of Sheba he vastly outranked me. But he bowed too, then approached and proceeded to kiss me on both cheeks as though we were equals. For he had come to seek my help.

Once we were seated and Hami had brought us refreshment, Luqman asked my permission to dispense with pleasantries and come straight to his point, for he did not want to be detained here long enough for anyone from the palace to find out where he was. "You see, Lord Tamrin," he said, honouring me with a title I did not strictly merit, "Queen Makeda was not taken back to Yeha because she was ill. It is true that she was in poor health, but this is not why she was sent home. She was expelled from Marib because she was in her father's way. If his power were not dependent on her continued existence, her fate would not have been exile from Arabia but execution."

I blew out the breath between my teeth as I sought to take in this all too plausible revelation. Meanwhile Luqman regarded me with melancholy gravity, but also with an unspoken question in his eyes, which was when I realized he was hoping I could somehow help him set things right.

I said, "Queen Makeda was not content for Sheba to be governed in the way it always has been, I gather? She wanted to change something, against her father's wishes?"

"She wanted to change *everything*, Lord Tamrin. She wanted to prevent rich farmers from enslaving their poorer neighbours and annexing their land. She wanted to pay architects and engineers to assess the feasibility of building public dams and cisterns to control the outflow of water from the mountains and to ensure it is distributed equitably and not wasted in flash floods that demolish poor men's homes. She wanted to reform the way justice is dispensed, even insisting on hearing some of the weightier cases herself. She wanted *all* her people to be happy and healthy and free, and for that she was driven from her palace by her own father."

When Luqman had begun this speech, I hadn't been able to tell whether he approved of what Makeda had been trying to do or not. By the time he had finished I was in no doubt. He worshipped the very ground she walked on, and his dearest wish was to see her circumstances and those of her father decisively reversed.

Yet in spite of his high status, he himself was in no position to bring this about, since Rafash controlled Sheba's army and treasury, and Luqman had no means of knowing who, if anyone, would dare to side with him if he sought a showdown.

"Lord Luqman," I said, "you may rest assured that if I knew how to dislodge Rafash from his seat and bring back Queen Makeda in triumph, I would do it. But I am a merchant, not a statesman, and certainly not a soldier. For surely what we are looking at here is civil war."

"But Rafash is not popular. If somehow we could rally the opposition... Not even the generals of his own army respect him. As for the chieftains of the other tribes, Rafash is not what the Crown Council thought they were getting when they handed him power on a plate. They would oust him tomorrow if they could, but only Rafash has the authority to call the council together."

"Rafash or Her Majesty."

"Her Majesty? What are you suggesting?" Luqman must have seen a gleam come into my eye even as the idea dawned in my head, for he leaned forward with as much alacrity as a man of his aloof disposition can be expected to show.

"Lord Luqman, I do believe I can see a way forward. You must come with me to Ethiopia, and in collaboration with Makeda we shall give out that the seat of Sheba's government has been shifted to Yeha. Then we reconvene the Crown Council and have them pass an edict exiling Rafash from the kingdom for daring to dishonour the queen. If the generals despise him as you say, they will be more than happy to arrest him and his brothers and have them removed from the palace, as long as they have the council's mandate to do it."

For quite a long time Luqman made no response. He went on scrutinizing my face with disconcerting intensity. Then he said, "Tamrin, for a merchant, you are a remarkably cunning thinker. Perhaps you should have been a politician after all."

"Perhaps I shall be one yet," I said ruefully, "though one does not succeed in business without a sharp mind, either."

And so it was that when I left for Ethiopia not many days later, I took with me not only my entire caravan, but Luqman the grand vizier of Sheba and a number of other ministers of government and senior administrators whom Luqman had known to be profoundly dissatisfied with the current state of affairs. There were even two seasoned generals with their regiments, and there would have been more, except that we needed them to remain on hand in Marib ready to round up Rafash and his brothers and send them packing once the Crown Council had given the order.

Even as we were taking our leave, with the bustle of packing and loading up all around me and the cries of the camel drivers ringing in my ears, part of me was finding it hard to believe that I had had it within me to act so decisively, or that so much could have happened so quickly. But the nature of the coup Luqman and I were attempting to stage precluded any hesitation, else our cause would be lost before we had even made our first move.

Nonetheless, Rafash must have learned of the disappearance of Luqman and his compatriots long before we reached the Arabian coast. Since it coincided with the departure of my own caravan, even he must surely have worked out that we had left together. Yet we were not aware of being pursued; I thought perhaps Rafash was merely relieved to be rid of these tiresome relics of the old regime who had always seemed to be in his way. Perhaps he had convinced himself that they had merely fled with me to Africa as refugees, intending to embark upon lives of harmless retirement far away from Sheba's capital, and that he was better off without them.

When we were making the Red Sea crossing I suddenly remembered what Solomon had said about the Tyrians swearing by ginger to protect them from seasickness. After tracking down a consignment of it among the merchandise we were transporting, and taking a couple of pinches neat at regular intervals, I have to say that I scarcely felt nauseous the whole time we were at sea.

Which is more than can be said about the way I was feeling as we came within sight of Yeha. For I was literally worried sick about Makeda, and the condition in which I might find her. She had been in poor health, after all, when her father had banished her from Marib, and who could say how low she would have sunk since then, having been shown so little respect? If she was being kept at Yeha's palace in secret, there was no guarantee that she would be being treated in any way like a queen. Perhaps she would have been confined to a single tiny room or even a dungeon, with no one to do any more for her than attend to her most basic needs. All that Rafash needed from her was for her to stay alive.

Had I shown up at the palace without Luqman or our considerable military escort, I think I might have been denied entry. Its precincts were heavily guarded, and I recognized none of the men who were responsible for vetting visitors. In the end I was admitted, but I had it made clear to all concerned that unless I was permitted to return safely to my companions within the hour, our soldiers would storm the palace and slaughter the entire garrison.

Once inside the walls I did begin to see servants I knew, and who knew me. They were as glad to see me as they had ever been, but they all looked anxious and cowed. Nor were they falling over one another in their eagerness to take me to Makeda.

At least she was being allowed to live in her old apartment with its window over her garden, and this was where she was standing when I was shown in, just as she had been when I had visited her after my first expedition to Israel. And as before, her handmaid, Sabla, stood beside her. But nothing else was as it had been. For Makeda's shoulders were hunched and her hair unkempt, as though she had only temporarily left her bed. Clad in a shapeless nightshift she looked thin rather than slender, and I realized that Sabla held a hand beneath her mistress's elbow to lend her support. When the two of them turned to face me I saw the rings under Makeda's eyes, and even Sabla wore no make-up. Clearly they were not used to receiving visitors.

Knowing how vain and coquettish Sabla had grown up to be, I would have expected her to turn from me in shame at being caught in this slovenly state. But for the first time ever she looked almost as relieved to see me as Makeda did. Neither of them ran forward, for I think Makeda might have fallen; instead I went to them, and a moment later, bizarre and inappropriate though it was, I found myself embracing them both, and all three of us were weeping.

"Oh, Uncle Tamrin," Makeda said eventually into my shoulder. "It has been so terrible, you can't imagine. I have seen no one but Sabla since they brought me here; they said I needed the mountain air, but I have not been allowed to leave this room. My father rules my kingdom, his servants here have charge even over the garden I used to tend, while I myself do nothing but fade away like a wraith. Not even you can save me this time."

"Actually," I consoled her, "I believe I may be able to." And as she raised her head and gazed at me, incredulous, I began to unfold before her the plan Luqman and I had devised. As I did so, it was like watching a miracle: the light came back into her eyes, her shoulders straightened and a healthy glow suffused her cheeks, which in spite of the darkness of her skin had still seemed somehow drained of colour. Sabla let go of her elbow, and when Makeda drew back from my embrace to stand on her own two feet, she did not fall.

"So," I finished up, "am I to understand that our plans have earned the royal seal of approval, Your Majesty? And that you will not shrink from giving the order that will drive your father into exile, if the Crown Council sanctions it? For it has to be said that you have always accorded him vastly more respect than he has ever deserved."

"No, Uncle Tamrin. I will not shy away from what has to be done, because this is not about me; it is about my people. My father has oppressed them more cruelly than they have ever been oppressed before. He has trampled justice underfoot even more savagely than he has trampled me. The time has come for me to act on their behalf, and with the support of you and Lord Luqman, I will do it."

"So, I shall return to Luqman and the men he has brought with him and assure them that all is well. Then we must proceed quickly, before your father can outmanoeuvre us." Embracing Makeda once more in farewell, I reflected that Solomon would have been proud of us both.

Once we had begun to put our plans into action there was no turning back. Luqman and his ministers set up their headquarters in what had once been Rafash's banqueting hall, and for the moment Makeda was enthroned on his old chieftain's chair, until the mighty throne of her predecessors could be wrested from the usurper. A proclamation was sent throughout the kingdom of Sheba to say that the queen would now rule from Yeha, whither all members of the Crown Council were requested to hasten in order to address the political crisis that was tearing the nation apart.

Even before the Crown Council had met, disaffected officials and palace servants began arriving from Marib. The little flock of handmaids who had served the previous queen arrived too, courtesy of the palace steward and his assistants who accompanied them to Ethiopia; they were as overjoyed to see Makeda as she was to see them, because in the short time they had been permitted to serve her she had won their love with her gentle and generous ways. By the time the council had assembled, the palace of Marib must have been all but deserted; certainly Rafash could not have been unaware of what was happening, but we heard nothing from him – presumably because the military units that Luqman had instructed to remain in Marib were preventing him from making contact with anyone outside his own city walls. To all intents and purposes he was already being held prisoner in Marib much as his daughter had been held in Yeha, so Luqman's prime objective had already been achieved.

The Crown Council might have taken many months to elect Makeda its queen in the first place, but it took no time at all to approve our proposals as put before it by Luqman. Before he spoke, Makeda herself addressed the gathering. She was dressed as she had been for her coronation, in the same elaborately pleated white robe; she wore the diadem of Sheba on her brow, the necklace of office upon her breast, the quadruple bracelets at her wrists and ankles, and dangling almost to her shoulders were the huge golden earrings that seemed to have been made for a queen of giants.

And she was so obviously well enough to undertake public duties that her absent father was exposed as a liar before she even opened her mouth. When she did open it, and the expectant chieftains heard her strong, low, musical voice and her eloquent words, she soon had them eating from the palm of her hand.

"Princes of Sheba," she began, turning her limpid gaze upon each man in turn. "Little did I know, when I accepted the honour you bestowed on me of reigning as your queen, how swiftly I would be stripped of my authority and prevented from carrying out the task with which you had entrusted me. If only you knew how reluctant I am to say a single word against the father who gave me life and the opportunity of serving you and the people of Sheba, and how my heart breaks when I think of the disrespect he has shown not only to me but to you, in the way he has sought to appropriate your wealth and prerogatives for himself. Power has undoubtedly corrupted him, it is sad to say, and you can all see as well as I can that he is no more fit than he is entitled to be acting as my regent – as though I needed one! For if he is permitted to continue behaving as though he and not I were head of state, he will make dupes and paupers of you all. Only give your consent, and I shall have him displaced forthwith; Sheba will be ruled for the time being from here in Yeha, where the esteemed Vizier Luqman will act as my chief adviser. I am sure that most of you already appreciate the depth and breadth of his experience of all things political, and with regard to Sheba's economy, who better could I have to give me counsel than my own Uncle Tamrin, who has amassed a truly prodigious fortune, yet without cheating a single client? My lords, if you wish to see Sheba ruled with equity, for the good of *all* her tribes and their clans, and in such a way that every other nation will acknowledge her worth, I beg you, restore me to my rightful place, and let us throw off the yoke of my father's tyranny before it crushes us all!"

A brief silence ensued. I saw Mafaddat, father of Sheba's erstwhile heir apparent Ghalilat, shuffle in his place as though he intended to get up and speak in opposition. Perhaps he thought the time was ripe to get Makeda ousted along with her father, but he rapidly realized his mistake and hunkered down once more as the mood of the meeting made itself felt. Kahalum of the Banu Waren was the first to stand up and applaud Makeda's speech, closely followed by Salamat, who had supported Kahalum in the past. One by one the other chieftains rose to their feet, and finally Yuhafri, aged father of Makeda's predecessor, got up and applauded her too. When Luqman had seconded all that Makeda had said, and the matter came to the vote, the procedure was nothing more than a formality because everyone could see which way it was going to go.

At dusk that evening, I received an invitation from Makeda to walk with her in her garden, from which she had for so long been kept out. The evening was cool and mellow, with the lightest of breezes ruffling the petals of the roses and wafting their scent into the air like incense. Though Makeda sighed frequently over things that hadn't been done to her liking by her father's gardeners, to me everything seemed perfect, and while her handmaids made an inordinate fuss of Hami, she and I were free to walk alone.

"Uncle Tamrin," she said, "I cannot begin to thank you for what you have done for me in the short time since you returned from Israel. You can see for yourself how my health has been restored and the purpose put back into my life. But what of you, and *your* health and welfare? When last I saw you, your heart was as heavy as mine has been these past few months. Yet now you seem changed; is it simply because you have been able to help me, or was it your time with Solomon that changed you? You have not told me anything of your most recent expedition, and surely you did not neglect to bring me a present?"

I glanced at her with a smile; for a moment she was the little girl again, divested now of her regalia and clad in a simple robe of pale cream linen, against which her dark skin glowed like the polished wood of a statue whose clothing has been carved from ivory.

And so as we strolled among the flowers and listened to the brightly coloured birds calling to one another in the fading sunlight, I began to share with her the insights that Solomon and his ministers had imparted to me. I explained as well as I could how his country was governed, and how justice was administered; I described the esteem in which his subjects held him, and enthused about the peace and contentment in which they lived. No doubt some cynical detractor could have interrupted with examples of occasions on which things in Israel had gone badly wrong, and come up with countless exceptions to disprove the rule, and I myself was of course well aware that nowhere and nothing in this world is perfect. But the gist of what I said was true, and my excitement about it was infectious. Makeda heard me out with wide and sparkling eyes, but as my eulogy drew to a close I saw them cloud over. Afraid that I had somehow caused her offence, I asked her what the matter was.

"The matter? The matter is that Sheba and Israel are as like to one another as the desert and the ocean; that while Solomon's subjects enjoy his care and protection, so many of mine languish in poverty, having been robbed of their land and of any means to make a decent living. Sheba is riven by corruption, exploitation, discrimination, and there is nothing I would love more than to cause it to resemble Israel, but I don't know where to start. When my hands were tied by my father it was all too easy to blame *him* for what was wrong; now, if nothing changes, the blame will lie with me. Solomon can rule as he does because both he and his people believe that the laws by which they live were given to them by their god; would that Almaqah or Shamash had seen fit to do the same for us! But our laws, such as they are, have been made by the rich and powerful expressly to keep the poor in their place. And no matter how much I impressed the chieftains today, if I do not rule them with a rod of iron they will fall to feuding among themselves as they have always done. Fear is what my predecessors and their kinsmen who ruled on their behalf have traditionally used to keep the Shebans from tearing one another to pieces, and if I cannot or will not make them afraid of *me*, all will be lost."

"The line between fear and respect is a fine one, Makeda. Surely it must be possible to make them respect you without resorting to terror to keep them in check?"

"I don't know; I suppose it may be. But I am so young, so inexperienced. I know what I want to achieve, but I am so afraid that men who are older and cleverer than I am will thwart me at every turn."

"You have Luqman to help you outwit them. He is a wise man and a good one, and he is already devoted to you."

"But he is one among many. If a league of chieftains rose up against him, he could not withstand them."

"You could seek an alliance with Solomon himself. He has chariots and horsemen by the thousand." And patiently I started to explain to her what Solomon was planning for Ezion-geber, and how eager he was to cooperate with Sheba in any way possible for the mutual benefit and prosperity of both nations. "He has invited me to return to Jerusalem for the consecration of the temple he is building for Adonai," I finished up. "If you were to send ambassadors with me, empowered to negotiate on your behalf, we might be able to come to terms there and then."

Briefly she weighed my words, and the face that had just now been that of a young girl had once again taken on the grave and ruminative aspect of a queen's. Then, while she was still deep in thought, I had another idea.

"Makeda," I said, "there may be a better plan yet. You could visit Solomon yourself."

"I beg your pardon?" We had continued walking slowly along while she had pondered the prospect of an alliance. Now she stopped dead in her tracks and looked at me as though I had suggested we swim the Red Sea.

"Why not?" I challenged her. "Heads of state frequently pay one another formal visits for precisely this kind of purpose. What better way for you to study statecraft than with Solomon himself? And you have always wanted to see the world… at least, you did before I took you to Marib. Naturally I understand if that particular experience has put you off travel for life."

"But Uncle Tamrin, I haven't yet definitively reclaimed power from my father. You can be sure *he* wouldn't let me go to Israel with things as they are. And if – when – he has been driven into exile, I shall need to be here to consolidate my position."

"Luqman is more than capable of holding the fort until your return, as long as he has the backing of the army and of the Crown Council. We can have the council sanction his regency tomorrow, while its members are all still here in Ycha. You can promise them that you will return with a code of law suitable for establishing Sheba on a secure footing as a sound modern state fit to be compared with Israel, Egypt, Assyria and the like, and one that can count upon Solomon's support in the future. Solomon believes that his God has entrusted him with the mission to spread his ideals throughout the world, so he is hardly going to refuse to share them with you."

"But Sheba's queen does not travel! She is not allowed to be seen by her own subjects, let alone by a foreign king."

"And since when has your life been governed by convention or tradition, Makeda? A chieftain's daughter does not consort with sailors or hold the dead bodies of salt cutters' children in her arms. Perhaps it is time for the queen of Sheba to be what her title implies. And if you are to rule over an entire nation, you must begin by taking charge of yourself."

"Uncle Tamrin, you are right, as always. Tomorrow we recall the council and I start my packing."

Chapter Nine

On the morrow Makeda addressed the Crown Council once again. With forceful words she painted for its members a sorry picture of Sheba's current predicament as she saw it: our nation was not truly a nation at all, but an uneasy, unstable agglomeration of disparate tribes whose only reason for suppressing their mutual hatred was the fact that they hated non-Shebans more. Indeed Sheba was a cesspit where theft, banditry and corruption bred and flourished, and ultimately this unhealthy state of affairs would bring about her destruction. If Sheba were to survive and prosper in the modern world of mighty states and empires, we must put our turbulent past behind us and embrace the opportunities the present was offering. Sheba needed a constitution and a way of administering justice that was worthy of her proud people – all of them, not just the rich and favoured few. She also needed powerful and dependable allies.

Makeda paused briefly when this tirade was finished; the assembled chieftains shifted uncomfortably in their places and eyed one another with a mixture of chariness and grudging acceptance that she was right. Yet how could the necessary changes be brought about? Happily, she was about to tell them.

The new picture she proceeded to paint, of Solomon's hallowed kingdom, was more appealing than even I could have made it. As she spoke, it was as though I was carried back there on the wings of her words, and I found myself marvelling that she who had not yet seen it could have described the place so persuasively. "And do you know the secret of Solomon's success?" she asked her now spellbound audience. "It is as simple as it is profound, and it is wisdom. Real wisdom, godly wisdom, not devious cunning which strives only to get its own way. It is from the supreme God himself, creator of the universe, that Solomon's wisdom came to him, through direct revelation! And it has been of vastly more benefit to him and to his subjects than all the gold and silver under the sun – though it has brought him untold riches too. Wisdom is sweeter than honey; it is a shield for the breast, a helmet for the head, a light for the eyes. But the most remarkable thing about Solomon's wisdom is that he does not seek to keep it for himself or to restrict its influence to his own territories and subjects. No; he has made it his goal to spread this wisdom throughout the world, and you, the princes of Sheba, may be among the first to benefit from his generosity! Only give me your blessing and I, your chosen queen, will journey to Israel and bring back this wisdom to you myself. It is my dream that before death compels me to hand on my kingdom to another, Sheba will have been transformed beyond recognition, and all of her people will enjoy such security and prosperity that there will no longer be a place for the corruption and violence that has blighted their lives until now."

Having said all that she needed to say, Makeda sat back on her temporary throne and bowed her head, no doubt exhausted by her efforts – for her health was still not strong – but also as a sign of her submission to the council's will. And notwithstanding their prejudices and entrenched commitment to tradition, the princes of Sheba rose to their feet as one man and gave her the blessing she sought.

Thus it was that while swift messengers were galloping away to Marib to set in motion the expulsion of Rafash and his remaining supporters, Makeda was commencing preparations for her state visit to Israel. Messengers were sent there too, to inform Solomon of her intentions; it would take them many months to reach their destination, but not as many as it would take the enormous, unwieldy cavalcade with which she would be obliged to travel as queen of a country seeking international recognition and respect. There were moments during the long days of planning when she threw up her hands in exasperation and asked me whether she couldn't travel in disguise with a mere handful of retainers and only reveal her true identity when she was introduced into Solomon's presence. But I quickly convinced her that this would never do. If the celebrated Solomon were to receive her as a potentate on a par with himself, she must take pains to look the part and behave accordingly. She must also take with her lavish gifts to assure Solomon of the respect in which she held him, which was only fitting when one considered that he would be obliged to entertain her and her retinue in royal fashion for some considerable time.

So while she and her handmaids put together the considerable wardrobe and fabulous array of jewellery and cosmetics to which a queen must always have access, I myself organized the procurement of gifts fit for a king. I heaped up bales of the sheerest silk from the distant lands of the Orient. I acquired sackfuls of the aromatic spices for which Arabia is justly famous, and others which I customarily imported from further afield: cinnamon and cassia, cumin and cloves. Of course, we merchants keep secret our sources for such exotic substances, some of which are literally worth more than their weight in gold. But as well as the sacks of spices already dried and ground, I obtained living plants from which some of them come, for I knew that Solomon had gardens of which Makeda would be fiercely jealous, in which he nurtured specimens of as many plants, shrubs and trees as could be induced to grow in the Jerusalem hills. Along with the spices, I heaped up vast quantities of myrrh and frankincense, and also more of the ebony, red gold and gemstones that Solomon had asked me to provide for him previously. He already had enough precious metals, stones and wood for the beautification of his temple, but once that had been consecrated, I knew that he planned to build himself a palace more in keeping with his magnificence than the modest affair built by his father David, in which he was still residing. Building a house for his God had taken precedence over remodelling his own, but achieving the latter objective was important to him also.

In the meantime, Luqman was forming his interim government, making appointments with Makeda's approval from among those men who had fled Rafash's court and who had been ministers of government under the previous queen. He tried to choose men who had at least some rudimentary sense of integrity, and who could see that perpetuating the old culture of bribery and favouritism was not in Sheba's best interests. He also sent to Marib for the great royal throne of Sheba, for only when that was brought to Yeha and Makeda had assumed her place upon it would the people of Sheba accept that Marib was no longer their principal city, at least for the foreseeable future.

A spectacular throne it was too, expertly fashioned from the blackest ebony and inlaid with ivory and gold. From its high back soared a canopy shaped like a huge spray of flowers intricately carved from polished wood, whose centres were clusters of jewels. At the canopy's apex was the symbol of Almaqah, a full moon riding on the horns of a bull, while along the panelling below the seat ran a row of bull and ibex heads whose horns were surmounted with elaborate graven chaplets.

As the day drew nearer upon which we had scheduled our departure, Makeda grew ever more excited and impatient to be gone.

"You do realize that this journey will take as long as it takes a child to reach full term in its mother's womb?" I reminded her. "We shall not be meeting with Solomon tomorrow, or even next week or next month. It is very much further from here to Jerusalem than it is to Marib."

"Uncle Tamrin, if you have told me once how long this trip will take us, you have told me a hundred times. And *I* tell *you* that I am ready, however long it takes and however arduous it turns out to be. Am I not completely recovered from my illness? Am I not as strong and healthy as you have ever seen me?"

And it was true; in the time it had taken us to get our expedition organized, all traces of her sickness had evaporated. Her skin glowed and her eyes shone; I had never seen her looking happier or more beautiful.

Sabla, on the other hand, was clearly dreading the day when she would have to leave her home comforts behind her. Naturally the queen and her handmaids would have a spacious pavilion to themselves whenever we pitched camp, and everything they might conceivably need would be unpacked for them each evening. But extremes of temperature and weeks of boredom would have to be endured, and our cooks would seldom have access to the kinds of delicacies to which the royal household was accustomed.

Once we had made the crossing to Arabia, our road would take us relentlessly north between the mountains in the west and the desert to the east; you wouldn't have caught me going by sea all the way up to Ezion-geber even if the port city there had already been built. Rather, we should be travelling by way of a series of trading colonies that Sheban merchants had established long ago, each of which I knew as well as I knew the route that linked them. But many of these places were little more than clusters of mud-brick hovels braced against the desert winds. I hoped that Makeda and Sabla would soon get used to drinking camel's milk and eating locusts, for to a desert dweller a plateful of crispy fried locusts dipped in honey is like a foretaste of heaven.

On the morning of our departure the entire population of Yeha turned out to wish us well. So much for the tradition that forbade the queen of Sheba's subjects from beholding her face; Makeda had resolved to follow my advice from day one of our journey and cast convention to the winds. Mounted upon her snow-white camel, enthroned on a contrivance that was half saddle, half palanquin, and clad in a golden cape that extended from its stiffened collar to halfway down the camel's flanks, she elicited cries of admiration from all sides. And was I imagining it, or were there tears in the dour vizier Luqman's eyes as he watched her ride away?

I shall not risk tiring either myself or you who are reading my account with a description of our crossing over to Arabia, since you have made that journey with me already. Suffice to say that Makeda was as friendly and familiar with peasants, sailors and salt cutters as she had been before being crowned their queen, and they were as charmed by her as they had been then, only now they were awed as well. Meanwhile Sabla was as flirtatious as *she* had been too, except that she was becoming disconcertingly interested in Hami in particular.

Once we got north of Sirwah we were entering uncharted territory as far as Makeda was concerned. In those early days everything was a source of fascination to her: the misshapen, dead volcanoes, the sudden verdant oases, the cacti and the spiny ziziphus trees... I began to wonder if we would ever reach Israel at all, not because of the perils of the journey, but because Her Majesty wanted to stop and look at every isolated structure or bizarre rock formation we passed, and to converse with anyone we met along the way. In the middle of nowhere one day, we sighted a sizeable Bedouin encampment of black goatskin tents some distance from the road, and Makeda insisted that we pay its occupants a visit.

"Makeda, we cannot descend upon them unannounced! We are a company thousands strong; custom will compel our hosts to slaughter their entire herd in order to try to feed us all."

"Don't be silly, Uncle Tamrin. We shan't all go to see them. You and Hami and Sabla and I shall go, with a platoon of soldiers for protection, and everyone else will stay here. Remember, the Bedouin are my subjects too; I want to understand how *all* my people live."

Once she had got an idea of this kind in her head it was useless to argue. Much against our better judgment, Hami, Sabla and I set off in Makeda's tracks, Hami on foot leading our camels and the rest of us mounted. I dare say if we hadn't been quick enough off the mark, Makeda would have left even us behind and gone on quite alone.

Long before we got there, children from the encampment had seen us coming, and would have run out to welcome us had it not been for the presence of the armed men who rode beside us. Sensing the youngsters' fear, Makeda directed the soldiers to halt and bade Hami lead the three of us on without them. I was feeling worse and worse about this escapade the more we became committed to it, but as I have said, there was no stopping Makeda once she got an idea in her head.

No longer afraid, the children raced out in excitement, vying with one another to seize the rope by which Hami was leading us and bring us to their parents' tents. They couldn't have had the remotest idea who we really were, though they could no doubt guess from our clothing and accoutrements that we were rich beyond their wildest imaginings. As we were climbing down from our camels, Makeda first as usual, some of the children ran to fetch their parents while others attended to our beasts with the expertise of men three times their age. Meanwhile the youngest ones sucked their thumbs and stared, and one little girl dared to touch Makeda's golden cape.

When the menfolk appeared from their tents, to begin with they had no more idea who we were than their children had had. After all, what previous queen of Sheba had ridden around in the desert with her face unveiled and a retinue of one handmaid, an ageing merchant and his valet? Then one of them recognized the royal monogram upon Makeda's breast, and another saw that beneath the flowing white scarf that protected her head from the sun the royal diadem sparkled on her brow. At once they fell on their faces in the sand, and their children with them.

But Makeda bade them rise again forthwith, even taking the little girl who had touched her cape by the hand and setting her squarely on her bare brown feet when the child was too terrified to stand of her own accord. Then Makeda knelt down so that her eyes and the child's were on a level and said, "Which is your tent, little princess? I should like to visit your father and mother."

Sabla, Hami and I could only follow like lambs as the girl held on to Makeda's hand and led her inside the nearest of the Bedouin's outlandish homes. Of course, Hami and I had been shown hospitality in many such dwellings before, but Sabla was visibly unnerved and would only sit down when Makeda ordered her to do so. She then sat down right beside Hami, who did not seem as displeased as I might have expected or hoped.

As for Makeda, she was in her element once again. Sitting on the carpeted floor with her new little friend on her lap, she drank the soured milk we were offered without wincing, and ate her way through a number of plump fresh dates with patent relish. Meanwhile she chatted easily not only with the head of the household but also with his wife, who would have served us in dutiful silence and then retired, had not Makeda urged her to stay.

Yet, as had happened so often before, the more Makeda learned of her hosts' harsh lives, the more distressed and angry she became. All the tents in the encampment belonged to a single extended family that had once owned a valuable herd of goats. But armed raiders had come in the night not so very long ago and stolen all but a few dozen, which some boys from the camp had fortuitously penned up some distance away where they had found enough grazing to last another day. The raiders had clearly come from a village not far from where the Bedouin had been encamped, but when an appeal was made to its council of elders for the goats to be returned, it was curtly refused.

"On what grounds?" asked Makeda, incensed.

"On the grounds that I had no proof of who the thieves were," the father of Makeda's new friend explained. "But this was not the real reason why my appeal was ignored. The reason is that I was of the Bedouin, and settled folk despise us. They steal not only our animals but even our children if they can, to sell or keep as slaves. We *never* get justice; abuse is what we have learned to expect."

"Have you lost a child yourselves?" pressed Makeda gently, noting that the Bedu's wife had turned her head and covered her face with her thick black veil.

"We lost our firstborn son," the man replied; his wife sobbed silently into her veil, and the little girl on Makeda's lap burst into tears as well, making dark damp blotches on Makeda's golden cape.

Not much later we got up to leave. Makeda took the woman's hand in hers and said, "I cannot promise to restore to you your son, or your goats, or your happiness. But I can promise you that I shall do all in my power to make Sheba a safer and fairer place to live, for *all* her people, farmer and Bedu alike."

For the rest of that day, Makeda was pensive and subdued; nor did the days that followed bring with them much cause for celebration. For now we had left the land of Sheba behind to traverse the territories of her often hostile neighbours, and never had our formidable military escort been more necessary. Of course, I had travelled this road before, and it had always been dangerous. But previously I had only had my own goods and chattels to worry about; now it was Makeda herself for whom I feared. For what more valuable hostage could kidnappers seize and hold for ransom than the queen of Sheba?

Nor did the grandeur of the landscape any longer offer much in the way of relief from the discomfort and tedium of travel. After days, weeks and eventually months on the road, the jagged mountains to the west seemed less fascinating than they were forbidding, and one red desert sunrise was much like another. For miles we rode without seeing a single fellow traveller, or even a herd of goats in the distance, or a solitary bird overhead. Our joints grew sore, our eyes and heads ached from the relentless sun, and even Makeda and I ran out of things to say to one another as day followed uneventful day. I suppose we should have been thankful that most days *were* uneventful, for anything truly out of the ordinary that had happened would undoubtedly have been something unwelcome.

And I suppose I should not have been surprised when at length Hami succumbed to Sabla's advances. He was a healthy, affectionate youth after all, on the very cusp of his manhood, and handsome too in his way, though I had never really thought about it before, since my tastes don't run in that direction. And Sabla was as skilled a seductress as someone in his position was ever likely to meet. So I couldn't honestly bring myself to begrudge him his pleasure when I happened upon them one siesta-time beneath a single blanket. I just wished he had chosen someone less flighty with whom to lose his innocence, for he was soft of heart and I knew that Sabla would break it.

Makeda too seemed more wistful than angry when I told her of my discovery. Perhaps for the first time she was wondering whether, in sacrificing marriage for monarchy, she had made the right choice.

There were certainly days on which both she and I seriously wondered if she had made the right choice in undertaking this foolhardy expedition. Though our military escort kept bandits at bay, it could do nothing to ward off the noontide sandstorms that became more frequent the further north we got. Late in the morning we would notice that the sunlight was dimming as the first clouds of sand blew across it from the open desert. Then we would have no choice but to halt and attempt to protect ourselves against the storm that would soon be upon us, blasting sand like burning needles into eyes, mouths and noses, penetrating our clothing and inevitably getting inside our luggage and sacks of provisions no matter how hard we fought to keep it out. Only the camels were untroubled by the onslaught; their nostrils can filter out the sand. In fact very little deeply distresses a camel apart from losing sight of its calf. This is why a calf is always led by the camel walking in front of its mother, rather than by the mother herself.

Once the storm was over, an unearthly greenish mist would shroud the landscape, a noxious blend of humidity, sand and particles of debris which the wind had picked up. We would be obliged to set off while it was still hanging over us, but it felt somehow like walking along the bed of the sea, with its choking green waters swirling above our heads.

Occasionally this mist was so thick and so persistent that we would happen upon the next trading post for which we were headed before we had seen it coming. One moment there would be nothing visible ahead but vapour, the next, there would be the inevitable squat mud-brick gatehouse where we must stop and pay our taxes to whichever chieftain or warlord controlled the stretch of road along which we were about to pass. Some of the settlements around these taxing and trading posts had grown to become small townships or even cities, and at the less primitive of these we would sometimes spend the night. I would send Mahiko and his colleagues to make overtures on Makeda's behalf to the local potentate and present him with gifts, and Makeda and her immediate entourage would then be received into his fastness as honoured guests. In this way, Makeda with her consummate charm made many more friends for herself along our route; my map of the Incense Road was soon studded with fresh inkspots marking the places where we knew we would be made more than welcome on our return journey.

However, there were great gaps on my map where I knew that for many days we should encounter nothing resembling civilization at all. At least this meant a respite from paying taxes, paying for water, and generally being fleeced by all and sundry for everything of which we had need. But it usually meant there would be no water or food to be had at all, and although our camels were capable of carrying supplies for many days, there were sections of the route where our provisions would run perilously low and we had no alternative but to subsist entirely on camel's milk. It is perfectly nutritious and one can live on it for a long time if one has to, but this was scarcely the kind of diet a gently born woman is used to, let alone a queen.

In the event it was Sabla who fell sick, not Makeda, for Makeda was sustained by the knowledge that her meeting with King Solomon would now be taking place sooner rather than later. But Sabla fell into a dangerous fever and had to be carried by litter like Makeda's other handmaids for several days, being quite unable to ride. Poor Hami was distraught, having come to regard Sabla as the love of his life. I hadn't the heart to tell him that she had already entertained two camel drivers at least since the time I had found her lying with him. Still, while she was burning up with fever she couldn't be seducing anyone else. Under Hami's assiduous ministrations she eventually recovered, having the constitution of a camel herself in spite of her pouting and whining, and for a week or even more she remained touchingly faithful to her devoted nurse.

The final leg of our journey involved crossing the plateau and mountains of Moab and then the river Jordan in one of the several places where it can be safely forded. The once independent kingdom of Moab had been conquered by Solomon's father, David, and now belonged to Solomon's empire, so as soon as we approached its borders messengers were no doubt galloping off to Jerusalem to apprise the Israelite king of our progress.

And as our road wended steadily uphill, so the barrenness of the desert gave way to rolling grasslands, and to fields of wheat and barley; the deep ravines which cut through the plateau, and which the road was careful to avoid, could not fail to remind us of Ethiopia, now so far away. I saw not only Makeda and Sabla but Hami too brushing brief tears of homesickness from their eyes.

But there was no time now for regrets or for looking backwards. Our nine-month ordeal was almost at an end; in a matter of days we should be encamped beneath the walls of Jerusalem.

Chapter Ten

The visit of the queen of Sheba to the court of King Solomon was the grandest state occasion Jerusalem had witnessed since Solomon's wedding to the daughter of the pharaoh. Arrangements were made for our entire caravan to process through the streets of the city to the palace, and just as in Yeha the whole population had turned out to see us leave, so in Jerusalem the streets and rooftops were thronged with men, women and children eager to make us welcome. Rumours of Makeda's loveliness had clearly gone before her – I had probably started them myself on my previous visit – and everyone was desperate to catch a glimpse of the celebrated beauty.

Nor were they disappointed, for she rode bareheaded and with face unveiled on her lofty saddle-cum-palanquin, the diadem of Sheba set high upon her brow and her mass of curling hair braided into glossy black plaits interwoven with gold. Her golden cape, impeccably arranged by Sabla, spread out from her shoulders like the halo of the sun, and in spite of the rolling gait of her fabled snow-white camel she seemed to be borne forward as smoothly as a galley on a calm flat sea.

Almost as impressive as the queen herself were the multifarious gifts she had brought with her to present to Israel's king. Though the jewels, silks and spices were hidden from view, the treasure chests in which they were carried were clearly visible stacked upon the camels' backs, and there were so many of these magnificent beasts in the queen's cavalcade that it must have seemed to the teeming crowds that they would never see the last of them as they went on filing past.

When at last we reached the palace gates we were ushered into the outer courtyard, which was of no mean dimensions, but there was still nowhere near enough room for the whole caravan to be accommodated. Accordingly the unloading of the treasures began straight away, so that the camels which had been relieved of their burdens could be moved aside to create space for those whose loads had yet to be unpacked. Meanwhile Makeda and her attendants, and I myself with Hami, Bijo and Mahiko, were welcomed with much bowing and scraping by members of the royal household and invited to refresh ourselves before being presented to His Majesty. There was scarcely any need, since the final stage of our journey had been as short as we could make it, and we who would meet the king had been bathed and oiled and perfumed only a short while before. So now we took as little time over the business as we could, for I do not think Makeda would have been able to bear it if the meeting had been put off for very much longer.

Great olivewood doors twice the height of a man closed off Solomon's throne room from the antechamber in which we stood while Sabla and her assistants straightened Makeda's cape and took up its train in their accomplished hands. I would have walked behind them, but Makeda said, "Solomon is your friend, Uncle Tamrin. You must introduce us." And she gave me her elbow so that I could escort her as the father of a bride might accompany his daughter to her wedding. As soon as we were ready, there was a blare of trumpets, the double doors swung open, and we commenced our stately progress towards Solomon's throne.

As I have mentioned before, Solomon was still residing in the palace built by his father, which was nothing like as grand as the one he built later for himself. But it still seemed a very long way – much further somehow than I remembered it – from the throne room's entrance to the dais upon which the great throne stood. It must have seemed further still to Makeda, who had to concentrate so hard to walk without a limp, especially when she was nervous. And she was certainly nervous now.

But long before we had reached the dais, the king had started from his throne and descended the steps of the dais to meet us. For he and Makeda were equals, after all, and it would not do for her to be made to feel that she was approaching one greater than herself. As he came towards us I was struck once again by his youthfulness and by the buoyant spring in his step. It was only when I heard Makeda catch her breath that I realized I had never told her what he looked like, and she had never asked. I suppose it was because all I had said about his wisdom and piety had led her to assume he was a man of mature years, and that his appearance was of little consequence. If so, then how wrong she had been.

And how foolish *I* had been for not anticipating the effect that the first glimpse of him might have upon her! No doubt it was because I *was* a man of mature years that I had forgotten what it is like to feast one's eyes upon someone who epitomizes everything for which one's heart has been yearning quite without the permission or even the knowledge of one's head. For the first time, I saw now that Solomon was not merely young, lean and lively, but also astonishingly handsome – much more so than Hami – with his clear fair skin, even features and dark, dancing eyes, and his loosely waving hair, which to African-Arabian eyes looked impossibly soft and smooth.

Nor was Makeda's beauty lost on him. I knew it because he did not address her at once, but rather allowed his eyes to meet with hers, and for once his searching gaze was still and steady, while the hint of a smile played on his lips. Perhaps it is just as well, I thought sardonically, that he is already married and believes himself to be subject to Moses' stringent ethical code, and that Makeda is wedded to her role as Sheba's virgin queen.

If we had been in Egypt, or indeed in almost any one of the other foreign lands I have visited on my travels, Pharaoh's daughter would have been present too, seated on a throne beside Solomon's. But this was not the way of things in Israel; Makshara was nowhere to be seen.

At length Solomon thought to speak the courteous words of welcome that protocol required, on this occasion employing scrupulously formal language even in addressing me, whose solemn obeisance he accepted without demur. Then Makeda motioned bearers to come forward with the chests of gifts we had brought for His Majesty's delectation; as each was set down before him, its lid was tipped back and the jewels and spices and sumptuous silks were revealed in all their colourful splendour. Even though Solomon was rich beyond belief, he exclaimed with delight at the queen's generosity and declared that the treasures would duly be exhibited in public for all the people of Jerusalem to see and admire.

Meanwhile he wished to honour Makeda in return, by granting her a lavish apartment near his own for the duration of her stay. Hither an array of magnificent robes would be brought each morning from which she might select whatever she wished to wear. At the same time she would be offered the finest foods and wines his steward could supply – these she might enjoy whenever she was not eating at the king's own table, which both she and I were warmly invited to do as often as we chose. The dedication of the temple was scheduled to take place in a month's time; we must stay at least until then, and afterwards for as long as we wished. This very evening a banquet would be held in our honour.

When this initial audience was over, servants came to show us to our accommodation. I was assigned rooms not far from Makeda's, hence not far from Solomon's either. There were quarters nearby for the more senior of my employees, though as usual their junior colleagues would have to set up camp with the camel train outside the city walls.

No sooner had Hami unpacked my personal belongings than Sabla appeared on my doorstep requesting me to wait upon her mistress.

If my own quarters were luxurious – and they were – Makeda's looked as though they had been designed for a goddess rather than a mere mortal queen.

"Look, Uncle Tamrin! There is gold and purple everywhere," she exclaimed, dancing from one elaborate wall-hanging to another, then drawing back the heavy embroidered curtain which shut off the great high bed from the rest of the room. The bed had been strewn with pink rose petals, there were living rose bushes in tubs by the window, and the air all around was thick with the scent of rose-perfumed oils being burned in little bronze lamp-holders that hung in bright clusters from walls and columns. "Have you ever seen anything so beautiful?"

"Apart from Solomon himself, that is." The interjection came from Sabla, impudent as always; if Makeda noticed the sly smile on her handmaid's face, she affected not to. Then Sabla looked sideways at me and went on, "I wonder why your kinsman did not think to tell you of Solomon's comeliness as well as of his wisdom?"

I did not deign to respond, regarding Sabla's comments as typically inappropriate. Makeda merely shrugged her shoulders and said, "Yes, I suppose the king is quite pleasing to look upon. But see how tastefully the cushions have been arranged on my couches. And look: from this window I can see gardens, just as I can from my rooms at home in Yeha. I cannot wait to explore them; do you think His Majesty will allow me?"

"He will probably guide you around them himself if you ask him," I assured her. "Though he has much larger gardens south of the city, in which he is minded to grow at least one specimen of every plant in the world, and he has collected a very large number already. He would probably take you there too."

"Solomon collects *plants* as other men hoard jewels and I have my little statues of the gods? But how wonderful! If I had known, I would have brought him plants from the forests of Ethiopia, saplings that would grow into mighty African trees..." Makeda was dancing again, flitting from window to couch, and couch to bed, as oblivious of her limp as she was of Sabla's wry disdain. Then suddenly the energy left her; overcome by the stress and excitement of everything she wilted upon the bed and said, "Sabla, we must rest before you have to prepare me for the banquet." And a moment later she was sound asleep. She was still so young, and she had journeyed so very far since leaving Yeha, in more ways than one.

I went back to my room to rest a while too, though I did not sleep. I read, and thought, and looked forward to being able to converse with Solomon and Jehoshaphat and the other friends I had made in Israel once again.

The banquet that evening was a very different affair from the one to which I had been treated on my arrival in Jerusalem the time before. Whereas that had been informal and relaxed, this one was the epitome of state magnificence. Tables had been laid the length of the longest hall in the palace; everyone who was anyone had been invited, and instead of cushioned couches for leisurely reclining there were as many chairs and benches as could possibly be squeezed into the space. At the king's own table stood a great high-backed chair almost as ornate as his throne, where he would soon take his place; to its right there was another chair, equally tall and grand, for Makeda. The back of each was surmounted by a kind of golden cupola embellished with a symbol of the royal house of the monarch who would sit beneath it: Solomon's was the six-pointed star of David, Makeda's an ibex head. I might have expected the horns and disc of Almaqah, but this was Israel, land of Adonai, who brooks no rival.

To the left of Solomon's seat was a lesser one, with a lower back and simpler adornment. This was for Makshara, the pharaoh's daughter. At least she would be accorded the honour of entering with the royal party; those of us who were not of royal blood were shown to our seats in advance, to await their majesties' arrival.

Another blast of trumpets announced its imminence. Everyone stood, with heads bowed in deference as Solomon entered, his left arm linked with Makshara's and his right with Makeda's. Makeda's radiant smile drew every averted eye irresistibly upward, but Makshara's lips were tight, and temporarily I forgot that I had once thought her the most ravishing creature I had ever seen. Behind the royal party walked a long retinue of their servants.

I myself had been assigned the place to Makeda's right; Sabla was obliged to stand with the rest of Makeda's handmaids behind their mistress's chair. Hami stood behind mine, wearing a fatuous grin on his face because this put him right next to his beloved. But Sabla wasn't in the least bit interested in Hami tonight.

When the opening formalities were concluded and the meal itself began, Solomon, Makeda and I talked easily and happily about our journey; the king made several valiant attempts to involve Makshara, but the more animated our conversation became the less she joined in, and the more strained was the smile that she had forced onto her heavily painted face. Meanwhile, as the buzz of chatter in the hall grew louder, I with my ageing ears found it increasingly difficult to distinguish Solomon and Makeda's voices from the background hubbub. I found myself withdrawing to concentrate on doing some small justice to the stuffed joints of lamb, roast duck, calf's sweetbreads and heaps of garlic-drizzled delicacies that Hami was piling onto my plate without really thinking about what he was doing. It wasn't long before I was feeling distinctly unwell. So it came about that Solomon and Makeda spent most of the evening talking exclusively to one another.

"He knows so much, about so many things!" she enthused to me the next morning. We sat by her window savouring the shade of the room while outside the climbing sun poured its fierce light into the garden. "Plants, tree, animals, even birds and insects! He has special names for different sorts of *beetle*, would you believe? And not even grass is just grass to him; he says it all depends on where it is growing."

"And did he agree to show you around his gardens?" I asked, genuinely relieved and pleased that they had evidently got on so well together, because to me it had not been a foregone conclusion that they would.

"Oh yes! We are to meet there this very afternoon, and you must come too, because it wouldn't do at all for he and I to go about together with mere servants as our chaperones. Besides, he may want to talk to me about affairs of state, and I shall need you there to help me keep up with what he is saying."

I laughed, for suddenly she sounded so disconcertingly like her father, when he had insisted I attend the Crown Council that had ultimately elected her as queen. But Sabla said archly, "He won't be thinking about politics, my lady; you needn't worry about that. Nothing of the kind will enter his head once he is walking with you among the roses." I chose to ignore her as usual; Makeda told her with uncharacteristic sharpness not to be silly, which only made Sabla smile her knowing smile before flouncing off to torment her fellow handmaids. She was forever setting them to some pointless task and then criticizing their performance, seldom giving them any peace or praise.

When the noontide siesta was over, Makeda had herself made ready for her rendezvous with Solomon in the garden. True to his promise, along with a breakfast that might have fed a small army, he had sent her that morning a huge trunk filled with spectacular dresses, some sewn all over with tiny gold beads, others embroidered with fabulous flowers, yet others as fine and transparent as a dragonfly's wing. But the one she chose was simple, white, with enamelled brooches shaped like little serpents to fasten it at the shoulders. I think it may have been Greek, for Solomon and Hiram's ships made regular calls at harbours throughout the Western Sea.

A simple dress, and her hair in a simple coil on top of her head, from which Sabla had teased out the occasional curling strand to hang as if quite without intention down the side of her face and over her smooth dark neck. Had she been festooned with all the heavy glittering regalia that as queen of Sheba she might have chosen to wear instead, Makeda could not have looked lovelier.

Solomon was clearly thinking the same as he strode through the garden towards us, quite alone, without a single bodyguard or valet in sight. Disappointed to find Hami, Sabla and the other girls waiting with us, he asked if they had no other duties to which they could be attending; discreetly I directed Hami to take the queen's attendants away somewhere, which he was predictably happy to do.

"Tamrin, my friend." Having kissed Makeda's hand, Solomon at last took the opportunity of embracing and kissing me, Sheban style, on either cheek. "Your charming cousin could not have been blessed with a more congenial protector. Come, let the three of us walk together, for now I think we are *all* of us friends, are we not?" And so we commenced our tour, with Makeda walking between us, one arm linked with Solomon's and the other with mine.

It was true that he had different names for every kind of plant and shrub we paused to admire. I was surprised how many were still in bloom, for it was late summer by now and in the wild the flowers had long gone to seed. But Solomon's were watered twice a day – night and morning – and he had taught his gardeners to prolong their flowering by pinching off any blossom that was past its best.

"That is a hollyhock," he told Makeda when she marvelled at an enormous spike of pink flowers almost as tall as she was. And, "No, that is an acanthus," when she pointed to another and asked if it was the same. When we came upon hollyhocks and acanthus again later on, she had remembered which was which, and Solomon rewarded her with a dazzling smile, for he said that nothing gave him greater pleasure than sharing his knowledge and love of nature with someone who showed a genuine interest in what they were looking at. This wasn't something that happened often.

"Doesn't your wife appreciate beauty when she sees it? Don't you come walking here with her?" Makeda asked in surprise.

"Makshara? I brought her once, but she said that flowers make her sneeze. She appreciates beauty, certainly, but chiefly the beauty of good craftsmanship in gold or silver. She does not see that God himself is the greatest craftsman of all; that a single petal can exhibit more evidence of fine design than the most intricate piece of filigree." Solomon paused in mid-step to pick an exquisite white lily, which he then held reverently under Makeda's nose. "There. Have you ever seen or smelt anything more wonderful? The costliest perfume could never hope to rival that scent. I had Hiram's craftsmen carve lilies like this on the pillars of Adonai's temple, and there are others to be seen on the Great Bronze Sea, a cauldron in the temple court. Yet no carving or casting, however expertly done, could compare with the living flower."

Makeda smiled and took the lily from his hand. Briefly their fingers touched, and more briefly still some unreadable emotion showed in Solomon's eyes, then it was gone.

We walked on, and turned a corner, and up ahead a little stream ran down among rocks, the whole feature created by artifice but made to look as much as possible as though nature had shaped it. Makeda was so entranced that she darted forward without thinking, and now it was Solomon's turn to catch his breath. Instead of hastening to join her, he put out a hand to detain me and whispered, "Tamrin, she is lame! Has there been an accident?"

"There has," I whispered back. "But it was many years ago."

"I see." He was still watching her; quite oblivious of his staring, she was cupping her hands in the stream to catch its bright water between them. "What happened?" he asked at last.

"That is not for me to say, I'm afraid. She doesn't like people to know unless she chooses to tell them. It may be that she will choose to tell you."

"Yes. In time she may." He nodded, and went ahead again to catch her up. I wondered briefly how much time he might decide to devote to the project, and how Makshara might feel about that.

Certainly he seemed in no hurry that afternoon to return to his kingly duties. Of course he had a plethora of ministers and officials who were perfectly competent to carry out the day-to-day administration of his government, but he always made a point of keeping a close eye on their activities.

In the days that followed, however, by his words and actions Solomon convinced me that he had not forgotten the real reason for Makeda's visit. He arranged meetings for Makeda, Bijo, Mahiko and myself with various ministers of the government, at which these eminent authorities explained to us the principles underlying the decisions they were required to make, and the direction in which Solomon wanted things to move; everything, ultimately, had its roots in the Law of Moses.

At some of these meetings Solomon was present in person, but at many he was not, since he not only had meetings of his own to attend, but also cases to judge and appeals to hear. For even the lowliest of his subjects had the right to appeal to the king for justice or assistance when in trouble or any kind of need. After a while, Makeda asked if she might sit in on some of these interviews herself, as long as she remained silently in the background and did not interfere. Solomon agreed with surprising readiness; I noted a few raised eyebrows among his ministers, but as far as I know, none of them complained. And because Makeda was allowed to be present at these royal hearings it followed that I was there too, for everywhere she went I went with her.

How different these occasions were from everything that had ever happened in Sheba! Far from the monarch being hidden away from the common people's sight, Solomon was petitioned in person by all and sundry: orphans, beggars, widows, and even prostitutes, for women as well as men could bring their grievances before him. So it was that Makeda and I came to be present at one particular hearing that has since acquired the status of legend – again, probably because I myself told so many people about it. After all, it is such a pertinent example of the everyday practical wisdom for which Solomon was equally and as deservedly famous as he was for his prodigious knowledge and understanding of natural philosophy.

Two women came before him together, both dishevelled, both distraught. It was clear that both of them were harlots of the tawdriest kind: their faces were gaudily painted, their attire shamelessly provocative, and they wore cheap perfume, the cloying scent of which was nonetheless insufficient to mask the stench of their unwashed flesh. It amazed me that Solomon would spare them a single moment of his time, at least without instructing them to bathe first and change their clothes, and come back when they had calmed down enough to stop clawing at each other's hair and spitting in one another's faces. However, he did ensure that some burly servants were on hand to restrain them, should it become necessary, before he permitted either of them to speak.

It was only when the king asked which of them would like to speak first that I noticed that one was holding an infant against her breast. She was already ranting so hysterically at her companion that even though the baby's mouth was wide open I couldn't hear it crying at all. So Solomon turned to the other woman and bade her explain what had prompted the pair of them to seek an audience with him today.

"Oh, Your Majesty!" she wailed, wringing her hands. "This woman and I live in the same house, and we both bore children, three days apart. One night only the two of us and our babies were in the house, and her son died because she lay on him accidentally in bed. So she got up and took mine away from me while I was sleeping. She put him to her own breast, and laid her child next to me. In the morning I got up to feed my baby, and he was dead. But when I looked at him, he wasn't my baby at all."

Scarcely had she finished speaking when the woman with the child at her breast started shrieking, "No! No! You are lying. This living child is mine; the dead one was yours!"

But the first one yelled back at her, "*You* are the liar! The dead baby was *yours*; you have stolen my son."

So there they were, arguing and swearing at one another in the king's presence like a couple of soldiers in a barrack block. Makeda's eyes were starting out of her head; of the various civil servants and courtiers who were present, a few of the younger ones were quietly sniggering while most of the others cringed with embarrassment. Meanwhile the burly servants were waiting for a sign from the king to drag the strumpets outside and send them packing.

Solomon, however, was looking intently at each woman in turn, making a conscientious effort to discern which of them was telling the truth – as if anyone else would have thought that it mattered.

"So," he said eventually, "let us get this straight. *You*" – and he waved his finger at the woman who had spoken first – "*you* say that this baby here is yours, and that hers is dead. But *you*" – and he waved his finger at the woman with the child – "*you* say that *her* son is dead, and that this child here belongs to you."

Both women nodded furiously through their tears; the young men who had been sniggering now stood with hands on their hips laughing out loud, presumably at the thought that Solomon's proverbial wisdom might have met its match in two feisty whores. But in an instant he wiped the smiles from their faces by instructing one of their number to fetch him a sword.

"Now," he said when the weapon had been brought to him, "I

assume that the dead child has been taken away for burial, which is why these two ladies are fighting over the one that is left. So, my young friend, take this sword, cut the remaining child in two, and give half to each of them. What could be fairer than that?"

For the first time since the hearing had begun there was silence. The young courtier with the sword stood goggling, unable to believe what he had heard, while the two women stared at Solomon in consternation. But when the king told the courtier to get on with the job instead of gaping at him like a fish, the woman who held the child suddenly thrust it into the arms of the other and wept, "Please, Your Majesty, give my baby to her. I'd rather let her have him than see him die as well."

Thereupon the king rose to his feet and declared, "This is the true mother. The living child shall be given to her."

Now that was wisdom if ever I saw it. I turned to Makeda to say so, only to find that there were tears pouring down her cheeks.

I have often wondered since whether that woman *was* the child's real mother, and whether Solomon knew it, or whether he only meant that she was the woman with a true mother's heart. Perhaps that isn't what matters; perhaps what the episode taught all those who witnessed it about Solomon was more important than what any of us thought of the two prostitutes themselves. But my own opinion, for what it's worth, is that neither of the loathsome creatures was fit to bring up a child.

As time went on, it wasn't only at the palace that Solomon and Makeda might be found in one another's company. He wanted to show her around the city, and in particular around the temple before its dedication, as he had done with me. And just as I had been, she was profoundly impressed with the interest he took in the lowliest of his subjects, for he always made it seem that each of the labourers on his building projects was as important to him as the architect, just as the squabbling prostitutes had been of no less consequence to him than a pair of rich, respectable matrons might have been.

When Makeda made a comment to this effect, Solomon beckoned to a workman who was passing by bearing a great capstone on his head and a skin of water round his neck, and whose ration pack and sandals were slung around his loins. His garments were ragged, sweat fell in droplets from his forehead, and water leaking from the skin made splashes down his bare dusty legs. Solomon bade him stand still, and said to Makeda, "Look at this man. In what respect am I worth more than him? We are each made of flesh and blood; the same worms will consume our flesh when we are dead, though we seem so different now. What grounds would I have for complaint if God decided to reverse our circumstances tomorrow?"

"You could complain that you wouldn't be strong enough to do his work," Makeda replied with a smile. "Whether he would be wise enough to do yours, who can say?"

Solomon laughed, evidently as taken with Makeda's wit as he was with everything else about her. But as he sent the labourer back to his work Makeda asked, "Surely kindness and respect for all men are not enough on their own to ensure that a ruler's subjects will love him – or her – in return? Surely there are times when one has to be harsh, to punish wrongdoing and ensure that it does not spread its poison through everything?"

"I have been continually surprised by what kindness and respect *can* achieve, as long as they are combined with integrity," Solomon answered. "After all, if people do not exercise kindness and love upon the earth, what is the point of mankind being here at all? For we were made in the image of God, and it is in the nature of God to love everything he created. But you are right: kindness and leniency are not the same thing, and sometimes a king has no choice but to punish, in the same way that God himself must do if he is to ensure that the strong do not terrorize the weak and that injustice and corruption do not swamp his entire kingdom."

Makeda nodded thoughtfully, and I noticed that the next time Sabla was cruel to one of the other handmaids, she received a much harsher reprimand than she was used to. She was taken aback, but in her brimming eyes I saw more respect for her mistress than I had seen there before.

Makeda and I were both to see evidence of the sterner side of Solomon's character only a few days later. One of the ministers of his government was found to have accepted a bribe in return for enabling a rich man to jump the queue for petitioning the king. The minister was dismissed forthwith and his considerable fortune confiscated. He was left with only his house and the patch of land he had inherited, so that he could continue to feed his family; the Law of Moses forbade a man to be deprived of the means to make his own living.

Nor was corruption the sole issue upon which Solomon took a firm line. He made no secret of the fact that on coming to power he had eliminated, one by one, every rival against whom his father had warned him. He had, however, been careful to wait until each of these men had committed a crime for which he manifestly deserved to die. For in addition to warning him against his enemies, David on his deathbed had also commissioned his son to rule in righteousness.

Because I was obliged to follow Makeda everywhere when she went abroad with the king, I had precious little time to renew the friendships I had made during my previous stay in Jerusalem. But now and again she would take a prolonged siesta or announce her intention to rest for the day in her rooms because of the heat, and then I was free to amuse myself. One of the first visits I managed to make was to the delightful home of Jehoshaphat the royal recorder, who had welcomed me so warmly in the past.

And he did the same again, but we hadn't been talking long before I detected a wariness about him that hadn't been there last time, and which became more noticeable whenever I mentioned Makeda. In the end I was compelled to ask him what was wrong.

He shifted uncomfortably in his seat and said at last, "There has been talk, Tamrin. Perhaps it is as well that you should know."

"Talk? About what? What kind of talk, and among whom?"

"About our king and your queen. That they are seen together too often, and that the king has been neglecting other business."

"And has he? Is it ministers of his government who have said so, or men who should keep their noses out of others' affairs?"

"Personally I don't think he has been remiss, nor do I think it inappropriate that he should be making a priority of devoting attention to a visiting head of state. But there are those among my colleagues who take a different view, as of course does the Lady Makshara. And Israel cannot afford to offend the Egyptians."

"Well," I said, "the dedication of the temple takes place not two weeks from today, does it not, at the beginning of the Feast of Tabernacles? After that there is no reason why the queen of Sheba and we who serve her should not return to our country. Then everything here will be as it was before."

"Will it?" Jehoshaphat suddenly peered at me very intently; he had bristling, bushy eyebrows and the acuity of his piercing eyes staring out from beneath them was decidedly disconcerting.

I chose not to pursue the matter any further, and we talked of other things, such as the cooperation between our two nations over the development of Ezion-geber, which had taken considerable strides forward during the course of the meetings that Makeda and I had already had with the king and the members of his council.

But I did commission Bijo to find out what he could about Makshara and the nature of her marriage to Solomon. It turned out to have been arranged for purely political reasons: Solomon and the pharaoh had wanted to form an alliance against the Philistines, who had been flexing their muscles along the coast of the Western Sea after the death of Solomon's father. The Egyptians had proceeded to lay waste the Philistine city of Gezer to safeguard their commercial ties with the Tyrians; Pharaoh had then given Makshara in marriage to Solomon and presented him with the territory of Gezer as a dowry. Although the royal couple had always got along with each other amicably enough and been faithful to one another throughout, there had never been much in the way of love or even understanding between them, and so far they had produced no heir. This wasn't altogether surprising since they rarely slept together, and Makshara didn't even share Solomon's private rooms at the palace. He had built her a mansion of her own, within the palace precincts but considerably further away from the king's chambers than Makeda's quarters were.

None of this was reassuring, and much as I relished spending time in Jerusalem I found myself beginning to be glad that we would soon be going home.

As the heat of summer abated and the Feast of Tabernacles approached, a formal alliance was drawn up between the king of Israel and the queen of Sheba, in which each promised to protect the interests of the other for all time to come. Each would guarantee safe passage over land and water to the other's caravans and shipping, and the Red Sea city of Ezion-geber would be developed to the advantage of both. If either was attacked by a foreign power, the armies of the other would hasten to its aid, and in all respects Israel and Sheba would henceforth regard one another as friends.

Chapter Eleven

The Feast of Tabernacles was one of three major festivals that the people of Israel celebrated each year. It was incumbent upon the head of every household to make a pilgrimage to Jerusalem on these occasions, but for Tabernacles in particular whole families would come, and spend the full seven days of the festival celebrating with their fellow Israelites on Zion, God's holy mountain, which Solomon's father had captured from his enemies.

The festival had been established to commemorate the exodus of the Israelites' forefathers from Egypt, when on their journey to the Promised Land they had dwelt in portable shelters, or tabernacles, made from skins and the branches of trees. But it was a harvest festival too, marking the end of the farmers' year and the safe ingathering of all their crops, so the people had more reason than one to be in the highest of spirits.

This year they had a third reason: for the first time ever, the sacrifices that the law required them to make for the feast could be offered in Solomon's magnificent temple rather than at the makeshift shrine where the Ark of the Covenant had had to be housed until now.

Several days before the festivities were due to begin, the streets of the city started to fill with pilgrims from every corner of Solomon's kingdom. Shelters sprang up everywhere – not mere tents or awnings made from whatever could be readily obtained, but special shelters diligently and lovingly constructed by parents and children to remind them of those of their ancestors who had travelled with Moses through the wilderness. Branches of palm, myrtle and willow were interwoven in elaborate symmetry on rooftops, in public squares, by the city gates, and even round the edge of the courtyard of the gleaming temple by those who got there first. The whole of Jerusalem was alive with anticipation, and the atmosphere was intoxicating. Yet astonishingly, intoxication with the fruit of the vine seemed to be the exception rather than the rule; yes, we did see people drunk, but they were in the minority, and outbreaks of violence and disorder were rarer still.

The dedication of the temple was due to take place on the first day of the festival itself. The Ark of the Covenant would be borne through the streets from the temporary home where it had been kept since David had brought it to Jerusalem, and set up in the Holy of Holies, the most sacred and secret part of Solomon's temple. Once established there beneath the wings of the golden cherubim, no one – not even Solomon – would ever set eyes on it again except the high priest himself, and even he would approach it only once every year, on the Day of Atonement. As many people as could pack themselves into the temple court would hear Solomon pray the prayer of consecration over the place that Adonai had chosen to make his dwelling for all time to come, and witness the sacrifices that would be made at the altar by the entrance to the Holy Place. The Law of Moses prescribed myriad elaborate sacrifices that must be performed at the Feast of Tabernacles as a matter of course: bulls, rams, billy goats, male lambs without spot or blemish, grain offerings, wine offerings and the like were all to be tendered in specific quantities on each of seven days, with more again on the eighth day to mark the festival's conclusion. But for the dedication of the temple there would be special sacrifices made in addition to all of these, and most of the meat from the slaughtered animals would be distributed for the sustenance and enjoyment of the jubilant crowds.

Of course, neither Makeda nor I would be obliged to mingle with the masses. We were to be assigned places of honour in close proximity to the king – who seemed genuinely taken aback at the furore that erupted when it became generally known that two Gentiles, as they called us – one of whom was a woman – had been selected for preferment at an event that they should not even have been permitted to attend. Naturally no one insulted us to our faces, but Jehoshaphat took it upon himself to make sure I was not under any illusions.

"Are you saying that we should stay away?" I asked him in some consternation. "It was specifically to attend the temple's dedication that I was invited back to Jerusalem in the first place."

"Invited by Solomon, perhaps, but not by the members of his council, or by the priests. They believe that the court of the temple should be reserved for Adonai's chosen people, and that Gentiles would defile its sanctity."

"But it is Solomon's vision that people of all nations should one day come to worship Adonai in Jerusalem alongside the people of Israel, since Adonai created the universe and is the supreme God above all others."

"Solomon's vision is not one that is yet shared by many of his fellow countrymen."

"Well, the last thing Queen Makeda or I would wish to do is to cause friction between the king and his own subjects. I shall speak to him about this matter myself."

And I did exactly that, as soon as I could contrive to speak to him alone. He was patently embarrassed and angered by the line which these blinkered critics of his had taken, and was minded to ignore them altogether. It was the first time I had ever found myself questioning his judgment. In the end, when I wouldn't let the matter rest, he summoned Zadok.

Zadok, high priest of Adonai, had already held the office for many years and was a man of prodigious piety. He had tiny, piercing eyes, and an enormous patriarchal beard that he could almost tuck into his belt. He and Solomon respected one another deeply, and I was even less keen to drive a wedge between the two of them than I was to cause unrest among the populace at large.

"Zadok, is it not true that Adonai ultimately wills all the peoples of the earth to be united in worship here on Zion, his holy mountain?" Solomon challenged the venerable holy man as the latter waited upon him in deferential silence.

"Yes, it is true, Your Majesty," Zadok replied, with the merest inclination of his greying head.

"And is it not also true that if all nations are destined to worship here, the representatives of the first of them must set an example to the others, and we, Adonai's servants, must demonstrate to all the world that they are welcome among us?"

"Indeed, Your Majesty, it is as you say."

"Then I enjoin you to assemble the priests whose turn it is to serve at the sanctuary during the festival and inform them that the queen of Sheba and her guardian the Lord Tamrin are to be regarded henceforth not merely as my guests but as the guests of Adonai the Almighty God himself. Their attendance at the temple's dedication is not only to be questioned no further, but to be celebrated by all the people as being in accordance with the divine will, and as a sign of what is to come. Then I shall assemble my counsellors and you will tell them the same thing."

Thus it was that when the day of the dedication came we were not heckled but hailed, and any opposition that remained was effectively muzzled, at least for the present.

And what a day it proved to be, with the autumn sun smiling down on the yellow-gold stone of Adonai's house, which had been seven years in the building, and even longer in the dreaming of both Solomon and David. Makeda and I sat with our attendants on a specially constructed platform only a little lower than the one that had been erected for the king; Makshara, who remained unswerving in her devotion to the gods of Egypt, played no part in the proceedings at all. Makeda wore full ceremonial regalia, as of course did Solomon; in his jewelled crown and purple robes he was the epitome of imperial magnificence. While Makeda's handmaids appraised the king's appearance with approval, then looked beyond him to appreciate the rest of the splendour around them, Makeda herself could look nowhere except at the king.

I don't think she saw any of the beasts being sacrificed. I don't think she saw or heard the priests marching round the temple court waving branches of palm and singing joyous psalms to Adonai. I don't even think she saw their colleagues bearing the Ark of the Covenant on its long poles through the teeming throng. (Ranks of armed Levites – apparently some lesser kind of priest – made sure that no one ventured to touch it or was accidentally shoved forward into its path.) I watched the ark being borne up the steps between the great pillars Jachin and Boaz, until it disappeared from view inside the Holy Place, and I remembered the little replica Solomon had had made for Makeda long before they had met.

But even Makeda saw what happened next at the entrance to the temple. For when the priests had emerged into the daylight once more, thick black cloud like billowing smoke began to spill out after them into the courtyard so that they disappeared all over again, along with the altar, Jachin and Boaz and the whole of the front of the temple building. I would have thought it a clever conjuring trick of the kind that wizards from Egypt favour, had I not seen Solomon fall to his knees, his face a mask of something midway between awe and terror. Then the priests fell prostrate too, and the crowd in its turn, from front to back, like a field of ripe corn bowing down before the wind. For it wasn't a fire that had broken out. There were no flames, and nothing was destroyed. Rather, Adonai had deigned to manifest himself before his people. The glory of God had filled the temple.

It was the king who recovered first. Rising to his feet once more he cried out, "Did not Adonai promise Moses and our ancestors who went out with him from Egypt that he would be present among them as a dark cloud by day and a fiery pillar at night? Behold, the sign of Adonai's favour; he has indeed taken up residence in the house which we consecrate in his honour today."

Thereupon the people rose up as one in reverential silence, waiting for him to say more. So he blessed them, and spoke at length about the plans he and his father had made for the building of Adonai's sanctuary, and what a joy it was for him to have seen them come to fruition. Then he raised his arms to heaven and recited the prayer of dedication that he had composed in advance, giving thanks for the covenant Adonai had made with his people, and binding himself and his subjects to keep it faithfully in the future. Then – and I saw him look more than momentarily at Makeda as he did so – he prayed for the Gentiles who were not as yet included within it.

"O Lord our God, for the foreigner who does not belong to your people Israel, but who has come from a distant land because of your name, when he comes and prays towards this temple, then may you be pleased to hear him from heaven and grant him his request, so that all the peoples of the earth may revere you." Finally he acknowledged that although he had built this temple for Adonai to possess in perpetuity, he knew very well that God had only made his presence felt among us today because he chose to. "The highest heavens cannot contain you!" Solomon proclaimed. "How much less this house that I have made."

It was clear to me even then that Makeda had been deeply moved by Solomon's words, and by the spectacular manifestation she had witnessed of Solomon's God. That night when festivities were still going strong in the streets outside, she sent for me to come to her room, where she sat on the enormous bed in a simple shift, her face scrubbed clean of its paint and her washed hair hanging loose. She looked very small and scared.

"Uncle Tamrin," she said in a tremulous voice when I appeared. "Have you ever seen anything like that before?"

"You mean sacrifices on such a scale, or the ark being carried to the temple?"

"No, Uncle Tamrin. You *know* what I mean. That cloud which came out of the Holy Place. It was a sign from God. It was a miracle."

"Yes, Makeda. I think it probably was."

"But you know what this means, do you not? Has Shamash ever shown himself to you like that, in all the years you have revered him? Has Almaqah ever put in a personal appearance at any of *his* holy temples?"

"Not to my knowledge. No."

"Not to your knowledge? Not to *anyone's* knowledge, for heaven's sake! Uncle, ever since I was a little girl you have been searching for truth, and today it smote you in the face! Are you not inspired? Are you not desperate to find out more?"

"Makeda, what exactly are you telling me?"

"I am telling you that we cannot simply go home – not after this. Solomon *prayed* for us today, but surely you see that in us Adonai has begun to grant him his heart's desire already! He longs for the nations to acknowledge his God, and we have done so. At least, *I* have done so. I want to make Adonai the God of Sheba as well as of Israel. And I want to make him *my* God too."

What was I supposed to say? For much as I longed to go home, much as I feared allowing Makeda to spend one more hour in Solomon's company, I could not deny the evidence of my own eyes. What I had seen at the temple rendered all philosophical speculation futile. Adonai was God; the God who had created the sun and the moon and everything else in heaven and on earth. If my search for the truth had ever been more than an idle fancy, it behoved me now to learn how I might become one of Adonai's devotees myself.

So it was that I resigned myself to our staying on as guests of the king of Israel and his God a while longer; how much longer remained to be seen. Meanwhile Makeda sent messengers back to Sheba to inform Luqman that we had been unavoidably delayed, but that this would prove to be all to Sheba's good.

When she also sent word to Solomon that she and I both wished to be received into the fellowship of Adonai's people, His Majesty was ecstatic. He came in person to Makeda's chambers as soon as he received her message, embraced each of us in turn without inhibition, and announced that our instruction in the faith would begin forthwith.

And thereupon he set about unfolding for us the sacred history of Adonai's dealings with mankind, and with Israel in particular, commencing with the creation of the universe, and incorporating the stories of Adam and Eve, the great flood, the covenants made with Noah and with Abraham, the wanderings of the patriarchs and the adventures of Joseph in Egypt. Then came the four hundred years that Israel had spent there in slavery, then the Exodus led by Moses, the conquest of the Promised Land by Joshua and his successors, and the period of the Judges, such as Deborah, Gideon and Samson, when law and order broke down and each man did whatever seemed right in his own eyes. Therefore Adonai had seen fit to appoint a king to rule over them: Saul had been the first, and when he had failed to live up to his calling, Solomon's father, David, had been anointed in his place. Many of these stories Solomon, Jehoshaphat or Zadok had told me before, but never so comprehensively or in their chronological order. The realization that so many men and women had experienced the power and love of the same God over so many hundreds of years left my mind reeling; Makeda too was enthralled. But the sacred history was only the first of many things we must learn if we were to be counted among the faithful.

There was the Law of Moses in all its complexity: the regulations concerning food and festivals, ritual and moral purity, and the requirement to submit every aspect of our lives to divine direction. For Israel's religion was like no other I had ever encountered; it simply wasn't acceptable to make bargains with God or try to bend heaven's will to yours.

Solomon had not the time or the expertise to instruct us in all this plethora of detail himself. So Zadok was prevailed upon to enlighten us further – "He is a true man of God who has supported me through thick and thin," Solomon assured us – and scribes were commissioned to copy out Moses' words for us to take back home when we went, along with Solomon's own book of Proverbs, which he said he had almost completed.

It was just as well that Hebrew was one of the scripts I could read already, for Israel's priests value literacy above every other skill, and children are taught to read almost as soon as they can speak. Once Zadok was satisfied that we knew enough and were prepared to live out our lives to the glory of God, we should each be required to swear an oath of allegiance to Adonai and take a bath of purification. And I must accept the sign of the covenant that all male descendants of Abraham bear.

Zadok, like Solomon, was overjoyed at the turn events had taken. He applied himself to his task with alacrity, exclaiming in delight that "Ethiopia has stretched out her hands to God", and with his honeyed words seducing us away from the gods under whom we had grown up. "Adonai covers the moon in full; his mists spread over its face," he lectured us, quoting some ancient hymn. "Do not let your heart be stolen by its glow, or by the radiance of the noonday sun." He needn't have worried; I had no intention of returning to my idolatrous ways. But circumcision was not a prospect I was relishing.

"It doesn't hurt at all if it is done when you are eight days old," Solomon informed me breezily. "I really can't say I remember mine in the slightest." This wasn't exactly reassuring.

But at last – or all too soon – the day came when Zadok pronounced us ready to undergo our initiation. I was relieved to discover that this at least was not to be a grand state occasion. Our oath must be sworn in front of official witnesses, but the bathing and the circumcision would take place in private, with the minimum of fuss.

We swore our oath by the altar in the temple court, before Solomon and Zadok and the priests whose lot it was to minister there that day. This was followed at once by prayers of blessing; both Solomon and Zadok laid hands on our heads and prayed that Adonai would strengthen and embolden us, and they exhorted us to pray aloud for ourselves as well. Makeda prayed for wisdom, just as Solomon had done so long ago, that she might always rule her people with equity, building on the firm foundation she had laid today. I prayed only that I might serve both my God and my queen with the devotion they deserved. Then we retired to the palace for the ritual bathing and, for me, the thing I was dreading the most.

The man who performed my circumcision was not a surgeon – though Solomon had many – but he had been specifically trained to do what he did, and he did it with exemplary speed and skill. I was given strong poppy wine for the pain, and took to my bed dreaming lurid dreams for several days. But the flesh healed cleanly and there was no infection.

So now, I thought, surely, we can and must go back home. But there always seemed to be one more thing Solomon wanted us to see or learn, one more hearing at which he thought we should be present, or one more godly man to meet and question. And the things we saw and learned were indeed beneficial, the hearings instructive, the godly men inspiring. Plus, we were each buoyed up by our new-found faith, by the knowledge that Adonai had promised to respond to the prayers of his people, that never again would either of us need to feel that we were merely shouting out into the void.

Yet at the same time, I was troubled. Makeda had prayed for wisdom in ruling her people, but had she given any thought to who was ruling her heart? And was it possible that Solomon's heart could be losing its way as well? Throughout the ceremony during which we had sworn our oaths, and he and Zadok had invoked God's blessings upon us, Solomon had scarcely taken his eyes from Makeda's face, and he had been smiling beatifically all the while, because – or so I assumed – a pagan monarch had chosen to espouse his religion. But afterwards, once I had returned to the land of the living from my dreamworld of pain and poppy, I found that he was smiling besottedly over her still, while whenever my path chanced to cross with Makshara's, her lips were pulled tighter than ever.

Nor was it merely Solomon's smile that struck me as being somehow out of order. His daily gifts to Makeda became ever more extravagant. He sent her necklaces, rings, bracelets and anklets to complement the dazzling costumes she still received from him every morning. He took to composing songs in her honour and sending a choir of fifty singers to perform them for her in her chambers. Then there came a day when we were invited, as we often were, to a session of hearings in the throne room, but Makeda's usual chair had been taken away. Instead a throne had been set up for her beside the king's, festooned with garlands made of gold and silver, its back and sides studded all over with jewels, and with silken cushions on its seat. Makeda was no longer to listen in silence; she was to voice her opinions and judge the cases alongside the king. Observing the horror etched on the faces of Solomon's regular counsellors, I wished the ground might open and swallow us both, but when I ventured to query things afterwards, Solomon brusquely informed me that it was good for her to gain experience in such matters before going back to Sheba to rule in her own right.

So I tried a different angle; I tried telling Solomon I was worried about his wife, because she looked so sad and angry all the time.

"Yes," he agreed. "I'm worried too. Perhaps I must treat her more firmly. My father did warn me to be especially on my guard against the intrigues of jealous women. It was Haggith, the mother of my brother Adonijah, who was behind the plot to get him made David's successor instead of me. And as for my mother, Bathsheba... I have always been glad she was my mother and not someone else's. But thank you for the reminder, Tamrin. I do appreciate your concern. I shall have Makshara closely watched."

A week or so after this, the king announced his intention to enjoy a few days' private retreat in the hills away from the city. He would go to his house near Bethlehem, which was where his botanical gardens were situated, leaving the ministers of his government to take charge of state business during his absence. But Makeda and I must go with him.

How could he not have sensed the outrage of his courtiers? How could he not have heard their mutterings or seen their knitted brows? Any criticism that did reach him he put down to base jealousy, in particular his blinkered countrymen's unwillingness to recognize that Israel's once exclusive relationship with Adonai was meant to be opened up to all the world. But mostly it was as I have said; he seemed to have lost the ability to see anything except Makeda's beauty, or hear anything but the music of her voice. And she was so excited at the prospect of seeing his complete collection of trees and plants at last that neither fire nor flood would have kept her from going.

The pain from my circumcision was as nothing compared with the agony of dread and embarrassment I suffered during those days away from Jerusalem. For I could see where things were headed as plainly as I could see the end of my own nose, yet what could I do to stop it, when most of the time my royal charges barely remembered that I was there? Still I followed Makeda about like a lamb, but at a distance now, for I was afraid to intrude. Nor was there anyone with whom I might share my anxieties, for Hami's mind was on Sabla and there was no one else in the house except the rest of Makeda's empty-headed handmaids and a handful of domestic servants of Solomon's, none of whom I really knew. All I could do was watch, while Makeda and Solomon strolled among the flowers, and fed the birds he had tamed ("You know, Uncle Tamrin, the sparrows will eat from his hand. And I swear they understand what he says to them!") and made music together by moonlight ("He plays the lyre more beautifully than my own mother did. And it moves him so deeply when I sing his songs.").

But it wasn't only plants and birds he kept in his gardens. He had animals too, in cages; mostly exotic creatures that his traders had brought him from faraway lands, or that vassal kings had presented to him as tribute. In one of the cages was a red Ethiopian wolf, which some call a jackal. Solomon pointed it out to Makeda specially, thinking it would please her to be reminded of her home. Instead she screamed, took to her heels and ran.

For once acknowledging my presence, Solomon turned to me in alarm and asked, "Does she really miss Africa so very much? Or does she want to forget she ever lived there?"

Knowing the cause of Makeda's distress full well, I said only, "We must find her quickly. Come."

So we searched the gardens between us, calling her name. Hami, Sabla and the other maids and servants heard our cries and rushed to our assistance. Eventually it was I who found her. She had taken refuge in a gardener's hut and barred the door. Solomon's servants staved it in with planks of wood; Makeda was cowering in a corner sobbing her heart out and veiling her face with her hair.

I would have taken her in my arms and soothed her, just as I had done more than once in her childhood, only Solomon got there first. To begin with she pushed him away, but when he persisted she curled herself against him and cried into his breast until there were no tears left. Then she remained there in silence, shaking like a bird which has flown into a wall.

When at last he deemed it prudent to ask what the matter was, I thought she would not answer. But he spoke so tenderly, and held her so respectfully, that the whole harrowing story came out.

"I was five years old. I had a jackal as a pet, a male, just like that one. His mother had rejected him; I'd raised him from a cub with my mother's help, and he was so gentle, so trusting. We called him Ginger, after the precious spice, because we loved him so much. But as he grew bigger my father used to fight him. He called it play, and I think Ginger thought he was playing too. They would wrestle each other to the ground, and Father would grab Ginger by the muzzle so he couldn't bite. But it made him excitable, aggressive even, and one day he went for me. He…"

She could not go on, and suddenly looked straight at me, appealing to me to finish the story for her. But I shook my head; she must decide for herself what to tell Solomon, and what to show him.

At length she cleared her throat and continued. "Ginger attacked me. He scratched me all down my body; it took months for the scars to heal. But while Father's men were trying to pull him away from me, Ginger bit my leg right through to the bone, and it has never healed, not properly. The skin there is thin and raw, and it breaks…" And then she showed Solomon what she had never shown anyone since childhood, save Sabla and myself. She drew up her skirts, peeled off her bandage, and showed him the cause of her lameness, and of her current distress.

Solomon studied the ravaged flesh without flinching, but rather with close attention, as though examining some novel specimen of butterfly or insect he had recently added to his collection. Then he announced, "My physicians could help you, Makeda, if you would permit them."

"Really?"

"Really. They and I have studied many manuscripts, Egyptian and Babylonian, and they have developed many effective treatments of their own, whose secrets are known only to them. They have taken on a number of such cases before."

Makeda was too overcome to say any more. Then quite without thinking she threw her arms about his neck and kissed him.

It was the chastest of kisses, on the cheek and not on the lips, but the same look came into Solomon's eyes that I had seen there when he had handed her the lily in the gardens of his palace and their fingers had brushed together. Then carefully, almost reverently, he rose to his feet with Makeda still cradled in his arms, and carried her back to her room.

Once we were back in Jerusalem Jehoshaphat lost no time in coming to see me. Though I had seen him troubled before, I had never known him angry; his great bushy eyebrows met in a bristling frown and he blustered without introduction, "Tamrin, this cannot go on. The Sheban party must leave at once. Our king and your queen are in love."

I winced at his choice of phrase, and said I wouldn't go as far as to call it that.

"Then what *would* you call it, I ask you? Tamrin, you and I have been friends for a long time now, and our two nations are sworn allies to boot. But all this is being jeopardized by the relationship you have allowed to develop between Solomon and Makeda."

"Relationship? What exactly are you suggesting?"

"Tamrin, ask *her* if you don't believe me. Ask your queen, your cousin, if she isn't in love with Solomon. Tell her to answer you truthfully, and you won't be able to bury your head in the sand any longer."

So I did ask her. I asked her that very evening while Sabla was taking the pins from her hair and brushing it out in shining coils upon her shoulders.

"In love with Solomon?" she repeated, laughing a nervous laugh which gave her away on its own. "How many times have I told you not to worry about ridiculous things?"

"Of course she's in love," Sabla interrupted. "It's written on her face, in her eyes, in her laugh, in her walk. It couldn't be more obvious if she went about with his monogram hanging round her neck."

For a moment I feared that Makeda was going to strike her. It wouldn't have been any more than she deserved, after all. But Sabla darted out of reach and left her mistress to vent her wrath on me.

"So what if I am in love with him? It isn't as though I have lain with him, nor could I, when you trail me everywhere like a wet-nurse! And in any case I wouldn't, and you know I wouldn't. I'm the virgin queen of Sheba. And if I want to fall in love with someone, I shall do!"

"So you admit it. You love him. A married man, a married *king*, whose wife is none other than the daughter of the pharaoh."

"But they have never been in love! He married her because the pharaoh gave her to him, like a lapdog! She never had a say in the matter, nor really did he. He has never known true love before, any more than I have, and any more than either of us is likely to do in the lives our rank requires of us. Do you really want to rob us of what little affection we can enjoy?"

"Yes, I do, Makeda, because I have no choice. Neither Sheba nor Israel can risk incurring the pharaoh's wrath; nor can Solomon risk losing the love of his people. That is as much a part of his greatness as his wisdom is – and now he seems intent on losing both."

"So you would have us go home before his doctors can look at my leg? You would rob me of that opportunity too?"

"Oh, Makeda, Makeda..." I put my head in my hands and shook it from side to side, because nothing on earth could make me unhappier than knowing that I had made her unhappy too. But she would not be swayed, though she could see very well that I was deeply upset.

I did not sleep at all that night. I tossed and turned, racked with remorse. I should have seen this coming; no, I *had* seen it coming, but had not prevented it before things had got out of hand. Part of me wished I had never introduced Makeda to Solomon in the first place, except that so much good had undoubtedly come of their meeting. But now the beautiful tapestry was unravelling, and I could only blame myself. Perhaps it was because I already felt so guilty for the part I had played in making her queen and robbing her of the chance to know the legitimate love of a man in the first place.

I should have thought to pray instead of fretting. Adonai's adepts say that if you know how to worry, you know how to pray. But I was as immature in my faith as I was mature in years; I simply wasn't used to believing in a God who might be personally interested in me. So instead of turning to Adonai, I got up early, went to Solomon and confronted him in turn. Unlike Makeda, he admitted the truth straight away.

"Yes, Tamrin. It's true. I *am* in love with her, in a way that I have never loved another woman before and never will again. Of course I know we can never marry; I could never insult Makshara or her father by taking another wife, nor could I take Makeda as a mistress when adultery contravenes the Law of Moses, and her own right to be Sheba's queen rests on her virginity. But there is no law against our being friends."

Nor was there any law against his physicians applying all their skill and care to the alleviation of Makeda's suffering. As Solomon had said, they guarded their knowledge closely, and I never found out exactly what they did for Makeda because they drugged her so effectively against the pain of their ministrations that she could not afterwards tell me what they had done. But she had hazy memories of maggots, and scissors, and stitching, and endless applications of special unguents, and all the while she was kept in a secluded wing of the palace that no one was allowed to visit for fear of infection. When the scarring from the treatment itself began to fade, its spectacular success was made manifest. Never again would Sabla have to bandage Makeda's leg, and although she would always limp a little, she would no longer be in pain. And as Solomon professed to find her limp endearing, she no longer cared to be rid of it.

Nor could we even think of going home until the doctors were satisfied that she was fully recovered…

However, now that Solomon and Makeda had each confessed to me that they were in love, from everyone's point of view except theirs things got worse rather than better. For now they felt able to tell one another of their love as well, quite openly, and no longer did they feel the need to pretend that things were other than they were. Makeda's anger against me was transformed into gratitude and joy. "I'm so glad you brought all this to a head, Uncle Tamrin. We don't need to hide our love from you any more."

Nor did they even attempt to. I was obliged to lurk in the background cringing with embarrassment as they walked with each other hand in hand, or rode out into the hills where they cast off their royal cares and fantasized about living as a shepherd and shepherdess tending their flocks as David, Solomon's father, had done in his boyhood. This was as ironic as it was irksome, since real shepherds and shepherdesses no doubt dream of being kings and queens. They made up songs together about their pastoral love and sang them to one another: "How beautiful you are, my darling; oh, how beautiful! Your eyes are as soft as doves," he would croon, and she would reply, "Dark I am but lovely; my lover is radiant and ruddy, his hair is as smooth as the feathers of a raven." Solomon wrote all their songs down and said he would give me a copy along with his Proverbs – as though I would welcome a memento of this, the most excruciating episode in my life so far.

I was obliged also to witness their first real kiss, which took place in the shade of an almond tree dripping with blossom. Its petals fell upon them in a shower of soft pink blessing as their lips came together for the first time and their arms went tight around each other's backs. Even from my judicious distance I could sense the keenness of their hunger to go further, yet they did not. They merely drew apart and devoured one another with their eyes, and I did not know whether to weep, intervene, be sick or conceivably cheer them on.

For much as I disapproved, much as I loathed being party to their illicit passion, there was something touching, heart-rending even, about the intensity of their doomed love. It *was* innocent, too, in its way, for neither had truly loved before. Sometimes the way they looked at each other, or touched each other's cheeks or hair, reminded me of the easy intimacy I had enjoyed long ago with my own peerless Zauditu, and when that happened I suddenly found to my horror that I *couldn't* begrudge them their joy. They were soul mates without question. The only tragedy was that they could never be anything else.

By now it was early spring – the almond trees are the first to flower in Solomon's gardens – and we had been guests at the Israelite court for almost six months. It was just about this time that the inevitable happened – not between Solomon and Makeda, I hasten to add, but

in Hami's affair with Sabla. We were staying at the king's estate near
Bethlehem again, and Hami discovered Sabla granting her favours
to a gardener in the very hut where Makeda had taken refuge from
Solomon's jackal. When Hami started shouting and accusing his
beloved of breaking his heart, she yelled back that he was blind and
stupid and should never have been naïve enough to imagine that he
was her only lover, or that she had ever really loved him at all.

Poor Hami. He came to me inconsolable, though I did my best
to comfort him, biting my lip and resisting the temptation to tell
him that this was one of the few times in her degenerate life that
Sabla had ever spoken the truth.

But Makeda was furious. "How *could* you treat Hami like that,
when he worships the ground you walk on? He loves you, Sabla; he's
not like those other men. You wicked, wicked girl!" And not only
did she beat Sabla with her own belt, a thing she had never done
before, but she promoted one of the other royal handmaids to be
chief over Sabla's head, while Sabla was made last in line.

Was it only because Solomon had told her she must be firm as
well as kind, that she had reacted with such ferocity? Or was it not
also because she knew how she would have felt if her own love had
been rejected or betrayed? Or even that she envied Hami and Sabla,
humble servants as they were, because they could have belonged to
one another in a way that she could never belong to Solomon.

Whatever her reason for chastising and demoting Sabla, she
remained firm in her resolve, and the disgraced chief handmaid was
not reinstated. But Sabla's reaction surprised me as much as Makeda's
resolve. Instead of smouldering resentment, I again saw respect in
her eyes and, more surprisingly still, a change in her behaviour. She
stopped seeing other men completely, and looked shamefacedly at
the ground whenever Hami crossed her path.

Then one day when I was visiting Makeda in her chambers, it
was announced that another visitor had arrived to see her. Her new
chief handmaid, whose name was Romna, showed the newcomer in,
and it was none other than Makshara, the pharaoh's daughter and
Solomon's wife.

Neither of us knew her at first, for we had only ever seen her with her face heavily painted like a mummy's mask. Now, instead of being blackened with kohl, her eyelids were red and puffed up from crying.

Makeda was distraught and did not know where to put herself. It was left to me to do obeisance and entreat the lady to be seated. But she said, "Don't bow to me, Lord Tamrin. I'm not a queen, and never shall be. Yet I haven't come here seeking pity, for that or for anything else. I have come to give Queen Makeda a warning, that's all – and I don't mean a threat. I have only her best interests at heart, as Her Majesty will learn if she will be gracious enough to hear what I have to say to her."

Makeda could not speak. She could only nod her head and stare.

"Your Majesty, I want you to know that my husband is about to propose marriage to you, so that when he does you will be prepared, and will have had time to decide in advance how to answer him. And I want you to know as well that if you decide to accept his proposal I shall not stand in your way. You need not feel sorry for me; he won't divorce me. He will keep me in splendour in the mansion he built for me when we were wed. But he'll never love me in the way he loves you. I know that now, and there is nothing I can do to change it. All I want for him is to see him happy, and you can bring that about." Then she lowered her head, put her hands to her face and wept.

It is hard to imagine how the colour could drain from a face as dark as Makeda's. But I have seen it happen, and it happened now. She began to stammer, to say it was all impossible: Solomon knew perfectly well that she could never marry him and he would never be foolish enough to ask her. Yet all the while Makshara just went on crying her heart out, until at last I said I thought she had better go home, and Romna led her quietly away, giving her into the care of her own women who waited outside.

"It cannot be true. It cannot," was all that Makeda would say to me when she was gone; but the next day a letter from Jehoshaphat came for me. He could no longer bring himself to visit me in person, it said, but he wished me to know that on account of my negligence Solomon had been led so seriously astray by the visiting temptress that he was ready to risk his entire kingdom to marry her. Jehoshaphat even suggested that Makeda's conversion to Solomon's religion had all been a sham, an excuse to allow her to remain at his court when she had clearly outstayed her welcome.

I showed the letter to Makeda. No longer able to pretend that none of this was happening, she broke down in remorse and repentance, and I had never been more sure of the sincerity of her conversion, or of mine, especially when at last she spoke the words I had so much been longing to hear.

"We must return to Sheba before he can do it," she told me through her tears. "He will disgrace himself in the eyes of all his subjects if he persists in this reckless insanity. You must make the arrangements straight away."

But it was already too late. That very evening the king fetched up in person on her doorstep, unannounced and uninvited, demanding to know why she and I had not joined him for supper as was our wont.

"Solomon, I can't see you. My handmaids have got me ready for bed. I'm not well…"

But he rattled at the door in exasperation until we feared he would break it down. In the end Romna let him in, and he fell at once at Makeda's feet.

"Makeda, my beloved, I can go on no longer with things as they are. I love you more than my own two eyes; I cannot bear to be apart from you for a single day. Marry me, Makeda. Be my bride."

"Solomon, how can I? I am queen of Sheba, sworn for ever to be married only to my country! How can you ask me to break my oath? How can you marry me when you are married to Makshara?"

"That is not a marriage; it never has been. It is a political convenience."

"It is not! Makshara loves you. I know she does!"

"Nonsense. You know nothing about Makshara. And did not David, my father, have many wives? Am I not myself the son of a woman he took from another man? Yet Adonai forgave him because he loved her."

"Adonai did *not* forgive him because he loved her. He forgave him because he repented, as you yourself need to do. And you needn't try to contradict me; thanks to Zadok I know the history of you and your people now as well as you do. I shall be returning to Ethiopia as soon as my caravan is ready to travel."

"Then you will know that Moses himself married an Ethiopian! There was opposition to their union too, but Adonai himself rebuked those who complained."

"I don't care who Moses married. You are married to Makshara."

"… who is completely incapable of giving me an heir! What kind of king risks going to his grave without leaving a single son to succeed him? Is that responsible? Is that what my people or my God would want me to do?"

"Perhaps if you had spent the occasional night with Makshara you might not have found yourself in this predicament."

"But she is an Egyptian, for God's sake! She worships foreign gods. No son of hers could ever be counted as one of God's people unless she embraced our religion, and that she will never do. Whereas you, Makeda, you are a daughter of Zion; in any case, your people and mine are cousins by blood, for Sheba, the father of your people, is mentioned by name among the ancestors of mine."

"Solomon, it's not where my nation came from that matters; it is where it is going. And it will be heading straight for ruination if I marry you and forfeit my right to be queen. It will be plunged into civil war."

"But who will rule Sheba after you in any event? Suppose you were to die in the desert on your way back home. Would there not be civil war in your country anyway? Whereas if you married me, our son could inherit both kingdoms together! Would that not be wonderful?"

"No it would not, because Israel would be plunged into war with Egypt."

"Egypt? Egypt is a spent force, Makeda! The pharaoh could no more threaten me than his daughter has been able to bear me a child. Whereas *our* child would cement the alliance between *our* peoples more firmly than any treaty. Our union would bring peace and prosperity to all our subjects and glory to our God."

"No, Solomon, it wouldn't, because my people would never accept it, and neither would yours. Any son I bore you would be driven into exile in the wilderness, if he wasn't torn limb from limb!"

Having exhausted his battery of arguments, Solomon did nothing for an excruciating interval but stare at Makeda in increasing desperation, while she stared back, simultaneously defiant yet devastated by love just as he was, which made her look as beautiful and terrible and irresistible as I had ever seen her. For Solomon this was the final straw. Still on his knees by the couch where she was seated, he laid his head in her lap and wrapped his arms around her legs as though physically to impede her escape. Then he whispered, "Lie with me, then, Makeda. Just once. At least grant me that. No one need ever know."

"I would love to do that, Solomon. Not even you could ever imagine how happy it would make me for that single night. But God would know. Then neither of us could ever be happy again."

Of course, in his heart of hearts he knew she was right. And so did she. But it didn't prevent him from pleading with her further, nor her from crying her heart out while she continued to refuse, nor from clinging to him wildly when at last he rose up to leave, for fear that she would never see him again.

But he said, "Don't be afraid, my beloved. I shall not leave you like this; this is not the parting we must have to remember. There will be a banquet on your last night here as there was on your first, and you shall sit beside me in splendour for the last time. Every Sheban you brought to Jerusalem will be invited, and as many of my people as can be accommodated in my largest hall. We shall preside over them as their rightful rulers, so that all the world will know that we parted as friends and as allies."

"No, Solomon. Over and over again you have contrived to keep me here just one more day, one more week, one more month. I have to go. I *have* to. In fact, Tamrin assures me that everything will be ready the day after tomorrow, and that is when my caravan will leave."

"Then the banquet must take place tomorrow night. Please, Makeda. Grant me this one small favour if nothing else. Do not refuse me again."

"Very well, you shall have your banquet. But that is *all* you shall have. You must promise me faithfully that you will not seek to ply me with drugged wine or try to take advantage of me when I am tired and not thinking as I should."

"Makeda, you know that I would no more rob you of your maidenhead against your will than you would steal the cups from my table."

"Then promise me, Solomon. Give me your word."

"Very well. I give you my word that as long as you steal nothing from me, so shall I steal nothing of yours. Will that be enough to keep you happy?"

"It is enough to reassure me, yes. But not to make me happy. For *you* must be assured that when the sun rises the day after tomorrow and I say goodbye to you for ever, I shall be saying goodbye to happiness also. I love you, Solomon. I always will. If there were any way that I could stay here and bear your son, I swear to you, that is the path I would take."

Chapter Twelve

As soon as the banquet began, I decided that Solomon intended to keep his word. He made no attempt to beguile Makeda into drinking more heavily than was prudent, nor had anyone tried to interfere with her wine or her food, for she was served from the same wine jar and platters as the rest of the guests at the topmost table.

And what a table it was! There was every luxury and delicacy you could imagine, and many more besides. Ten courses of fabulous foods were ceremonially carried in and the leftovers whisked away in their turn: venison, peacock, duck and goose, as well as the tenderest beef, lamb, goat, and every conceivable kind of fish. Everything was cooked to perfection in the peculiar Hebrew fashion to which Makeda's own royal cooks would have to become rapidly accustomed, though I noted that it was much more generously spiced than the Israelites are wont to prepare it – out of special deference to Sheban taste, or so Solomon professed. After the savouries came the sweetest of sweetmeats, and pastries soaked in honey; even these were spiced with cinnamon and saffron. All the while myrrh and cassia burned in golden lampstands, rose petals were scattered constantly by pretty little servants, and the whole atmosphere was utterly exquisite.

Makeda herself was calm and composed now too. She seemed to have done all her weeping by the time she took her seat beside Solomon, and to be fully focused on presenting herself to her subjects and to his as the proud and dignified monarch she truly was. In fact, I had ceased to worry about her almost entirely since earlier that afternoon when she had made me kneel and pray aloud with her to Adonai. This was something we had not really tried until then, and an indescribable peace such as neither of us had ever experienced descended upon us both, and convinced us that in returning to Sheba now we were acting fully in accordance with the will of God himself.

Would that my stomach had felt as settled as my soul. But the longer the banquet went on, and the more of that spicy food I permitted myself to eat, the iller I started to feel. Of course, I knew it was only my stomach's notorious queasiness that was to blame; no one was trying to poison me, because just like Makeda I was being served from the communal plate. But from the initial hint of discomfort, the griping in my belly grew steadily worse until the perspiration was pouring down my face and I seriously feared that I might be going to collapse.

I bore it as long as I was able. I remained stolidly upright in my seat even when I could no longer make sense of a single word that was being said to me. Soon Solomon and Makeda, as they chatted and smiled and laughed and did everything they could to preserve decorum and keep their mutual sorrow at bay, were just blurred, muzzy shapes swimming somewhere in the middle distance. Standing behind me in his place, Hami was bending over with his mouth to my ear, desperately trying to make himself understood, no doubt begging me to let him take me away. But how could I leave Makeda unchaperoned now, in the presence of so many courtiers, ministers and merchants? How could I disgrace myself and dishonour my host by walking out of a banquet arranged in honour of myself and my queen?

Then again, I was hardly going to disgrace myself or dishonour my host any the less by throwing up all over his table. So when Hami left off trying to harangue me and instead hoisted me bodily from my seat to drag me outside, I let him get on with it. I could but hope I would be fit to travel in the morning.

And miraculously I was, though I didn't surface as early as I had meant to. Hami left me to sleep off my malaise until all the work of packing up my personal possessions had been done for me; as for those men whose job it was to draw up the caravan ready for the road, they were sufficiently well drilled to get on happily without me.

By the time I saw Makeda she was already ensconced upon her famous white camel, the diadem of Sheba glittering on her brow, her face a regal mask and quite unreadable. Solomon and all his court came out to watch us leave; Solomon too wore his kingly gravitas along with his crown and ceremonial robes, so if the crowds had been hoping for – or dreading – an emotional scene, it certainly wasn't forthcoming.

As for Solomon's ministers and courtiers, their faces were wreathed in smiles: the shameless foreign seductress was leaving at last, and although their king's reputation had been tarnished, there was every chance that the damage would only be temporary, and that in due course a few of his spectacular solutions to intractable lawsuits would enable them to win back for him the renown he had previously enjoyed.

While these men looked on benignly, officials from the king's treasury brought forth chest after chest stuffed with gemstones and gorgeous garments to present to Makeda as parting gifts – as if she didn't have enough of such finery already – and fresh camels to carry them.

Finally, Zadok the high priest invoked divine blessing on our journey, and even Jehoshaphat appeared sanguine and relaxed, having evidently decided to forgive me my shortcomings, for he inclined his head when he saw me and his bristling eyebrows no longer met in a furious frown.

Thus, to my immense relief, we set out at last upon the long and arduous road back to Sheba, though for the first time in my life I did begin to wonder if I was getting too old for the itinerant existence. There would be no fresh vistas to inspire Makeda, either, since we would be retracing the same route we had taken to get here, and every step the proud white camel took her along it would be one step further away from her precious Solomon. When she rode for miles without speaking I was scarcely surprised, nor did I feel the need to ask her what the matter was when from time to time I saw her face awash with silent tears. I was sure that as the days slipped by she would begin to look forward to being home as much as she was looking backward to what she had lost, and that in time she would once again become the vivacious, effervescent Makeda I had known and loved.

Yet this did not happen. If anything she grew more morose and withdrawn with each mile we covered. She seemed to be losing her appetite too, in particular refusing to have anything at all for breakfast, claiming that she had never been one for eating much before midday. Of course, our cooks weren't yet used to preparing meat without the blood in it, but they were doing their best, as was Hami, who strove tirelessly to come up with something, anything, to tickle the royal palate, all to no avail.

After the first month or so on the road she even gave up praying with me in the mornings – instead of making offerings to Shamash as we had done on our way to Jerusalem, we had adopted the custom of praying in the direction of Solomon's temple. But now Makeda left me to pray on my own, while she got up later and later, causing us to lose valuable time when we should have been travelling during the coolest hours of the day.

"Makeda, are you ill?" I ventured to ask her at last, when she emerged from sleep one morning even later than usual, looking wan and hollow-eyed and somehow as though her mind was very far away. She was fiddling with a ring on one of her fingers which I didn't recall having noticed before, but which seemed to be too loose to stay snugly in place – as indeed were all her other rings, for she was visibly losing weight.

"No, Uncle Tamrin. I am perfectly well," she lied, but would say no more. And later in the day, as on most days, she did seem to rally a little, never becoming too ill or too weak to ride.

Then early one morning when we had been on the road for six or seven weeks, I heard a woman's voice quietly but urgently calling my name from outside my tent. I sent Hami to find out who was there but he said, "I know who is there. It is Sabla." And without meeting her gaze he showed her inside.

She fell at once at my feet and stammered, "Lord Tamrin, forgive me for coming to see you uninvited, but I have to speak to you about Her Majesty."

I had never known Sabla so distressed on her mistress's account. The strict discipline to which she had recently been subjected, or conceivably something else, had certainly wrought some changes in her character. More kindly than I'd been wont to address her in the past, I asked her, "Does she know you are here?"

"No, my lord. But I have to tell you: Queen Makeda is with child."

She might as well have struck me with a shield boss. I went instantly cold all over and had to sit down on a handy bale of clothing that Hami had been repacking. As though from a long way away, I heard my own voice saying fatuously, "No. It's not possible. How could it have happened? When?" But already I knew exactly when, and in spite of my futile protests I didn't need any further convincing.

Sabla wasn't to know this, of course, and said desperately, "You have to believe me, Lord Tamrin. I know the signs. I have been as she is myself." Hami's eyes almost started out of his head. "If only things had been as they used to be between my mistress and me, and she had been confiding in me all along! If only I hadn't offended her, she would have told me earlier what was wrong, instead of my having to guess. Then I might have been able... I mean, there are herbs which sometimes... But it's almost certainly too late now. She has missed her bleeding twice."

"She has told you this? She has confessed?"

"No, Lord Tamrin." Sabla sniffed and brushed a hand across her nose. "I had to question Romna whom she made chief handmaid in my place."

"Then you and I must talk to Makeda together, immediately. Hami, bring me my robe."

He did so, though not without fumbling. (Might a child of *his* have succumbed to Sabla's expertise?) Then he and I accompanied Sabla back to the royal tent.

I called Makeda's name to warn her that I was about to enter, but when Romna attempted to have me wait outside I took no notice and blustered my way in. The queen of Sheba crouched in the dust being sick into an earthenware pot.

When at length she looked up and saw me, she knew that I knew, and that nothing could be gained by attempting to hide the truth from me any longer. I didn't ask her outright to give me the sordid details, but now that I knew the worst, it seemed that she wanted to tell me the rest as well.

"Oh, Uncle Tamrin, what can I say? Ever since we left Jerusalem I have been so frightened, I didn't know what to do, what to say, how to talk to you… and then when I did not bleed, and I began to be sick… You see, on our last night in Jerusalem, after the banquet… It was so late, and everyone else had gone to bed or fallen asleep where they sat; even my handmaids and Solomon's servants had gone to sleep at their stations. Only Solomon and I were still there talking, for neither of us wanted the evening ever to end. But I was so tired, I could neither sit up any longer nor face walking back to my chambers. So he carried me away to his own, and laid me on a couch in the room where he has his bed. I went to sleep – I did, I swear it! And so did he, alone! But after eating so much peppery food I awoke in the night with a raging thirst. There was a pitcher of water beside his bed, and I didn't want to wake him, so I went and took a sip without asking. Then he put out his hand and seized my wrist and said he had only promised to take nothing of mine if I took nothing of his."

"You mean… he tricked you? He *raped* you?"

"Yes! I mean, no… I mean… He said I had broken my word, and I suppose I had, in a manner of speaking. But it was only water I took, and I entreated him, 'How can I have broken my oath merely by drinking water?' But he said, 'Water is the most precious commodity on earth. Shebans of all people must know this.' So then, when I couldn't think how to plead my cause any further, and while he still had hold of my arm, he said, 'Do not merely sip from my pitcher, Makeda. Drink your fill. For when will either of us be able to love like this again?' And then he… he *knew* me, he possessed me, there on the royal bed that he must surely have shared so many times with Makshara without ever his seed taking root within her. But really… Uncle Tamrin, I wanted to lie with him as much as he wanted to lie with me. And it was beautiful. I have never known such bliss in all my life."

By the time her confession was complete she was crying against my breast, and in spite of everything a tiny misguided part of me rejoiced because once again she was my neglected little cousin who had always needed me. I rocked her against me, waiting for her sobbing to abate. But when it did so, instead of falling silent she blurted, "It's so unfair! *Once* I lay with Solomon, *once*, when he hasn't produced an heir with Makshara in all these years! And when Sabla… Sabla has… But Sabla has never fallen pregnant in all this time."

A horrible awkwardness ensued, which Sabla herself ended by saying, "With respect, my lady, there is much about me you do not know. But I *do* know things. If you had told me earlier I could have helped you. Even now it might be possible, with wormwood, perhaps, or pomegranate seeds, or rue. But it would be dangerous, because of the quantities that would be needed."

It took Makeda several minutes to assimilate what Sabla was suggesting, and for the mingled horror and hope to show on her face. Then she whispered, "You know how to make the medicine I would have to drink?"

"Yes, I know. But some of the ingredients could poison you as well as the baby."

The substance of what I was hearing made me sick to the pit of my stomach. If somehow a child had been growing in *me*, I could not have felt sicker were it being torn out with a fish-hook. But Makeda was desperate, distraught; any unmarried woman in her predicament would have been, and she stood to lose far more than most women can ever have dreamed of having in the first place.

"Sabla, it is a risk I must take," she concluded after frantic thought. "If I die, then so be it. It's no more than I deserve. And if we don't try, my life hereafter will not be worth living in any case." Then the hope faded once more as she added, "But where shall we find the ingredients we need in the desert?"

Sabla lowered her head before replying, "I carry them with me, my lady. It is only prudent."

"Then we must waste no more time. You must mix the potion straight away."

So Sabla set to work there and then, boiling, crushing, pounding, while Makeda retired to lie down on her mattress, with the rest of her handmaids fussing around her. I sat and stared at the floor, and Hami stared at Sabla's nimble fingers as they went about their business.

Eventually he stood up and approached her, standing over her without uttering a word. He didn't need to. She in her turn answered his unspoken question without looking up or pausing for a moment in her task. "I destroyed no child of yours, Hami. You have my word." Then she did look up, and her skilful hands suddenly fell quite still. She said very quietly, "And I want you to know that I never would. Not any more."

Relieved and bewildered in equal measure, Hami went back to his place and rested his head on his knees. Presently Sabla announced that the medicine was ready, if Her Majesty was ready to drink it.

Would I have stopped her, if she had said that she was? Would I have dashed the cup from her lips, as I knew with all certainty that I ought to do? I have always been a man of conscience, though like any other man I haven't always heeded its warnings. But the stirring I felt inside me now was something other than my natural conscience, and stronger than mere revulsion. That is, it *was* that conscience, and revulsion, but heightened by something I know now to have been the Spirit of Almighty God – to whose suzerainty Makeda had submitted her life, just as I had.

So there was no need for me to act upon my conviction, because she must have felt the same prompting herself. Although she raised Sabla's poisoned cup to her lips, she could not bring herself to drink. Tears sprang in her eyes afresh as she thrust the cup back at Sabla and clasped her hands together, clutching at the new ring I had seen on her finger before. It was quite distinctive, a heavy gold signet ring engraved with the six-pointed cipher of the House of David. With her brimming eyes fixed upon it she whispered, "Solomon said that if there were a child, and if it were a boy, I must send him back to Jerusalem with this ring, so that there can be no doubt as to his identity. And it *might* be a boy, it might! How can I kill the only son of the only man I shall ever love? Sabla, thank you for trying to help me. I know you had only my best interests at heart, but I cannot do this evil thing. Take the cup away and pour its contents in the sand outside the camp, where the earth is barren already."

It was while Sabla was still hovering there, uncertain whether to do as she was told or to try to persuade her mistress to think again, that the wild idea came to me which was to change the course of Sheban history and which came, I was certain, from the same source as the conviction I had felt before. "Sabla," I said, "you may be able to help your mistress after all."

Naturally she had no idea what I was talking about. Neither had Makeda, and neither, really, had I, for the idea was only forming itself in my mind while my lips were speaking it aloud. So I was as startled by what I was saying as Sabla and Makeda were, and as Romna and the rest of the royal handmaids must have been, though they were trying to pretend they weren't listening.

"You and your mistress are very much alike in build and in colouring – I have always thought so – since you are cousins, after all. No one but the people here in this tent knows that Makeda is with child, and no one else would ever suspect that she could be. You, on the other hand…"

"Uncle Tamrin, whatever are you thinking? Tell me at once!" Makeda interrupted, suddenly and unexpectedly sounding so much like her feisty old self that it gave me the courage I needed to go on.

"Is it not obvious?" I all but taunted her. "Once the pregnancy begins to show, you and Sabla will change places. Sabla will ride your camel, heavily veiled of course, and you will be carried in a litter. The story will be put about that your handmaid is with child, and must remain out of sight because of her shame. Once the child is born – which will certainly be before we get back to Ethiopia – you will resume your rightful seat upon the camel you have always ridden, and Sabla will bring up the baby as her own until – assuming it's a boy – he is weaned and can be safely smuggled back to his father."

"Uncle Tamrin, have you taken leave of your senses? I never heard anything so ridiculous in all my life. Sabla doesn't walk like me. She doesn't *talk* like me."

"She won't need to walk; she will be mounted. As for talking, you have barely opened your mouth since leaving Jerusalem. It will excite no comment if she does not speak at all."

"But how will Sabla feed a baby? She won't have any milk."

"A wet-nurse can be bought or hired en route. We shall have to acquire a midwife, after all. It shouldn't be a problem."

Another silence ensued, during which Hami raised his head and tried to make sense of the baffling conversation he had just become aware of. Then Makeda said firmly, "No. I cannot ask this of Sabla. It is too much. I shall bear the consequences of my sin for myself, and cast myself upon the mercy of my people. If they demand that I be exiled or put to death for my iniquity, then so be it. If my child is allowed to live when I am gone, Sabla may decide for herself whether she wants to take care of him or not."

Thus my plan for changing history might have been aborted as swiftly as Makeda's baby, had not Sabla made her choice already and infused the madcap proposal with life. "My lady," she murmured, "please, let us do as Lord Tamrin suggests. To do this thing for you will make me the happiest woman alive, if only it helps you see your way to pardoning me the offence I caused you by humiliating Hami. Don't misunderstand me – I'm not asking you to restore me to my place as chief of your attendants. I have been selfish and wicked all my life. I ask only for your forgiveness, and for the opportunity to make amends for my many transgressions."

During the course of this startling speech, Sabla had fallen to her knees beside the bed where Makeda had lain down to drink the poison. Makeda now stared at her handmaid's bowed head in astonishment and said, "You would agree to this madness, of your own free will, because you are sorry for what you did to Hami?"

"Yes, my lady. Hami loved me and I was cruel to him, and it made you hate me. I would do anything to have things back as they were between us."

Then, sensing the warmth of a hand laid in blessing on her head, Sabla ventured to look up. But it wasn't Makeda who had blessed her. It was Hami.

"You are wrong when you say that I loved you," Hami corrected her. "The truth is that I *do* love you, and I always will." Then he took her in his arms, where she broke down and wept. Next Makeda was weeping too, and so was I, and I'm sure that God and all the hosts of heaven were weeping with us, and laughing and dancing into the bargain. For I have learned that there is nothing Adonai prizes more than a contrite heart, and to see forgiveness and reconciliation flourishing in soil where previously the root of bitterness has prevented their germination.

So it was that our frankly desperate scheme was put into action. Romna and her girls were sworn to secrecy on pain of having their tongues cut out, though the threat was probably superfluous because every one of them had come to love their mistress in a way that they had never had the chance to love their own mothers, and they would never have betrayed her confidence. From that moment on, Makeda studiously avoided speaking to anyone at all, except for those of us who knew the situation, and took care to be seen abroad as little as possible except when mounted on her camel. Until such time as her pregnancy became visible, she continued to ride as she had always done, except that now and again she and Sabla took to changing places for a day as a sort of trial, to convince themselves that their subterfuge would not be discovered straight away. They need not have worried; since Makeda had lately been accustomed to riding in stony silence with her veil drawn over her face, purportedly meditating on the many things she had learned at Solomon's court, no one perceived the exchange. Daring to hope once more that her life and reign might not be over after all, Makeda grew stronger and her appetite returned; Solomon's ring was no longer loose on her finger and her hollow cheeks filled out. Though she still wouldn't eat in the mornings, later in the day she had cravings for the strangest of delicacies, which the permanently euphoric Hami did his best to procure.

Though she was careful not to engage anyone in conversation during the day as we travelled, in private during the evenings Makeda was keen to make up for lost time. Now that the air was clear between us, Sabla and I were her confidants once again: to

Sabla she spoke of her concerns as a woman, to me of the things of the spirit, of philosophy and statecraft, and the wonders of nature which we had discussed together since she was a child. But she spoke of Solomon too: to me, to Sabla, to Romna, and to any of her women who seemed happy to listen. For she loved him still, in spite of all that had happened.

"Aren't you angry with him even a little, for taking advantage of you when you were at your weakest?" I asked her one sultry night as we sat out under the stars. The two of us had evaded all our companions and sat well away from them, hidden behind a rampart of baggage. Here Makeda could gaze up at the sparkling firmament unobserved, absorbing its beauty as though to preserve it intact in her memory ready for when she would have no choice but to hide inside her tent whatever the weather.

"No," she answered promptly. "And I'm no longer angry with God because of what happened to me, either. The fault was all mine. I am queen of Sheba and a daughter of Zion too. I should not have *had* a weakest moment. But I have repented and made my peace with God. I can only pray that Solomon has done the same, for he showed himself as weak and irresolute as I." She sighed, and passed a hand across her belly as she had begun to do often, involuntarily; you couldn't yet see it swelling up, but no doubt she herself could tell that its shape was changing. "Besides, there was a part of me that wanted to lie with him, for I loved him as I love my own two eyes, and love him still, and not a moment goes past when I do not think of him and wish he could be mine."

"Just as there is a part of you that wanted to bear his child?" I suggested gently; straight away she took her hand from her belly, but then put it back and left it there as though to embrace the child that was growing inside.

"Yes," she admitted in a small voice, and said no more for some time, but then continued, "And just as a part of me does not want to send the child back to him, boy or no. For he will have Solomon's face and Solomon's eyes, and every time I look upon him I shall feel that a part of his father *will* be mine, forever."

"Well, did Solomon give you any instructions as to *when* exactly he wanted you to send him the child?"

"When? I'm afraid I don't understand."

"Did he specify when he was weaned, or when he was grown?"

"He did not say, precisely, but I do not doubt what he meant. If the boy is to be his heir, his upbringing must prepare him thoroughly for what his future will demand of him."

"*If* the boy is to be his heir. But the people of Israel will not accept a child of yours as their king if Solomon has any other son. Let Sabla keep the child as you suggested yourself, boy or no, till it is grown. If no legitimate heir to the throne of Israel has been produced, *then* if your child is a boy they will welcome him with open arms."

"So he cannot be told the truth until he is a grown man? He can never be told that I am his mother and Solomon his father, until he is nearly as old as I am now, and never at all if Solomon has another son? He must grow up the son of a slave, the *bastard* son of a slave, whose father could be any one of the many men his promiscuous mother has lain with?"

"That is what he will have to believe until the time comes – if it ever does – for him to return to Jerusalem, lest he involuntarily give away the secret himself. But you will be able to watch him grow up; he will still be nearby to remind you of the father he must surely resemble more closely every day. The worst thing you will have to endure will be hearing him call Sabla 'mother' and seeing him raised with none of the rights or privileges that a prince ought to enjoy. And if Solomon does beget a legitimate heir, the truth about *your* son's birth will have to be withheld from him forever."

"Poor little boy. For he will be a boy; I know it." Both Makeda's hands were pressed to her belly now, and her hair, unbound, hung down about it like curtains to protect its treasure from the prying eyes of the world.

Poor Makeda, I thought but did not say, because I did not think she yet knew how hard the thing was that she was asking herself to do.

"You know," she said presently, when I did not speak, "I can at least ensure that he grows up free, if not a prince. When he is born, and I have given him over to Sabla, I shall grant her her freedom. I shall provide for her to go on living with him in my palace if she chooses to do so, since it is her right as cousin of the queen. But if she wishes, she may take him far away where she need not listen to the wagging tongues of those at court who would condemn her for bearing a child out of wedlock. I could not make her endure that humiliation along with everything else. She could go somewhere where the people would believe she was a widow."

"I could free Hami, and they could marry and bring up your baby together," I said on an impulse, but then both of us laughed, because of course it could never be. Sabla was nobly born and had sunk into slavery only through her father's debt; Hami was a slave born and bred, and could have coped no better with freedom from serving me than I could have coped without him. Nor would Sabla's family ever have sanctioned her marriage to such a base-born creature, though they had had no qualms about selling her; this was simply the way most self-respecting Shebans thought.

Thus the decision was taken that Solomon's son – if indeed the baby was a boy – should not be sent back to him directly, nor should Solomon even be told of the child's existence. Let him produce an heir by Makshara if he could, and let Makeda's son grow to manhood incognito, unthreatened by the jealousy of those who would fear him.

So the months went by, and Makeda grew large and heavy and was carried through the desert in curtained seclusion, while Sabla rode the white camel with her veiled head erect and the strangers we encountered prostrating themselves before her, which once upon a time would have represented the fulfilment of all her dreams. Now it brought her only the pleasure of knowing that she served her mistress, who had always loved her in spite of her faults, which were many. And Hami would look up at her in doglike devotion, content in the knowledge that although they could never be married, her heart would always belong to him. As for her body, she had taken a vow of chastity to atone for her past promiscuity and would never allow a man to invade it again.

In spite of the delays Makeda's sickliness had caused when our journey was getting under way, in its later months we made good time, and in the end had to slacken our pace lest we find ourselves back in Yeha before the baby was born. Nevertheless he was born on African soil, because once it became feasible that he might be, Makeda resolved that it should be so. Therefore instead of loitering in Arabia we made the crossing to Aduli as hastily as we could, and found midwives and a wet-nurse readily enough in its needy streets.

A healthy boy he was too when he came, and large, so that I feared he would tear his slender young mother apart as he fought his way out into the inhospitable world of men. When the midwife put him to Makeda's breast for the first and only time she would ever suckle him, she wept and wept to see that he had Solomon's fair skin, and would have his waving hair and not the thick black curls he might have inherited from his mother.

"You must name him, Makeda," I told her through my own tears, for I was weeping too, in relief that she had survived her ordeal and in sorrow as I reflected that his name was just about all she would ever be able to give him.

"Menelik," she said at once, surprising me with her decisiveness, because I wasn't aware that she had given the matter any thought. But clearly she had made up her mind that since she could not call the child openly after his father she could in one small way recognize the connection between them. For in the language of her mother's tribe, "Menelik" means "son of the wise man".

Then, gently, little Menelik was prised from his mother's embrace and handed to the wet-nurse who would suckle him until he could be weaned. And Makeda dried her tears and set about preparing herself to become the virgin queen of Sheba once again.

PART TWO

Chapter Thirteen

It was an unusually hot afternoon in the upland city of Yeha, and the boy and I sat in the shade of a portico in its much extended and beautified palace. Between us on a low table rested an ebony game-board, exquisitely carved for the playing of mancala. In each of its cup-like indentations the little ivory counters in their various combinations told me, with my years of experience, that my opponent had undoubtedly won, as long as he did not throw away his advantage at the last minute. Of course he would not do so; he was much too clever for that. Nevertheless I kept my knowledge from showing on my face, because if he did win, it would only be the third time I had been beaten at mancala since I'd been his age, and the first time I had ever lost at any game to him.

Gradually coming to appreciate the strength of his position, the boy leaned forward with renewed concentration, hands on his knees and forehead furrowed above knitted brows. As happened so often when I looked at him these days, my heart missed a beat, not merely because his fair-skinned, twelve-year-old face was becoming so strikingly handsome, but because he so closely resembled the father he had never known. It wasn't surprising that their faces should have shared the same noble contours, and their eyes the same intelligence and intensity. But that their mannerisms should be so similar had never ceased to amaze me.

Suddenly he looked up at me with such a quizzical expression that I feared my discomfiture might have given itself away. Then I realized it was his own incredulity that had prompted his sudden change of focus, rather than mine.

"Master Tamrin, I have won, have I not?" he exclaimed, more mystified than triumphant. I smiled, pleased and impressed that he could see the inevitability of the outcome so far from the end of the game.

"Yes, young Menelik, I do believe you have," I conceded, still smiling so broadly that he was driven to ask me whether I had allowed him to win on purpose. But I had not, nor had I been tempted to let him win at anything for a very long time, for he would certainly have seen through me with his father's legendary perspicacity.

Unexpectedly our absorption in the game was interrupted by a clattering of weapons and studded sandals in the far corner of the courtyard, and by a hubbub of semi-broken voices. These belonged to Menelik's classmates, the sons of palace officials and civil servants, all of whom I had been engaged to tutor together since I had given up my life of travel and trading. I was still the owner of the business empire I had built up, but nowadays Mahiko managed it for me, and stood to inherit a substantial share of it when I was gone. Already I felt the weight of old age heavy upon me; my vision was clouded and my hearing poor, and every joint in my body ached when the weather was damp or cold. The heatwave we were currently experiencing was actually a relief to me rather than a burden.

"Hey, Menelik! Lessons are over," shouted one of the noisy youths across the wide expanse of the yard. "Get up off your backside and come play some real men's games, son of the wise man!"

"Son of the wise man! Son of the wise man!" echoed the youth's companions, twisting Menelik's name so that its meaning, less obvious in the dialect of Yeha, became abundantly clear. They didn't mean it as a compliment.

"Son of the wise man? Son of the *woman*!" shouted another, and then they were all shouting it, taunting him as they did mercilessly whenever there was no one in authority close enough at hand to give them the beating their bullying deserved.

Menelik's hackles rose visibly, but he did not lose his temper. He could not afford to; there was only one of him and a whole herd of them. I wished I could have knocked their heads together myself, but if I had tried to hobble over to their corner I would only have made a laughing stock of myself and caused them to start yelling all over again.

As it was, they ran away jostling and shoving one another before I could do or say anything at all, no doubt to go hunting or practising with their spears and wooden swords, as was their habit. Menelik could handle a weapon as well as any of them, but by inclination he was a scholar like his father, and thus a closeness had grown between us despite my resolve to treat him no differently from his peers.

The insults he endured for being studious were bad enough, but I knew it was the "son of the woman" jibe that hurt him more. It was painfully clear what they meant by it: that his mother had never had a husband, and that he didn't even know his father's name. Sometimes, when they were being particularly cruel, the boys would change "son of the woman" to "son of the whore", and once when that had happened Menelik *had* lost his temper completely and wrestled one of his persecutors to the ground. The others had kicked him black and blue for his offence until they had been hauled away by palace guards, but although Menelik had come off by far the worst, they would never have dared to take him on one by one. For he wrestled as well as he read Sheban script, and Babylonian cuneiform, and Egyptian hieroglyphics – and played mancala.

To take his mind off his troubles I started to praise his skill, and to analyse our game out loud to ensure that he understood fully why it had gone for once in his favour. But although he did not interrupt me I could tell he wasn't listening, and when I had finished, he asked me, "Master Tamrin, do *you* know why they hate me so?"

"Because you are cleverer and braver and more handsome than all of them put together," I answered him perfunctorily, leading him to suspect that I was teasing him too, which indeed I was. My strategy had always been to make light of his companions' jealousy, to distract him from asking me too many awkward questions that I couldn't afford to answer. Neither his real mother nor Sabla had ever lied to him about his identity – Makeda would not have it – but they had nevertheless successfully avoided telling him the truth. As he got older, this was becoming more and more difficult for us all.

"I so much wish I wasn't sometimes," he said, with a desolate sigh, so that I knew he wasn't going to let me so easily off the hook. "Why did I have to be born with such pale skin and such strange straight hair? Why couldn't I just be like *them*?"

"You know very well that you were conceived when your mother was in Jerusalem for the queen's state visit; all the men there have skin even paler than yours. And your hair isn't straight, not by their standards. As for your wanting to be like those oafs who harass you – I can only be thankful that you are not, because then I should derive no pleasure from my teaching whatsoever."

He sighed again, having heard me talk in this way so many times before. But then he said, "*You* went to Israel with them, did you not? When my mother was in service to the queen you must have seen her every day. You must surely have some idea of who she was – seeing."

But I could only shake my head and trot out the official story: that Sabla in her younger days had known so many men that no one could have been sure who the father of *any* child she bore might have been. I hated having to say it, because ever since then she had kept her vow of chastity, and it was no wonder that Menelik found my words hard to swallow. Besides, my respect for her had increased with every year that passed as I saw her being the best of mothers to her foster son, and simultaneously bearing her base reputation with equanimity.

In the end he accepted that he was going to get no further with me than usual, and wandered off in the direction his classmates had gone. I watched him cross the courtyard, a tall, graceful, slender figure silhouetted against the sunlight. But there was no pride in his gait, no self-esteem. I was glad he could not see the sorrow in my eyes as I mourned my part in the deception that had robbed him of all joy in his own existence.

I got up and went my way then too, to take my daily turn around the palace roof. I knew that if I made no effort to exercise regularly, my joints would seize up altogether. So every afternoon when lessons were finished, I would go to a part of the palace where the roof was flat and bounded by a solid balustrade, and I could walk about in safety while enjoying an extensive view of the city and of the forest and mountains beyond.

Sometimes I still missed the travel and adventuring of my younger days, but mostly I was content to contemplate the beauty I saw close by, in and around Yeha itself, and to reflect upon the extraordinary changes Makeda had wrought in her capital city and in her kingdom as a whole in the years since she had returned from the expedition to which Menelik owed the existence he found so hard to endure.

Yeha had been declared the permanent centre of Sheba's government and chief residence of the royal court and of the queen herself, and so magnificently had she embellished it that one often heard it referred to these days as Debra Makeda, the Citadel of Makeda. The palace that had once been her father's tribal stronghold had been extended and refurbished beyond all recognition, and was now as impressive (albeit not as tall) as any building in Marib, or even in Jerusalem, with the exception of Solomon's temple itself.

But Adonai now had a temple in Yeha as well, though not especially large or ostentatious, because Makeda had no desire to wean her people from their idolatry by crass intimidation. She had simply made it known throughout her kingdom that she herself now honoured a different god, the God who had *created* the sun and the moon that she had worshipped as deities herself before her enlightenment, and that her hope was for her subjects to come to worship him too. Yet no one would be forced to, or even bribed into doing so. They could simply witness for themselves the difference her new faith had made in the life of their queen and in the principles by which she and her trusty vizier Luqman and his fellow ministers now governed them.

For corruption and exploitation had been all but eradicated from Sheba's burgeoning economy. In the arid desert regions of Arabia, new dams and irrigation canals had been constructed, creating work for thousands of engineers, craftsmen and labourers, and bringing the bounty of the mountain rainfall to all, not merely to the unscrupulous rich who had previously hoarded it all for themselves. So nowadays the peasants could grow enough food to feed their families and even have surplus to sell at market, as only the favoured few had been able to do before.

Meanwhile in the cities there was no longer filth and excrement everywhere; men were employed to remove it in carts. Then it would be burned in a furnace at one of the new public bathhouses to heat the water, and the resulting ash would be distributed to farmers to fertilize their fields. Thus everyone's diet and health improved, and fewer of their children died in infancy.

In short, prosperity had increased throughout the nation, benefiting everyone from the greatest to the least. Even the homes of the poorest were better built and more proudly kept these days, and those men who had lost their land or even their freedom through debt or misfortune found that measures had been put in place for them to recover what had been taken from them. Along the lines of the Hebrew model, no native Sheban could be kept in slavery against his will for more than seven years; Makeda had declared Menelik's foster mother legally free as she had vowed she would, and I had even offered to free Hami. But, as I had suspected and very much hoped that he might, he had begged me not to send him away from me, and now he wore a ring through one ear as a sign that he was pledged of his own free will to serve me for life. This was another of the many Israelite practices that Shebans were rapidly adopting.

They were adopting the worship of Adonai too, just as Makeda and I had been hoping and praying that they would. Of course there was no Ark of the Covenant in Yeha's temple as there was in Solomon's, but it had been built to face Jerusalem and, as Makeda pointed out, if God was everywhere, the distance between us and the earthly symbol of his presence scarcely mattered. She did suggest with a smile one day that we should put in Yeha's sanctuary the tiny replica of the ark that Solomon had sent to her before they had even met. I wasn't entirely convinced that she spoke in jest. But for now the Holy of Holies at Yeha remained quite empty.

Presently, as I stood leaning on the parapet and gazing contentedly out over the roofscape, my attention was diverted by raised voices coming from below. Hard of hearing as I was these days, I could not make out what they were saying. But I knew very well whose voices they were, and made all the haste I could to descend and, if necessary, intervene.

"Not a day goes by when they don't mock me!" Menelik was yelling as I came within earshot. "You know what they said to me today? 'Your father must have been clever indeed if he managed to run off before even your *mother* could find out his name!' And some of them call me 'son of the white man' and others 'son of the woman' or 'son of the whore'. How do you think it makes me feel? How do you expect me not to lash out at them when it's you they are insulting as much as me? Do you *want* me to stand there and take it when they call you a harlot? You're my *mother*, for God's sake, and I love you! And if you love me you'll tell me the truth about who I am!"

"Menelik, I've told you the truth! I have been honest enough to tell you what I was like as a young woman; what more can you ask than that? I had many lovers in Jerusalem, as I had in every place I went, because I was a slave, and I did not care, and I looked for love wherever I thought I might find it!"

"But why did you call me 'son of the wise man' if you didn't know which of these shameless fornicators my father was?"

"It's just a name, Menelik, as Sabla is mine. In fact it's a popular name among *my* father's people; in their dialect it means 'how handsome he is'. And you *are* handsome, just as you are wise! Isn't it enough for you to have your father's gifts, without needing to know his name? You're becoming obsessed."

"Obsessed? Are you surprised? How can I not be obsessed by the need to find out who I am?"

"Because you never will find out! I cannot tell you."

"Cannot, or will not? Cannot or will not?"

At this point, the unstable adolescent pitch of Menelik's voice rose to become more of a scream than a shout. Then came the noise of a struggle, and a stifled scream which wasn't Menelik's at all, and I realized I had no choice but to get involved.

The argument was taking place inside his foster mother's quarters, which could not be reached from the courtyard directly except through an open window. Not being agile enough to gain access that way, I had to go round. By the time I had barged my way in, Menelik had the terrified Sabla pinned to the wall by her throat. For at twelve years old he was already taller and stronger than she.

"I demand that you answer me directly, Mother: yes or no. Do you know who he was?"

"I cannot…! I don't…!"

"Yes or no. Yes or no! Do you *know*?"

And before I could think how to pull him away from her, or even call out his name to distract him, Sabla had stammered, "Yes."

At that he let go of her straight away. Sobbing and shaking, she slid down the wall against which he had held her, and fell in a heap at his feet.

For a while he just stood over her, open-mouthed. Before he could take it into his head to do anything else, I had interposed myself between them and begun to help Sabla stand up. Shoulders heaving, and streaming eyes locked with his, she said then, "But I cannot tell you his name nonetheless. I swore an oath. It would be more than my life is worth."

"You swore an oath to my father?"

"No, Menelik. Not to your father. To the queen."

For a moment he obviously thought she was mocking him just like everyone else; if I hadn't been protecting her, he might even have struck her. Then all at once the fire went out of him, and his eyes flicked in entreaty from her face to mine as if he somehow hoped that I could magically make everything all right. But I just said quietly, "Menelik, please respect your mother's wishes and don't question her any further. Do not force her to choose between her love for her son and loyalty to her queen. No mother should ever have to face such a choice – certainly not at her son's insistence."

So without a word he strode out of the apartment, making no attempt to disguise his disgust with us both, though now he was clearly more shaken than enraged.

Sabla pressed her face into my shoulder and said, "I'm sorry, Lord Tamrin. I shouldn't have admitted that I knew. But I couldn't help it, and sooner or later, if no one tells him the full truth, he will force it out of me. He is strong now, and angry, and every day his strength and his anger increase. I have done my best by him, but I am afraid."

"Afraid of *him*, or of what you might say to him?"

"Both, Lord Tamrin. I admit it."

"Well, perhaps the time is coming when he will have to be told the whole truth after all," I conceded, and resolved to speak of it to Makeda at the earliest opportunity.

In fact, a number of matters were coming to a head about which I thought that the two of us needed to talk. Not least of these was the question of the succession, for more and more people were starting to ask who would inherit Makeda's throne when she was gone, and Solomon was not alone in appreciating the importance of having a recognized heir. For him and for Israel it was all about his begetting a legitimate son, but for Sheba things were not quite so straightforward. Of course, Makeda herself was still young; she wasn't much more than thirty years old, and mostly enjoyed good health. But few of her predecessors had lived on into grand old age, and there was a very real fear among her countrymen that if Her Majesty were to die before her time, Sheba might sink rapidly back into the mire whence the reigning queen had dragged her. Without Makeda's restraining influence, benign as it was, the tribal chieftains would still have been at each other's throats, and although she deserved her reputation for benevolence, she had certainly learned from Solomon how to be ruthless when it was required. On her return from Israel she had efficiently eliminated every individual whom Luqman had identified as a threat, and any rival who had arisen since had been similarly liquidated if no other option were available. But when Makeda was gone, would everything return to square one? Would there be another Crown Council quarrelling and conceivably coming to blows over who was fit to succeed her? Might even the spurned Ghalilat reappear to claim the throne of which she had once, as she believed, been cheated? She hadn't been seen or heard of since, but as far as anyone knew, she was still alive, either in exile or living in secret much closer to home. Had she abandoned her royal ambitions, or was she merely biding her time? Would she even be content to wait for the reigning queen to die? Would she even need to? I couldn't believe I was the only person who had noticed that Makeda's gait was becoming increasingly uneven. The ulcers that had once troubled her so grievously had not returned since Solomon's doctors had treated her, but no physician would ever be able to rectify the damage done to her muscles and sinews. So she had never lost her limp, and as the years went by she was finding it harder and harder to conceal. If someone who hated her could convince the Crown Council that she should never have been accepted as eligible for the throne in the first place on account of this imperfection, there could be civil war.

As for Solomon, as far as anyone in Sheba was aware, he still had not fathered a son. I no longer maintained the elaborate network of spies I had employed in the past; Mahiko, I knew, had agents of his own, but they had not to my knowledge heard anything to suggest that an heir had been born to Israel's throne. Throughout the first few years of Menelik's life, Solomon had sent messenger after messenger to Yeha to ask if Makeda had borne him a child, but she had merely instructed them to tell him that she was well, and remained a faithful servant of Adonai.

For my own part I endeavoured to make Menelik one too, but even though he had been circumcised on the eighth day like a true son of Abraham, his foster mother had never renounced her idols, so it was inevitable that Menelik should be seduced by them. Not so many months ago, I had found him making offerings before the little figures that populated his mother's domestic shrine, and had been moved to tell him one of Solomon's stories of Abraham, who at exactly Menelik's age had taken a hammer to *his* parents' idols and smashed them to pieces. When his father had come upon the scene and demanded of Abraham whether he knew who was responsible for the sacrilege, Abraham told him that one of the idols had attacked the others and then run away. "Don't be ridiculous!" his father had shouted. "An idol couldn't do that. Idols can't do anything." "Exactly," Abraham replied, and probably received a beating for blasphemy.

But before I could go to Makeda with any of my mounting concerns, someone of consequence came to see me.

I did not know him at first, so old and infirm had he become, and when at length I did recognize him from his great bushy brows I was astonished that a man of his age, frailty and station should have embarked upon a journey that would certainly have seen off many much younger travellers. But Jehoshaphat, royal recorder at the court of King Solomon, was a desperate man.

He and his party had already been warmly received by Makeda on their arrival, and Jehoshaphat had been given guest rooms at the palace, where he had allowed himself a day or two's grace for rest and recuperation before nerving himself to see me. But although the signs of exhaustion were still etched deeply into his white-bearded face and the hand that grasped his staff shook alarmingly, his errand could wait no longer.

"Jehoshaphat, my old friend!" I greeted him incredulously when Hami led him into my presence. I embraced him as closely as I dared, for he looked as fragile as a cracked clay pot. "May Adonai grant you his peace."

"And Adonai's peace to you too, Tamrin, my brother. You cannot begin to imagine how happy it makes me to find that you and your queen have held firm to the faith you found in Jerusalem, especially when I think on what has become of Solomon. I was wrong in my hasty judgment of you both, and for that I am sorry and crave your forgiveness."

"There is nothing to forgive," I replied. "It was only right that you should be concerned for your godly king, and fear the pernicious influence that a beautiful pagan queen might exert upon him. But he was so much wiser and surer of what he believed than she or I had

197

ever been that there wasn't much doubt as to who would influence whom."

"Oh, if only things were so simple! For if you could see what he has become, your heart would break as mine has broken."

"*Solomon* has become an idolater? But how can this be?"

"It wasn't your fault, or even Queen Makeda's. He should have known better than to beg her to stay so long, or to let himself love her so besottedly when he was already wed to another. But after she left him he fell apart like a wall built without mortar. He feared he would never find love again, and never have an heir. So he took another wife, and another, and concubines too, in the forlorn hope of finding someone like your queen. Some of them are the daughters of heathen kings, and he let them bring their idols with them, just as the pharaoh's daughter, Makshara, brought hers. One of them, Naamah of Ammon, told him that her god would give him a son, and almost at once she was found to be with child."

"And was the child born safely? Was it a boy?"

"Yes, it was a boy; there is an heir. But is he truly of Solomon's blood? So many wives, so many concubines, and in all this time only one of them has borne him a son? So vehemently did Naamah maintain that the child was a gift from Molech, her god, Solomon was almost persuaded to sacrifice the wretched creature in order that he might be given more."

"To sacrifice his son to Molech?"

"Yes, that's what the Ammonites do. They feed their firstborn to the god in return for the promise of more."

"I know, Jehoshaphat; I know perfectly well what the Ammonites do. But that *Solomon* should contemplate doing such a thing… It makes no sense. He was the shrewdest, most prudent and pious man I have ever met. How can he have changed so completely?"

"Because he loved a woman more than God."

I didn't know what to say, any more than I knew what to think. If anyone other than Jehoshaphat had been telling me these things, I should not have believed them. At last I asked him, fearfully, "Have you spoken of these matters to Makeda?"

"No, brother Tamrin. I have spoken like this to you alone, because you were my dearest friend. You *are* my dearest friend."

"And it warms my heart to hear you say so. But why would you come all this way to tell me something I can do nothing to change?"

"Because perhaps you can, my brother; perhaps you can. You see... Prince Rehoboam is not an intelligent child; he is not a pleasant child, either. Indeed, in my bleaker moments I could almost wish that Solomon had given him to Molech after all. But rumours have become rife in Jerusalem that Solomon lay with Makeda the night before she left, and that Rehoboam may not be Solomon's firstborn after all. I *had* to come and find out for myself, for even an illegitimate son of Solomon would make a better heir than one who may not be his at all, and whose character is the very opposite of what one would look for in an Israelite king."

"But Solomon has made enquiries here before. He has never been given any grounds for supposing that Makeda might have borne him a son."

"I know, Tamrin, I know. But I also know what the prompting of God's Spirit feels like in my heart, and I know that it was such a prompting that sent me here. Moreover, in the few days since I arrived I have twice seen a boy at the palace who looks so much like Solomon that my heart almost failed me altogether at the sight of him. I would wager my life that he is twelve years old, and that he is Solomon and Makeda's child."

What was the point of my trying to deny it? Jehoshaphat had fixed me with those penetrating eyes that had read me like a scroll so long ago; the bristling eyebrows above them, now whiter even than the beard that flowed over his chest, somehow made me feel that I was under the scrutiny of Almighty God himself. So I whispered, "It's true, Jehoshaphat. The boy *is* twelve years old, and he is clever, and good, and exactly who you say he is. But he does not know. *No one* knows, except his mother and I, the woman who has brought him up, and a handful of our most trustworthy servants. For if the truth were to get out, Makeda would lose her throne and perhaps her life, and the boy would be offered up to Almaqah long before Solomon could offer him to Molech."

"Offer *him* to Molech?" exclaimed Jehoshaphat, with tears pouring down his ancient face. "Solomon wouldn't give a child of Makeda's to Molech! He would make him his heir straight away."

"No, Jehoshaphat. He might want to. But his Ammonite wife and her supporters would be only too quick to change his mind, and besides, you seem to have forgotten how desperate the elders of Israel were – how desperate you were yourself! – that Solomon should *not* have the opportunity to sire a child upon the queen of Sheba."

"But everything has changed now, don't you see? If I could take the boy back with me, Solomon could send his foreign wives and concubines packing, and the noxious Rehoboam with them."

"And risk offending these women's fathers, some of whom you told me were powerful kings? It's a miracle that he wasn't attacked by the pharaoh the moment he took a wife alongside Makshara."

"The pharaoh is weak, and beset by troubles within his own borders; he is in no position to contend with an empire such as Solomon's. But Tamrin, unless I take the boy with me, Solomon will go on and on acquiring wives and concubines until he finds one who makes him forget Makeda! And I dread to think what will become of Israel in the meantime."

"Well," I said, "I shall inform Makeda that you have uncovered the truth for yourself, and that unless we keep you a prisoner here in Yeha, Solomon will duly learn it too. So she might as well send you to him with a letter confessing all, in her own words. Then it may be that he will refrain from taking further wives or concubines to provide him with heirs, even if he has not found love such as he knew so long ago. But he must swear by Adonai himself to tell no one else. Nor can the boy go with you, for the danger to his life would be too great. He will be told who he is, since it would not be right to withhold the truth from him any longer. And who knows? It may be that when he is older, things in Sheba will have changed, and the Shebans too may be told that wisdom was not the only thing their queen and her entourage brought back from Solomon's court. Then he may go openly to see his father if he chooses to, and even be made heir to the throne of Israel, if by then that is what Solomon and his people really want."

Jehoshaphat nodded slowly, and all at once looked simultaneously so weary and so relieved that the thought struck me that he was not much longer for this life. But his mission would not have been fully accomplished until he had returned safely to Israel with his sensational news, and with the letter which Makeda must unquestionably write for him.

Hami guided him gently to the door, where a servant of his own was waiting to take him back to his rooms. But when Hami returned, he had a wan-faced Menelik by the scruff of the neck. My own face must at once have turned paler even than his.

"Menelik? What were you doing, skulking outside my doorway?"

"That old man, the one who was here… he was staring at me. Who was he?"

"Menelik, I am asking *you* the questions. What were you doing outside my door?"

"The old man… I saw him when he first arrived at the palace, and he stared at me so hard I thought he was putting a spell on me. Then just now I heard his voice coming from your apartment through the window. I heard…"

"You heard what, you meddlesome boy? What did you hear?"

Hami still had hold of him, and when he didn't answer immediately, Hami shook him until his eyes were almost rattling in his head. Then everything came tumbling out at once.

"I heard that there is a boy here at the palace who is Solomon's son! And that Solomon loved the boy's mother, *really* loved her. It's me, isn't it? 'Son of the wise man'; it all makes sense. King Solomon was one of the men my mother slept with when she was in Israel with the queen. I'm the son of King Solomon, Master Tamrin, am I not? You have to tell me the truth!"

"Yes, Menelik. You are. But even that is not the whole of the truth you need to hear."

"I don't understand. There is more? How can anything else matter, compared with this?"

"Menelik, the time has come for you to be told something that you may find harder to believe and possibly more upsetting than what you have learned today already. But first I must go to see the queen."

Chapter Fourteen

It was not until the following morning that Makeda felt ready to have Menelik brought before her. The evening in between we had spent sharing our fears and daring to voice our hopes for what the future might hold, now that mother and son were to face one another at last. But she knew as well as I did that the moment could not be put off any longer. Jehoshaphat knew the full truth, and Menelik knew that he knew. If the boy did not hear it from us, he would not hesitate to extract it from him.

Of course, when I told Menelik where I was taking him that morning he could not understand what the queen should have to do with any of this, nor was he keen to see her. To him she was a remote, all but irrelevant figure, distant and aloof, for this was how she had had to seem in his eyes, until today.

So he expected to be led into her throne room where she would be ensconced in splendour like a goddess, a vision of glittering jewels and sumptuous silks, with the diadem of Sheba gleaming on her brow and courtiers grovelling appropriately at her feet. Instead we went to her private apartment where she sat alone and bareheaded on a low-backed couch. Beside her there was room for another person to sit; she patted the vacant cushions with one hand and said, "Come, Menelik. Sit beside me. Do not be afraid." And she spoke so kindly, and smiled so tearfully, that without a murmur he did exactly as he was told.

"Menelik," she continued when he was settled, "for many years you have been asking people to tell you who your father was, when all the time it was your mother's identity you should have been questioning." Bewildered, he stared at her with his father's eloquent eyes, so that any solemn speech she might have had ready for him was forgotten in an instant and she could barely stammer, "Embrace me, my son, for that is who you are. Your father was king of Israel and your mother is the queen of Sheba."

Naturally he could no more embrace her than he could find his voice to speak. But she, who had been unable to hold her own son since the hour of his birth, could restrain herself no longer, and folded him into her breast, where she held him as though she never meant to let go of him again. She wept uncontrollably, surprising even herself, I think, with the strength of the emotion that for twelve long years had been pent-up inside her. So for a very long time none of us said anything, because none of us were able.

At length, however, her tears subsided and she released her grip on Menelik sufficiently for them to look one another in the face. His eyes were dry; he had been too shocked to cry. But on seeing his own features reflected so undeniably in hers, even though her complexion was dark and his was fair, and even though he resembled his father much more closely than he did Makeda, it was Menelik's turn to be overcome by the strength of his feelings. A potent mixture they must have been, but as he gave in to them and wept, Makeda's face became radiant with joy because for the first time ever she was able to give comfort to the child she had borne and from whom she had been so cruelly kept apart. Having had no children of my own, I was unable to appreciate fully the poignant nature of her experience, but having been more of a father to Makeda than her own father had been, and something of a father figure to Menelik too, I felt I could understand it at least a little.

Very much later, when mother and son had dried each other's tears, she told him the whole story of the night on which he had been conceived and showed him the ring his father had given her. Briefly he was as bewildered as before, and even angry: "My father tricked you? He… raped you?" he demanded, echoing almost exactly the words I had used myself when long ago Makeda had told the story to me. But when she told him how deeply Solomon had loved her, and how desperately she had loved him in return, and how for six whole months they had longed to consummate their love and yet held back from doing so, he was reassured. He had been so afraid that he was the product of a loveless, fleeting, carnal coupling of slaves that to know that his royal parents had loved one another passionately was enough to render him content.

"But how could you not have told him in all this time that he had a son?" Menelik asked, once he had grasped that Solomon was yet to learn of his existence. "How could you not have sent me back to him with the ring, as he had bidden you?"

"Alas," she replied, "it breaks my heart to think that I have so long kept him from finding out that our union bore the fruit he was so keenly hoping it might. But it would have been too dangerous, both for you and for me, if the truth had got out. I should certainly have lost my throne, and both of us might have lost our lives."

"But you will tell him now? You will send me to him, with the ring, when Jehoshaphat returns to Jerusalem?"

"Certainly I shall tell him. That is to say, I shall write him a letter, which Jehoshaphat will give to him in secret. But as for sending you, the time is still not ripe. Your life would still be in danger, as would mine if the Shebans were to learn that their virgin queen has mothered a son. Besides, how could I bear to part with you when you have only just been restored to me? No; you must continue to live with Sabla and to call her Mother as you have always done. For she *has* been a mother to you, the best mother you could ever have had."

"I know she has, it is true. Yet I have reviled her and accused her of deception, when she has never wished anything but the best for me. I must go and beg her forgiveness, though I do not deserve it."

"Yes, you must – presently, when you and I have finished saying to one another the things which have to be said. But you must not breathe a word of this business to another living soul, Menelik. You must swear on your father's life that you will mention it to no one, excepting only Sabla and my uncle Tamrin here, who will now be your uncle too, though you must not call him such in the presence of anyone else. Do you swear, Menelik? Do I have your word?"

"Yes, Your Majesty… Mother." He smiled at his own embarrassment, and she smiled too. "I swear on my father's life and on my own. But must the secret be kept forever? Shall I *never* be allowed to go to him and claim my inheritance? Must the spiteful boys who mock me never see me as anything but the son of a whore?"

Makeda winced visibly; then, for the first time since setting eyes upon Menelik this morning, she turned to look at me, and indicated that I should explain to him the ideas we had shared between us the evening before, concerning the succession.

So I said, "Prince Menelik, your mother and I both hope very much that the day will come when *everyone* can be told who you are, and that you can be acknowledged as heir not necessarily to your father's throne but certainly to your mother's. For hundreds of years Sheba has been rocked by political instability every time she has buried a queen, and this can go on no longer. If a royal dynasty with clear principles of succession could be established, Sheba's future security and prosperity would be assured. But a great deal of preparation must be done before this can happen. The chieftains must be convinced that it would be in their own best interests as well as in that of their nation, and that your mother is not merely seeking her own glory and immortality. I scarcely know where we shall begin, but begin we must, for all our sakes and for Sheba's."

"So I would be king of Sheba." Menelik looked from me to his mother and back again, his face alight with wonder, then with amusement. "King of Sheba," he repeated. "It sounds so strange. It would be a privilege indeed for me to be the first one ever – the first of many, if the gods so will it. But Israel will need a good king too, to carry on the work my father has begun, and it seems that Solomon also lacks the kind of heir that he needs. Might I not inherit both my parents' kingdoms one day, and unite them into a mighty empire fit to rival what Egypt once was, or the Hittites, or ancient Babylon?"

"This was Solomon's dream too, once upon a time," Makeda told him with a wistful distance in her eyes. "And yes, it might happen, depending on how events turn out. But not unless you can convince the elders of Israel that you are a worshipper of Adonai."

"I do worship Adonai!" Menelik exclaimed. "Master... I mean Uncle Tamrin has seen to that."

"You worship Adonai and your foster mother's gods besides," I reminded him gently. "That would have to stop."

"Oh, Menelik, I wish it would stop in any case!" Makeda leaned forward and took hold of her son suddenly by both his arms so that he had no choice but to meet her earnest gaze. "Adonai alone is God, Menelik; he made everything that is: the sun, the moon, the stars and the earth and every living creature that walks upon it or flies in its skies or swims in its seas. No other god is worthy of your veneration, for they have no power over anything. Renounce them, Menelik; have nothing more to do with them. Then Adonai will bless you beyond your wildest imaginings."

"You would have me smash my foster mother's idols as Abraham did to his father's? Then she would *never* forgive me."

"You need not do anything quite so dramatic – unless you become convinced that this is indeed what Adonai would have you do. But you don't need to bow to them yourself."

"I won't, Mother. I promise you. I shall never bow down to an idol again. I shall honour Adonai, and him alone, as long as he grants me life. For I can see how he has blessed and guided you, and Uncle Tamrin, and how much better life in Sheba has become for those who were once oppressed and exploited by men who should have known better. If I could build on the foundation you have laid, I should be a good king indeed."

"You will, my son, I am sure of it. But in the meantime there is much that you must learn, and not merely from the books you love so much. You must learn how to manage men as well as you manage weapons, and how to rule them according to the Law of Moses. You must learn how to remove those who threaten your supremacy, yet without laying yourself open to accusations of injustice. In short, you must learn all the things that I learned from your father when I visited his court, and you must learn them in secret, lest anyone question why the son of a freedwoman should need such specialist knowledge."

"And who will be my teachers?"

"You will continue to study with Tamrin and his other pupils, irksome though their company may be. But you will also come daily to me, without telling anyone except your foster mother where you are going. You will come late in the evenings, when you would usually be in her apartment preparing for bed. Then no one will notice that you are absent from any of your regular activities. Do you find these arrangements to your liking?"

"Of course." Menelik shrugged his shoulders, not used to being given any kind of choice, and apparently unsure if he had one now.

And so this new routine was duly put into practice. Menelik continued to attend my classes each morning, to call me "Master Tamrin", and to say nothing to his fellow students about the astonishing truths he had learned in the past few days. To begin with I feared they might find out nonetheless, for now there *was* a nobility in the set of his shoulders and a swagger in his step when he crossed the courtyard. But mostly they paid him too little attention to notice the change, being much more interested in their games and their military training and, lately, in each other's blushing sisters, than they were in him. I don't think they even noticed that because he was no longer rising to their bait, they were mocking him less than they had previously been accustomed to do.

Meanwhile Jehoshaphat returned to Jerusalem armed with a secret letter from Makeda to Solomon, the first she had sent him in the thirteen years since their parting. I wondered how he would react to the momentous news contained within it: with joy, with dismay, or conceivably with anger? Might he even refuse to keep it to himself, as Jehoshaphat and the letter itself would entreat him to do? From the little that Jehoshaphat had had time to tell me about the changes he had seen in Solomon since Makeda had left him, I no longer felt confident that the Israelite king could be relied upon to do the wisest thing. The only thing that was certain was that we would not find out about his reaction for well over a year.

If I had my doubts about Solomon's current disposition, no such concerns disturbed Menelik's new-found happiness. His confidence in himself and his readiness to assume the role he believed history would require him to play was growing daily, along with the knowledge he would need to perform it. No doubt Makeda was as responsible for bequeathing to him an idealized portrait of his father, the epitome of kingly beneficence, as she was for preparing him to be a king in his own right. For who else but Menelik would listen with such appreciation when she extolled Solomon's virtues or waxed lyrical about the esteem in which his subjects held him? Who else would agree so readily when she maintained that he must be the greatest and wisest king who had ever lived?

"Uncle Tamrin, if only you knew how badly I long to see him," he confessed to me one day, when we were alone and I had rebuked him for harping on the subject of his father yet again. "If only there were some magic that could transport me to his throne room and let me look upon his face, even if he couldn't see *me*. But how much better still if he *could* see me, and recognize me at once as his son, and proclaim me his heir in front of all the elders of Israel.'

Certainly the briefest glance at Menelik would have told Solomon that this was indeed his son, though when he spoke so excitedly he reminded me much more powerfully of his mother.

"Menelik, I thought it was Adonai you had promised to worship, not Solomon," I chided him. "It is just as tempting to make an idol out of a man as it is from stone or wood."

But Menelik only laughed, and said that if Adonai would only make it possible for him and his father to be reunited, he would sacrifice everything he possessed on Adonai's altar and never eat another slice of bacon as long as he lived.

As the weeks and months passed by, he did at least keep his word not to bow before Almaqah or Shamash or the gamut of gods that Sabla kept in her household shrine. If Sabla was offended by his neglect of them, she kept her thoughts to herself, as she knew she must. The prince she had raised as her son was hers no longer; ever since he had been a baby, she had known that this time would come. Now she must bear any pain she felt in silence, just as her household gods had to do.

But Menelik's faith in Adonai was not deep; not yet. Whether it would ever become so remained to be seen.

Alongside the work she was doing with Menelik, Makeda had already begun to work upon the Sheban chieftains with a view to their accepting that changes in the procedure as regards the succession would have to be considered seriously if Sheba were to hold her own in the modern world. This was a world of powerful rival empires, and one that seemed to be growing ever smaller as merchants and explorers travelled further and further afield. For the first time in many years, Makeda called an assembly of Sheba's Crown Council, a thing that no queen of Sheba before her had ever done on her own initiative, and which she herself had only ever done in the gravest of political or military crises.

It took the chieftains many weeks to muster, and much fuss they made about it too, grumbling that they were having to forsake their ivory towers for another perilous ocean crossing and another exhausting trek along precipitous tracks through the highlands of Ethiopia to get to Yeha, the furthest-flung city in the whole of Sheba.

But they couldn't grumble once they got there, for they were put up in the most luxurious apartments and provided with veritable armies of servants to indulge their every whim. By the time the official proceedings began, most of them were already eating from Makeda's hand as they had found themselves doing in the past. Besides, they agreed, was it not better to be seated in the airy spaciousness of her light, bright hall, cooled by Yeha's gentle mountain breezes than squatting cheek by jowl as they once would have done in the stifling heat of the ancient palace at Marib? When Makeda appeared in their midst, clad in a golden gown just like the one she had worn on the day they had elected her to rule over them, all banter among them ceased, and they beheld her in reverential silence.

"Princes of Sheba," she began, her low, musical voice effortlessly smoothing down any feathers that might still have been ruffled, "it will not have escaped your notice that many things have changed for all of us over the years since you did me the supreme honour of making me your queen. I have done my best to prove myself worthy of that honour, and have striven with all my strength to rule over my people with equanimity and integrity, seeking only the best for

210

everyone, from greatest to least. But you must have noticed too that I am not as young as I was when you elected me, and how can any of us know for sure how many years God has allotted us to walk upon the face of the earth? Sheba as a nation has taken great strides forward in my time as queen, yet I fear that when I am taken from you she may slide back into the mire from which she has struggled so hard to escape."

At this point she paused, letting her eyes come to rest upon each attentive face in turn. None of the men could have guessed where her speech might be leading, but they must have had their ideas. Here was the fearsome Kahalum of the Banu Waren, whose daughter had been ten years old at the time of Makeda's succession. Now she was in her twenties; was he hoping that Makeda had decided to designate a successor, and that this time his daughter might be chosen? Here was Salamat, whose daughter had been just a baby; had her turn come this time? And there was Mafaddat, father of the jealous Ghalilat, whose whereabouts no one ever spoke of any more. Sullen and surly as ever, I could not begin to fathom what might be going through *his* mind. As for his stepfather, Yuhafri, father of Makeda's predecessor, he had long since passed away.

When none of the chieftains ventured to voice any thoughts aloud, Makeda took up the thread of her speech where she had left it.

"Now perhaps you are waiting for me to suggest some means by which this council can avoid the usual wrangling when God sees fit to take me from you. But the truth is that I have no intention of doing so. I am merely asking that you give the matter your consideration now, when – God willing – we still have plenty of time to debate any alternatives that may present themselves. Make your suggestions here, today, if you wish, or return to your homes and turn the matter over in your minds in the weeks and months ahead. And if you have cause to travel beyond Sheba's borders, make it your business to study what is done in other countries to ensure that the transition from one administration to the next is a smooth one. But whatever suggestions are put forward, it is my firm belief, and that of Luqman my vizier, that if we continue to appoint our rulers in the way we have always done, sooner or later Sheba will be torn apart by civil strife."

And on this occasion, this was as far as she wanted, or indeed needed, to go. She had sown the seeds of change in their minds; soon they would come to see for themselves that it was imperative. Yet the nature of that change would remain undetermined until, perhaps, such time as one of *them* thought to suggest that the greatest queen they had ever had should establish a dynasty. Then, provided that everything was expertly managed, the disclosure of Menelik's existence might be greeted with delight rather than with horror.

In the meantime, Menelik would continue to learn and to mature, and to grow more handsome with each week and month and year that passed. Soon the sisters of his companions had eyes only for him, for now he was undeniably taller, wittier and more self-possessed than any of his peers, in addition to being more accomplished than any of them at anything he put his mind to.

Nor did he resent the attention they lavished upon him; on the contrary, he revelled in being the focus of pretty girls' admiration rather than the butt of rude boys' jokes. Whenever there was a feast or a festival – of which there were many in Yeha just then, for Makeda had introduced several Hebrew holidays alongside the native Ethiopian – the girls would seek to charm him with their dancing, or their singing, or the way they carried themselves in the solemn processions, and he was only too willing to be impressed. All I could do was hope that he would refrain from playing too active a part in furthering his mother's dynastic plans until he was crown prince in name as well as in notion, and safely married to a lady of suitable rank. As I said, his devotion to Adonai did not yet run deep, and his respect for the Law of Moses was more formal than profound.

When more than a year had passed since Jehoshaphat's departure for Jerusalem, I began to wonder how soon it would be before we received word of Solomon's reaction to the letter that the old man had carried with him. Would he send back a letter of his own, and if so, what would be the tone of it? Would he send an escort to whisk Menelik off to Israel, whether we liked it or not? Might he send an army to bring him back by force? Or might he disown Menelik altogether? But as more and more time went by and we heard nothing at all, I began to be concerned that Makeda's letter might never have reached Solomon in the first place. Jehoshaphat had been aged and infirm, and the expedition he had undertaken would have been arduous even for a very much younger man. It was all too likely that my dear old friend had not survived the return journey, and if that were the case, what might have been the fate of Makeda's letter? Perhaps, instead of being duly delivered by his companions, it had been buried with him, or blown away in the desert dust. But it might just as easily have found its way into hostile hands.

Still, there was nothing to be gained and potentially a great deal to be lost by making direct enquiries. If the letter had fallen into hostile hands, we should likely find out all too soon; if it had simply disappeared into the desert, then as far as Solomon was concerned it would be as though Jehoshaphat's visit to Ethiopia had never taken place. From the perspective of Makeda and Menelik's security, this would surely be all to the good.

Presently some of the members of the Crown Council did come up with proposals about the succession, but none of them were the ones Makeda and Luqman wanted to hear. It was suggested that the tribe from which the new queen would come should be chosen by lot; another idea was that the priests of Almaqah should make a special sacrifice and determine heaven's choice by inspecting the entrails of the victim. It was even mooted that the new queen should be the first baby girl born to the wife of a chieftain after the reigning queen's death, the child being regarded as her predecessor reincarnated. Reincarnation was not a belief indigenous to our part of Africa; it was one of the more exotic ideas that traders had brought back from the East along with silks and peacocks and which, like them, was gaining admirers. But it certainly wasn't a doctrine that Makeda as a daughter of Zion could endorse.

Thus it came about that Menelik attained the full stature of a man without any change in his status becoming apparent. Having graduated from my classes, along with those of his weapons trainer and wrestling instructor, he had undertaken training as a palace scribe, for there had to be some pretext for his remaining at court. His mother and I could only pray that Adonai would reveal to us a way forward with regard to the succession before it was too late.

Chapter Fifteen

On Menelik's twentieth birthday, Sabla threw a party in his honour.

There was nothing particularly special about being twenty according to the Law of Moses; in Israel a boy becomes a man at thirteen, when he is judged old enough to take on the responsibility of keeping God's commandments for himself. But in the tribe from which Sabla's father had come, twenty was apparently the age at which a young man would be ceremonially expelled from his parents' household and would set up home in a new hut with a new wife, and Sabla obviously felt that she could not allow this important day to pass without it being marked. I don't suppose she had ever imagined that Menelik at twenty would still be living with her as her son.

Of course, his real mother was not present; there was no reason why the queen would deign to attend the birthday celebrations of a lowly scribe. But as his erstwhile tutor I was invited, as were most of the pupils I had taught with him. Now that they were all grown up the merciless bullying had mellowed into mostly harmless banter, and Menelik would give at least as good as he got.

A goodly number of the youths' fathers were present too, as company for me and for Menelik's other teachers; many of these men were educated and cultured, being civil servants of appreciable standing. Meanwhile most of the girls who had worshipped the ground the adolescent Menelik had walked on were now married with children of their own; some of them were at the party too, but they mostly sat in a corner, with their babies on their laps, and only stole the occasional guilty glance at the handsome young scholar in whose honour they had assembled.

It was a quiet party by Ethiopian standards, more Arabian than African, and more Hebrew than Arabian. There were no naked jugglers or acrobats, no drummers or fire-eaters or warriors in feathered headdresses strutting about like displaying peacocks. Rather, there were harpists and flautists and elegant dancing girls modestly clad, and enough erudite discussion over decently watered wine for me to find it a surprisingly enjoyable occasion.

Then, just as I was beginning to think about turning in for the night, a new pair of entertainers were ushered into our midst. Not that they looked very much like entertainers at first sight: one of the pair was an elderly woman, wizened and bent, with a heavy veil shading much of her face, and the other seemed to be her servant, a girl on the brink of womanhood who might have been pretty had she condescended to smile. I fancied that there was something vaguely familiar about the older woman's features, but thought little of it. I've often thought that one old woman looks much like another, and I couldn't see her face clearly because of her veil.

It transpired that she was a travelling teller of fortunes who had arrived in Yeha some days before and put it about that she was seeking engagements at which to practise her craft. In return for a fee and a share of the feast, she would delight the guests at any gathering with the uncanny accuracy of her intuitions and the unambiguous detail of her predictions. Whether any of the latter would come true, only time would tell.

Makeda would have given the crone short shrift, having been convinced by Solomon that there could be no place for divination in the life of a worshipper of Adonai; one must trust *him* for the future, and him alone. But Sabla was no daughter of Zion. She escorted the fortune-teller and her servant into the hall herself, and seated them among the men.

"Oh, what fun!" cried the women from their corner, when they heard what the newcomer claimed to be able to do. They descended on the visitors like a flock of jackdaws, their children hopping and squawking, and all intellectual discussion came abruptly to an end. "Tell *my* fortune!" one girl exclaimed, thrusting a tiny gold piece into the old woman's face. "No, mine first. Mine!" another one demanded, addressing her claim to the servant, whose chief role was evidently the collection of payments. "How many children have I got?" another piped up, challenging the girl's aged mistress to prove her credentials before any more pieces of gold or silver changed hands.

And so the session got under way, the flock of women cawing with delight when the old woman correctly asserted how many children each had borne, and how many of these were sons and how many daughters. Not that this was an especially impressive feat, since the aforesaid children were mostly hanging spellbound to their mothers' skirts or clamped against their breasts.

Next it was the turn of the men, most of whose questions were much like each other's: will I live to be old, and will I have sons to make me proud and to whom I can pass on my good name? The old seeress would examine the palms of their hands and the lees of their wine, but most intently their avid faces, before telling them pretty much what they wanted to hear.

All the while Menelik had remained in the background studiously avoiding my gaze. He knew very well what I thought of diviners, whether accomplished or not; in fact, incompetent quacks I abhorred far less than those whose evident skill was seductive. But it was only a matter of time before his companions clamoured, "Where is the birthday boy?"

"Let Menelik son of Sabla come forward and have *his* fortune told!"

"Perhaps we shall find out his father's name at last!"

This prompted Menelik to back away still further, but he had left it too late to make his escape. Impatient hands grasped hold of his and dragged him forward, while the girls who were still unmarried giggled and cooed, "Will he marry *me*?"

"Will the handsome son of Sabla choose one of *us*?"

Meanwhile the boys, noting his distress, urged him, "Don't be afraid, birthday boy. It's only a bit of fun. What harm can some crazy old charlatan possibly do to you?"

By the time he was seated with his hands palm up in the old woman's lap, there was sweat gleaming at his temples and his fair-skinned face was paler than ever.

The woman barely glanced at his palms, and pushed away his wine cup when someone helpfully proffered it. Instead she looked him full in the face and said only, "You are not who you appear to be, Menelik, son of the wise man. Everyone wants to know who your father is, but not one of them has asked if your mother is truly your mother." And because she had raised her head to study his face, her veil had fallen back from her brow, and suddenly I knew exactly who she was.

She was nowhere near as old as she had made herself out to be, though her face was genuinely lined and her hair was streaked with grey. But it was her thin bitter lips that gave away her identity, and her eyes, haunted by the spectre of lifelong disappointment.

For a long time no one spoke. The sweat that had glistened at Menelik's temples now dribbled slowly down his cheeks like oil from an anointing. It wasn't until the not-so-old woman rose to her feet, pointing ahead of her with a trembling finger, that I noticed Sabla standing aghast behind the dumbfounded audience. "You!" the seeress shrieked like a screech owl. "You are not his mother! You have *no* living son, though the gods know that Sheol is full of your dead ones! It's time to tell the truth, Sabla the child-killer. I think we should tell your guests who the birthday boy's mother really is!"

Before the stupefied Sabla could react, Hami, who as usual was standing at my shoulder, shot forward like an arrow from a bow, seized her accuser in a wrestling hold and clapped his hand across her mouth. "Silence! How dare you insult your hostess in this way," he denounced her, and I marvelled that he should have it in him. "Master, what shall I do with this wretched creature who has flouted the laws of hospitality so flagrantly?"

"Keep hold of her while I summon the palace guards," I replied tersely, and almost at once men came running. By the time they arrived, Hami and I had succeeded in gagging our prisoner with her own veil, bound several times between her teeth. Both she and her servant were dragged away struggling; I would interrogate them later myself.

When they had gone, the silence that had greeted the fortune-teller's revelation prevailed once again. Neither Menelik nor Sabla had indicated that they thought her anything other than a malicious liar, but the guests were not fooled. I knew there were some who would not rest from now on until the deepening mystery of Menelik's parentage was solved to their satisfaction.

Taking charge of the sorry situation, I spread my arms wide and said, "Ladies and gentlemen, I regret to announce that the party is over. You can see that your hostess and her son have been sorely distressed by the insults of this troublemaker. I beg you to be gone as quickly as you can, so that they may be granted space to recover their dignity."

The guests were only too happy to do my bidding, and departed without a word of objection, though I could hear the hum of their voices outside as soon as they had left the apartment. When only Sabla, Menelik, Hami and I were left, Hami took Sabla in his arms. I sat down beside Menelik and laid a reassuring arm across his shoulders.

"What do we do now, Uncle Tamrin?" he asked me forlornly, suddenly sounding very much younger than his twenty years. Accustomed as he had always been to seeing me as the fount of all knowledge, it was only natural that he should look to me for direction in this unexpected crisis.

I said, "We go to the queen and tell her that the whereabouts of Ghalilat, daughter of Mafaddat of the Banu Marthadam, are no longer a matter for speculation."

Menelik's mouth fell open. "I beg your pardon? Ghalilat? Mafaddat? Who are these people?"

"The old woman, who is nothing like as old as she appears, was once your mother's rival for Sheba's throne, and almost certainly made an attempt on her life in order to wrest it from her."

"What! Has she come here to take it from her now?"

"To topple her from her pedestal, perhaps, or else to blackmail her. Who can say? I shall find out from her if I am able. But I do not doubt that the time has come for Makeda's subjects to find out who *you* are, from their own queen's lips, before they learn it from someone else's."

"I'm sorry, Uncle Tamrin. I should never have let that sorceress read my fortune."

"Sorceress? She may be a sorceress, I suppose, but it is more likely that she is merely a very clever woman whose ability to gather intelligence would cast Bijo's into the shade. But she would have said what she said whether you had agreed to sit down with her or not."

"I don't understand. How could she possibly have learned the truth if she isn't a witch, when no one else has uncovered it in all these years?"

"Again, I shall do my best to find out. Of one thing I am certain, however, and that is that she didn't learn the truth from your palm, or the dregs of your wine, or from some unfortunate sacrificial victim's entrails. Come, Prince Menelik. We must go to the queen with all haste."

Makeda received us at once, for Romna could tell from one glance at our faces that our business was urgent. Without preamble I related exactly what had happened, assuring Makeda that Ghalilat and her servant would remain in custody until they had been exhaustively interrogated, and then until Makeda had told her subjects whatever she deemed it best to tell them. For Ghalilat could not be muzzled all the time; she would have to be given food and water and no doubt the moment her gag was removed she would start screaming out all she knew about Menelik and his origins to her guards and to anyone else who happened to come within earshot of the place where she was imprisoned.

"I'm sorry, Mother," Menelik murmured when I had finished. "It was all my fault. If I had refused to have anything to do with that woman; if I had ordered that she be ejected from our gathering as an affront to Adonai – "

"It would have made no difference at all," Makeda assured him exactly as I had done. "She would have shouted out everything she knew to all and sundry even while she was being escorted away, and then things would have been much worse. No, Menelik; if anyone is to blame for our predicament, it is Sabla. But it may be that this is the moment we have been praying for. It may be Adonai himself who has brought these things to pass, or at least, if it was not, he will still use them to his glory and to the good of us all."

Menelik sat briefly in silence, weighing the implications of what she was saying. Then he ventured in a small voice, "Mother, you could just have this Ghalilat quietly strangled in her cell before she can say anything to anyone. That's what most kings or queens would do."

"And since when have I been known to base my decisions on the opinions of the impious and ignorant? Is threatening to tell the truth a capital offence in Sheba now? No, Menelik. You still have some growing up left to do before I would be happy to entrust my kingdom to your care. Besides, Ghalilat must have learned the truth from someone, so having her silenced would most probably achieve nothing in the long term other than the staining of our hands with her blood." As Menelik dropped his gaze in acknowledgment of her wisdom, Makeda turned to me and said, "Uncle Tamrin, I shall meet with Luqman to discuss what and how the people will be told. Meanwhile you will interrogate Ghalilat to find out how she learned the truth, and who else knows it. Nothing will be firmly decided until you have reported back to me."

By this time it was late; I needed to rest, to pray, and to collect my thoughts before presuming to pit my wits against such a shrewd and slippery opponent. So Hami and I went at first light the next morning to the strongroom where she and her servant were imprisoned. I bade the guards leave us and stand outside; they barred the door behind them. Then Hami removed the veils that were wrapped around the captives' mouths, though the ropes that bound their hands and feet remained firmly tied. If they had been thrown into the dungeon where common criminals were held, they would have been chained to the wall. But such treatment would not have been appropriate for women, one of whom was a chieftain's daughter who if things had turned out differently might so easily have been a queen.

The girl said nothing when her gag was removed; she seemed almost too terrified to breathe. But Ghalilat hissed at once, "I do know who the boy is, and I can prove it."

I said, "Yes, and so do I. What is more, I know who you are too."

Taken aback, she narrowed her eyes; her tight-lipped face was rigid with the venom of spite. But when she did not speak I went on, "What I want to know is how you know the boy's identity, since I am certain it was no god or demon who revealed it to you. Moreover, I want to know who else knows, and if I do not find your answers convincing, both you and your servant will be put to death."

"I am the daughter of Mafaddat, and this girl whom you call my servant is my niece, Masqal, who would have been queen after me were it not for your meddling, Tamrin the Merchant. You would not dare to harm us."

"Probably not, if anyone other than the rightful queen and her closest associates knew who you were. But fortunately for me, in your haste to tell the world who Menelik is, you neglected to inform anyone here that you are anything more than a wandering seeress whose disappearance no one would notice, let alone question. So I suggest you tell me what I want to know, without delay."

"And if I do?"

"If you do, you and your niece will be freed."

"I don't believe you. You wouldn't dare free us, knowing what we know."

"Once everyone in Sheba knows the truth, your knowledge will be neither valuable nor dangerous."

"Everyone in Sheba? If anyone outside of Makeda's immediate household learns that she has a son, it will not be my niece or I who faces the executioners."

"That must be for the people of Sheba to decide. Your concern is only to tell me the answers to my questions."

"Very well." Ghalilat shook her greying hair from her eyes and continued to look at me disdainfully down what had once been a noble Arabian nose. "I learned the truth from Naamah the Ammonite, mother of Rehoboam, *legitimate* son of King Solomon of Israel."

"From Rehoboam's mother? You have been in Israel?"

"Yes, I have been in Israel. For many months."

"And Menelik's existence is known there to the whole population?"

222

"No. To Rehoboam's mother only, and for obvious reasons she has told no one. She only told me because when she learned who I was, she imagined that I would want to destroy Menelik as badly as she does."

"So from whom did *she* acquire her information?"

"From Jehoshaphat the recorder, or rather from a letter he was carrying back from Ethiopia. She knew that he had left for Africa to find out the truth about Solomon's relations with Makeda for himself, so she had him intercepted when he was on his way home. After her men had extracted the letter from him by force and made him tell them how he had prevailed upon Makeda to write it, they put him out of his misery. By then it was probably the kindest thing they could have done."

"They murdered him? Rehoboam's mother had Jehoshaphat killed?"

"But of course. She could not risk Solomon discovering that Rehoboam was not his firstborn son after all. So, Tamrin the Merchant, are you convinced?"

"Yes. I am convinced." I could not have been more completely satisfied that Ghalilat was telling me the truth. "And *your* motivation?" I continued, when she went on glaring at me, in triumph as much as in bitterness. "Did you mean to expose Makeda, or to blackmail her somehow, to extract something from her in return for your holding your tongue?"

"Blackmail? What use would I have for blackmail, or for anything Makeda could be persuaded to give me? She has one thing I want, and one only, which should have been mine in the first place! I want her *throne*, Tamrin, and by all the gods, I shall have it. You may delude yourself into thinking that the people of Sheba will forgive her her fornication and her twenty years of deception, but they will not. They will see that in choosing her over me they handed themselves over to a harlot and a liar, who has tried to make fools of them all into the bargain. I have given you the information you asked for, Tamrin the Merchant. Now you give me and my niece what you promised *us*. Our freedom."

"You shall have it," I assured her. "Once the people of Sheba have made their choice. In the meantime, you will say nothing to anyone." And I bade Hami tie the prisoners' veils tightly between their teeth once again before we left.

Hurrying back to Makeda, my heart felt very heavy in my breast. I could not help but fear that Ghalilat might be right, in that despite all the good their reigning queen had done for them, the Shebans might decide that her crimes outweighed everything else. I was not sure which of her two great offences would anger them the more: the single act of fornication in which Makeda had surrendered her virginity, or the duplicity that had led her to pull the wool over their eyes for twenty years. There was no denying that she had transgressed their laws outrageously and then covered up her iniquity to save herself. If her people decided to have her ousted and stoned to death, and her bastard son with her, and to have the woman who had exposed her villainy invested in her place, they would be perfectly entitled to do so.

I did consider as I bustled along that it might not be too late even now to avoid the truth coming out. Orders could be given for Ghalilat and her niece to be killed instead, as Menelik had suggested. Since no one in Yeha had been able to uncover the facts about Menelik's parentage before, it was by no means inevitable that they should succeed in doing so now.

But as soon as the idea had reared its ugly head I dismissed it. I had given my word to Ghalilat that if she answered my questions she and her niece would go free. It was not for a servant of Adonai to break a promise so heinously. Nor would I be gaining any advantage for Makeda or Menelik by doing so. The longer Menelik's identity remained a secret now that he was grown to manhood, the less likely his eventual acceptance by his mother's subjects would prove to be. Besides, those who had grown up with him would now have stronger motivation than ever before for trying to discover who he really was. For they would never again believe that Sabla was his mother, especially if the fortune-teller who had sown the suspicion in their minds were to disappear, never to be seen again.

There was nothing else for it: Makeda would simply have to throw herself upon her people's mercy and trust that the love they bore her would atone for the sins she had committed against them. And when I told her what I had learned from questioning Ghalilat, Makeda agreed.

Therefore a proclamation went out throughout the kingdom that at the Festival of Passover, which was due to be celebrated in Yeha as in Jerusalem in a month's time, the queen would make an important public announcement with regard to the succession. All members of the Crown Council were required to present themselves, along with as many people as could possibly make the pilgrimage to Adonai's temple for this his most important annual feast.

Accordingly during the course of the following weeks, the pilgrims began to arrive and to set up their tents in the streets and open spaces of the city, and in a vast sprawling encampment outside its walls. The air became thick with the smoke from thousands of fires and noisy with the bleating of the lambs that would be slain in the temple to recall the slaying of Egypt's firstborn, when Moses had led his people from slavery to freedom. Of course, it was Solomon's ancestors who had marched with Moses, not Makeda's, but when Adonai had promised Moses' forefather Abraham descendants too many to count, he had not referred solely to progeny according to the flesh. Everyone who called upon the name of the Lord would have the right to be numbered among his people, whether Israelite, Ethiopian, Arabian, or dweller at the bottom of the sea.

On the eve of Passover, the momentous announcement would be made. With Ghalilat and her niece still languishing in custody, Makeda, Sabla, Menelik, Hami and I kept vigil together in Makeda's chambers the night before. None of us slept or even tried to, knowing only too well that this could be our last night together, and that for some or conceivably all of us it could be our last night on earth. Sabla, distraught because it was she who had invited Ghalilat to the palace and brought this calamity upon all of us, wept inconsolably, but Makeda's eyes were dry and her spirit calm.

"Sabla, I forgive you, and Adonai forgives you for this and for all your iniquities, just as he has forgiven mine," she assured the penitent who had once been her slave. "Only reach out to him from your heart and receive the mercy he offers you, and you will know his peace in the depths of your soul and be able to trust him for the future, as I do."

"What future? None of us is likely to have a future because of what I did. What use is peace in your soul if you are about to die?"

"I am ready to die if that is what is asked of me. But Sabla, what was asked of you was greater by far. For to die takes but a moment, whereas you gave twenty years of your life to bring up my son. I can never, never thank you enough for that. Even if he too must die tomorrow, you have given me the joy of watching him grow into the clever and capable man he is today. And while I have had to live all these years apart from his father, whom I truly loved, every day I have been able to behold his image in Menelik's face, for they are so alike that sometimes I have had to look twice to persuade myself that Solomon has not been walking among us."

This only made Sabla cry harder; Hami embraced her, then Menelik embraced them both, and soon all five of us were weeping and embracing one another, until Makeda's voice rose above the noise of our grieving in fervent prayer to Almighty God, calling down his mercy and blessing on us all. Then I was praying aloud and extemporaneously too, and then, one by one, so were Menelik and Hami, and eventually even Sabla. And gradually our tears turned to laughter as the divine peace of which Makeda had spoken flooded all our hearts to overflowing, and we knew ourselves united in the joy of Adonai. Her eyes alight with happiness, Makeda said, "I once asked Solomon what he thought was the ugliest thing in the world, and what he thought the most beautiful. He told me that the ugliest thing is when a faithful man becomes unfaithful, but the most beautiful is a repentant sinner. And here there are five!" Now there was nothing the multitude who would gather on the morrow could do to separate us from the love of God or of one another.

The following morning, Makeda stood on the steps of the temple she had built and addressed the members of the Crown Council and as many of her subjects as could cram themselves into the open court below. Every person present gasped at the sight of her, for she carried no sceptre and wore no diadem on her brow. A plain linen shift was her only garment; her feet were bare, and her mass of curling hair hung loose to her waist like a mourner's. She extended her arms, devoid of any bracelets or bangles, and as she held out her hands palm upward in contrition, there were no rings on her fingers but for the single one that Solomon had given her.

"Princes and people of Sheba," she cried, her voice ringing clear and loud above the heads of all assembled, "I have indeed called you here to make an announcement about my successor. But before I do so, I must tell you that I have sinned, and beg for your forgiveness. If you withhold it I shall understand, and if you condemn me to death I go to face it willingly, knowing that whatever awaits me on the other side, my God will be there."

A murmur passed through the crowd, but so far it was only a murmur of sympathy mingled with surprise. For Makeda, although she stood now with bowed head and hands hanging loose at her sides, presented such a picture of simple dignity that they could not be offended by her demeanour, unqueenly though it was.

When no one ventured to move a muscle or utter a word, she raised her head and spoke again.

"Most of you know that over twenty years ago I paid a visit to Solomon of Israel. He taught me all he knew about ruling a nation, and I have sought to rule you all in accordance with the wisdom of his teachings ever since. I have laboured day and night to enforce justice and vanquish corruption, to protect the weak against the strong and the innocent against their oppressors. I have kept order among chieftains and warlords, encouraging them to cooperate for the good of Sheba rather than allow their rivalry to tear her apart. I have provided you all with clean water for yourselves and your families to drink, and for your crops to grow healthy and tall. I have restored to you your children whom you were forced to sell into slavery, and your fields that were confiscated when you could no longer pay your debts. And everything I have given you, you owe to Solomon, because it was he who gave such wisdom to me.

"But he gave me something else as well – something I ought not to have taken and he should never have given, yet which I do not and cannot regret that I received. Princes and people of Sheba: Solomon gave me a son, whom I present to you today as the heir to whom I would bequeath my throne and all that I have achieved. He will be all you could ever wish for in a ruler, and it is my profoundest prayer that you might accept him as such when I am gone, and pledge yourselves to accept his descendants as your rulers after him. Menelik, son of Solomon and Prince of Sheba, come forth and be acclaimed by your future subjects."

No murmur arose after this, of sympathy or otherwise. The crowd stood silent in shock as the aforesaid young man stepped forward from the vestibule of the temple where he had been waiting unobserved in the shadows. He took his place beside his mother: tall, handsome, broad of shoulder and lean of hip, his bearing proud but not arrogant, his expression grave yet quite without guile. In short, he was hope for the future personified, a fresh-faced youth in the prime of his life, and no one but a mindless savage could have wished to see him or the woman who had borne him condemned to death.

Then from the ranks of the Crown Council who had seats on the temple steps rose the voice of Luqman the grand vizier, who had served not only Makeda but the two queens before her. "Hail Menelik, Prince of Sheba!" he cried out into the silence. "May his dynasty reign forever!"

For an excruciating interval after that, the only sound was the echo of his cry ringing round the sunlit courtyard. Then Kahalum of the Banu Waren called out, "Amen! Hail Menelik, Prince of Sheba!" And Salamat shouted the same, and another chieftain, and another, and as each one voiced his support for Menelik and Makeda and the new principle of succession, so the men and women of his tribe chimed in with him. Soon the entire temple court was a sea of waving arms and open mouths, and if some of these were crying out in protest, their dissent could not be heard above the deafening roar of acclamation. Makeda had fallen to her knees in gratitude to Adonai, and as a symbol of her recognition that a great king or queen is as much a servant as an overlord of the people.

When at last the roar subsided, Luqman demanded in a deep, commanding voice whether there was any member of the Crown Council present who wished to register his objection to the nomination of Prince Menelik as the queen's successor, or indeed to call for Makeda's abdication in the light of the sin to which she had confessed. For without a doubt their queen was no longer a virgin; moreover, she had also been suffering since childhood from a disfigurement which under the old dispensation should have disqualified her from holding royal office in the first place. Now was the time for any such objection to be made; once this convocation was over, it would be too late.

The howl of outrage that greeted Luqman's words was so ferocious that briefly I feared for his safety. Certainly Mafaddat, father of Ghalilat, who alone might have been tempted to rise to his challenge, had more sense than to pit himself against the baying unanimity of the mob. And if he did not speak up now, he must forever hold his peace.

Once it was clear that no one was going to clamour for her resignation, Makeda stood up once again and raised her arms for silence.

"Princes and people of Sheba," she cried, her voice now hoarse with emotion. "Words cannot express my gratitude for your indulgence and for the confidence you are prepared to place in my son. But I owe it to you all to prove his paternity beyond any shadow of a doubt. Behold!" – and she removed and held aloft the single ring she had been wearing – "This ring was given to me by his father, King Solomon of Israel, at the time of his conception, and Solomon bade me return it to him along with the child, if such there should be, and if it were a boy. The time has come for Menelik to undertake the journey I myself undertook more than twenty years ago, and to be recognized by Solomon as his son. Along with the ring he will carry a letter, requesting that Solomon provide him with testimonials to present to you all, and to anoint him heir to Sheba's throne with the holy oil with which he and his father David before him were anointed as rulers under Adonai.

"Furthermore, I shall ask Solomon for a fringe from the mantle that covers the holy Ark of the Covenant for us to place inside the sanctuary of this temple where we stand today. Then we shall have a symbol of Adonai's presence in our midst; his sanctuary will stand empty no longer, and you will have proof that every word I have spoken today is true."

So it was that Makeda and Menelik's prayers were answered: hers, that her son would be accepted by her people, and his, that he would at last be allowed to travel to Jerusalem and present himself to his father. While mother and son were still standing arm in arm acknowledging the adulation of the multitude, Ghalilat and her niece were released from prison and reunited with Mafaddat; we never saw them again. I learned much later that Ghalilat had died embittered and crippled by her jealousy, but that Masqal had married and had children and been as happy as her aunt had been miserable. It was not only Sheba as a whole that would benefit from the establishment of a royal dynasty, but the many daughters of chieftains who would have continued to be denied the consolations of love and marriage in the forlorn hope of one day wearing a crown.

The following day, Sabla, Hami and I sat down to share the Passover with Makeda and her son. And yes, even Hami sat down for once among us, for at Passover there can be no masters or servants, no slaves versus free. As we ate the special foods and drank the wine that symbolized Adonai's redemption of his people, we had never felt so free ourselves, because there was no more need for secrecy or pretence, no more fear that the truth would break out and destroy everything. Now truth was not our enemy but our friend, and Menelik, from being son of the whore, was heir to a kingdom, and possibly two.

Yet still our joy was tinged with sadness, for very soon mother and son must once more be parted, not to see one another again for very many months.

"You could come with me, Mother," Menelik entreated her. "Wouldn't it make you happy to see my father again, if you loved him so much?"

"No, my son." She shook her head sadly, the faintest ghost of a smile playing on her lips. "I loved him with all my heart, and I love him still, but time cannot be turned back. Nothing would be the same, and I would rather treasure my dream untarnished."

"But how shall I manage without your wisdom to guide me? We have talked every day since I was twelve."

"Yes, and now you are twenty – old enough to make wise decisions for yourself. Besides, you will have Uncle Tamrin to keep you in line."

Uncle Tamrin? I sat up with a start, almost spilling my wine. "Makeda, I retired from travelling a long time ago. I cannot go with Menelik to Jerusalem."

"Cannot? But you must. There is no one who knows the deserts and the seas as you do; no one who can steer his way safely through dens of robbers, nests of vipers, and who knows what other dangers that may beset an unwary traveller en route. Unless you go too I shall not get a wink of sleep until Menelik returns. You must promise me that you will go, and that you will guard my son's life with your own."

And how could I not, when she fixed me with those beseeching brown eyes that had been able to disarm me since her childhood, and when needing to be needed by her had given my life its meaning for so many years?

"Very well, Your Majesty," I consented. "Your word is my command." And the smile that had played on her lips spread and lit up her face like the sun breaking through clouds, for she knew that in spite of my words I was doing her bidding from love and not as a subject's duty.

"And you, Menelik, must promise to return when your uncle bids you," she said to her son. "No matter how well you are received by your father, how highly he praises you or how extravagant the promises he gives to you, you must give me your word that you will come back here with all haste, or I shall not let you go."

"Upon my honour, Your Majesty, I shall return as soon as I am able."

"Then you go with my blessing, both of you. And may the blessing of Adonai be upon you also."

Chapter Sixteen

In the event, the expedition Menelik and I undertook to Israel could not have been more different from the one on which I had accompanied Makeda. There was no great cavalcade of camels, no procession of chests full of treasure. Instead we went in disguise, as traders of modest means, for no one could predict how Solomon would react when he learned that the queen of Sheba had borne him a son after all. Yes, we took him gifts, but only as much as could be carried by a couple of donkeys, and we had a military escort to protect us, but only a squadron of half a dozen men dressed in civilian clothes, their swords and knives carefully concealed. Hami came along to see to my personal needs, and Menelik had a manservant of his own. This was our entire party.

Nor did we take the same route along which I had guided Makeda. Menelik was minded to pass through Egypt and see the pyramids and temples and mighty cities of the Nile rather than traverse the emptiness of the Arabian desert. So we went on foot through the mountains, and by boat on the Nile where it was navigable, though there were many stretches where it was not, and we had to pick our way over rocks and through tangled undergrowth while the river plunged down beside us in foaming waterfalls.

To begin with I thought it would be nothing short of a miracle if I came back alive, but the further we trekked the more the years seemed to fall away from me. I began to feel younger and fitter than I had in a very long time, though I must confess that I seldom walked once we had descended from the mountains and it became possible to ride. Meanwhile Menelik grew stronger and hardier and more and more able to fend for himself in the forests and marshes. He hunted deer and waterfowl and even crocodiles once the Nile was broad and slow enough to support them. With a turban wrapped tight around his brow and his teeth flashing white in his sun-browned face, he looked more like a bandit than a trader by the time we came to the Valley of the Kings.

Yet he had never been happier, for like his mother he loved being outdoors, and like her he derived endless pleasure from talking with peasants and fishermen and even collectors of taxes, of which Egypt has very many. Whenever there was fertile ground along the banks of the river it was farmed intensively, and wherever there was farming there were tax-collectors with their scales and tablets and excess of bureaucracy. Thus Menelik came to appreciate at first-hand how much better was the lot of the common people in his own country than that of those who toiled and sweated on the estates of the pharaoh.

Disguised as we were as humble traders, we had no cause to present ourselves at the pharaoh's court, and we left Egypt as anonymously as we had come, by boat from an unprepossessing little port at one of the mouths of the Nile delta. The Egyptians have never been particularly keen on sailing or even on trading, and the port was a ramshackle, rundown affair utterly unworthy of a nation that boasted such a glorious history. But then again, Egypt as a whole was fairly run down these days too, and though her history might be glorious, her present left much to be desired.

From the wretched little port we sailed east along the coast as far as Gaza, the southernmost city on the Israelite seaboard. For hundreds of years it had belonged to the Philistines, Israel's neighbours and enemies; now it had been swallowed up in Solomon's empire. But its inhabitants were a rough and ready mix of sailors and adventurers of every colour and creed.

In search of a place to stay, we wended our way up and down its narrow streets, our donkeys stepping nimbly over the piles of multifarious wares, rotting rubbish and dung that characterize every seaport under the sun. We were doing an excellent job of blending in with the motley crowds, no one giving our dusty robes or scruffy animals a second glance, until a raggedy pedlar-boy with a tray of trinkets on his head ran into our path and shouted, "Hey! King

Solomon! Look! It's Solomon himself in disguise!" And all at once every beggar and street vendor in town descended upon us to see what the fuss was about.

I don't know how the impudent little urchin had come to be face to face with his king before, but he was firmly convinced that Menelik was indeed he. No matter how vociferously we protested that neither of us was King Solomon, that we were simple traders from Africa come to buy and sell like everyone else, a crowd had soon gathered round us, and a goodly number of the folk who were pointing and shouting claimed to have seen their king at close quarters before, and that Menelik was unquestionably his spitting image.

"No, he is younger!" someone called out, and another said, "No, he is darker!" But all alike agreed that they had never seen anyone who looked more like King Solomon in all their lives, and try as we might we could not get away from them.

Inevitably the commotion soon attracted the attention of the city garrison, who turned up in force, prepared to quell a riot. Our own soldiers' hands hovered over their hidden weapons, but the last thing Menelik or I wanted was any sort of ugly scene. So I motioned them to wait patiently to see what the captain of the approaching detachment might have to say for himself.

He perceived at once that our party was the focus of the disturbance but that we ourselves had done nothing to provoke it. When at last he got the street hawkers to stop shouting all at once and tell him plainly the cause of their excitement, he strode purposefully up to Menelik and peered straight into his face, nose against nose. Almost at once he sprang backwards again as though Menelik had punched him in the belly.

"By Molech's gaping jaws," he exclaimed, "you *do* look like King Solomon. In fact, you look more like Solomon than Solomon himself does these days, I swear it. Who are you, boy? Tell me your name at once, and where you have come from."

"I am Tafari of Aduli, a spice dealer from Ethiopia," Menelik replied at once, giving the details we had dreamed up for him before leaving Yeha.

"Ethiopia?" repeated the officer scornfully. "You don't look like an Ethiopian to me. I've seen Greeks with darker skin than yours." Which was doubly ironic, because Menelik was currently darker than he had ever been in his life. "Tell me the truth, boy. It will do you no good to waste my time."

"I *am* from Ethiopia. I swear it on my mother's life."

"Your mother, eh? And who would she be? The queen of Sheba, I suppose." Then his suspicious soldier's mind must have started making connections all by itself; his jaw went suddenly slack and he started peering at Menelik even more intently than before. "Ibhar?" he called out, snapping his fingers at one of his men without taking his eyes from Menelik's face. "Return to barracks and see if Commander Benaiah has arrived yet to conduct his inspection. If he has, please ask him if he would be so kind as to accompany you straight back here."

On the latter part of our journey I had done a great deal of thinking about how and when we were going to reveal our true identity and to whom, so that we might be presented to Solomon at the most opportune moment and in the best light. Now it seemed that with regard to Menelik's parentage events were once again to be taken out of our hands. Benaiah was commander-in-chief of Solomon's armed forces and his close personal friend; presumably, coincidentally, he was due to be in Gaza today.

At least *we* weren't being taken to *him*, but the captain who was still staring fixedly at Menelik had no pretext for placing us under arrest. Still, I don't know what would have happened if we had simply attempted to leave then and there and go on our way.

The crowd, which was growing larger by the minute as more and more people sidled over to see what was going on, now stood in a silent and expectant ring ranged about us; our own armed protection had withdrawn so as to blend in with it rather than too obviously seeming to be with us. Menelik and I exchanged charged glances but said nothing, while the captain who had waylaid us took to pacing around us in circles as though he expected us to vanish into thin air at any moment.

Presently his lieutenant returned with Commander Benaiah in tow. I had encountered Benaiah on my previous visits to Israel, but only ever briefly and not for more than twenty years. Nonetheless, his hazy recollection of my face probably confirmed his intuition that Menelik's striking resemblance to King Solomon was more than a coincidence.

"So you swear on your mother's life that you are Tafari the spice dealer from Ethiopia, do you, boy?" he challenged Menelik gruffly. He was a grizzled, humourless old veteran who had been a soldier more than twice as long as Menelik had been alive; he had served under David before Solomon and must have been well over sixty years old.

"No," answered Menelik evenly. "I swear I am from Ethiopia, but Tafari is not my real name, nor am I a spice dealer."

Benaiah's eyes narrowed, then alighted and lingered on the signet ring that Menelik wore on his little finger. Eventually he said, "If you are who I think you are, you had better come with me when I return to Jerusalem tomorrow morning to report to the king." Then his eyes flicked sideways to me. "*Both* of you must come."

"We should be honoured, Commander Benaiah," I said on Menelik's behalf. "Tamrin of Yeha at your service, sir, and I *am* a trader, or at least I was. May I present to you my kinsman Prince Menelik, crown prince of Sheba, only son of Makeda and firstborn son of Solomon, your king. We shall gladly accompany you when you appear before him tomorrow, and ask only that we be furnished with accommodation for tonight in keeping with our station."

Briefly the crowd remained silent, stunned by the revelation to which they had so unexpectedly been party. Then the pedlar-boy who had first accosted Menelik when we had merely been minding our own business shouted out to no one in particular, "I told you he looked like the king. I told you! I told you!" And he started scampering about like a magician's monkey, his tray of trinkets quite forgotten.

So after months of sleeping in tents and under bushes or lying out under the stars, we were welcomed that night at the imposing residence of the city governor. Here we feasted on delicacies that were not only ravishing enough to have tempted the most jaded of palates, but also prepared scrupulously in accordance with the Law of Moses. We slept in magnificent beds rather than on flea-ridden mats on the floor, and altogether revelled in the delights offered by civilization and in the luxury of being ourselves once again. The following day we were escorted by Benaiah to Jerusalem.

We rode in a carriage as was fitting; this too had been supplied by the city governor. Menelik's servant and Hami walked behind with our donkeys, and our military escort marched behind them. But now we had fifty of Benaiah's men to protect us too, and to enhance our prestige in the eyes of those we passed along the road.

At first we were both too exhilarated by the turn of events and too full of anxious anticipation to pay much attention to our immediate surroundings. But gradually things began to impinge, and as they did so our excitement was overtaken by dismay.

For Israel did not seem at all as I remembered it, nor as I had described it to Menelik so enthusiastically in the past. Alongside the dusty road there were abandoned homesteads whose buildings had gone to rack and ruin, and whose fields were overgrown with briars. In the villages there were empty workshops with doors hanging off their hinges and scrawny sheep running loose in the streets and squares. Worse still, there were beggars: men, women and children with hollow cheeks and hollower eyes, holding out chipped earthenware bowls in the hope of receiving a copper piece or some grains of corn. It was as though everything Sheba had once been, Israel had become, while Sheba now enjoyed the good fortune Israel had lost. It was all very disconcerting, and when Menelik turned to me with enquiring eyes, all I could do was shrug my shoulders, my expression as perplexed as his.

Worst of all, as we began the gradual ascent to Jerusalem we saw that on the tops of the low wooded hills round about stood shrines, sacred stones and pillars such as I would never have expected to see mushrooming on Israelite soil in a thousand years. These were not altars to Adonai erected by local communities in honour of their national God. No; they were unmistakeably pagan sanctuaries, so-called "high places" for the offering of sacrifices – conceivably human as well as animal – to Baal and Asherah of the Canaanites, Chemosh of the Moabites, Molech of the Ammonites, or to one or more of the grotesque bestial deities of the Egyptians.

Never would the Solomon I had known have sanctioned the building of such abominations on his very doorstep. Nor would he have permitted his subjects to fall back into the savage idolatry of the unenlightened. When Jehoshaphat had visited Ethiopia more than eight years before and told me of Solomon's backsliding under the influence of his foreign wives, I had never for a moment imagined that things might sink as low as this. With a pang of regret and of grief for my murdered friend, I realized that my incredulity had prevented me from listening to him as attentively as I should have done, and that I had subsequently thrust the uncomfortable truths he had told me from my mind. Now, before Menelik and I were presented to the king I'd thought I knew, and had for many years counted as a friend, I had to find out more about what had gone so radically wrong.

"Commander Benaiah!" I hailed our venerable guide as he rode stiffly ahead of us; after a lifetime in the saddle he was very much at home there, but his age was apparent in the visible tautness of his spine. "Commander Benaiah, I beseech you, call a halt for a while; I am distressed."

He did as I requested, supposing, I think, that I must be feeling my age as he was. When he wheeled his horse around and frowned into my face I said, "I beg your pardon, Commander, but what is the meaning of these standing stones and pillars that desecrate every hilltop? Is this not Israel, the Promised Land, and are we not bound for Zion, the holy mountain of Adonai?"

Benaiah's frown became a grimace and his eyes mere slits in his contorted face. He said, "I regret that you will not find everything in Israel as you left it, Lord Tamrin."

"Everything? I see practically *nothing* as I left it. But how can this be? Does Solomon no longer rule here? Surely he cannot have entered his dotage; he is a younger man by far than you or I."

"Entered his dotage, no," Benaiah replied through gritted teeth. "But whether or not he remains in his right mind, you and Prince Menelik may judge for yourselves when you meet him."

His response was scarcely reassuring, but he would say no more, doubtless afraid that he had said too much already. Yet the faces of his men told me all too clearly that Solomon was no longer the model king loved unreservedly by his grateful subjects.

So now we were doubly anxious about meeting Solomon, for we had no longer to worry only about the impression Menelik would make upon him, but also about how *he* would seem to *us*.

In stark contrast to the poverty we had noted in the countryside, the city of Jerusalem had never looked so magnificent. For Adonai's temple was no longer by any means the sole object of wonder. Adjoining its sacred precincts Solomon had since constructed a palace for himself on an altogether grander scale than the one built by David, in which he and his court had been content to reside when I had been in Jerusalem before. In addition he had extended the city walls to incorporate swathes of new territory, on which the mansions of men he had enriched had sprung up, built of fine yellow limestone like the temple and palace. In the blazing sunshine it seemed that Zion's citadel had been crowned with a diadem of gold.

Without troubling to comment on the grandeur of our surroundings, Benaiah steered our column into the outer courtyard of the palace. Messengers were dispatched hotfoot to the king to warn him of the arrival of foreign emissaries of the greatest importance. Every courtier, valet or groom who crossed our path or rushed to attend to our needs or to those of our animals reacted with the same hastily concealed amazement when he first saw Menelik. No one needed to ask why it was imperative that we be presented to the king as speedily as possible.

And so, after the briefest opportunity for refreshment, Menelik and I were led through tapestried vestibule, frescoed anteroom, and one pillared hall after another into the vast shimmering throne room in which Solomon was to receive us. The principal palace of the pharaoh might have cast it into shadow, but no other in which I have ever set foot, and in my time as a traveller of consequence I have set foot in many. Of course, there was no reason why the king of Israel should not live in opulence; Makeda did, after all, and it was only fitting that a monarch of Solomon's repute should have built for himself a residence appropriate to his exalted status.

But to be living like this when there were beggars in his streets, and the signs of hardship everywhere? And whence had the resources come to appoint and furnish the edifice so lavishly? Yes, Solomon and his ally, Hiram of Tyre, had their Red Sea fleet and their Western Sea fleet and their overland caravans, and Solomon had his copper mines at Timna. But I couldn't help remembering that the bulk of the funding for Pharaoh's palaces had come from ruthlessly taxing his own people, and I began to wonder if the scowls on the faces of Benaiah's soldiers and the undeniable impoverishment of the Israelite peasantry might not be attributable to a similar cause.

It was so very far from the throne room's threshold to the dais on which the king's throne stood that he could not have seen either Menelik's face or mine at all clearly until we had advanced more than half the distance towards it. Nor could we see him, especially as protocol demanded that we keep our heads bowed until invited by the king to lift them. The further we progressed, the more hopeful I was that he would see all he needed to see and jump down from his throne to welcome us, in just the way he would have done in his youth. Yet we reached the very foot of the dais without detecting the slightest movement on his part, and neither of us dared to look up or to utter a word until he invited us to do so.

However, when we had been standing there some considerable while and still the king had not moved or spoken, I decided that on the strength of his once having been my friend, I would venture to raise my eyes.

I saw at once why the captain of Gaza's garrison had declared that Menelik looked more like Solomon than Solomon did himself nowadays, for I should never have known him had we encountered one another out of context. Solomon was thin now, rather than lean; his purple robes hung loose on his wasted body. His hair beneath his crown, once so lush and lustrous, was as thin as he was himself, and greyer than it was brown. His face was lined, pallid rather than fair, his once full lips were taut and white, and altogether he looked older than me – or at least, older than I felt, honed as I was from the travelling that I'd begun to feel I should never have given up. But the most distressing thing of all was that he was weeping, silently but copiously, as I had never seen a grown man weep before.

I glanced at Menelik to catch his eye, but failed, because he was already staring transfixed at his father, not knowing where to put himself. The heralds who had shown us into the royal presence having withdrawn, no one was there but the three of us. So I said to the stricken prince, "Go to your father, Menelik. Show him your ring. He will want to embrace you."

He nodded and obeyed me, though I was sure that those few faltering steps he took up the stairs that separated him from his father required of him more courage than any of the hunting forays he had undertaken in the hippopotamus and crocodile-infested marshes of the Nile. Having mounted the stairs, he knelt at Solomon's feet and attempted to show him the ring, but I could see straight away that Solomon neither needed nor wanted to see it. He pushed it away, shaking his head and weeping more bitterly than ever.

Knowing full well who Menelik was, did Solomon intend to reject him out of hand? For a few terrible moments I thought that he might, and the wretched young man, who was still a vulnerable child to me, must have thought so too.

Then Solomon extended both his hands, which shook like a wizened old man's, and pulled Menelik's head onto his lap.

Briefly Menelik retained his formal posture, as much from embarrassment as from any sense of propriety. Then I watched his rigid muscles give way and his arms go around Solomon's legs; Solomon's head fell forward over his son's, and for a very long time this was how they stayed.

Now it was my turn to be embarrassed, or at least to feel that I was intruding where I should not be. I resolved to creep away in silence and leave them together, but the moment I moved, Solomon's head came up and he looked me straight in the eye.

"Why, Tamrin?" he implored me, his swollen, red-rimmed eyes so horribly bright that they gave him the look of a man who was sick unto death. "Why now, after all this time? Why did nobody tell me? Why did *she* never tell me?"

Did he really want me to answer him? And if so, where was I to begin? While I stood there wringing my hands Menelik said, "But she did, Father. More than eight years ago. She sent a letter, with Jehoshaphat."

"Jehoshaphat? Jehoshaphat went away and I never saw him again. I received nothing from your mother, nothing! And she should have sent you to me as soon as you were born; she *knew* that was what I wanted. All these years believing that our union had borne no fruit, or that Makeda had miscarried, or that our child had been born dead! So much grief, when all the time you lived and breathed, and were learning to walk and to talk, and cutting your teeth, and practising your letters and your numbers, and I did not know…"

"I'm sorry, Father. Truly I am. But – there is another letter now. Please…" And Menelik took from the folds of his garments the letter Makeda had entrusted to him, in which she asked Solomon to anoint his son king of Sheba, and to give him a fringe from the mantle of the Ark of the Covenant to place in the Holy of Holies at Yeha.

I watched Solomon's face as he read, and saw that his misery only intensified to find that the letter contained no profession of undying love, no words even of remorse or regret – in fact nothing genuinely personal at all. When he had read it, and read it again without speaking or even looking up, Menelik said, "Well, Father? Will you grant her requests?"

"Requests? Requests? I don't see how she can have the effrontery to ask me for anything." Then observing that Menelik drew back in consternation, Solomon repented of his anger and said faintly, "We shall see, my son. We shall see. After all, you are not going anywhere yet." And finally, on a fresh tide of grief, "I could not bear it."

"I'm sorry," Menelik said again. "Perhaps I should not have come even now, and brought this distress upon you. But *I* did not know who I was until I was twelve years old, and never for one moment from that day to this have I ceased to dream about coming here to find you. I thought it would bring happiness to us both. Instead – "

"Instead? No, my son, do not say 'instead'. Your coming here *should* have made me happy. And indeed it *will!* I shall have a proclamation made throughout my kingdom that my son, my son…" But all of a sudden he was weeping profusely once again, as it came to him that he didn't even know how to say his own son's name.

"It's Menelik, Father," the young man prompted him gently. "My name is Menelik, 'son of the wise man' in the dialect of my mother's people."

"Menelik ben Solomon from today," his father declared. "Menelik ben Solomon ben David; for to me it is *my* father, David, whom you resemble above all, when he was in his prime." And I recalled the stories I had heard about David when he was younger still, before he was even king, in fact little more than a bandit with a gang of rogues for followers. Menelik probably did look like him, with his turban wound like an adventurer's, tight around his brow.

Then Solomon remembered and picked up the thread of his previous pronouncement. "I shall have it given out that my lost son, Menelik ben Solomon, has been found, and there will be a public holiday for all my subjects, with feasting and merriment across the land!"

At long last Solomon was smiling, and something of the old vivacity danced in his too-bright eyes. Menelik was smiling too; they embraced, then, man to man, Solomon kissing his son all but triumphantly on both cheeks. Then he held out one hand to me, bidding me climb up on the dais beside them, and he embraced Menelik and me both together, one with each arm.

"Tamrin, my friend," he saluted me, "I do believe that today you have brought me back to life. You have braved the sands of the desert once again to present me with treasure that I thought could never be mine. I thank you from the bottom of my heart."

Who was I to deflate his swelling joy with my presentiments of doom? Who was I to point out that a great public welcome for Menelik just now might not be the best way to celebrate his coming? Neither Rehoboam nor his mother would be in the mood for feasting, that was for sure; they would be obliged to watch from the wings while the kingdom made merry, weighing up what the advent of Solomon's firstborn son might mean for them.

Nor would they lack sympathy. Much as Rehoboam might not be the sort of crown prince many Israelites would have wished for, at least he had not been born out of wedlock on foreign soil to a wanton African temptress.

Chapter Seventeen

At first light, swift horsemen fanned out across the kingdom to inform all and sundry that the following day was to be kept as a holiday by every man, woman and child in Israel. Sheep and goats would be provided and slaughtered at royal expense in the principal city of every district so that even the destitute could eat fresh meat and be satisfied; wine would be supplied in plenty also, and there would be music, dancing and other entertainments laid on to encourage the people to flock in from the villages and celebrate the king's good news together. For those who could get to Jerusalem itself, the gates of the palace would be thrown open, and food and drink would be served free of charge from the royal kitchens; Menelik himself would appear alongside his father on the palace rooftop where all would be able to see and acclaim him. For this handsome prince who had not existed, now was, he that had been dead was alive, and his father desired that every one of his subjects should have cause to remember this momentous day with fondness.

And it seemed that they were minded to do so. Even within the palace itself, courtiers and civil servants who dined magnificently at the royal table daily and had no reason to relish the prospect of sharing this privilege with the masses were going about with smiles on their faces and a spring in their step. I didn't attribute their high spirits to their delight in Menelik for his own sake – they knew nothing as yet of his character and had no reason to suppose him any different from Rehoboam – but rather to their relief at seeing Solomon cast off the cloak of depression which it seemed he had been wearing for a long, long time. Generosity too was a quality in which for years the king had apparently been sadly lacking. Thus the very air seemed charged with the possibility that the Golden Age

Israel had enjoyed during the early years of Solomon's reign might be on the point of restoration.

Not that Solomon had said anything so far about making Menelik his heir, or even recognizing him as having any sort of priority over Rehoboam. It would have been hasty of anyone to assume that Menelik's acceptance implied Rehoboam's rejection, or even relegation to second place in his father's estimation. For the time being, Rehoboam would be well advised to welcome Menelik as a brother, but not to betray the slightest hint that the newcomer could be seriously regarded as a rival.

If I had been imagining that Solomon would want to spend the day before the festival catching up in private with his long-lost child, I would have been much mistaken. For it seemed that before Menelik could be presented to the public at large, he must be introduced to anyone who was anyone at the palace. Clad in glittering golden robes that his father had lavished upon him, he was brought first of all before the high priest, Zadok, who was as spare and austere as ever, but even more commanding a presence now that he wore a crown of snow-white hair. Next Menelik was paraded before the chief ministers of the civil administration, many of whom had also been in post since my previous visit: the secretaries of state, Elihoreph and Ahijah; the chief of the district governors, Azariah ben Nathan; Zabud, the most senior of the royal advisers; Abishar the palace steward, and Adoniram ben Abda, who was described rather worryingly as being in charge of forced labour.

After these came the lesser ministers, then a host of courtiers who were related to Solomon either by blood or by friendship, or who had earned the right to eat at his table as a result of heroism in war or having performed some particularly laudable public service.

Finally, there was a large company of younger men, mostly sons of the dignitaries mentioned already, many of whom were roughly of an age with Menelik himself. Foremost among these was Azariah, one of the sons of Zadok, already practising as a priest in his own right, and quite ferociously devout. Nevertheless he made a great show of bowing deferentially before the young prince and stating his conviction that the two of them would become firm friends.

I would have expected Menelik to endure all this formality with his customary good-humoured grace, but he did much better than that. He charmed, disarmed and impressed everyone in accordance with what was appropriate, as only his mother could have taught him to do. Now I could see them all thinking: he is *everything* that Rehoboam is not. I began to doubt that he would ever be allowed to return to Sheba.

When Menelik had assured the earnest Azariah that his friendship would be more than welcome, Solomon seemed to think that his son had met everyone he needed to meet at last. So his face fell when Menelik said, "But Father, you have not introduced me to Rehoboam or his mother, or to any of your other wives. And people have told me that you have daughters living in the palace as well as a son? I want to meet my brother and sisters."

"Have you not seen enough new faces for one day?" Solomon objected in return. "Rehoboam will not be as keen to be your friend as young ben Zadok is, you know."

"But he will be offended if I am not introduced to him today, when I have met everyone else of consequence here in Jerusalem. Besides, he has nothing to fear from me. I have come here only to make your acquaintance and to have myself anointed king of Sheba, and I shall tell him so, too, when I am given the chance."

Solomon made no response to this statement other than to glower non-committally. But he acquiesced, albeit reluctantly, in arranging to have his two sons meet face to face.

He summoned them both to the throne room, where he himself would be present to preside over their altercation, since he seemed to think there was little prospect of their engaging in civil conversation. Rehoboam's mother, Naamah, would accompany her son; Menelik would be supported by me.

It was clear from the moment we saw them that both mother and son were disposed to be our enemies. Rehoboam was an ill-favoured youth: stocky, bow-legged and overweight, with coarse, heavy features that wore the expression of a man who has found something very unpleasant under a stone. His mother, icily beautiful, looked nothing like him, and since he certainly didn't favour Solomon, one could not help but wonder where he had come by his uncouth appearance.

"Prince Rehoboam," Solomon said in his starchiest voice, "may I present to you Menelik, my African son."

"Your *bastard* son," growled Rehoboam, loud enough even for me to hear, with my leaden ears. But Menelik chose to pretend that he had heard nothing, and advanced with arm extended to clasp Rehoboam's in friendship. Rehoboam kept his arms firmly folded over his ample stomach. He said, "I rather think it is fitting for a visitor to the court of a king to *bow* before a member of the royal family, don't you?"

"Very well." Menelik smiled, as though the whole affair were amusing rather than insulting, and bowed with enough aplomb to retain his dignity, but not so much that Rehoboam could object to being mocked. Then he straightened up again, and doing the best he could not to look down at Rehoboam – for he was very much the taller – he said, "Prince Rehoboam, I understand perfectly well that my arrival in Jerusalem when you did not even know of my existence will have been perceived by you as a threat. But you have no need to fear me at all. I have come here merely to ask our father to anoint me king of Sheba, and when he has done so I shall go back there quite content. It may be that in years to come, you and I will have the pleasure of meeting again as rulers of our respective countries." He offered his hand once more, and this time Rehoboam took it; clasping one another hand to forearm they had sworn by gesture at least to lay enmity aside. But there was no such swearing in Rehoboam's eyes.

Solomon's daughters were presented next, each with their respective mothers, neither of whom was the daughter of the pharaoh. The girls were both still children, and they curtseyed prettily, one of them gazing at the exotic young prince in awe, the other averting her eyes with bashful blushes. Then Solomon asked Menelik rather pointedly how many of his other wives he seriously wished to meet, since at the last count there had been well over five hundred.

"Five hundred?" Menelik repeated in undisguised astonishment, while my own mind was doing cartwheels, thinking: five hundred wives, and only four children? And how could Solomon have so totally forgotten both what the Law of Moses taught about marriage and the appalling conflicts that tore apart his own father's life and household as a result of his marrying a mere handful of different women? The more I saw and learned of the new Solomon, the less he had in common with the wise scholar—ruler who had been my friend.

"There are many kings and chieftains eager to be allied with the kingdom of Israel," Solomon explained with patent satisfaction. "If I marry the daughter of one to cement our friendship, how can I refuse another without giving offence? But you may meet them all if you wish." Then he smiled almost archly and added, "Of course, they are all exceptionally beautiful."

Menelik said simply, "I should like to meet one in particular. Queen Makshara, the pharaoh's daughter. But – not here."

I began to wonder what was going through Menelik's mind and, simultaneously, whether he might be going to make a habit of surprising me by acting unexpectedly on his own initiative just as his mother had been inclined to do at his age.

"There is no queen of Israel," Solomon informed him, and I could see that he too was pondering what motivation lay behind Menelik's unforeseen request.

"But Makshara was your first wife, Father – your *only* wife until after you met my mother. Is she not still foremost among them?"

Solomon admitted that she was; she had her own mansion, after all, which had been entirely subsumed by the new palace complex but which had been built for her long before any of it. "You may meet with her in private," he conceded. "But only if you tell me why you wish to do so."

"Because she knew you intimately as a young man, when my mother knew you," Menelik answered promptly, making no attempt to dissemble. "She alone can help me to understand why it was that my mother fell so deeply in love with you that she was prepared to risk her kingdom and her very life to bear your child."

Momentarily Solomon turned away, not wanting Menelik to see that he was profoundly moved. I believe I knew what he was thinking: that Makeda had not pretended to her son that she had had no choice, that the wicked king of Israel had forced himself upon her against her will. Eventually he murmured, "It will be arranged."

Of course, when Solomon had said that Menelik could meet with Makshara privately he had meant only that he himself would not be present. It would not do at all for the young prince to be entirely unchaperoned; I must go with him to Makshara's palace-within-the-palace, where her guards and her ladies would also be on hand to ensure that all was seemly and in order.

We were shown into a leafy courtyard open to the sky; there was a pool in the centre where orange and turquoise fish swam to and fro, and elegant stands of papyrus reeds swayed gently in the breeze, a continual and poignant reminder to Pharaoh's daughter of her distant home.

But it was quite some time before Makshara appeared. When at last she did so, with an elderly Egyptian kinswoman at her shoulder, I could see at a glance how reluctant she was to receive us. I was also struck by how markedly she had changed, just as her husband had done. It was not merely that she was older; it was rather that the light had somehow gone out inside her, and the lines on her face, which even her heavy Egyptian make-up could not disguise, had clearly been formed by years of resignation rather than by laughter or by passion of any kind. She greeted us formally, without either spite or warmth, and said, "Prince Menelik, I am told that you wish to hear about your father as a young man. Pray, tell me what it is that you want to know."

"Oh, my lady, please forgive me," Menelik exclaimed, falling at once to his knees and pressing Makshara's hand to his lips. "I had not considered how painful it would be for you to revisit those memories; how could I have been so thoughtless? Please, forget that I even asked. My uncle and I will go at once and leave you in peace."

Visibly disconcerted by his abject apology, Makshara responded awkwardly, "No, Prince Menelik. There is no need for you to go anywhere." She stretched out her free hand and laid it on his bowed head, then withdrew it hurriedly, as though the gesture had taken her as much by surprise as it had him. "My days here can go by so slowly sometimes. It is refreshing for me to receive visitors."

He kissed her fingers again, then bestowed upon her his most winning smile, and I thought: he will soon have added even the pharaoh's daughter, who has as much reason as Rehoboam to resent his very existence, to his train of admirers.

"Please," she said, almost effusively now, "sit beside me by the pool, both of you. If it lies within my power to tell you what you wish to know, Prince Menelik, then I shall do so."

"I am sure that it does, my lady, for I could not think of anyone more qualified than you to paint a picture for me of what my father was like back in the days when I was a little boy growing up far away in a foreign land. For if I had been your son, rather than supposedly the son of a freedwoman, I should surely have been brought up by the best father in the world. I shall be forever in your debt if you can help me salvage something from the wreckage of my childhood."

The appeal in his eyes might have won over a tigress, let alone an unhappy woman such as Makshara whose maternal instincts had languished untapped through the whole of her childless and loveless marriage. She sighed, rearranged her veil, and allowed her eyes to look wistfully back into the past rather than fixing them on Menelik's face. "He was handsome, just as you are. And witty, and knowledgable about so many different things. He would have taught you all there is to know about the plants and trees in his gardens and the animals in his menagerie. He was generous, and merciful, but he never let anyone take his kindness for granted. He would not have spoiled you, that is for sure. Yet it seems to me that even without his fatherly influence, you have still grown up into the sort of son he would be proud of."

"You flatter me, my lady," Menelik said with another smile. "But Prince Rehoboam… did my father not seek to impart his knowledge and wisdom to him?"

"Ah. Rehoboam," said Makshara heavily. "You have heard something about him?"

"I have heard many things. And I have met him for myself. But he doesn't seem like my father at all, either as you say he was, or as he is today."

"There are those who say that this is because Rehoboam is not Solomon's son at all."

"And what of you, my lady? Is this what you think also?"

Momentarily I feared that he had gone too far and that Makshara had taken offence. Then I saw that although she was indeed upset, it was not because Menelik's words had offended her. With her eyes gazing back into the past once again she responded at last, "For many years I believed that I was barren, and many others believed it too. They pitied me, but I knew they were encouraging Solomon to divorce me, or at least to take another wife and keep us both. I shall always be grateful that he did not for very many years, though I know now that it was out of duty and piety rather than love that he remained faithful to me. For it was only when he met your mother that he learned what love was meant to be like."

Menelik began to protest; to say he was sure that Solomon had loved Makshara too, but she said wearily, "No, Prince Menelik. I know you mean only to be kind to me, but I could see for myself that he would never love me in the way he loved Makeda. He married me to confirm his alliance with my father, and never pretended otherwise, though he has always provided generously for my needs, and been courteous and considerate and all that my father or I could have expected him to be. But with Makeda it was different. When she returned to Sheba he went completely to pieces. I knew he had slept with her on their last night together – don't ask me *how* I knew – but when no word came of a child I began to wonder for the first time whether I might not be barren at all, but whether the problem might be with him. And that was when he began to take wife after wife in his desperation."

"His desperation for an heir to his throne?"

"Yes, but that was only a part of it, and not the larger part. Really he was desperate to find love again, to recapture what he had only ever known with your mother." When Menelik looked away and did not speak, Makshara continued, "When his hundreds of wives produced only three children between them, I became convinced that it was he and not I who was infertile; that even the few children he had were not truly his. It is possible, you know, for a man to be infertile, though if a couple are childless it is invariably the woman who is blamed. And so I believed this of Solomon for a great many years."

"Until..?"

"Until I set eyes on you today." Impulsively she took both of Menelik's hands between her own. "That is why I was so reluctant to meet you. When they said that you resembled your father so closely that you had to be his son, I wanted to run away from this place and never come back. I wished I were dead."

"My lady, do not say such dreadful things! You will break my heart."

"Break *your* heart? Why should you care whether I live or die? I am nothing to you, just as I am nothing to your father but the seal on his alliance with mine."

"Because you *could* have been my mother! And because both of us were denied the happiness which real family life can bring: you, because you had no children, I, because I had no father, and because the woman I grew up believing was my mother was not my mother at all."

So raw was the pain in Menelik's eyes that any remaining resentment which Makshara was harbouring against him was swept away on a tide of unleashed emotion. "Oh, Prince Menelik!" she cried. "If only you *had* been my son. How different things might have been, and how happy you and I might have made your father. Perhaps then he wouldn't even have noticed the queen of Sheba's comeliness when she came here to visit him. There would have been no need for any of the searching, any of the ridiculous marriages. And Solomon might still have been the man he used to be."

Then all thought of keeping things seemly and in order was abandoned as Menelik took the distraught Makshara in his arms, and neither her attendant kinswoman nor I lifted a finger to intervene. In fact we exchanged a silent nod of understanding as Makshara poured out the grief of more than twenty years on the shoulder of her rival's son. When at length her tears abated, Menelik helped her sit up straight again and then asked gently, "My lady, would you allow me to visit you again while my uncle and I are here in Jerusalem? I should very much like to talk to you further, if I may, especially since my own mother is so very far away."

As she gazed back at him, incredulous, I feared that her tears would start falling afresh. "Of course, Prince Menelik," she managed to reply. "I should be honoured."

"But you must not call me Prince Menelik. Menelik is quite enough on its own."

"Menelik. Yes, I shall remember. But are you to call me 'my lady' while I call you by your name?"

Menelik hesitated only a moment before venturing, "If you will permit me, I should like to call you 'Mother'. After all, I have two already, and if Solomon can have an African son, why should I not have an Egyptian mother?"

Now Makshara's tears did fall afresh, but as Menelik embraced her once again they both began to laugh as well as cry, and it was all I could do not to start laughing and crying myself.

When later we came to leave, and I looked back at Makshara across the courtyard, I saw that although her face was streaked with kohl-stained tears and her eyes were rimmed with red instead of black, the light in them had been rekindled. In fact, she looked happier than I had ever seen her.

The next day was the holiday on which all Israel was ordered to be happy. And I'm sure almost everyone was, with the exception of Rehoboam and his mother. There was food in abundance, wine flowed freely, and Jerusalem was thronged with teeming crowds wielding branches of palm, throwing flowers and shouting, "Hail King Solomon! Hail Menelik, Solomon's son!" The golden-clad Menelik was in his element, waving and smiling from the palace roof at the multitudes gathered below, but acknowledging their adulation from a distance was never going to be enough for this young man who was as much Makeda's son as he was Solomon's. "Come, Father," he exhorted the startled king. "Let us go down and meet the people face to face. They can scarcely even appreciate the resemblance between us from so far away." And before Solomon could find the words to protest, Menelik had taken his arm and was leading him down the stairs from the roof into the courtyard and then plunging in among the people to shake their hands and accept their congratulations. At first they shrank back from him in awe, but when he only moved undaunted towards them they were soon vying with one another to thrust their flowers into his hands or scatter the petals over his hair and clothing. Solomon they regarded more warily; once they had loved him as they were now minded to love Menelik, but much had changed, though I still wasn't sure exactly what had happened to sour Solomon's relationship with his subjects so drastically. Was it merely his many wives that they resented, or something more? Was he crippling them with heavy taxation, or was there more to it even than that?

On the morning after the festival, I began to get answers to some of my questions. For Azariah ben Zadok, the pious high priest's even more pious son, turned up on the threshold of the apartment in which Menelik and I were staying and asked if he might speak urgently with us both.

Hami showed him in: a tall, gaunt young man with a grave face and deep-set dark eyes as sharp and fierce as a hunting hawk's. Hami offered him refreshment, but he refused, being preoccupied with more pressing concerns than yet more food and drink.

Menelik had only just got up, for the previous day had been as exhausting as it had been enjoyable. No longer the glittering prince, he wore only the tunic he had slept in, and his untamed hair fell tangled into his eyes. Nevertheless, he welcomed Azariah with enthusiasm and bade him sit down and share what was on his heart.

"Prince Menelik, when I said that I wanted to be your friend, I meant it most sincerely. For if you are going to retain the favour both of your father and of his chief ministers you will need a friend who understands the political situation here in Israel very keenly, and who can help you navigate its turbulent waters without running aground. I believe that I am the man to help you."

Menelik responded with his customary warmth, seizing firm hold of both his visitor's forearms in appreciation of his overtures. "Your friendship I welcome, as I told you before. But rest assured that your assistance with diplomacy will not be required, since I do not intend to stay here long enough to risk incurring anyone's displeasure. I shall return directly to Sheba once my father has agreed to anoint me as its king."

"With respect, my prince, what you intend and what is permitted may turn out to be two different things," Azariah demurred, reinforcing my own suspicions. "For neither your father nor his advisers are remotely interested in who becomes the next ruler of Sheba. But while they are very interested indeed in who stands to inherit the throne of *Israel*, they do not by any means agree about the kind of heir their country needs."

Menelik leaned against the back of his couch and rubbed the sleep from his eyes. Fixing them hard on the young priest's face he said coolly, "Perhaps you had better go on."

"Prince Menelik, it cannot have escaped your notice that your father no longer walks in the way of the Lord. He has taken a great many wives – and concubines too, though he may have been even less keen to introduce you to any of them than he was for you to meet his wives, to whom he is at least formally bound. Not only has he polluted his marriage bed with these foreign women, but he has allowed them to bring their abominable idols with them. Did you not see the high places on the hilltops on your way here? And yet he claims that the presence of these loathsome shrines does not detract from the glory of Adonai; that it is only right that we respect the beliefs and customs of the foreigners who live among us and accommodate them with tolerance and forbearance. But how are we to tolerate human sacrifice, and the abuse of children? For it is not merely animals that are being offered up to idols on Zion's holy mountain. Children are being cast into the jaws of Molech every day; the bones of murdered infants defile Jerusalem's sacred soil. And

Molech is the god of Rehoboam's mother. The only heir there has ever been to Solomon's throne until you came here shares the blood of child-killers!"

Menelik said rather stiffly, "My mother is a foreign woman too. Does this not make me as much of an abomination in your eyes as Rehoboam is?"

"I do not doubt that there are members of the Royal Council who would rather Solomon adopt a dog as his heir than a foreigner, as long as its Israelite pedigree was unassailable. But to men like my father and myself it is not who your mother is that counts, but who your God is. And your mother renounced her ancestral deities, did she not? Am I not right in thinking that both you and she are worshippers of Adonai?"

"It is true that we do not bow down to idols. My mother and my uncle Tamrin here worship Adonai with exemplary devotion."

"You mean that you yourself do not?" Azariah's eyebrows went up; beneath them his deep-set eyes sparked with disapproval.

"I mean that I am circumcised, and that I pray, and that I have known the joy of Adonai in my soul. But I am a young man, Azariah, and a prince. Conspicuous piety may be regarded as a virtue in a woman, or among the elderly, the weak and the poor. But it ill becomes a self-respecting youth of royal blood, or so I have always thought."

"Then, Prince Menelik, you must think again. For my father, and those ministers of government who remain faithful to the God of Moses, will only give you their support if they believe that you will restore what *your* father has allowed to be destroyed."

"I have already told you, Azariah: I do not need their support. The last thing I want is to rob Rehoboam of his birthright."

"So you would condemn the people of Israel to a future of tyranny and oppression when it lies within your power to set them free? Rehoboam is a bully, Menelik; he wants Solomon's power only to abuse it, and his wealth only to squander it upon himself."

"But if I were to set myself up as Adonai's champion come to restore Zion to her former glory, I should thereby be insulting my father as well as Rehoboam. And it is Solomon's favour I came here to seek – no one else's."

"Which is precisely why you need me to guide you, to ensure you retain *everyone's* favour! Your father is not an apostate, not in his heart of hearts. He has been led astray, but you could lead him back. You could heal the divisions that have cut him off from his godliest counsellors, to whom he no longer listens. You could help him to see that his wives have bewitched him; that the taxes he has imposed upon his subjects to indulge his women's extravagant tastes and to build their abominable sanctuaries are driving good men into debt and even to starvation; that the programme of forced labour he has inflicted on them in addition is making them hate him with the same passion that they loved him before!"

Menelik had at last been rendered speechless. I could see that his mind was reeling, for the visit he had been eager to undertake for predominantly personal reasons seemed to be turning into something different altogether, for which he obviously felt entirely unprepared. While he sat there kneading his temples, I decided it was high time to ask Azariah some of the questions that were troubling *me*. Evidently I had been right about the taxes, but was it possible that Solomon could really be using forced labour too? I recalled that when Menelik had been presented to Solomon's ministers, one Adoniram ben Abda had been described as being in charge of it, but there can be no swifter way for a king to turn his subjects against him than by making them work as his slaves. Israelites would resent it more than most, since their ancestral hero Moses had won his fame by freeing them from forced labour under the pharaoh. So I interjected tentatively, "Solomon makes *every* man do forced labour?"

"To begin with it was only the Canaanites he drafted, descendants of the idolatrous tribes who occupied the land while our ancestors were slaves in Egypt," Azariah explained. "But there are not very many of these aliens left – certainly not enough to provide the manpower that Solomon's ostentatious building schemes have required. It's not merely the palace here in Jerusalem, or all these pagan temples he's been building, but elaborate fortifications, barracks and stables in all the major cities of Israel. So he drafted Israelite labour too – but only from the northern tribes, not from Judah or Benjamin whence the support for his father's house has always chiefly derived."

"And the taxes?" I pressed him. "Are these the kind of projects that the taxes have been paying for?"

"Yes, and paying off Solomon's debts to Hiram of Tyre, whose help he has relied upon throughout his reign. But the taxes have not been imposed equitably either. The northern tribes have paid vastly more than their fair share." Here Azariah paused, and suddenly threw up his hands, as though describing the national crisis to me had somehow made it worse. "Solomon has overreached himself, Lord Tamrin," he finished off. "And now he is reaping what he has sown."

I shook my head in perplexity. "Yet he used to be so scrupulously impartial in his dealings with everyone. It's hard for me to understand how everything could have gone so wrong."

"Gradually," Azariah answered with a grimace. "So imperceptibly at first that hardly anyone could see what was coming. My father saw, and tried to warn him to repent and turn back to Adonai with all his heart, because this was the root from which all his problems stemmed. A king faces many more challenges and temptations than a peasant or a pedlar, and this is why it is essential that he remain in close communion with God." Azariah paused again, to look Menelik in the eye. "This is why *you* must commit yourself fully to Adonai's cause, my friend, for surely you shall be a king one day, though whether over one nation or two remains to be seen."

After that there was no more to discuss, but very much to be thought about. Azariah took his leave, having charged Menelik to devote serious consideration and prayer to the things he had told him. But as soon as he had gone, Menelik leapt from his couch and paced about the room, saying half to himself and half to me, "This is not what I came here for. I came to meet my father, to discover what I could about the man who induced my mother to give up everything she was to love him. I didn't come to steal another man's kingdom, still less to be lectured in the affairs of the gods! Did I not promise my mother that I would return to Sheba as soon as I possibly could? Perhaps I was wrong to accept Azariah as a friend."

But I wasn't in the mood just then for bringing him comfort, or even for using reason to calm him down. For I myself was distraught, beside myself with grief over what my own friend and his kingdom had become. Injustice, oppression, even rivalry between Israel's ancient tribes... Had Makeda been with us, she would have been pacing the room as Menelik was, but not out of pity for herself. She would have grieved for Solomon's people, and for Solomon himself, and for the near-paradise over which he had ruled, now reduced to dust and ashes. Most of all, she would have grieved because God himself and all the hosts of heaven must be grieving too.

Chapter Eighteen

When I entered Menelik's chamber to rouse him from sleep the next morning, he was gone.

There was no sign of his manservant either, so briefly I wondered if he might have had enough and decided to quit Jerusalem altogether. I doubted he would have set off back to Sheba without me, but it was possible; he could be as stubborn as his mother once he took an idea into his head. If he had made up his mind that it was too risky for him to remain at the palace even for as long as it would take to persuade me to leave with him, he was perfectly capable of absconding on his own.

Then I found that his belongings were still in the chest at the foot of his bed. So I sent Hami to see if he had gone to visit Makshara, or even Azariah, but neither of them had seen him. It was only when I had begun to consider the possibility of foul play on the part of Rehoboam that Menelik reappeared, having been with the king.

He was in as dark a mood as I had ever seen him, throwing himself down on his bed without a word and lying there with his arms under his head, glowering at the ceiling as though daring it to fall on him. Not caring to have my own head bitten off, I refrained from asking him what the matter was. He would tell me in his own good time.

Which he did later that morning, bursting in upon me while I was studying my daily portion of the Hebrew Scriptures. "Surely it isn't too much to ask of him, that he hail me king of Sheba and pour a little holy oil on my brow, and write a letter acknowledging me as his son so that I can go back home where I belong?" he fulminated. "It's all that my mother has ever asked of him, yet you would think she had asked him for the jewels from his own crown."

"She did ask him for a piece of fringe from the mantle of the Ark of the Covenant as well," I pointed out diffidently.

263

"And so? These things are nothing to him, nothing! Yet he says, 'Why the rush, my son? You have only just arrived here; surely you cannot want to desert me and return to Sheba so soon? Let us get to know one another before you disappear again into the desert whence you came.' But the longer I stay here, the more complicated things are going to get."

"So, did you tell him the reason for your impatience? Did you mention your conversation with Azariah?"

"No, of course I didn't. I didn't want to give him ideas. He may not even have thought of proclaiming me as *his* heir, and I can only pray that he won't."

"So how did the audience end?"

"He said, 'It may be that I shall comply with your mother's requests, even though she never complied with mine. But first I must be sure that you are ready for the kind of responsibility she wants to give you. We must spend time together so that I can assess your suitability for kingship.' How pathetic is that, coming from him as he is today, I ask you! It's nothing short of hypocrisy."

"But you agreed to wait, and to spend time with him as he suggested?"

"I didn't exactly have much choice, did I? So yes, I did. I am to wait upon him every afternoon, when he has finished consulting with his ministers and judging cases and whatever else he does with himself in the mornings. He will show me round the royal estates, and take me hunting in the hills, and…" Seeing that I was suddenly smiling, Menelik gave in and smiled too, and said, "I suppose it may actually be quite pleasant."

"I suppose it will be the very thing you really came here to do," I corrected him. "Make the most of it, Menelik. For once we return to Sheba, who knows when – or even if – you will ever see your father again."

"As long as I don't see Azariah again in a hurry. He can take his piety and his lectures somewhere else."

Thus it was that Menelik and I both resigned ourselves to a longer stay in Israel than we had anticipated. I reflected ruefully that this was how things had started to go wrong when I had visited Solomon with Makeda, but I was in no better position to change things now than I had been then.

Most mornings, Menelik took to visiting Makshara – as much to avoid Azariah, should he put in an appearance, as for any other reason. But I don't doubt that there was a kind of affinity between the lonely royal consort and the affectionate prince, and that they genuinely enjoyed each other's company as much as they enjoyed talking about Solomon as a younger man. In those days, Makshara had respected him deeply, and Menelik could see that he himself would have done so too. Then, in the afternoons, Menelik would go off to see his father in person, and often I would not see him again until nightfall.

In the meantime, therefore, I was free to pursue my own studies and interests. This I did with relish, befriending the royal archivists and the curators of the various specialist libraries that Solomon had acquired and augmented over the years. These men in their turn were only too happy to share with me their knowledge, and their regret that they saw so much less of the king these days than they had once been wont to do; he still hadn't finished compiling his own collection of Proverbs, of which he had promised me a copy twenty years before. When I asked them why they thought he consulted them and their books so infrequently now, they all said the same thing: his affair with the queen of Sheba had been the undoing of him as a scholar, and they hadn't been in the least surprised when Menelik's arrival on the scene had proved that the relationship had been sexual all along. In fact, one reason why Solomon had failed to finish his collection of Proverbs was that he had been distracted by another project: the making of a book out of all the love songs he had written for Makeda. So Makeda's salvation and Solomon's backsliding ironically went hand in hand.

But it was my own salvation and spiritual enlightenment that I was eager to work on while I was in Jerusalem with time on my hands and access to men and materials that I knew could assist me. For back in Ethiopia, neither Makeda nor I had any mentor in the

Hebrew religion to whom we could turn for advice or direction, and no access to accounts written by saints or sages of the past whose knowledge of God had been real and intimate. In Jerusalem, I could – and did – read voraciously of the history of Adonai's dealings with his chosen people, and I could question men who had worshipped and communed with Adonai their whole lives.

I missed Jehoshaphat, to whom I had turned for such fellowship in the past, but found a new confidant in the aged Zadok. I must confess to having found him somewhat forbidding as a teacher when he had undertaken to instruct Makeda and me in the Hebrew religion over twenty years before, yet there was no one who understood more keenly than he the necessity for daily prayer and meditation if one was to deepen one's personal awareness of the divine. He had rarely been granted spiritual experiences of a spectacular kind, but he enjoyed a continual sense of Adonai's presence in his life, and communicated a profound peace to all those around him without even opening his mouth. The fiery devotion of Azariah he smiled upon with indulgence, confessing that he himself had been consumed with a similar zeal at Azariah's age. But now the blinding flames of fanaticism had subsided into a sort of serene glow which gave the old man a strange unearthly beauty, such that he seemed to be simultaneously an inhabitant of this world and the next. To behold the face of Zadok at prayer was like contemplating the countenance of God himself.

Inevitably, when I spent time with Zadok I rubbed up frequently against Azariah, and against Eleazar, his younger brother, who was as energetic and highly strung as Azariah, but not so self-consciously devout. (There was an older brother too, Ahimaaz, but he was already married, with a home and sons of his own.) Every time I met Azariah, he would ask me whether Menelik had had any further thoughts about the future or taken any steps to consolidate his personal commitment to Adonai. I said only that Menelik was his own man and would make his own decisions in his own good time. As far as I knew, the only thing he really wanted was to return to Sheba at the earliest opportunity.

Nevertheless, Azariah insisted on apprising me of the political situation as it developed, and of Rehoboam's state of mind in particular. He claimed to know for a fact that Rehoboam was acutely jealous of Menelik, not only because he so obviously enjoyed their father's favour, but also because he seemed to be popular with everyone. But since Rehoboam had scarcely any friends at all, he would not be so rash as to move against Menelik directly. Rather, he would wait for Menelik to compromise himself in some way, or for Solomon's counsellors to become disgruntled with the amount of time the two of them were wasting on frivolous pursuits, just as had happened with Makeda. At that point, Rehoboam would begin to exploit the general disillusionment to his own advantage.

"You see, Lord Tamrin," Azariah stressed to me, pounding about the room as he spoke, for he had too much pent-up energy to sit in one place for long, "the longer Menelik waits before listening to reason, the more precarious his own situation will become, and the more danger the nation of Israel will be exposed to. Solomon's very empire may disintegrate, and he himself may be deposed or even murdered by a usurper."

"Come, come, Azariah," I cautioned him. "Surely you know better than to try to scare Menelik into complying with your wishes. From what quarter is Israel threatened, and what usurper would dare to try to wrest the throne from Adonai's anointed?"

"The security of Solomon's empire is threatened from at least two different directions. And I know of at least one would-be usurper who has intelligence as well as ambition, and no more respect for Adonai than he has for Solomon."

"But is not Adonai God of the whole universe? And has he not promised to preserve Solomon's kingdom forever?"

"Only for as long as Solomon honours his side of the covenant. If the ruler of God's people fails to live up to his calling, God himself will raise up enemies to destroy him. And those enemies are already waiting primed and poised on the sidelines."

"Really? So who are these paragons of virtue who are worthier of ruling over Israel than Solomon is? I take it you are not referring to Menelik."

"No, it is not for Menelik to depose the Lord's anointed! Just as David refused to destroy his predecessor Saul when *he* had become unfaithful, so Menelik must wait until Adonai himself sees fit to bring Solomon's reign to an end. But there are others who will not wait, nor are they paragons of virtue. For God can use men as his instruments of judgment whether or not they knowingly do his will or even acknowledge his existence."

"Azariah, you are beginning to give me a headache. Pray tell me who these enemies are instead of running theological rings around me, poor foreign convert that I am."

"Very well. The enemies who threaten Israel's security from outside are Hadad of Edom and Rezon of Damascus. The Israelite who would usurp Solomon's throne is one Jeroboam ben Nebat of the tribe of Ephraim."

As soon as he spoke their names, I knew that I had heard of Hadad and Rezon before. Jehoshaphat had told me about them twenty years earlier; in all that time neither of them had ever dared challenge Solomon outright, but if Azariah was to be believed, they had not grown tired of waiting for his hold over Israel to weaken. Hadad had by now returned to Edom from exile in Egypt, having ingratiated himself with his former opponents by masterminding attacks on Solomon's caravans and on the Red Sea port of Ezion-geber, the jewel in the crown of Solomon's achievements as a builder. To general acclaim, he had ousted the vassal king who ruled with Solomon's approval, and was now refusing to pay the annual tribute that Edom was required to tender.

Meanwhile Rezon had apparently won a number of skirmishes against Solomon's garrison troops in Damascus, and at one point it had seemed possible that he might seize control of the city itself. Furthermore, his raiding parties were a persistent threat to trade routes between Israel and the Euphrates.

As for Jeroboam, son of Nebat, his was a name I had not previously heard, and I told Azariah so.

"This does not surprise me," Azariah responded. "For he can only have been a child when you were in Israel before. But he's a dangerous man: clever, tireless, and hungry for power. He used to be one of Adoniram's henchmen, in charge of the forced labour teams from Ephraim and Manasseh; his workers built the supporting terraces for Solomon's palace, and some of the extensions to the city walls, in record time. It was obvious to everyone how capable and enterprising he was; then some prophet called Ahijah of Shiloh started giving him grandiose ideas by telling him that Adonai was going to take all the northern tribes away from Solomon and hand them over to him. Solomon got to hear of it and tried to have Jeroboam eliminated."

"Was the prophet truly sent by Adonai? And where is Jeroboam now?"

"I know nothing more about Ahijah than what I have told you. But Jeroboam fled to Egypt."

"Jeroboam found sanctuary in Egypt, just like Hadad? What can the pharaoh be thinking of, giving refuge to all these enemies of Solomon, when he is Solomon's ally and his daughter is Solomon's wife?"

"Siamun is hedging his bets, and who can blame him? Perhaps he fears that Solomon may divorce Makshara even after all this time, because she has borne him no son."

"Well, I shall tell Menelik what you have said, Azariah. But whether he will take any notice is another matter. He may simply be angry that when he would not listen to you, you started haranguing me instead."

But I did not mention any of these things to Menelik when he returned from Solomon's apartments that evening, because he was so obviously troubled already. In fact, during the course of the past few days he had been growing increasingly morose, though I had not been able to draw anything out of him except a complaint that instead of taking him hunting or to watch his troops in training or his teams of chariots racing, Solomon only wanted to talk. This evening, however, it was Menelik who wanted to talk, so I laid Azariah's concerns to one side and encouraged Menelik to share his.

"I wouldn't mind if he wanted to talk about things that will be of use to me when I become king of Sheba one day," he protested. "But all he wants to talk about is how much he still loves my mother, and what I believe she feels for him now. He's obsessed with her, Uncle Tamrin, even after all this time. He keeps telling me how beautiful she was, and how special, and how he used to write songs for her, and how he has written them all down in a book. Then he tries to justify himself for sleeping with her, by saying, 'My father David slept with my mother Bathsheba when she was someone else's wife, but God allowed him to keep her for himself in the end, or I myself would never have been born.' Then he says, 'Do you think she *hates* me, Menelik, if she really doesn't love me any more?'"

"And what did you say to that, I wonder?"

"I told him I didn't think so, no. But that only seemed to distress him the more. I think he would rather she hated him than didn't feel anything for him at all. I said she had simply had the good sense to realize that she could not afford to dwell on what had happened between them, and that this was why she had broken off all contact. She had repented of her sin, and put the past behind her. Yet it seems that my father cannot do so, because he cannot accept that when they slept together it *was* a sin at all."

"Well, when he looks at you and sees what a fine son he has now, it cannot be easy for him to do so," I pointed out with a smile.

"But Uncle Tamrin, you have always told me that God can bring good out of any situation, no matter how much sin and evil are mixed up in it. That is what my mother has taught me too: that she would never, ever wish to be without me, but that God made me such a blessing to her because she repented with all her heart of what she and my father had done."

"And it blesses me too, Menelik, when I see how wise you are becoming," I exclaimed, and my smile must have broadened, because I was thinking: He *is* beginning to think more deeply about what he believes. His conversations with Solomon may yet make of Menelik a true man of faith, though not at all in the manner I might have anticipated. I became more hopeful still when Menelik continued tentatively, "You know, Uncle Tamrin, although my father says all the time how much he misses my mother, I think it is his fellowship with God that he misses more. He says that if Adonai truly loved him and wanted to bless him, he would have found a way to enable him and my mother to stay together, just as had happened with *his* parents. But if he were to repent with all his heart, and resolve to do God's will instead of wanting God to do his will, his fellowship with Adonai would be restored, and he could become once again the wise and virtuous king he used to be. Don't you think that's true?"

"I *know* it is true," I replied with conviction. "And Solomon used to know it too. I'm sure you remember your mother telling us that she asked him once what the most beautiful thing in the world was, and what was the ugliest, and he said that the ugliest thing is when a faithful man loses his faith, but the most beautiful is a repentant sinner."

"Do you think *I* might be able to help him recover what he has lost, then? Might that be why Adonai has brought us here to Jerusalem, and kept us here so long?"

"It might be, Menelik, yes. But I think there may be work you need to do on your own faith before you can help your father rekindle his."

Menelik only pursed his lips at this. Still, I could see that he knew exactly what I meant, and when he returned to his own chamber not long after this, I knew that he would pray before he slept.

Thus it came about that in the following days it was Menelik who encouraged Solomon to talk, rather than the other way around. He let his father talk about Makeda, yes, but gradually, gently, he tried to shame him into facing up to his failings, to convince him that it was repentance he needed, and to rediscover the love of God rather than the love of any woman. Solomon did reach the point of confessing that it was his multiplicity of marriages which had been his undoing; that he had repeated the mistakes of his own father many times over.

"If I had been truly wise, I would have learned from my father's experience," Solomon told Menelik. "Yet how often it seems that a man merely does the stupid things his parents did all over again instead of resolving never to be so foolish! Yes, Adonai allowed my father to marry my mother in the end, because after he had had her true husband murdered, who else would have taken care of her? But their first child died, as his punishment... just think, Menelik, I could have lost you in the same way, had not the Lord chosen to be merciful! For over twenty years I believed that this or something like it was what must have happened. Yet all the time, you lived, while I have been so ungrateful, so unfaithful. You know, Menelik..." – and here, Menelik told me, Solomon lowered his voice, conscious that he was divulging to Menelik something he had never told another soul – "the night I seduced your mother, I had a dream which greatly disturbed me. I dreamed that the sun departed from Israel and flew to Ethiopia. I did not know what it meant, yet for years the fear haunted me that *God* had left me; that in sleeping with your mother I had forfeited God's blessing forever, and from now on would have only my own resources to fall back on."

Menelik said, "It's not too late, Father. It is never too late to repent before Adonai, make the sacrifice the law requires, and be restored fully in his favour."

But this was a thing which Solomon still was not ready to do, preferring now to harp on about his failings than to have them dealt with. "It is because I did not keep faith with the Lord my God that I have sired so few children; I know that now," he said forlornly. "The Law of Moses makes it clear that if we seek God sincerely we can expect prosperity, wholeness and peace – and a great many sons, if that is what we desire. But I have done as Abraham did; he did not believe that God could bless him with sons in his wife's old age, so he took the matter into his own hands and slept with her slave girl. Such faithlessness always leads to disaster." But when Menelik opened his mouth to advocate repentance once again, Solomon only said, "At least *you* can learn from *my* mistakes, my son. Take one wife – take an Israelite wife, who honours Adonai – and establish your dynasty with her, as God commands us. Take no other woman to your bed as long as you both shall live." And Menelik simply nodded, now too distracted himself to pursue the question of his father's repentance any further because, as he told me now, he was thinking: If my father is talking of my establishing a dynasty, surely that means he *will* soon anoint me as Sheba's king, and let me go home to my mother and the people and the mountains and forests that I love?

Solomon may not have been ready to change, but Menelik was changing now by the day, determined that he would indeed break the cycle of sin and stubbornness which had blighted the lives of his father and grandfather before him. He was praying formally at least three times daily, as I had discovered from Zadok that Hebrew custom requires, and as I myself had newly resolved to do. He was often to be found at the temple, making offerings or deep in conversation with the priests. Eventually, he even stopped avoiding Azariah, and confessed to him that he was prepared to do whatever Adonai asked of him, though he was yet to be convinced that this would entail breaking his promise to his mother and remaining indefinitely in Israel to become his father's successor.

"I must do what Adonai calls me to do, not what *you* demand of me, Azariah," he pointed out. "And does not the law require us to honour our mothers as well as our fathers?" Azariah could only nod, and accept that Menelik was right.

But Menelik did tell him about Solomon's dream in which the sun had departed from Israel and flown to Ethiopia. Perhaps he thought it would help Azariah accept that his new friend would one day have to go home. But Azariah only opened his hawk-like eyes very wide and lapsed into silent thought for a very long time. The next day, when Menelik told him in my hearing of another inconclusive discussion he had had with his father about repentance, Azariah declared, "You are wasting your time with him, Menelik. It *is* too late; God has abandoned him because he knows he will *never* repent. How can he, when he has all those women to look after? Can he send them all back to their fathers? He would have every tribe and nation from which they come taking up arms against him! He *dare* not repent, because he cannot bear to imagine the consequences. It may even be that God has abandoned Israel altogether and is seeking a new people with whom to work."

"No, Azariah. That cannot be true," Menelik objected, simultaneously convinced of his own theology, I was sure, yet unnerved by Azariah's long experience in the faith. "Adonai made an everlasting covenant with the Hebrew people. He may break faith with a faithless king, but never with Israel as a whole." But Azariah would debate the matter no further.

A few days after that, Menelik returned from his daily session with Solomon looking distinctly bemused, as though he had been given a wonderful but somehow inappropriate present. He said, "My father says that our conversations have gone on long enough, and that he is now completely satisfied that I am suited to kingly rule. He says the time has come to make the announcement for which I've been waiting, and that tomorrow there will be a plenary meeting of the Royal Council to which you and I will also be invited."

"He is going to anoint you king of Sheba in front of his entire council? And will he give you a fringe from the mantle of the ark in front of them as well?"

"I don't know; he didn't really say any more than what I told you."

"So we can go back to Sheba at last! Yet you don't seem as ecstatic as I might have expected."

"No." Menelik pulled a wry face and shrugged his shoulders. "I suppose I'd begun to hope I might see some change in my father's frame of mind before we went. I just can't see why he should want to recapture something from the past that is dead and can never be revived, instead of putting it behind him and moving forward in faith."

But I wasn't sure that this was the only reason for Menelik's ambivalence. I ought to have questioned him more closely as to what exactly Solomon had said about the meeting of the Royal Council which we would both be attending the following day.

When we duly presented ourselves on the threshold of the chamber where the council habitually met, we were redirected at once to Solomon's great throne room. Here we found not only the members of the council but also a number of priests from the temple, Zadok and his sons included, already seated close to the dais. Upon the dais, a second throne had been erected to the right of Solomon's – less ornate and not as high in the back, though by no means unimpressive – but so far neither of the thrones was occupied, for there was no sign as yet of the king himself.

His son Rehoboam, however, was very much in evidence. He was esconced on the middle one of three chairs that had been placed at the very foot of the dais, in full view of everyone assembled. He wore a flamboyantly embroidered robe and a superior smile that only broadened when Menelik and I were motioned to sit down beside him, one to his right and one to his left.

What had Rehoboam been told about the purpose of the gathering? Why was he even there? Was Solomon planning to confirm Rehoboam's status as heir to the throne of Israel by anointing him at the same time as anointing Menelik heir to Sheba's? It would be a shrewd move to make in a way, I decided, for it would reassure Rehoboam that he did indeed have nothing to fear from Menelik, and it would strengthen the bond of friendship to which the two half-brothers had committed themselves in the shaking of hands.

But how different the two of them looked as they sat there together waiting for their father to appear! Rehoboam smug, self-satisfied, hands folded over his substantial paunch, Menelik on his guard and distinctly underdressed. Even sitting down it was obvious that he was almost a head and shoulders taller than his brother, but although Rehoboam probably still had some growing to do, he must already have measured twice as far around the waist. Menelik was tanned, Rehoboam pale; Menelik's shoulders were broad, Rehoboam's round. It was almost impossible to believe that these were sons of the same father, but then, if the rumours were to be believed, perhaps they were not.

At length a blast of trumpets announced the king's arrival. All the men present rose to their feet and bowed before their sovereign, who was decked from head to foot in gold and purple, with full ceremonial regalia. He took his seat and gestured for everyone else to be seated also.

"Elders and priests of Israel, my brothers," he addressed the assembled dignitaries, over our heads. "You know as well as I do that in recent years I have not always exhibited the wisdom with which you associated me in my youth. I have strayed from the path the Lord our God laid before me for me to walk, and both you and I have suffered as a result. Today I mean to make amends for my transgressions by relieving you all of the burden of anxiety with which you have been living almost as long as any of us can remember. We all know that over a nation where there is uncertainty as to who will succeed the reigning king there hangs the constant threat of rivalry between contenders for the throne, and even of civil strife. Even before Menelik of Sheba set foot on Israelite soil, there was widespread recognition that my son Rehoboam would never be fit to rule over Adonai's people. Therefore today I am minded to make it clear to all of you, my sons included, whom I have appointed as my successor, and why."

At this point he paused deliberately, and though nobody spoke, the very air in the throne room seemed suddenly to be humming with pent-up energy. Charged glances were everywhere being exchanged, for it seemed horribly likely that Solomon was about to make the announcement so many in the room must have been dreading for many and varied reasons. Surely, I was thinking, he cannot intend to declare Menelik heir to the throne of Israel in front of all these eminent personages when he knows that Menelik himself does not want it? And what will Menelik do if he does? Catching a glimpse of Rehoboam, I saw that he had broken out in a visible sweat, and he was breathing as heavily as a man who had run from Jerusalem to Jericho and back without so much as moistening his lips.

But before Solomon or anyone else could say another word, a commotion broke out at the far end of the throne room. A scrawny derelict dressed in rags came hurtling at the king as if from nowhere, hotly pursued by a pack of palace guards. Just as they were falling upon him he swung about wildly, knocking his closest assailant off balance and leaping up onto the dais like a grasshopper in spite of all efforts to prevent him. There he poked a bony finger in Solomon's face and shrieked, "Since when has the nation of Israel been an item of your personal property, Solomon ben David? Was the Promised Land promised to you alone? Is God's kingdom no more than a piece of merchandise to be bought, sold or bequeathed according to your personal preference? Any authority you have ever wielded has been yours solely by appointment of Almighty God! Woe to you, proud king, who threw away your wisdom along with your respect for the God of your fathers! You already know the future that Adonai has ordained for this nation after your death. Ten of the twelve tribes of Israel will be torn from the hands of your son and given to another man to rule, and it is only for the sake of your father, David, that this will not happen in your lifetime, and that all twelve tribes will not be wrested from your control. Mark my words, Solomon the proud, for they proceed from the mouth of Adonai himself!"

Though many of those present seemed not to know who the ragamuffin was, I myself was in no doubt that this was Ahijah of Shiloh, the prophet who had been inciting Jeroboam ben Nebat to rebellion. By now the royal guards had at last succeeded in wrestling him to the ground and dragging him away to spend the night in a dungeon. But the damage was already done. Solomon sat as stiff as a corpse against the back of his throne, as though transfixed there by a spear. Rehoboam's face had turned pasty white like curdled milk, and he was trembling. The members of Solomon's council sat open-mouthed, while the majority of the priests stared impassively before them, giving nothing away as to whether they believed they had been listening to the voice of God or not.

But Zadok had fallen to his knees and wept unashamedly from unblinking eyes which seemed to be gazing in awe at something no one else could see; his face was transfigured by wonder, joy and sorrow all at the same time. I knew that he grieved for Solomon's fall from grace, yet rejoiced because the voice of prophecy was not silent in the land.

So ecstatic was his countenance that it was some while before I could tear my eyes away from it to study the reaction of his sons, and of Azariah in particular, to the scene that had been played out before us. When I did, I saw that Azariah was staring directly at Menelik with the astonished eyes of a man who has received a revelation.

The nature of this revelation I was to learn as soon as the stricken king had been prevailed upon to dissolve the assembly. For Azariah pursued Menelik and myself to our apartment with all the tenacity of a hound that has picked up the scent of its quarry. There would be no opportunity for Menelik or me to unburden ourselves to one another before Azariah forced his own interpretation of Ahijah's intervention upon us.

Chapter Nineteen

The whole way back to our apartment Azariah danced about us like a tumbler working his audience for tips. While Menelik and I maintained a grim-faced silence, Azariah was jabbering with excitement: "It's all come clear to me now, Menelik. I know what you must do; Adonai has shown me the whole picture. Stop and hear me out, I tell you; I have discerned the will of God!"

Eventually I admonished him in no uncertain terms that priest or no priest I was very much his elder, and if he wanted Menelik or me to pay him any attention at all, his revelation could wait until we were in the privacy of our own rooms and I invited him to share it.

Once we were back there with the door shut and Hami had brought us all refreshment, I bade Azariah have his say, but preferably without bursting our eardrums, and with some attempt at coherence. Well nigh beside himself, the young priest could barely contain his elation sufficiently to speak at all. When he did so, the essence of his garbled pronouncement seemed to be that he had been right all along: Adonai had resolved to abandon the renegade Israel to her fate and choose a new people through whom to reveal himself to the world. But now it was crystal clear to Azariah who the new chosen people would be: the people of Sheba, with Menelik ruling over them as their faithful king-under-God.

"Don't you see, Menelik?" he cried in frustration when Menelik and I only stared at him nonplussed. "It's so obvious; your desire to return home to Sheba and Adonai's desire to fashion for himself a people worthy of their calling are not incompatible after all! Solomon is finished; his kingdom is about to be torn apart in inter-tribal strife. One of the psalms his own father wrote declares, 'Ethiopia has stretched out her hands to God.' It was a prophecy, and now its time of fulfilment is at hand."

I pointed out reasonably, "But Azariah, this is not what Ahijah of Shiloh said. He said specifically that Solomon's son would retain a part of his father's kingdom, for the sake of Solomon's father David."

"A mere concession, and a temporary one at that! How can the tiny southern tribes stand alone? You must have nothing to do with them, Menelik; leave them for Rehoboam, since Ahijah neglected to say *which* of Solomon's sons would retain them. You must have Solomon anoint you king of Sheba, and give you some sign of Adonai's presence with you to take home to your people, to convince them that they are now God's people too."

"Which is precisely what I have been asking my father to do all along," said Menelik with quiet exasperation. "If he would not do it before, I hardly think he is going to do so now."

"But he will. I know he will! *My* father will prevail upon him; after what has happened today, Solomon will be like clay in his high priest's hands."

"And what makes you think that your father will have reached the same conclusions about all this as you have?" I probed more keenly.

"The fact that this is Adonai's will, and that my father will have discerned it just as I have."

"Well," I said, motioning Hami to open the door once more, "perhaps you had better leave us and go to him directly, to check that your interpretations tally."

The tide of Azariah's zeal was stemmed at last; he glared at me as though I were an infidel, and left.

When he was gone Menelik said, "So you don't believe he was spoken to by Adonai?"

I said, "Do *you*?"

"I don't know. He is a priest, and the son of Zadok. He has walked in the ways of his God for much longer than we have. I should hesitate to contradict him."

"But Menelik, he did not say *how* God had spoken to him, only that the upshot of what Ahijah said was 'obvious'. Besides, from my own study of the Hebrew Scriptures I do not believe that Adonai would simply abandon the covenant made with his chosen people. He might rebuke them, or punish them, or conceivably replace their king. But reject them utterly? It would take more to convince me of this than the ranting of a young radical like Azariah."

"Perhaps you are right. But does it really matter to *us* whether Adonai has rejected Israel or not? All that *we* need is what we have needed from the outset: for Solomon to sign a document recognizing me formally as his son, anoint me king of Sheba, and give me a piece of fringe from the mantle of the ark. If Azariah and his father can convince him to do that, afterwards they can spend all the time they want worrying about Israel's eternal destiny while we get out of here as fast as our donkeys' legs will carry us."

"I cannot fault your logic, Menelik; you were always an avid student of philosophy. Yet at the same time I cannot help but be wary of Azariah's impulsiveness. I hope he will content himself with browbeating his poor father, and not do anything rash into the bargain."

"Anything rash? Like what?" Menelik demanded, but I merely shrugged my shoulders and threw up my hands. In fact, if I could but have guessed the direction in which Azariah's obsession was driving him, events might have turned out very differently.

The following morning he was back, more cocksure and irrepressible than ever. "Menelik," he announced, "it is all arranged. You are to wait upon your father this afternoon in his private apartment as you have been wont to do these past few months, and he will explain to you the procedure for your anointing as king of Sheba."

"And how do I know that he does not have some bizarre trick up his sleeve as he did before?" The more ebullient Azariah became, the more suspicious Menelik grew in response. "Look what happened last time he promised he would comply with my mother's requests."

Azariah's exuberance abated temporarily as he admitted the truth that could have made the most sanguine of saints despondent: that Solomon was presently in no fit state to think for himself at all.

Later, while Menelik was closeted away with his father, I repaired to the temple in search of Azariah's. I wanted Zadok's perspective on the events of the previous day, and to discover if he really did share his son's conviction that Adonai's covenant with Israel was irrevocably broken.

I found him at home, sitting out the hottest part of the day in his vine-shaded courtyard. His house stood within the great palace-cum-temple complex that now monopolized Jerusalem's highest ground. The venerable priest, being heavy with age these days and easily wearied, had delegated most of his routine duties to his subordinates, though he maintained an incisive grasp of what went on, and very little of political or religious import escaped his notice or his comment. When I was shown into his courtyard, his wife was there too, and his youngest son, Eleazar; of Azariah there was no sign, and Eleazar and his mother made themselves scarce as soon as I had been welcomed.

I was about to apologize for disturbing the old priest's rest, but his wrinkled face broke into a beatific smile and he said, "Tamrin, my friend, as it happens there is no one I should rather have had come to visit me this afternoon. Sit down; let us talk, for there is much to be said."

I smiled too, flattered that he should deign to spend time with me in the midst of this national crisis. But he recognized me as a man of integrity and a diligent student of the Law of Moses, and he had told me often enough that he knew far too may Israelites who were neither.

"You are aware, no doubt," he began, "that Solomon would have named your young cousin crown prince of Israel, had Ahijah not interrupted him before he could do so."

"Yes, I am aware, and so is Menelik," I responded. "In this respect, if in no other, we were relieved that the interruption occurred when it did."

"As was I, my friend, as was I. Had Solomon named Menelik his heir *before* Ahijah's disclosure, things would have been even worse for everyone than they are going to be in any case."

"For everyone?" I repeated, surprised, because I had almost begun to think that most Israelites would rather have had Menelik rule over them than Rehoboam, even though this was the last thing Menelik himself would have wanted.

"Oh, there is much talk about Rehoboam's shortcomings and lack of princely virtues, but I know my countrymen, Tamrin, and when faced with a choice between a bastard from a foreign land, however plausible and charming, and a bully born within wedlock here in Jerusalem, most of them would choose the bully over the bastard every time. Menelik would never have been accepted, notwithstanding the good impression he has created. Jeroboam would have risen up against him and hived off his ten tribes in rebellion, just as he will against Rehoboam. Menelik is well off out of the way – and the further away the better."

"So you believe that Ahijah speaks for Adonai? He is a genuine spokesman for the Almighty?"

"Yes, I do, both because I know the man himself and the exemplary life he leads, and because when he spoke, Adonai's Spirit within me leapt up in witness to what he was saying. His prediction will come true, of that I am sure, if only because Rehoboam will set about exploiting everyone he can, and turning them all against him, as soon as his father is improvident enough to pass away."

"Then Israel is finished? Adonai's covenants with Abraham, with Moses and with David have all come to nothing?"

"Oh no, Tamrin. Far from it. Adonai will always preserve a remnant within the nation that will retain its faith and inherit the promises made to our forefathers. Remember that he promised Solomon's father David that he would never lack a successor to sit upon his throne."

"But – might that remnant not belong to some nation other than Israel? And might not the throne be a foreign one too?"

Zadok's eyes narrowed; he stared very intently into my own and said, "To whom were you talking before you came here to see me, I wonder? I had thought you a scholar, not a pedlar of wild speculations."

Deeming it prudent not to beat about the bush I said, "Your son Azariah has told Menelik that Adonai has abandoned his commitment to Israel because of Solomon's transgressions and decided to take up with Sheba instead. Sheba will emerge as the new chosen people." And when Zadok's narrowed eyes opened as wide as libation bowls I added, "Moreover, Azariah is confident that you will have reached the same conclusions yourself, since both you and he are such discerning men of God."

"Well," said Zadok, "I can only say that whether Azariah's revelation came from Adonai or not, this is certainly the first I have heard of it."

"So Azariah has not discussed any of this with you already?"

"He urged me to have Solomon sanction Menelik's anointing as king of Sheba as a matter of urgency – which I was intending to do in any case, and which I have now done. The arrangements have already been made for me to perform the ritual myself within the week. But as for the notion of Adonai abandoning Israel in Sheba's favour... I think Azariah probably knew better than to speak of it in his father's hearing."

"So you don't believe he heard from Adonai at all? You don't believe the prophecy that 'Ethiopia has stretched out her hands to God'?"

"Of course I believe the prophecy, but only in so far as it means that Ethiopia will be among the first of the nations to acknowledge the supremacy of Adonai and thus come to share in Israel's destiny. The vision of the psalmist is that one day *every* nation will recognize the sovereignty of Adonai over all creation, and that all other gods are impotent in comparison."

"Yet Azariah seemed convinced enough to be convincing in his turn."

Zadok shook his head with a smile, and said, "Tamrin, my friend, it is God to whom each of us should listen, not to the persuasiveness of silver-tongued men. If Adonai has decided to change his mind utterly about Israel's election, and wants men as old and obstinate as you and me to believe it, he is going to have to choose a more reliable channel of communication than a hot-headed boy, even if that boy is my own beloved son."

"So you will speak to Azariah and urge him to think again?"

"I shall speak to him, yes, but only to caution him to be especially on his guard if it seems that Adonai is telling him something so very astonishing. I should not venture to undermine his belief that God can speak to him directly should he choose to, let alone suggest that he should listen to me rather than to the still small voice of the divine."

So it was that I returned to our apartment with plenty to think and to pray about. But when I got there, Menelik was already back from his latest interview with Solomon, and was sitting with his head in his hands.

"The talk with your father did not go well?" I asked him, in a tone that encouraged but did not oblige him to go into detail.

"It went well enough," he answered, looking at me but without raising his head. "He promised that Zadok would anoint me with the holy oil from the temple sooner rather than later, but in private this time, not in the presence of his council. He said it would be sacrilegious to cut a fringe from the covering of the ark, so I am to have the mantle in its entirety; a new one has already been commissioned to replace it. I shall have a written testimonial to take home confirming me as his son, signed by his own hand and sealed with the royal ring. I could not have asked for anything more." Then he closed his eyes and whispered, "It is my father himself who is not well. He looked sicker than he did the first time I ever saw him."

"He is depressed because of what happened with Ahijah?"

"He is like a man who has died, yet his body does not know it, and still walks and talks and breathes without any soul to give it life. He did not look me in the eye even once in all the time I was with him. It may not be too late for Israel, but it's too late for Solomon. I know that now, with no shadow of a doubt."

Briefly I laid one hand on his head and mussed his tumbling hair: a gesture of blessing and affection combined, which he accepted with a sort of rueful resignation.

Not many days after this, the ritual for which we had been waiting so long was finally enacted, in the Holy Place of Solomon's temple. Zadok was the celebrant; with none but the king and myself as witnesses, he took the jar with which Solomon himself had been anointed, and poured the holy oil over Menelik's forehead. Thereupon Solomon proclaimed him king of Sheba, with the throne-name of David, his grandfather, whom, according to Solomon, Menelik so strikingly favoured. Just as though this were the coronation of a king of Israel, Zadok recited a litany of blessings and curses that would descend upon the fledgling king depending on whether or not he remained faithful to his overlord, Adonai. Then two of Zadok's acolytes came in and stood beside their master, one to his right and one to his left. The one on his right held the mantle of the Ark of the Covenant, rolled and tied up like a scroll, while the other bore the letter from Solomon, written on papyrus and also rolled up, but without any fastening because Menelik must read it before it was sealed. Zadok took both the mantle and the letter and placed them in Menelik's hands.

Here the ritual ended; Zadok invited Solomon, Menelik and me to accompany him to a private room which adjoined the temple building, where Menelik could read and approve the letter and Solomon could stamp it with the royal seal.

I watched my young cousin's face as he read it, his eyebrows twisted in concentration, for although he read Hebrew well enough these days, he wanted to be sure that the wording left nothing open to dispute. I saw him nodding with satisfaction as his eyes moved along; he was presumably happy with the confirmation Solomon had given to the people of Sheba that Menelik – or David, as he would now officially be known – really was his son by their queen, Makeda.

Then suddenly his eyes opened wide and his eyebrows shot up out of sight beneath his hair. He turned to his father and demanded, "Does Azariah know what you have decreed concerning him? Does his brother know, or Zadok here, their father? And what of the other young men you have named, and their fathers too?"

Solomon did not react except to close his eyes as though Menelik's tirade had given him a pain in the head. Then as Zadok and I exchanged uneasy glances, Solomon said absently, "You will need advisers. A king cannot rule without advisers. And a king under God cannot rule without advisers who are steeped in the Law of Moses and know what a godly king should look like."

Menelik turned towards Zadok to gauge his reaction and then towards me; noting our bafflement and apprehension he thrust the letter into my hands and said, "Read it, Uncle Tamrin. And you too, please, my lord Zadok. I cannot agree to what is stipulated here unless all those whom it affects have agreed to it first."

Having skimmed the letter's opening, I lighted at once on the part to which Menelik was objecting. It made provision for twenty-four young men of noble Jerusalem families to accompany King David of Sheba back to his homeland to form the backbone of his Royal Council. All were youths as yet unmarried, whose fathers were priests, politicians or senior military officers known to be true to Adonai. Almost all were firstborn sons, but two of them were Azariah and Eleazar, and if Solomon's will prevailed, they might never see their father, Zadok, again.

What could have prompted the ailing Solomon to take such a radical step? Did he want to punish these youths and their fathers because of the latter's unremitting criticism of his foreign wives and their idolatrous ways? Had he resolved that since he must give up his own precious son, so must they? Or did he genuinely want to lend weight to his affirmation of Menelik as his son, and to see the boy succeed where he had failed? Whatever his motives, it was clear that I was never going to tease them out of him, because it was obvious that he had no intention of discussing them with me or with anyone else. In fact, he looked so very afflicted and weary that I began to think he was not much longer for this life at all.

Zadok, by contrast, did not exhibit the consternation which a less holy man in his position might have shown. Having read the letter himself, he maintained a reflective silence, merely nodding his head from time to time as he pondered the implications of

Solomon's decree, until finally Solomon himself said, "You do not speak, old man? Yet I don't doubt that you hold an opinion of your own concerning the measures to which my son appears to object?"

"Your servant would not venture to voice his opinion about any royal proclamation unless he were invited to," Zadok reminded him evenly.

"Well, I do invite you," snapped the king. "Come, learned priest. Tell me what you are thinking."

"I am thinking that if you send all of Jerusalem's most promising young men south with Menelik, then when Rehoboam comes to form *his* Royal Council only godless and greedy idlers will be left – along with a handful of toothless old relics like myself, should Your Majesty pass on before I do."

"Since godless, greedy idlers are precisely the kind of companions Rehoboam prefers, I scarcely think it will make much difference," was all that Solomon would say in response. With that he snatched back the letter from Menelik, stamped it hard with his seal-ring whether his son liked it or not, and swept out of the room, leaving us to our own devices.

Menelik protested at once. "Surely he cannot uproot freeborn sons of Israel from their families against their will and make them exiles as though they had committed terrible crimes? How am I to form a council with men who have left their hearts behind in their homeland? They will come to resent my very existence, just as Rehoboam does, even if they don't already. I will not take *anyone* with me who does not choose to come."

Zadok said, "Oh, they will choose to come if Azariah asks them to, especially if he can convince them that it is what Adonai requires. Every young man in Jerusalem looks up to Azariah, and the fathers of all the youths named here will have taught them to follow where the Lord leads them, whether or not they would have gone that way of their own free will."

"But what makes you think Azariah himself will want to come?" Menelik retorted, then obviously realized straight away that he knew the answer already; there was nothing Azariah would relish more, given the conclusions he had reached as to where the future of God's people lay.

"And you would part with two of your own sons without so much as a murmur of protest?" I enquired of Zadok myself.

"It is not the high priest's place to murmur against the express will of the king merely to please himself," Zadok replied. "Besides, they will have you to watch over them, my faithful friend." I could only purse my lips and wonder if a time would ever come when it was no longer my mission to bring up other men's children. Then again, the fiery Azariah and Eleazar were unlikely to prove any harder to handle than Makeda or Menelik had been in their younger days, and at least they had been brought up in the knowledge of Adonai.

Predictably, Azariah appeared on our threshold that very evening, having learned of Solomon's decision and embraced his commission with alacrity.

"Truly our God is the greatest!" he enthused, seizing Menelik by the shoulders and kissing him hard on both cheeks. "Everything is coming together; the dullest dunderhead could see that all this is the work of Adonai. We need never say goodbye to one another after all, Menelik, for I shall serve you faithfully forever!"

"And your brother Eleazar? Is he as eager as you are to leave behind everything he has ever known and journey to the ends of the earth in my service?" Menelik asked as he shook himself free.

"Eleazar? Oh, he will get used to the idea soon enough; he enjoys an adventure as much as anyone. The other fellows too will be raring to go once they realize that there is no future for them here. You need only leave them to me – though I think it would not hurt for you to spend a little more time in their company before we depart for Ethiopia."

"Indeed."

It had not escaped my notice, either, that the young men at court were the group of people with whom Menelik had fraternized the least during his time in Jerusalem; I knew it was because they reminded him rather too much of the boys at the court of his mother, who had made his childhood a misery. Older men, women, girls and younger boys he won over with minimal effort; his peers, however, he had always found more of a challenge, and one to which he was frankly reluctant to rise. "There will be plenty of time for them to get to know me on our way back to Ethiopia," he assured Azariah. "I intend to leave Jerusalem as soon as these adventurous friends of yours have packed their bags."

"Yes, of course, my prince, and I fully understand your impatience to be gone from this godforsaken city. But I have taken the liberty of commissioning another artefact, something very special to be made for you to take home with you as a gift for your people, and it will not be delivered to my father's house for at least another fortnight."

"An artefact? What sort of an artefact? As the Lord lives, Azariah, am I never to be allowed to leave this place? I do believe I shall be older than your father by the time I see the mountains of Yeha again! I don't need anything to take away from here for my people apart from the things my father has given me already."

"With due respect, my prince, there is little point in possessing the mantle of an ark unless you have an ark for it to cover."

"I beg your pardon?" Menelik gaped at Azariah in mounting disbelief. I too was beginning to suspect that Zadok's son had altogether taken leave of his senses.

"When the children of Israel fled Egypt for the Promised Land, the Ark of the Covenant was carried before them as a sign of the presence of God. So how can we set out for Ethiopia without such a symbol of our own? No one sees the ark any more except for my father, once a year, when he enters the Holy of Holies on the Day of Atonement, but all the instructions and measurements needed to make it were recorded in the writings of Moses. I have simply commissioned a master carpenter to fashion a replica, that is all. It won't be overlaid with gold, of course – at least, not until it has been brought to Ethiopia, where I know you mine gold by the cartload. But with the true ark's mantle to adorn it, it will not matter for the duration of our journey that our ark is made only of wood. It will go before us just as proudly, and inspire us just as gloriously to remember that Adonai is always with us. Rejoice, Prince Menelik – King David! – for the second exodus is about to begin."

What was to be gained by objecting? It seemed that the deed was already done; in any case, it would take the twenty-four youths who were to accompany us a week at least to come to terms with their fate, to say their goodbyes to their loved ones, and to make their arrangements for travel. Menelik gave a snort of resignation and said to Azariah, "Very well, my friend. I thank you for the trouble you have gone to on my account. But remember that from this moment on it is *I* who make the decisions and *you* who obey. So long as we both understand it is *I* whom your father anointed king, I trust we shall manage very well."

There was something in Menelik's tone that brought Azariah up sharp; with as much surprise in his eyes as new respect, he said, "Yes, Your Majesty," without a trace of irony.

Yet at the same time he looked distinctly uncomfortable too. Had he already taken some other decision that Menelik would not have wanted him to take? As he went on his way I followed him pensively with my gaze, but I was thinking as much about Menelik as about Azariah. I was thinking how much he had changed and grown in the time we had spent at his father's court. By the time he got back to his homeland everything about him would testify to his right to rule over it.

The following morning Azariah returned, but this time at Menelik's bidding. Menelik instructed him to gather the youths who were to go with him to Ethiopia and inform them that the man who was destined to be their king would address them as a body at noon. "But you shall come with me, Uncle Tamrin," he enjoined me. "Azariah may fancy that no one is more important to me than he is, and indeed I should not get far without him, at least until I have won the confidence of his peers. But you will always be foremost among my advisers. Only the counsel of Adonai himself could weigh more heavily with me than yours."

"As long as you listen to Adonai's voice rather than to mine if our counsel differs, you will make as wise a king as your father once was," I said with a smile. "But I thank you for your affirmation, and for placing your confidence in a mouldering old merchant who has seen better days. I ask only that you promise to pension me off if I enter my second childhood and can no longer be relied upon to talk any sense."

"I promise," Menelik laughed, but the shadow that passed fleetingly across his eyes told me that he would consider himself quite bereft without me.

Chapter Twenty

At noon, Menelik stood for the first time before the twenty-four men who would one day help him govern the people of Sheba.

An unnerving audience they made too: all of them silent, all of them inscrutable, charily studying Menelik's face and his every move. None of them betrayed their true feelings. Were they excited at the prospect of adventure and responsibility, or were they inwardly calling down curses on Solomon and Menelik's heads? While it was true that their fathers were all known for their devotion to Adonai, who could say what these young men themselves believed, or what they had previously hoped that the future might hold for them? Some might have had sweethearts to whom they were betrothed; some might already be carving out for themselves promising careers at the temple or at Solomon's court. All of them would be leaving their homes, families and possessions to follow an enigmatic African stranger into the desert. Whether Azariah had had any success whatever in inspiring them with his vision of a second exodus remained to be seen.

Their names we knew already, and could match most of them with the diffident faces. Eleazar sat with his brother, whom he resembled much more closely when neither of them was speaking. Next to them sat Zechariah, son of Benaiah, who commanded Solomon's armies. Then came Elimiah, one of whose kinsmen had been the great prophet Nathan, who had exposed King David's adultery with Bathsheba. There was Machariah, son of Ahishah, who had oversight of all the palace servants, and Samnaiah, whose father had replaced Jehoshaphat as royal recorder. The names of the others I need not set down here; suffice it to say that they were all of them youths of exceptional talent and potential.

Menelik said to them, "Gentlemen, I do not know what King Solomon has told you of the task with which you have been charged, nor what has been said to you as to why you in particular have been selected to accomplish it. But you may rest assured that as far as I am concerned, you have each been personally chosen by God himself to assist me in spreading his light in a very dark world, and in establishing the first royal dynasty inaugurated with his blessing beyond the borders of Israel.

"I cannot promise you that your mission will be an easy one, or that you will not wish you had never been required to be part of it. But I can promise you that violent and wretched days lie ahead for the country you are leaving behind you, and that those who love you will be forever grateful to God that he called you away from it when he did. I can also promise that your willingness to go with me and the sacrifices you must make to do so will win you universal respect in the land to which you are going. On the journey you must undertake to get there, you will not face any hardship which I do not face myself, nor will any complication with which we must contend be beyond Adonai's ability to handle.

"Moreover, because of the trouble taken by Azariah ben Zadok out of the love and deep respect he has for me, for you and for his God, you will have before you at all times a powerful reminder of the Almighty's presence and protection. It is in Adonai's name and for his eternal glory that we embrace the vocation he has given us, and neither he nor I intend to let you down."

During the course of Menelik's speech – which lasted for quite some time, for I have given merely a summary of what he said – it was a joy to behold the young men's attitudes softening and their hearts warming towards him. It was not simply the words that he spoke, but the manner in which he spoke them, looking each of his hearers approvingly in the eye one after another and striving to convince every one of them individually that he was already a valued member of an exclusive team.

However, when he reached the part about Azariah's ark – though he did not refer to it in quite so many words – the tension that had been in the atmosphere before he had begun to speak was evident again, accompanied by some distinctly uncomfortable glances and shifting in seats. Azariah himself seemed to have found a knot in the grain of the table in front of him worthy of his rapt attention, but I decided he was only embarrassed to have been singled out for special praise.

All in all the meeting went very well, and no one took issue overtly with anything Menelik said. When he asked if anyone had questions there were many, but most were genuine requests for information rather than thinly veiled objections. How far was Yeha from Jerusalem, and how long would it take us to get there? Would there be food and water available, sufficient for ourselves and the servants and pack animals we would need to take with us? What about the bandits and wild beasts we should undoubtedly encounter along the route; would we have troops to protect us? And when we arrived, would Menelik be invested as king straight away, or would his mother go on ruling until her death, and what would his counsellors' role consist of until the time came for him to assume her responsibilities?

Menelik fielded their questions as well as he could, though not all could be answered directly. Some he referred to me, and I shed what little extra light I could.

But at last came the question that sooner or later had to be asked: was it true that Adonai had turned his back on Israel for good? In other words, had Sheba not merely been grafted on to the people of God, but taken Israel's place?

"In all truth I do not know," Menelik replied, with an eloquent glance at Azariah. "It may be that only time will tell. It is not for us to fathom the mind of Adonai; only to trust him, and walk the path he has set before us."

When the questions had all been asked, and most had been answered, Menelik reaffirmed Azariah by bidding him invoke Adonai's blessing on us all, since he would soon be Sheba's high priest. Then he had every man present swear a solemn oath that he would serve both his God and Menelik – David – his king with unswerving loyalty as long as he lived. Finally, he said that from now until the day of our departure his door would always stand open; if anyone wished to come to him with a question or concern in private, such visits would always be welcome. After they had all departed, Menelik blew out his breath in a long, slow sigh, and went to lie down to recover his strength. He had done very much better than he might have done, but it had not been easy.

Not a day went by after that without one or more of his neophyte counsellors calling in to discuss some development or problem that had freshly occurred to him. Zechariah, son of Benaiah, wanted to know who would be commanding the troops that would form our guard. Elimiah was concerned about Menelik's understanding of prophecy: did he believe that Ahijah of Shiloh was a man of God? Then Eleazar appeared, and harped on all kinds of trivialities that were clearly nothing to do with the real reason why he had come. But at this point his brother Azariah turned up to deliver his daily report on the progress on his copy of the ark, and Eleazar took flight as though all of the pharaoh's chariots were chasing him.

"Do *you* know what that was about?" Menelik demanded of his latest visitor, who was plainly disconcerted by the way his younger brother had behaved.

"No. Not exactly," Azariah responded, but he delivered his report as tersely as possible and left in haste, which was so completely out of character that even Hami, the embodiment of discretion, registered surprise.

"He is plotting something. I am sure of it," I said when Azariah had gone. "Menelik, we shall have to confront him."

"Azariah – or Eleazar?" Menelik challenged me in turn, and I was forced to acknowledge that Eleazar had indeed been acting the more strangely of the two. Not that this wasn't troubling in itself, but as Menelik pointed out, each of them had sworn an oath to serve his God and his king with an undivided heart, and as sons of Zadok the brothers must surely be men of their word.

For Azariah was indeed delivering on his promise to excite his companions' enthusiasm for the adventure on which they were embarking. When they came by Menelik's chambers it ceased to be questions or worries that brought them, but their desire to assure him that they were more than happy to follow him even to the ends of the earth, for they knew now that their God would be with them and nothing could stand in their way. They were urging Menelik himself to be of good cheer and have faith, for soon he would understand why they had cast their fears to the winds, and why their sadness at leaving their homes and families had been swallowed up by the thrill of anticipation. Even Eleazar seemed buoyant; whatever it was that had vexed him was evidently disturbing him no longer.

Slowly but surely, the faith and friendship of the young men he had previously doubted brought Menelik to the point where the time he spent in their company became a joy to him rather than a trial, and their fellowship built him up rather than grinding him down.

At last the day came when Azariah announced that his copy of the ark was finished. Let Menelik but specify a date for our departure, and we should be gone.

All became a bustle of activity. In the courtyard of Solomon's palace, hundreds of mules and their drivers were assembled to carry not only our belongings and those of our Israelite companions, but also the inevitable surfeit of treasures that Solomon insisted on sending with us. (Among these was the book of Proverbs that he had promised me so long ago – still unfinished, but he knew that if he did not give it to me now, he never would.) He insisted too on an obscenely extravagant sacrificial ceremony in the temple; literally thousands of bulls and rams were slaughtered to mourn the departure of the king's firstborn son and to commend him and his companions to God. Copious tears were shed by these young men's parents, convinced though they were that their sons were doing God's will.

But no one was more distraught than Makshara, Pharaoh's daughter, who had no faith in Adonai to sustain her. She loved her surrogate son as devotedly as any mother has ever loved the fruit of her own womb, and Menelik adored her in return. She gave him an exquisite Egyptian ring with a stone in the shape of a beetle, the bluest thing I have ever seen, and asked him to wear it always. He has done so, and I do believe it means as much to him as all the treasures Solomon lavished upon him put together.

The climax to the temple ceremony was marked by the entry at the last possible moment of Azariah, who appeared on the steps between the pillars Jachin and Boaz dressed in priestly robes identical to his father's. From one of the rooms abutting the Holy Place came four more priests, bearing Azariah's ark on their shoulders. Shrouded in its mantle it could have been the real thing, and so awesome was the sight of it that an audible gasp arose from every quarter. The four priests who carried it then descended the temple steps to take up their position at the head of our cavalcade; they had volunteered to bear their weighty burden all the way back to Ethiopia and then to minister before it in the temple at Yeha.

Had the choice of route been left to me, I should again have elected to take the desert road through Arabia which I knew so well. Menelik, however, was minded to go home by the way we had come – not to admire the pyramids this time, or in the guise of an anonymous adventurer, but specifically to visit the pharaoh as a fellow king. He wanted to introduce himself as the anointed ruler of Sheba, to extend the hand of friendship to his elderly Egyptian counterpart, and at the same time to convey Makshara's greetings to the father she had not seen for so many years. Accordingly we were obliged to retrace our steps towards Gaza, where a flotilla of ships stood ready to carry us along the coast to the mouth of the Nile.

This first stage of our journey was remarkable only for its sheer uneventfulness. In fact, everything went so uncommonly smoothly that I began to think I must be dreaming and that we had not actually left Jerusalem at all. We made Gaza in two days – not an especially noteworthy achievement for a single rider on horseback or even for a well-disciplined military unit on the march, but for an unwieldy multitude including pack animals and many civilians who were not accustomed to travelling any distance at all, it was truly an astonishing feat.

Fortune continued to favour us as we struck out over the sea; a following wind drove us all the way to the Egyptian coast in record time. With the minimum of inconvenience we succeeded in chartering enough river-going vessels to carry us up the navigable stretches of the Nile. Though Siamun's capital was at Tanis, not very far inland, he was currently staying at his palace in Memphis, much further upriver. So we sailed there with all haste; and still we seemed to be leading a kind of charmed life, for we encountered no dangerous beasts, the river teemed with fish for us to catch, and the thickets of reeds by its banks supported so many game birds that we were bringing down more than we could eat.

The aged pharaoh received us politely, but he became positively fulsome in his commendation of Menelik once the latter had shown him the ring he had been given by Makshara and told him that she had permitted him to call her his "Egyptian mother". Siamun was assured that his daughter was being well looked after, and that although sadly she had never borne Solomon any children, he continued to treat her with respect.

It was while we were camped at Memphis – for Menelik insisted on camping everywhere with his companions rather than claiming any regal privileges – that I first began to suspect what the cause of our uncanny good fortune might be. For one chilly evening as Menelik and I sat with the young men of Jerusalem eating and talking by our campfire under the stars, Menelik said amiably to Azariah, "Come, my pious friend, you have not yet shown to me your precious 'artefact' which you were so determined we should bring with us. Isn't it time we took off the mantle to admire your carpenter friend's handiwork? What did he put inside it, I wonder? Is it empty, or are there copies of the Ten Commandments in there too, and Aaron's rod, and the jar of manna, and whatever else is supposed to be inside the real thing?"

The hum of conversation around the fire fell immediately silent, as though water had been poured on the flames. In the flickering orange light, every eye was fixed upon Azariah, who shuffled uncomfortably in his place and muttered, "It is not fitting to joke about holy things."

"Joke? And who exactly is joking?" Menelik retorted. "I do want to see your ark. And in any case, it isn't a holy thing, is it? It's just a wooden copy. It's no more holy than the box I keep my boots in."

Azariah winced as though a scorpion had stung him. "You must not say such things – Your Majesty. For the real ark is but a copy of the celestial ark that is in heaven. Any copy of that ark which is made according to the divine instructions is holy and constitutes the presence of Adonai among his people."

Not relishing the prospect of a confrontation between the two of them with so many people listening, I intervened tentatively, "Constitutes or represents, Azariah? Surely the former is not what you mean at all, for the term could lead men to suppose that the ark itself is a thing of magic, not merely a reminder that the invisible God goes before us always, to guide, protect and inspire."

"It is not a thing of magic," Azariah concurred. "Yet if Adonai chooses to focus his power in a certain object or place at a certain time, he is at perfect liberty to do so. Did he not manifest his glory to Moses in a burning bush? And did not the ark itself wreak havoc among the Philistines when they captured it in battle? It threw down the idols in their temples onto their faces, and smashed them to smithereens."

"All the more reason why I am intrigued to know what it looks like," said Menelik in the same playful tone with which he had introduced the topic in the first place.

"Well, you cannot," Azariah snapped. "And pray, do not ask me again unless you wish to make it appear that I have broken the oath I swore to you, when in truth I have not."

And this was the end of the matter, at least for the moment. But when we set off once again on our journey the following day, and during the course of the several days that followed, Azariah seemed increasingly nervous, literally looking over his shoulder every other minute. Eventually I said to him, "Azariah, you need not fear that Menelik will snatch the mantle from your ark without your consent. I know that he would not do so."

"He would only do it once," said Azariah, in a peculiar tone whose significance I did not care to interpret. "But that is not what I am most afraid of, as it happens." I raised an interrogative eyebrow and he said, "I fear that Solomon's men may already be after us."

"Why ever should they be? Solomon has accepted that Menelik will never sit upon Israel's throne. He won't seek to bring him back now."

"He may not be able to bring *Menelik* back, it is true," Azariah conceded, but although his remark sounded incomplete, he would not add any more.

"Well," I said, "considering the astonishing speed with which we have been travelling until now, he is unlikely to catch up with us, whatever his motives." As I spoke I looked Azariah hard in the eye, but he did not rise to my bait.

And indeed, the further south we got, the more prodigious our good fortune seemed to become. The only whiff of danger we smelt was when a band of Bedouin travelling in the opposite direction warned us with much waving of arms that we were headed straight into the path of an almighty sandstorm. We took the precaution of digging ourselves into safety, but when no storm was forthcoming several hours later we pressed onward regardless. Then we saw, from a trail of devastation including half-buried villages, dead animals, and huge fresh dunes where none had been before, that a sandstorm of epic magnitude and ferocity had indeed passed within a mile or so of our position and had been heading straight towards us along the road. But unaccountably it had changed direction, veering off into the deep desert, and left us untouched.

Then as we approached Egypt's southern border, the scouts who habitually rode ahead of our lumbering cavalcade came racing back to inform us that there was a large tribal stronghold in the wild country ahead of us. We had already been spotted by its lookouts, and its warriors were not minded to grant us safe passage. They were already massing, fully armed, in a steep-sided gorge through which we should be obliged to pass, and a military engagement was inevitable.

Menelik at once summoned Zechariah, son of Benaiah, and Jozabad, the commander of the troops who protected our column, to meet with ourselves and the scouts and decide how best to respond.

"They are merely spear-rattling savages with no discipline or strategy," one of the scouts reassured us. "They have no iron weapons, only bronze – in fact, many of them have only sticks and clubs."

"True, but they are many hundreds in number, perhaps even more than a thousand," a second interposed. "We cannot hope to defeat them head-on. And there may be others hidden among the rocks, waiting to take the places of the fallen."

"Have you not searched for an alternative route so that we might avoid these barbarians altogether?" asked Jozabad, who obviously had no desire to squander his men's lives in a futile struggle they could not win.

"We have searched, but found no trace of any sort of passage besides the road itself."

"Surely we should attempt to negotiate terms with these people before resorting to violence?" I could see that Menelik was determined to explore all options available. "We have no shortage of treasure with which to buy them off."

"As they themselves will certainly have deduced," said Zechariah. "And why should they be content with taking some of it, when for the price of a few of their uncircumcised hides they'll be reckoning that they can have it all? No, we must fight them, Menelik, and trust that our superior weapons and discipline will win the day."

"With respect, young sir," said the scout who had spoken second, "no amount of discipline or technical superiority can defeat a foe who outnumbers you ten to one. We should need magical weapons, not merely iron."

It was at this point that another man added his voice to the discussion – one who had not been bidden to the enclave but who had since deemed it appropriate to invite himself. Azariah said, "There is no need for magical weapons when one is already carrying the vehicle of the Lord's presence."

As had happened so many times in recent days, the briefest of references to the Ark of the Covenant gave rise to an excruciating silence. While Zechariah's eyes lit up with sudden hope, Jozabad fumed with anger; Menelik, seated between the two of them, glanced

302

several times at one and then the other before looking daggers at Azariah and demanding to know what he had in mind.

"I believe that our troops should form up in battle order and prepare to engage the enemy, but that the ark should be carried in front of them. The power of Adonai will rout the barbarian horde before a single arrow is fired or spear thrown."

Jozabad growled, "Don't be ridiculous. We are not living in the days of Joshua now. Walls no longer come tumbling down when a few crazy priests blow their own trumpets."

And Menelik added, rather more tactfully, "Azariah, your ark is but a replica, remember? We cannot expect it to achieve the same kind of exploits as the original is said to have done."

"*Said* to have done? My lord, there is no 'said' about it. But the Ark of the Covenant never achieved anything of itself; you know that as well as I do. It did what it did because God's power was focused upon it, and that was because the faith of God's people was focused on it too."

"You mean that if *we* have faith, we shall witness a miracle such as Moses and the liberated slaves saw during the exodus, and Joshua saw in the conquest of the Promised Land?" asked Zechariah, eyes still shining; his faith was flaring up already.

"Yes, I mean exactly that. For have we not been experiencing miracles ever since we left Jerusalem? The speed with which we have travelled, the dangers through which we have been preserved… you all saw for yourselves the destruction wrought by the sandstorm that passed us by."

"Insane. The lad is insane," Jozabad was muttering to himself, and I began to think that if Menelik did not assert his authority soon we should have a mutiny on our hands.

But then, unexpectedly, Menelik turned to me. "Uncle Tamrin," he said, "did I not say that you would always be chief among my advisers? Come, give your opinion, and I shall make my decision based upon it."

Now all eyes were fixed on mine: Azariah's bright with challenge and Zechariah's with hope, Jozabad's narrowed and as black as

303

pitch, Menelik's suddenly as trusting as they had been when he was but a boy, my pupil who believed I knew everything. All too aware that many men's lives rested on the wisdom of my judgment, I said, "Menelik, we must pray. Here and now. Azariah, gather all the young men appointed to Menelik's council, and we shall seek Adonai together."

Only Jozabad objected; he was a soldier through and through, with no time for fatuous mumbo-jumbo. He said he would go and consult with his lieutenants; Menelik could summon him again when he was ready to give him some coherent orders.

So it was that the twenty-four sons of devout Israelite fathers gathered and knelt by the roadside with Menelik and myself, bowed heads covered with the prayer shawls they wore beneath their cloaks, palms upraised to heaven. Azariah, who would one day be Sheba's high priest, invoked Adonai's name in a traditional chant to which the other young men added their voices one by one.

This was the first time either Menelik or I had prayed like this, in a company of Zion-born men whose need to hear a word from their Lord was both desperate and boldly expectant. We had prayed before on our own, or with Makeda, Sabla and Hami, all of us novices in the faith together. Or we had stood in the temple court with a multitude who were more or less involved in what was going on too far away for them to see or hear distinctly. But now we were surrounded by ardent young men whose faith was as informed as it was intense. As their youthful voices mingled together, and they began to sway back and forth as they prayed, any observer could have watched the Spirit of Adonai falling upon them and been left in no doubt as to what was happening as the outstretched hands and closed eyelids began to tremble and the syllables whispered by the moving lips no longer belonged to any human language. One by one the young men's faces were transfigured, until Menelik himself succumbed; then all of a sudden I myself was caught up too. I found myself chanting and singing in some heavenly tongue I had never learned and did not even understand. I knew only that I had never experienced such euphoria in all my life. I was quite sure that if the feeling lasted much longer I should fall to the ground as one dead, yet I did not care.

Then as swiftly as it had descended, the Spirit released us; we were left staring dazedly at one another as though we had all been awoken from some strange shared dream. All, that is, except for Azariah. He knelt in the midst of us with arms held high, head thrown back and bared hair streaming, still in the grip of his trance. In a voice that was not his own he cried out, "Take up the Ark of the Covenant and I the Lord will do amazing things among you! Do not be afraid of the enemy; I have given them into your hand. Not one of them will be able to withstand you." Then he collapsed in a dead faint.

The words he had spoken I had heard before; they came from the account of the hero Joshua's victories over the tribes that had occupied Israel while his ancestors were slaves in Egypt. But there was no questioning the fact that they were also the word of the Lord for us this very day, and that we should reject them at our peril.

While Eleazar tended his stricken brother, Menelik recovered himself sufficiently to recall Jozabad and instruct him to draw up his men in battle order. "But they will not need to fight," the sceptical old soldier was assured. "Nor will even one of their lives be lost, for today's victory belongs to Adonai alone."

Then Menelik bade the four priests responsible for the ark to raise it high above their shoulders on its long carrying-poles in full sight of our entire company, and proceed with it along the road ahead of us. The main body of our troops would march behind it, but at a distance, so that there could be no doubt in any man's mind but that it was Adonai who wrought our victory, not weapons of war.

What were any of us expecting to witness? Would Azariah call forth fire from his ark to consume the enemy in scorching flames? Would the divine power focused upon it cause the earth to split apart and swallow our opponents whole?

In the event, we didn't see anything – but the barbarians must have done. For without warning their battle cries became screams of horror; they turned tail, flung down their weapons, and started trampling one another to death in their desperation to escape whatever it was that threatened them.

Of course, they were superstitious savages, and they must have deduced that the thing being borne aloft ahead of our troops was the symbol of a god. But there was no obvious reason why they should have concluded that our God was more powerful than their own, unless they had been able to see some evidence of his supremacy. By the time the bearers of the ark entered the narrow passage between the rocks, it was deserted. The only enemy warriors who remained were dead ones, their skulls crushed by the feet of their fleeing comrades.

That night, the noise of celebration coming from our camp must have been audible in heaven itself. Priests, soldiers, muleteers and everyone else raised their voices in praise of Adonai; praise that grew more fervent and then more raucous as dozens of bulging wineskins were pulled from our animals' packs and handed out with reckless abandon. Solomon had intended the young men of Israel to have wine to enjoy upon their arrival in Ethiopia to assuage their pining for home, for the vine does not flourish in the mountainous country of Yeha and wine for most of its inhabitants is a rare luxury indeed. But no one cared about any of that just now. All that anyone wanted was to rejoice in Adonai's sovereignty and to show their appreciation in suitably extravagant style for his spectacular intervention in delivering us from the deadly clutches of our enemies.

So the wine and the praises flowed on together, and no one praised more loudly or drank more freely than the vindicated Azariah. It was not long before both he and Menelik were being paraded about the camp on men's shoulders, faces flushed with joy and with the juice of the grape. I had never seen Menelik truly drunk before, but didn't think it could do much harm as long as I stayed sober myself and made sure he didn't do anything to disgrace himself beyond redemption.

Azariah, on the other hand, had no one to exercise similar discretion on his behalf, since his brother Eleazar was in no fitter state than he was. And the drunker he got, the louder Azariah became in his acclamation of Adonai; certainly his religion was no flimsy veneer that alcohol might strip away. It was only a matter of time before the equally drunken men who carried him around stumbled and toppled him from his pitching throne, and as fate would have it, when they did so they lurched into Menelik's porters and knocked them over too. Thus their helpless soon-to-be king and his likewise incapacitated high priest finished up rolling on the ground together. Then, laughing like a madman, Azariah threw his arms around Menelik's neck and blurted out, "I have to tell you, Menelik, my friend; I can't keep you in the dark any longer. It's the real thing! The ark we brought from Jerusalem – it isn't a replica at all. It's the one Moses made, as sure as I'm Zadok's son. The Ark of the Covenant, the Glory of Zion… whatever you want to call it, we have it with us! I took it, right from under my father's nose, I swear it. Rejoice with me, Menelik, for your people in Ethiopia will be guardians of the ark forever."

Silence at once fell about him, and thenceforth spread so rapidly that a few moments later all you could hear was the spitting of campfires as the fat from roasting meat dripped onto the flames. Meanwhile Menelik stared muzzily at Azariah as though he was still speaking in some angelic tongue that no one else could understand. Then as his addled mind put two and two together and made five, he grinned and jeered in slurred speech, "Azariah, you should be ashamed of yourself! 'It is not fitting to joke about holy things.'"

"Oh, it's no joke, I assure you. Your ark is the very Ark of the Covenant that was fashioned by Moses in the wilderness. It's the ark that led my forefathers to the Promised Land. And now it's yours. Aren't you going to say thank you?"

"Thank you? *Thank* you?" Gradually the focus was returning to Menelik's eyes as anger got the better of his merriment. "I don't believe a word you are saying."

"Then ask Eleazar, my brother. Ask Zechariah ben Benaiah. Ask Elimiah. They will all tell you the same."

"And why should *they* know all about this when I don't? Has everyone been told this story but me?"

"No, not everyone; of course not. Not your uncle Tamrin, or Jozabad or any of his soldiers. But all twenty-four of the men whom Solomon appointed as your counsellors know the truth. How else do you think I could have persuaded them to follow you into the desert without complaining?"

Now Menelik was on his feet; his hackles were up, but he was just as drunk as before, a lethal combination in any high-spirited young man. He growled, "I warned you, Azariah. I warned you to remember that *I* am the anointed king of Sheba, not you. It's for me to take decisions and lead my people, and it's your business to do as you're told and keep God on our side so that they follow."

"Which is exactly what I have done – Your Majesty. How better to keep God on our side than by taking his holy vehicle with us? Besides, when you started laying down the law to me, the decision had already been made. Nor did I take it on my own initiative. I had a dream. An angel of Adonai appeared to me."

"An angel? As the Lord lives, Azariah, do you take me for a complete idiot?"

"Not a complete one, no. But do you seriously think I could have smuggled the Ark of the Covenant out of the Holy of Holies without Adonai's approval? He would have struck me dead the moment I entered the sanctuary. No one can go in there except my father, once a year on the Day of Atonement, and even then he must wear a cord around his ankle lest God decide to strike him dead after all and his body must needs be dragged out by the foot! Yet I went in, and three others with me – all of us ritually pure, of course – and we exchanged the ark for our replica while the priests and Levites who guard the temple just stood there motionless like pagan statues! We took the new mantle and draped it over our ark-shaped wooden box without any of them noticing at all. It was as though we were invisible, or as though time had stopped in its tracks for everyone except us! I tell you, Menelik: the miracles began before we had even left Jerusalem."

At the beginning of Azariah's explanation Menelik had still been on his feet, fists clenched, face like a storm-cloud. By the end he was grovelling on his knees in the dirt, shoulders slumped, head down, rubbing dust from the ground into his tumbling hair. When at last he ventured to look up, eyes still bloodshot through the filthy tangle of his locks, he could see not only Azariah but every one of his twenty-four counsellors staring at him and waiting to hear what he would say next. There was no need for him to ask any of them to verify Azariah's story, for their pinched faces were more than eloquent enough in their own right.

So quietly that I could barely distinguish his words, Menelik said, "I journeyed to Israel only to look upon my father's face and receive his blessing, and to bring him the joy of knowing that he had another son besides Rehoboam. Instead I have robbed him not only of his most precious possession, but of all joy, all hope, and even of his God. I might as well have slept with his wives and burned his palace and temple to the ground. There is nothing left for me but to die here in the desert before we cross over into Ethiopia and I defile her sacred earth with my blighted blood. Take my sword and kill me, Azariah, for I am undone."

"Kill you? You are insane! You are a prince who is about to come into his royal inheritance, and you have the Almighty God of the universe as your patron. No man in all the world has a brighter future ahead of him at this moment than you do, Menelik… David ben Solomon."

"Do not call me by a name of which I am not worthy. I have broken my father's heart. He has no choice but to disown me."

"You have done nothing of the sort. He may not even know as yet that the ark is gone; indeed, he may never find out! Even when *my* father enters the Holy of Holies on the Day of Atonement he does not take the mantle from the ark, and in any case, the sanctuary is almost totally dark."

"And it does not disturb you at all to think that you have made your own father a victim of the most heinous deception? He *will* find out, they will both find out, you can be sure, because you are not the only one who has dreams. *My* father told me of a dream he had on the night he lay with my mother. He dreamed that the sun set over Israel and rose over Ethiopia, but he did not know what it meant. Now I think it is obvious."

"All the more reason to rejoice, Your Majesty, for it shows that everything which has happened has been in accordance with the will of Adonai."

What was Menelik to say? He could see as well as I could that anything he did say would be taken by Azariah as further proof of his own interpretation of events. Noting his hesitation, Azariah went in for the kill, crouching down to grasp Menelik by the shoulders and exclaiming, "Now you see, don't you, why I cannot show you what the ark looks like, much less let you look inside it? No one must ever lift the mantle from it again. After we have arrived in your capital city and it has been placed in the sanctuary of your temple, even I shall see it only once a year. And I shall have a cord tied around my ankle just as my father does."

Then softly, almost insidiously, he began again to intone the chant with which he had inaugurated our prayer vigil by the roadside, and one by one his companions again took it up. And as their voices rose, so the Spirit of God descended gently to meet them like mist through a forest, to my mind a surer sign of Adonai's presence than any Ark of the Covenant would ever be.

Was it also a sign that Azariah had been telling the truth? Was it possible that our ark could be the genuine Ark of the Covenant as he was claiming? Could it really be true that Solomon, who had once sent a tiny replica of the ark to Makeda as a girl, was now unwittingly sending her the original? And if so, could Adonai truly have sanctioned its removal from the temple in Jerusalem, which was meant to have been its final resting place after all those years when it had been carted about in a glorified tent? Certainly it did seem unlikely that anyone, even Azariah, could have stolen it against the divine will.

Yet even as these questions flooded my mind, the conviction rose within me that the answers to most of them were unimportant. All that mattered was that Adonai was with us now, and that if we resolved, as of this moment, to accord him the respect which was his due, he would use everything that had happened to accomplish his own perfect will. He would weave together the strands of hope and despair, of expectancy and dread, of piety whether misguided or not, and even of outright sin, to create a tapestry of exquisite beauty which would cause whoever beheld it to fall on his knees and worship the One who brings order from chaos and eternally makes all things new. Whether or not the sun was destined to set over Israel, it must certainly rise over Ethiopia and shine there forever, even as it was shining now from the faces of the twenty-four sons of Israel who stood with arms stretched up to heaven, singing in angelic tongues and laughing, with tears streaming down their cheeks.

Nor could Menelik's spirit remain downcast any longer. Slowly I watched him rise to his feet, more as though lifted by invisible hands than as though he stood of his own accord. Then his own hands rose up to heaven, but rather than adding his voice to the soaring chant he opened his mouth in prophecy, addressing his words to the ark itself. And his voice was no more his normal speaking voice than Azariah's had been when he had spoken for Adonai concerning the battle.

"Praise to Adonai Elohim, King of the universe!" he cried. "For in all things it is your own will that you accomplish, and not the will of men. The counsel of the cunning you confound, and the injustice of the oppressor you overturn; you raise the humble man from the pit and set his feet on solid rock. A full cup of glory you hold out for those who love you, while those who reject you will drink the dregs of shame. For salvation shines forth out of Zion; everywhere where men and women cry out to you their sin will be expunged, for your goodness and mercy will be poured out over all the earth!

"This is only the beginning; there will be salvation wherever you are honoured: salvation in the house and in the field, salvation in palace and cottage, on the sea and on the land, in the hills and the mountains, the gorges and valleys. Do but be our guide, O Lord our God, and we will follow wherever you lead us; do but give us strength and we will serve you as you deserve, and make known your name and your glorious deeds until all of humanity comes to see that there is but one God in heaven, and that your love for your creation is as boundless as the universe you have made."

As Menelik's voice had risen, so the voices of his counsellors had fallen silent; as he had risen to his feet and somehow seemed to grow taller while he was speaking, so they had fallen one by one to their knees and prostrated themselves upon the ground – not before him, but before the ark of Adonai's presence. It was only when Menelik himself lapsed into silence and fell upon his knees with the rest of them that I felt the moving of God's Spirit once more within myself.

It did not make me laugh or cry or sing in some heavenly tongue this time. It only bathed my soul in warmth and whispered that at last my own mission was accomplished. I had watched over Makeda until she had become the greatest queen of Sheba there had ever been. And now her son, Menelik, who had also been my charge, was ready to succeed her. I, Tamrin the Merchant, would go to my grave content, not because I had built the biggest business empire in Ethiopia, but because Menelik was now a man, and not only a man, but a man of God.

Historical Note

Ever since it was first written down, the story of the queen of Sheba's visit to the court of King Solomon has fascinated Jews, Christians and Muslims alike. This is partly because the Bible introduces this powerful, rich, exotic woman and then tells us so little about her. In the Old Testament she appears only briefly in 1 Kings 10:1–13 (and in the parallel 2 Chronicles 9:1–12) and we are not even told her name, nor where exactly Sheba was. There is no indication that the relationship between Solomon and this foreign queen was romantic, much less sexual, except that many readers have taken verse 13 ("King Solomon gave the queen of Sheba everything she asked for") (GNB) as a hint that there was more to their liaison than politics.

All we are told specifically is that the queen of Sheba came to visit Israel because she had heard of Solomon's fame, wealth and wisdom and wished to question him to find out for herself whether the reports she had received were true. Perhaps she merely asked him the kind of riddles with which philosophers and rulers in the ancient world often tested one another's intellects. Or perhaps she had more serious questions about God and the gods – the first-century Jewish historian Josephus suggests that she was "inquisitive into philosophy"[1]. It may also be the case that she desired to forge a political alliance between her kingdom and Solomon's, which might otherwise have been rivals, or at least to reach some agreement concerning trade, involving access to various markets or control of the routes taken by caravans through the deserts of Sinai and Arabia. The fact that her own expedition included camels loaded with spices has led most readers to suppose that Sheba was itself located in Arabia.

---

1 *The Works of Flavius Josephus: Antiquities of the Jews* Book VIII, chapter 6; trans. William Whiston, 1737.

Whatever the truth about her visit, few readers have been able to resist the temptation to speculate further about its nature, and a bewildering variety of folk tales have been generated as a result, some of them demonstrably ancient, others dating back no further than the Middle Ages. Much of the Jewish and Muslim material is fanciful to say the least, complete with magical artefacts, jinns and talking birds. However, some of the most intriguing and least far-fetched of the stories are the ones from Ethiopia, principally those to be found in the Ethiopian national epic, the *Kebra Nagast*.

This document dates from the medieval period, though the bulk of its content may have much earlier origins. Whereas in the Islamic legends the queen of Sheba's name is given as Bilqis, and Josephus calls her Nicaule, the Ethiopians have always known her as Makeda, and have been convinced that Sheba, far from being in Arabia as has often been assumed, was in fact located in eastern Africa. There is still a region of Ethiopia known as Shewa, and while it is often claimed that no Solomonic connection can be found in Ethiopia before the Middle Ages, according to an ancient inscription one of the rulers of the much earlier Ethiopian kingdom of Da'amat was named Salamam-Fataran.

In fact, archaeology has established that there was an advanced civilization in Ethiopia centred on the city of Yeha dating back almost certainly to the time of Solomon, and that there were undoubtedly links between Ethiopia and southern Arabia at least as early as the first millennium BC. It may well be (as I have taken to be the case for the purpose of this novel) that Sheba's territory extended over parts of Africa *and* Arabia. After all, the gap between Africa and Arabia at the southern tip of the Red Sea (the Bab el-Mandeb Strait) is only twenty miles wide. And even in Ethiopian accounts, the route Makeda took to visit Solomon is usually taken to have been the caravan route overland through Arabia rather than alternative routes through Egypt or up the Red Sea.

There is considerable variation even among Ethiopian versions of the queen of Sheba legend. For example, her palace is variously described as being at Yeha, Axum and Debra Makeda. Again, in some accounts, Angabo (also known as Angabos or Angaboo) who rescues the child Makeda from the dragon is actually her own father; in another, Makeda's father *is* the dragon; in others, it is Makeda herself who kills a dragon or serpent and thus wins the right to rule over Sheba. In the struggle she injures her leg; in fact, the reference to some disability or disfigurement with regard to one or both of her legs is a recurring feature of Jewish and Muslim legends as well as Ethiopian. Some say that the queen's legs were unusually hairy and that she had the feet of a goat, despite being otherwise exceptionally beautiful (and prodigiously intelligent). The version of the story where Makeda is mauled by her own pet jackal is Ethiopian; a rival Ethiopian legend claims that when she was about to be sacrificed to the serpent, some of its blood splashed onto her foot, causing ulceration.

Whichever version seems the most plausible, in all of them Solomon plays some part in alleviating the queen's condition – if only by inventing a depilatory! Solomon's wisdom is in itself the stuff of legend; there are Jewish and Islamic tales in abundance eulogizing his encyclopedic knowledge and even magical abilities. Many of these tales credit him with the ability to communicate with birds and animals, and have them do his bidding. No doubt a scholar of such eminence may have given the impression of knowing what no mortal man could ever know, and in common with many kings in antiquity, Solomon probably kept botanical gardens, and specimens of animals and birds from every corner of his realm and from the far-flung countries his merchants visited. According to Josephus, Solomon owned extensive parks and gardens near Bethlehem.

Closely connected with the legends about the queen of Sheba is the intractable mystery of the disappearance of the Ark of the Covenant. The latest reference in the Old Testament to this powerful symbol of God's presence among the Jews is in 2 Chronicles 35. Here King Josiah instructs the Levites to put it back in the temple, whence it had presumably been removed either during the reign of the idolatrous King Manasseh or for the purpose of the renovations Josiah himself had been carrying out.

However, even in 2 Chronicles it is not specifically stated that the Levites obeyed Josiah's instruction; it may be that the ark had already gone missing and that its disappearance was subsequently covered up. Jeremiah 3:16 may constitute an oblique reference to this. It states that in the future the ark will never be remembered – "it will not be missed, nor will another one be made" (NIV 1984). Certainly this is what the Ethiopians have traditionally believed, for the *Kebra Nagast* states quite categorically that the ark was taken from the temple, with divine approval, by Azariah, son of Zadok. Azariah and his companions are said to have been distraught at the prospect of leaving their homeland, on Solomon's orders, to accompany his illegitimate son by Makeda back to Ethiopia, where Menelik was to rule as king under God. So they contrived to take the Ark of the Covenant with them to assuage their homesickness and punish Solomon for their harsh treatment at his hands. Azariah and his companions are believed by many to have been the ancestors of the enigmatic Ethiopian Jews, the question of whose origins is yet another mystery connected with the figure of the queen of Sheba.

Many Ethiopian Christians today firmly believe that the Ark of the Covenant now rests in the Church of Our Lady Mary of Zion at Axum, but since no one other than its guardian is permitted to see it, the truth of this claim is yet to be tested.

According to later Ethiopian legends, it was Menelik who founded the royal dynasty of Ethiopia that ruled almost without interruption for three thousand years, ending after two hundred and twenty-five generations with the fall of emperor Haile Selassie in 1974. However, it is difficult to verify whether the "Solomonic" dynasty which "re-established" itself in AD 1270 after wresting power from the rival Zagwe dynasty was in fact the same dynasty from which the Zagwe had taken over in the first place. (The Zagwe also claimed to be descended from Solomon as a result of his sleeping with Makeda's handmaid.)

Whatever the truth about its origins, it became customary for the Ethiopian royal family to choose each new ruler after a meeting of its Crown Council, a gathering of kinsmen of the late monarch and of representatives of other noble families. The reigning monarch was supposed to designate an heir, but the heir could not assume the throne without the council's approval, and would sometimes be rejected in favour of a rival claimant. I have taken the liberty of supposing that this custom prevailed in the days of Makeda and Menelik too.

There is some disagreement in the Ethiopian accounts as to whether Makeda was one in a long line of virgin queens, or whether she actually inherited the throne from her father. According to Arabic legends, the rulers of Ethiopia (or Abyssinia) from the earliest times were "royal princesses". We do know that in early Arabia there were female rulers; both Arabian and Assyrian inscriptions testify to their existence as early as the eighth century BC. Before this time it seems that Arabia may not have had kings or queens at all, but there were certainly "super chiefs" called *mukarribs* who prevented feuding among the lesser chieftains. Under the Sabaeans (a later Arabian empire whose name is clearly linked with Sheba) we know that the throne would pass to the first male born to one of the leading families after the accession of his predecessor. It is easy to imagine that a similar system could have worked with rulers who were female and not permitted to marry or bear their own children.

Almost all the characters in this novel first appear either in the Old Testament or in the *Kebra Nagast*. The Bible does not tell us the name of Solomon's Egyptian wife nor which pharaoh was her father, but the *Kebra Nagast* calls her Makshara, and a comparison of Egyptian and Israelite chronologies has led a number of scholars to conclude that her father was Siamun, the sixth king of the twenty-first dynasty. Others claim that Siamun died before Solomon's accession, and that the most likely candidate is Psusennes II, but the chronology of this period is fraught with difficulties.

Did the queen of Sheba truly renounce her pagan gods and resolve to govern her realm in accordance with the Law of Moses? It is suggested in 1 Kings 10:9 that she did at least come to acknowledge Solomon's God and appreciate the unique quality of his relationship with his people. But it is from Jewish, Muslim and Ethiopian Christian sources that we learn of her complete abandonment of paganism in favour of worship of the one true God. And presumably there is truth in what they say, because in Matthew 12:42 (and Luke 11:31) Jesus himself plainly regards the queen of Sheba as one of history's most famous penitents. She will even be present on Judgment Day to accuse those who refuse to accept the words of Jesus.

However, this by no means implies that God had abandoned the Jews in favour of the Ethiopians. Even if the Ark of the Covenant does reside in Axum, this is not to say that the Ethiopians are the new "chosen people", unless the *Kebra Nagast* is to be taken as a document with equal spiritual authority to that of the Bible! In the New Testament, Paul states emphatically (e.g. in Romans 11:1) that God has not rejected the people with whom he initially chose to work. Although the Ark of the Covenant was once the symbol of God's presence, it could no more "contain" him than could Solomon's temple. As Solomon himself proclaimed, the heavens themselves could not contain the Almighty God (see 1 Kings 8:27). Perhaps the ark *had* to be lost, so that Jews and Gentiles alike could learn the lessons not only of Jeremiah 3:16 but of Jeremiah 31:31–34:

> **"The time is coming," declares the LORD, "when I will make a new covenant with the house of Israel and with the house of Judah. It will not be like the covenant which I made with their forefathers... I will put my law in their minds and write it on their hearts. I will be their God, and they will be my people... [and] they will all know me, from the least of them to the greatest..." (NIV 1984)**

Further Reading

Francis Anfray, *Les Anciens Éthiopiens,* Paris: Armand Colin, 1990.

Nicholas Clapp, *Sheba: Through the Desert in Search of the Legendary Queen,* New York: Mariner, 2002.

Stuart Munro-Hay, *The Quest for the Ark of the Covenant,* London: I.B.Tauris, 2005.

H. St John Philby, *The Queen of Sheba,* London: Quartet, 1981.

Randall Price, *Searching for the Ark of the Covenant,* Eugene, Oregon: Harvest House, 2005.